HOT LEAD, COLD IRON

HOT LEAD, COLD IRON

A MICK OBERON JOB

ARI MARMELL

TITAN BOOKS

Hot Lead, Cold Iron
Print edition ISBN: 9781785650833
E-book edition ISBN: 9781781168233

Published by Titan Books
A division of Titan Publishing Group Ltd
144 Southwark Street, London SE1 0UP

First mass market edition: June 2016
1 3 5 7 9 10 8 6 4 2

Ari Marmell asserts the moral right to be identified as the author
of this work.

www.titanbooks.com

A CIP catalogue record for this title is available
from the British Library.

Printed and bound in the United States.

To Jaym, for giving Mick his first chance in *Broken Time Blues*—but more importantly, for helping me to make the most of my second. You're amazing, Little Dragon.

A BRIEF WORD ON LANGUAGE

Throughout *Hot Lead, Cold Iron*, I've done my best to ensure that most, if not all, of the 30s-era slang can be picked up from context, rather than trying to include what would become a massive (and, no matter how careful I was, likely incomplete) dictionary. So over the course of reading, it shouldn't be difficult to pick up on the fact that "lamps" and "peepers" are eyes, "choppers" and "Chicago typewriters" are Tommy guns, and so forth.

But there are two terms that I do want to address, due primarily to how they appear to modern readers.

"Bird," when used as slang in some areas today, almost always refers to a woman. In the 1930s, however, it was just another word for "man" or guy."

"Gink" sounds like it should be a racial epithet to modern ears (and indeed, though rare, I've been told that it *is* used as such in a few regions). In the 30s, the term was, again, just a word for "man," though it has a somewhat condescending connotation to it. (That is, you wouldn't use it to refer to anyone you liked or respected.) It's in this fashion that I've used it throughout the novel.

CHAPTER ONE

I really feel that fewer of modern society's bits and pieces are sadder—more *banal*, I guess—than a big office. It's kinda like, once mankind perfected the assembly line, there was nothing left to do but live on it. Desk after bulky desk, endless rows reaching into the distance like railroad tracks to nowhere; constant monotonous clacks and dings of typewriters and adding machines; tacky marble floors—and maybe columns, in the swankier joints—trying to echo the glories of ancient temples and libraries, and miserably failing at it. Honestly, I dunno if it's more depressing or more boring.

Unless someone's trying to rub you out in one of 'em. Then I'm pretty damn confident in telling you it's a *lot* more depressing than it is boring.

Right that minute, I wasn't looking at the desks, or the typewriters, or the pillars, because I was staring blearily at the growing puddle of red soaking into the piss-yellow carpet between my scuffed Oxfords. (Yeah, carpet. This was the second story, so no marble flooring here.) It wasn't a whole lot of leakage, not yet, but the brick-fisted galoots flocking around me seemed right eager to help me add to it. We were having a friendly little get-together, me and the four of them, wherein I was helping them to relax by massaging their knuckles with my cheeks and my gut. Repeatedly; they musta been *really* tense. But hey, at least the coppery scent in my nose kept me from gagging on the mixed bouquet of old sweat, typewriter oil, and carpet shampoo.

How the hell, I wondered, *can people work in this kinda hole?*

And then a refrigerator all dolled up as a fist tried to offer me a backrub through my navel, and I remembered that I had more important things to worry about.

They were pretty much all of a type: big fellas in cheap suits, breath reeking of bootleg eel juice and cheap cigarettes. It wasn't too warm in there, but they were sweating from the exertion of working me over, so their jackets were draped over the backs of chairs or hanging limp over one shoulder. I think the fact that I *wasn't* sweating was making them even more steamed.

Wonder what they'd have thought if I told them straight up that I don't do that? Ever?

I hadn't caught any of their names—if they'd been spoken at all, I'd had other things to worry about at the time—so as far as I was concerned, they were Mustache, Muscles, Edgy, and Egghead. Muscles was the guy who was doing most of the actual pounding on me (big surprise there, right?), with Mustache watching over his shoulder—maybe to see if Muscles was doing it wrong. Edgy kept a few steps away, fist wrapped around the only heater in sight—a Colt semi, if it matters—though I knew the others were packing in their coat pockets.

Egghead had also moved back a little, wiping the perspiration off his head with one hand; in the other, he was holding a length of polished whitewood, just a little curved, not quite twice the size of a fountain pen. He was noodling over it like it was the most confounding thing he'd ever seen.

Which maybe it was. He'd pulled it from the shoulder holster under my jacket, so I gotta imagine he was anticipating something else.

But ultimately, none of these fellas was my *main* problem. No, *he* was sitting way over at the front of the office, his keister planted on the manager's desk. Tan slacks, navy sportcoat, and a pressed shirt with a collar big enough to serve as a parachute—spitting image of a rich man's idea of "casual."

His name I knew. He was part of the reason I was here. The *other* part was the big brown envelope currently in his hand, and that used to be in my coat pocket.

Floyd Winger, committeeman of Chicago's 34th Ward, went red as a honeymooning bride and started spitting words he'd never let his constituents hear as he tore open the flap and looked inside.

Muscles—who, I guess, assumed that the parade of profanity was born of his boss's frustration— knocked on my ribs again, maybe to see if anyone was home. I think I probably grunted, and struggled to keep my focus on Edgy and Egghead.

Almost there…

"Who sent ya?" Muscles demanded. "What'd ya break in for? I swear, bo, you don't start talking, we're gonna—"

"It's all right, Ronnie." Committeeman Winger

waved the envelope at me. "I know everything I need to know."

Yeah, you keep right on thinking that, you dumb bastard...

Egghead, his curiosity piqued, turned to face his boss. Without even thinking about it, he slipped the length of wood into the pocket of his coat, which was hanging on the chair behind him.

Well, finally! The strings and strands of his thoughts had felt so greasy, I thought for a while there I was *never* gonna make him do that. I was disgustingly out of practice; no way that shoulda taken me more than a couple of minutes.

"So who is he, Mr. Winger?" Egghead asked, shoving a cigarette in his trap and digging in his pocket for matches. I struggled to pay attention to the conversation, all the while turning my focus back to Edgy's Colt...

"Oh, I don't know his *name*, Benny." Of course he didn't; I'd left my wallet back in my office. Didn't want my name on me during a B-and-E job, did I? "But I know *why* he's here."

He aimed his narrow, lying peepers my way. "And we both know who sent you, don't we?" Even here, with an audience of five—four on the payroll, and one that he was probably measuring for a pine overcoat—he couldn't switch off the politician. His voice was sharp, clear, echoing in the massive room; he coulda been addressing a rally of hundreds.

"I don't know what you're talking about," I told him, grinning around a mouthful of blood. "I'm just a janitor. Had to break in, 'cause I forgot my key. And my uniform." I shrugged, as much as the rope binding my hands behind the back of the chair would let me. "What can I say? I'm new at this."

Either I wasn't nearly as funny as I thought I was, or Muscles laughs with his fists, not his mouth. I'll let you decide which. Either way, I quit talking for a spell.

"Now, Ronnie," Winger said, "that shouldn't be necessary any longer." Something in the committeeman's voice made me look his way, almost losing my concentration on Edgy in the process. His tone hadn't changed much, but his words tasted wrong. Angry. The lines around his eyes and mouth were sharp enough to shave with.

"So this is how Baskin wants to play it?" he asked me. "Send some sap to come and burgle my place? Fine. We'll play. This is on his head, and yours." Winger brushed a few strands of thin hair from his face with the back of his hand, shoved the envelope into the inside pocket of his jacket, and reached for the office phone. He actually turned back toward me, as he lifted the receiver to his ear, so I could watch.

Louse. I *hate* politicians.

"Operator?" His lips were practically *on* the candlestick's mouthpiece, making love to the thing. "Glenview 0898, please."

I knew that exchange; he was calling Baskin at *home*. Nice guy.

"You'll want…"

He and the gang of four barely glanced my way as I paused long enough to spit out the last of the blood. "What was that?" Winger asked. I could faintly hear the sound of ringing on the other end of the line.

"You'll wanna put down the blower," I said. "Before you embarrass yourself."

Three chuckles and two pairs of rolled blinkers were all I got from *that* pronouncement. And why not? Even if I hadn't been tightly roped to a heavy wooden chair, I'd already taken a beating that'd keep a strong man down for hours, and put a weak one in the hospital.

Two things they mighta wanted to know right then. First, I heal fast. *Damn* fast; it takes a lot more than a beating to lay me up longer than a few minutes, no matter how bad. And second, I coulda been free of the ropes half a minute after they tied me up. Not only are my joints a *lot* more flexible than most, but Mustache left a lot of slack in the loops.

Why? Because it's an easy mistake to make if you don't know your knots, and I'd been concentrating *real* hard on how much I wanted him to make it, that's why. All I'd been waiting for was…

(I felt the aura of luck around Edgy's roscoe, the chains of cause and effect that had to go just right for the mechanism to function, finally deflate beneath the pressure I'd been willing into it on and off for the past ten minutes.)

…*That*.

I stood up—rope dangling loosely from around my left wrist—spun the chair around me like it was my partner on the dance floor at the Savoy, and used it to return some of the loving attention that Muscles had been giving me over the course of the evening. He doubled up around the wood and hit the carpet, puking up bloody chunks of what might once have been cheap sausage.

It *still* didn't smell as bad as the rest of the damn office.

For a heartbeat or two, everyone just gaped at me as though I'd sprouted a zeppelin. The receiver fell from Winger's fingers, a nervous, twitching tail dangling at his side. The cigarette tumbled from Egghead's kisser and bounced across the carpet in a mini-Fourth of July; the room was so quiet, we could actually hear the embers sizzling as they scattered. It was just luck that they didn't ignite anything.

Or maybe it's because I didn't want them to. I'm not always entirely sure, when it comes to little quirks of fortune like that.

Edgy was, well, on edge, and acted before any of the others. He raised the Colt in a trembling hand— but not trembling enough to throw off his aim at *this* range—and squeezed the trigger.

Something inside—probably the firing pin, by the sound of it—snapped with a dull twang, and Edgy found his fist wrapped around a Browning Colt M1911 doorstop.

I was off and running before any of 'em had quite doped out what was happening. I put a haymaker across Egghead's chin hard enough that he wouldn't have to shave for a week, and he collapsed in a heap that I mighta called boneless if my throbbing knuckles didn't prove there was a pretty solid jawbone in there. I yanked his coat from the chair where he'd draped it and spun, beating feet toward my favorite public servant, Committeeman Winger.

Who was, himself, making a pretty convincing sprint for the closest door.

Mustache moved to intercept me, yanking a .38

special from his jacket. No way I could deal with that one the way I had Edgy's; even if I'd had the time to focus on it, it's a *lot* harder for me to disable a revolver than a semi. Simpler mechanism, older technology. Maybe if I'd pulled my own piece from Egghead's jacket, but I hadn't had even a second to dig for it yet...

So I did what any normal Joe does when he's got the pipe of a gun pointed his way: I ducked.

More accurately, I hurled myself frantically to the side, plowing into one of the desks so we went tumbling in a splayed mess of limbs both flesh and wood. (Bad enough that the corners of the damn thing dug into my ribs something fierce, but they managed to catch three different spots that Muscles had already tenderized like a cheap steak. Of course.)

It did the trick, though. I heard the boom of flying lead, and the softer crack as the slugs chewed through the far wall or into the wooden shield I was hunkering behind, but other than an ugly splinter across the back of my left hand, it didn't cause me any pain.

I may heal fast, and I may die a lot harder than you mugs, but that don't make getting shot any *fun*.

So, I couldn't hide here forever. The desk was already about ready to disintegrate, I couldn't be sure how long the other guys were out of the fight, and Winger was getting farther away with every breath. I stood up from behind the broken heap, shoved the luck I'd pulled from Edgy's Colt into the short length of rope still coiled around my wrist, and threw it.

Mustache tried to knock it aside so it didn't hit

him in the face, tried to shoot me at the same time—and the .38's hammer came down and lodged in the hemp fibers.

You can do a lot with a little extra luck, if you know how.

But it was only a little. Mustache was frantically tugging at the loose strands, trying to clear the hammer, and it probably wouldn't take him long to pull it off. Edgy was digging in Muscles's coat over one of the other chairs, probably going for the larger man's roscoe, and Muscles himself was groaning and starting to struggle upright.

On the other hand, I was packing now, too.

From Egghead's jacket pocket, I slid the wand he'd found so damn peculiar: a Luchtaine & Goodfellow Model 1592. It sat in my hand like it was a part of me. No surprise there; considering how long I've had it, I've actually worn down the wood to fit my fist. The *dverga* who sold it to me so long ago swore up and down that it actually contains a sliver of the raft that carried King Arthur to Avalon; I don't know if I buy any of that, but on the square or not, the wand's never let me down yet.

I raked the L&G across Winger's goons, reaching through the mystic conduit to fiddle with the images behind their eyes. I gathered strands of shadow from the blind spots at the corners of their vision, smeared it across the rest of their sight; not as elegant as just painting myself out of the room, or making them see me somewhere I wasn't, but even with the wand, this was a *lot* faster. For just a few moments, their worlds went dark as the inside of a gas tank.

"What the fuck?"

"Hey, who killed the lights?"

"Ronnie, that you? Where are you?"

"I'm over here!"

"*Who's that?!*"

At which point, genius that he was, Edgy started squirting metal at every sound he didn't immediately recognize. Powdered plaster and chipped marble fell from the walls and the columns, steel crumpled and typewriter keys flew free, and Mustache and Muscles dove blindly for cover. I heard a loud thunk, a pained squawk, and another of the desks collapsed, putting Muscles completely out of action for the second time.

Figuring that oughta keep them all busy for a few minutes, I snuffled once—the smell of burnt gunpowder always makes me wanna sneeze—and went hunting for Floyd Winger.

I practically skidded across the rough carpet, doors banging behind me, and slid into the brass railing on the balcony beyond. A quick peek down into the first-floor atrium didn't show me much of anything useful: big honking secretary's desk, bunch of potted ferns, marble flooring with swirls the color of watered-down Pepto-Bismol. Of course, I couldn't see anything *beneath* the balcony, but at least the front door was firmly shut and there was no sight or sound of Winger anywhere near 'em.

The gink was probably hoping to stick around and make sure his boys took care of me. Good decision—for me.

I paused a minute, took a deep sniff. Winger

had to have been sweating something fierce when he took the run-out; he'd be leaving a trail of stink better'n any roadmap. And yep, there it was. Hell, I didn't even need the sweat; I could actually taste the lingering aura of his fear in the air.

L&G held straight and ready, I crept along the open hall on the balls of my feet; atrium to the left of me, thick doors and dark windows to the right. And I guess he knew I was coming, 'cause he bolted from his hiding hole and made a mad dash for the stairs.

He'd been skulking in the washroom. Of course. Where else would you find a Chicago politico, but with the rest of the shit?

I maybe coulda caught up with him, but why do things the hard way? I aimed the L&G and shouted, "That's far enough, Mr. Winger."

He froze, his hands high, and turned—at which point he saw just what it was I was pointing his way. If nothing else, at least I'd wiped the smug public-servant veneer off his mug. He gave me a sneer that woulda done any Mafioso proud. "You think you're funny?" he demanded. "You think *any* of this is funny?!"

I shrugged. "Yeah, I think there's maybe something funny to it."

"Fine! I'll send that stupid little stick to Baskin— along with a free copy of the headlines when the photos go public." He was starting to step away again, ready to bolt. "I'm sure he'll think the joke's absolutely hysteri—"

The hallway shook with the cough of a .45-caliber slug, and my "stupid little stick" spit fire. It wasn't any of it real, of course—just another illusion, sound and fury and all that—but it sure as shooting seemed real to *him*.

Uh, pun unintended.

Winger cried out, and before he could realize that he hadn't actually been shot, I was on him like a troll on a wounded kid.

For a minute we rolled back and forth between the office walls and the half-wall that marked the balcony's edge, fists flying, but I'm not being cocky when I say that he never had much of a chance. I got myself a nice, solid grip and started whaling on him.

I also got into the inside pocket of his coat— *twice*—and he never noticed. I wish I could pretend it's because I'm just that keen, just that sneaky. But in this case, to be completely on the square about it, I think he was mostly distracted by the fact that I was slamming his head into the floor by his hair, and jamming my knee into his groin hard enough to flatten a tire.

I was about to stop anyway—no, really, I was!— when I learned that I'd badly underestimated at least one of the committeeman's thugs.

Mustache flew from the office, one ace of a shiner decorating the left side of his face and a nasty little switchblade in his right hand. I really thought he shoulda been blind for another couple minutes. Maybe his loyalty to Winger was more than money, and hearing his boss yell out gave him the willpower to break my hold on him. Hell, maybe I just got careless, or I only winged him back in the office. Didn't know then, don't suppose I ever will. Can't see how it matters much, either way. Whatever the reason, he was up and about.

I heard him coming, despite the muffling carpet and Winger's groans; he musta still been disoriented from the magic I'd throw at him. Hell, *I* woulda been! He came at me and I stood, grabbed his arm, and spun him aside easy as duck soup.

He tottered, looking for all the world as though he was lit on cheap hooch—and went over the balcony railing with a girlish squeal.

Not my intention at all!

Winger and I just stared at each other, jaws hanging stupidly. It woulda been funny if, you know, it'd been funny. Then, reluctantly—not sure why; I'd seen, and done, a lot worse—I took a few steps and leaned over the edge.

You wouldn't have believed it, but damn if Mustache wasn't alive! He wouldn't be jitterbugging any time soon, I could see that from the new and fascinating ways his drumsticks were bending, but one of those goofy potted ferns had broken the worst of his fall.

Sometimes, I can't believe my luck.

I was still looking over the brass railing at the guy mangled and leaking right beneath me when the front door burst open like a belt at a banquet and a dozen coppers stormed the lobby. I actually *felt* more than twenty peepers focus on Mustache lying in the wreckage of the big terracotta pot, covered in blood and soil, and then rotate on up to focus on my gawping mug.

Sometimes, I can't *believe* my luck.

At which point, Winger—clever weasel that he was—began screaming for help. And shouting his name. And claiming that I was holding a gun on him.

I'm pretty sure there wasn't a lawman in the joint who didn't know just how much of a highbinder the dirty bastard was. But that didn't mean I wasn't trying to kill him; hell, far as they were concerned, it probably made it more likely! Plus, there was no telling just how many of 'em might be on Winger's payroll.

So it probably shouldn't have come as any surprise to me that four of 'em drew heat and started shooting at me before I even had the chance to raise my hands.

I threw myself back from the railing hard enough to crack the office window behind me—thankfully, it wasn't actually a mirror, despite the reflection; I normally carry enough salt on me to counter even *that* kinda bad luck, but right now it was sitting in the office, in my overcoat pocket—and I'm not sure the first of the slugs actually missed me by more than a mouse's pecker. I let myself hit the floor as I rebounded off the glass, and started crawling. I heard feet pounding on stairs across the atrium, and I knew that if the wrong bull found me, I'd be sporting some extra holes before I had the chance to explain.

So I was going to have to do something—even if it meant making a bunch of policemen think I was attacking 'em. I couldn't remember right at that point how many plans and contingencies I'd come up with, but the evening wasn't going according to *any* of 'em.

I slipped my wand from my holster again and grabbed it in my teeth, crawled a few more yards, and—wincing in anticipation of another fusillade—peeked up between the wall and the railing.

Most of the bulls had spread out throughout the lobby, taking what cover they could around the desk or in various doorways; I assumed the ones I couldn't see had already made it to the upper floor, and were somewhere close. I couldn't help but notice that nobody was actually paying much attention to Mustache; they must have really believed someone was about to start sniping from up here.

I saw, also, that three plainclothes cops had come in behind them, weapons drawn—and thanks be to whatever gods are left in this day and age, I recognized one of them!

"Keenan!" I ducked as a shot careened off the railing inches from my nose. "Lieutenant Keenan!"

The man I'd called, a hawk-faced, dark-haired fella in a brown fedora and matching trench coat, aimed his stubble my way. "Oberon? That you?"

A second slug dug into the wall I was hiding behind, a third whined overhead and thunked into an office door. "Not for much longer!"

"Hold fire! *Everyone hold fire!*"

I didn't actually know Keenan too well—mostly through a mutual friend on the force—but I coulda kissed him right about then.

It took a lot more yelling, and a few minutes of coppers running pell-mell through every room, accompanied by repeated shouts of "Police!" and "Get your hands up!" and "Grab some air!" but eventually, everyone was gathered downstairs around that humongous desk. Winger was smoothing his wrinkled coat and wiping the blood and sweat from his face with a handkerchief; Muscles and Mustache were receiving medical attention; Edgy was slouched over, his hands cuffed, since he'd taken a swing at the first lawman to come through the door; and Egghead was still snoozing.

For my part, I'd taken the opportunity for a quick, pinpoint illusion...

"Now," Keenan said, moving in my direction, pad, pencil, and unlit cigarette all dangling from his left hand. "Someone had damn well better start telling me what—"

"I can tell you everything you require, lieutenant," the committeeman said, stepping forward to intercept him. "This—this *hooligan* broke into the offices of my firm here and *assaulted* me and my employees! Why, there's no telling what violence he might have inflicted on us if you hadn't arrived when you did!"

"I attacked five guys?" I asked. I felt my lips curling despite my best efforts not to laugh in his face. "Alone? Unarmed?"

Keenan coughed and, transferring his cigarette to his right hand, used it to point at the obvious bulge in my coat. "Unarmed?" He stuck the butt in his mouth, looked around more or less aimlessly until one of the uniformed officers produced a lit match.

Being *very* careful to make every move slow and obvious, I pulled open my lapel and showed him the holster—and the wand.

"What the hell, Oberon?"

I smiled at him. "It's intimidating; makes it *look* like I'm packing. But I don't carry, lieutenant. Get Pete on the horn, if you don't believe me; he'll vouch."

"I see. And Committeeman Winger's claims?"

"Bunk from soup to nuts. Even for a politico,

it's one heck of a pack of lies."

I always thought someone "puffing up" was just an expression until right then, but I swear Winger's face actually inflated. "Now, see here—!"

"In fact," I continued, "I'm here on official business. On behalf of ASA Daniel Baskin."

That bought me a few raised eyebrows. But it was Winger who reacted first. "I think, lieutenant," he said, speaking to Keenan even as he did his level best to stab me through the eyeballs with a vicious glare, "that there's something you ought to know about Assistant State's Attorney Baskin before you consider giving this matter any further credence." And just as I knew he would, he stepped toward Keenan, hand reaching for the inside pocket of his sportcoat, greasy smile already oozing from his pores to cover the front of his head.

The same pocket I'd gotten into twice while we were tussling upstairs.

I'd been all set to give him a quick mental nudge, but it wasn't needed. He was so anxious, so eager to bring the man down, I don't think he realized until he'd already pulled it free that the paper in his hand was *not* the envelope he'd shoved in there earlier.

Floyd Winger could only stand there, paralyzed and perspiring, as Lieutenant Keenan leaned, squinting, to peruse the subpoena, inked beneath the formal seal of the Cook County courts.

"Looks like you've been served, Committeeman Winger," Keenan told him. Was it my imagination, or was the flatfoot maybe gloating just a little bit? "I'm sure the court appreciates your willingness to testify." He looked again. "March 28th? Okay. I appreciate you trusting us with this, committeeman. I'll be sure to have officers ready to escort you. For your protection and comfort, of course."

"I... I..."

I think I'd have taken this job from Baskin for free, just for the chance to hear a Chicago committeeman stammering.

"We'll have to take you in, too, Oberon," Keenan said then. "I don't buy that you attacked these men, but until we determine exactly what *did* happen—especially to that fellow there," he added, jutting his chin so the smoldering butt pointed vaguely at Mustache, "—we've got to treat you as a suspect."

Yeah, I'd expected as much. "Come on, lieutenant." I made a show of rubbing my aching ribs, carefully slid my hand up in case I needed the L&G for a little extra wow. "I've got an appointment with my client." I tilted my head toward the subpoena, as if he was somehow going to forget who I meant. "You know you can get everything from him during office hours tomorrow."

No way he should have gone for it—but then, I wasn't just asking. I'd been sending him waves of willpower the entire time we talked, softening him up; now I pushed at the membrane of will behind his eyes, blew on the embers of his thoughts, igniting what little trust he had for me—and, more importantly, his respect for Dan Baskin—into a raging fire.

Wound up that I didn't need the wand. "All right," he said finally, drawing a strangled gasp from Winger and a few puzzled looks from the other (thankfully lower-ranked) detectives. "But I'm still going to need you to come in some time soon and give your own statement about what happened. Just to keep things formal."

"Understand completely, lieutenant. Much obliged."

He nodded, then glanced down at the small bloodstains all over my shirt and suit. "You need to see a doc before you go?"

"Nah." I pulled my collar aside, showed him just a few minor bruises and abrasions. "Just a good tailor. Guys aren't as tough as they make out."

Keenan smirked and wandered away.

I ambled up to the second floor, collected my overcoat, and was back downstairs and out the door before I let the illusion fade and the ugly contusions and lacerations reappear. I knew I'd be seeing Keenan again before too long—maybe when I next went to call on Pete, and if not, when I went to give my statement—and by then, the wounds actually *would* be gone. I didn't want him noticing and asking questions.

Hmm. I guess, at this point, I really should put a few cards on the table. I'm a private investigator, licensed and accredited. My name is Mick Oberon, or at least it is now.

And like some of you have probably already figured, I'm not human.

CHAPTER TWO

I've had a lot of names before this one, and you ain't hearing any of 'em. I'm... I don't know exactly know how old. Time doesn't flow entirely right for us even in *this* world, and *all* bets are off once you step Sideways. Decades can drift by, like a soothing song, and you'd never know until you shake it off and look around; we forget so much of what we knew, and who we were.

I can tell you this. I've seen woad-painted Celts and war-painted Indians; Vikings on longships and knights on horseback; French revolutionaries and Italian inquisitors and Spanish conquistadors. I've slept on jagged rocks and woven moss, mite-infested straw mattresses and perfume-scented silks.

Today I sleep on a dilapidated Murphy bed in a cheap office, with wrinkled sheets and springs poking into my back, and believe you me, it ranks nearer the bottom of that list than the top.

I was among the last of the Tuatha Dé Danann, lords of the Emerald Isle, conquerors of the Firbolgs. We ruled as princes, in our world and yours, until you grew too many, your devices too intricate. We became the *aes sidhe*, the People of the Mounds, through which we retreated in our return to the

Otherworld. And we lost so much of what we'd been.

You call us Fae, and our world Faerie, or Elphame, or a dozen other names. And for longer than I can remember—literally—I remained a prince, an aristocrat of the Seelie Court.

Now I'm a PI in a filthy, crime-ridden city, where I gotta talk like I've got a beef with grammar if I wanna halfway blend in, in a world that actually *hurts* me. Any of you saps honestly believe there's any justice in the universe, c'mon over and see me. I've got a bridge to sell you. It's all kinda sparkly colors, and it takes you right to fucking Asgard.

And that's all you need. Or all you get, anyway.

Well, no, I'll give you *one* piece more: I had my own damn good reasons for walking away from the Courts and everything I was, and I've got my own damn good reasons for never wanting to go back.

That'll be important for you to know, later. You can probably imagine why.

The wind was faint and only a little chilly. It whispered in my ears and kicked the hem of my overcoat around my ankles, making it dance a quick waltz with bits of old newspaper, sandwich wrappers, and a few stray leaves that had survived the winter only to fall with spring just beyond reach. (I knew how they felt.) Dark cars grumbled past me on the street, beaming their ugly yellow light at me through big froggy eyes and leering through grills of metal teeth. I'd taught myself a long time ago not to shudder every time I got near one of the damn things, but the urge remained, waiting to conk me on the back of the head.

ARI MARMELL

Even this late, I wasn't hardly the only bird strolling down Michigan Avenue, and by the time I got where I was going, I thought my head would fall off my neck, I'd nodded so many polite greetings. If I wore a hat, I'd have worn through the brim from tipping it over and over again.

The sound of people laughing and dishes clattering, the smell of greasy meats and something slick burning off the stove, all hit me before I even opened the door. I have to admit, I was a little perplexed that we were meeting at a Thompson's— or "mpson's," at the moment, since someone had covered half the name with a poster supporting Smith over Roosevelt at the upcoming convention. Sure, it was *my* sorta joint, since it kept the same hours I did, and it doesn't much matter to me how lousy the food might be; but I didn't figure it for *his*.

But then, maybe that was the point. Not as though anyone would think to look for him here, right?

The crowd inside was just big enough to make me wait in line at the counter: businessmen and shopkeeps grabbing a bite after a long day, a few young couples riding the high of a great date, a handful of professional skirts fortifying themselves for another hard night.

And probably a few trouble boys planning something illegal for later in the week, but that'd be none of my business, would it?

I waited in the line, tapping my foot—because it's expected, not because I actually do that—and slowly slid my way completely past the food, ignoring the whole smelly mess of it. Finally, I got to the drink counter and the harried slob behind it.

"You got any of those warm?" I asked, pointing to a row of glasses made visible as one of the other workers opened the refrigerator behind him.

"Huh? Warm? Why would we do that, mister?" His face looked about as expressive as the grease stains on his apron.

I sighed. You wouldn't think it'd be that hard an order, would you? "Okay, fine. Just a glass of milk, please."

He gave me a funny look—proving that he could, at least, manage an expression—and delivered. I dropped a few cents in his sweaty palm and turned to get a slant on the room.

Took me a minute, since he was wearing a much cheaper suit than when I last saw him—anonymity again, I supposed—but I finally spotted him. No amount of shabby dressing was going to hide that five-dollar haircut, or the immaculately shined shoes. I found him off to the side, in a row of chairs lined up against a wall. Cheap, cramped little dinguses, with trays nailed to the left arm instead of any sorta legit table—but it put us out of earshot of anyone else in the joint, and it kept either of us from having to sit with our back to the room.

Thoughtful gesture on his part, but honestly, with my hearing, I don't much mind putting my back to a room.

Much.

He nodded as I approached but didn't bother to stand, finished chewing a mouthful of pastrami on rye, washed it down with a big gulp of a Coke that was just about the same color as his hair. I sat, giving him a pretty solid up-and-down—I'd only met him the couple of times, and trusted him roughly not at all—and he returned the examination in kind.

I wondered exactly how I looked to him.

You see, that's one of the things about me—about most of the *aes sidhe*, actually. None of you mortal-types see us exactly the same way. Sure, I knew *basically* what he saw: little taller than average, kinda skinny, narrow nose and chin, sorta sandy hair and ocean-colored blinkers. (Between the sand and the water, I used to tell people I was a son of a beach, until I realized, way too late, that it wasn't even a little bit funny.) But the *details*, the angles, the exact shades, the wrinkles and freckles and whatnot; those coulda been anything. It's never *dramatic*—show any handful of people who know me a photo, and they'll all recognize me; they'll just think it's a bad picture— but I'm always curious. I was wearing the same overcoat I usually wear, kinda dirt-colored and well loved. (Which I'm sure most of you mugs'll take as a euphemism for "worn and threadbare." Okay, fine, it *is* worn and threadbare, but damn it, it's *comfortable*.)

I knew he'd finished his studying when he blinked and sniffed once. "New suit?"

Yeah, it did have that clothing shop smell to it. I'd decided buying a new suit was probably less expensive, and certainly less hassle, than finding a tailor *and* a drycleaner to fix what Winger's thugs had done to my old one. Of course, even new, the blue pinstripe would have to be pressed twice to look good enough to be called "cheap."

"Wanted to dress my best for our meeting, Mr. Baskin," I said, making no effort at all to sound like I meant it.

He chuckled politely, then lifted a napkin, wiped a tiny bit of soda from the corner of his mouth. "It's done, then?"

I nodded, reached into my overcoat and produced the envelope. "It's done." I slapped it down on the table beside his sandwich wrapper.

His shoulders visibly sagged, his expression softened. For a man accustomed to standing in front of judges, juries, and crumbs who'd happily whack him for a shot of whisky, he was showing an awful lot of emotion.

Then again, I'd seen the pictures. If I'd been an Assistant State's Attorney, I'd have been relieved to get 'em back, too.

"The negatives?" he asked.

"Inside, with the prints."

He swept the envelope off the table and into a waiting leather briefcase. "And the subpoena?"

"Served." I grinned. "And he actually flashed it to Lieutenant Keenan, in a room full of bulls. No way he can make like he never got it."

Baskin laughed aloud. "Well done, Mr. Oberon, *very* well done."

"Yeah." My smile fell a little. "Maybe not *that* well done. There were, uh, complications." Briefly, and leaving out pretty much every mention of magic (as well as any reference to how bad I got pummeled), I gave him the skinny on what had occurred.

He was shaking his head long before I'd finished. "Not very subtle, were you?"

"It wasn't the clean sneak I was hoping for, no. I'd cased the joint for three straight nights; just my bad luck he decided to come in late today." I shrugged. "But it worked out, minus a few bruises I could do without."

"And the police report?" he asked. I watched him rotating his glass around and around, his fingers leaving streaks in the condensation, and I knew what he was asking.

"Won't mention the photos. I'll cop to the B-and-E, say I was just trying to make sure to deliver your summons and I didn't think Winger's boys would let me get near him." I paused, then, "You *can* arrange to have the breaking-and-entering charge dismissed, right?"

"I can. You'll get a slap on the wrist, I'll cover the fine, we'll make some noise about pulling your PI ticket if it happens again. No big deal."

"Swell." We sat for a moment, letting the ambient voices wash over us. I took a swallow of milk, and tried not to pull a face; still cold, damn it.

"Look, Mr. Baskin," I asked finally, "put me wise about something."

"Yes?"

"I understand why everything had to happen all at once. You snatch the photos before you serve him, and Winger might take a powder somewhere you can't reach him. You deliver the subpoena first, and he leaks the pictures. I get all that.

"But why subpoena him? Why not have the cops pinch him? You obviously had them in the area in case of trouble—no other way they'd have gotten there so quick once the shooting started—and I know you've got enough on him to send him over for years. So why isn't he in jail right now?"

Baskin leaned toward me, and damn if his eyes

weren't almost glowing like will-o'-the-wisps. "Because I don't just want Winger. I want Surrey!"

Made sense. Alderman Joel Surrey was the man who'd appointed Winger as his committeeman for the ward. Had to figure that, corrupt as everyone *knew* Winger was, Surrey must be in on it.

"I've been trying," Baskin was saying, "to get Surrey since before we nailed Capone! If I can get Winger to testify against him…"

I nodded slowly. "And in the meanwhile, Winger gets to think about how long you can lock him up if he doesn't cooperate—and to think about what Surrey's going to do when he hears about the subpoena."

"Exactly."

There was more to it than that. Baskin's words tasted like lies—or some of them did, anyway. Maybe he had other plans for Winger, or for Surrey; maybe he had something else going, investigative or political, that he didn't want to tell me about.

Or hell, maybe I was wrong. I can't always tell, especially with accomplished liars, and I've been way off before. Frankly, it didn't matter. Everyone in this town plays their little games, and everyone's corrupt or dirty *somehow*. If Baskin wasn't on the up-and-up, well, that was none of mine.

I took another sip—a bit warmer now, thankfully—and held out my hand. "You've got something for me?"

He frowned. "Yeah." He reached back into his briefcase, brought out something wrapped in crumpled brown paper and tied with twine. "A few bucks to cover expenses, and the, um, item. This wasn't easy to get, Oberon, not even for me. If it's some kind of joke…"

"No joke. You asked what my services would cost, this is what they cost. This time."

Shaking his head in such clear bewilderment I wanted to burst out laughing, he handed it over. It sat in my hands, feeling *right*. I got a charge just holding it.

You'll chuckle at that, later.

I squeezed from my chair, leaving most of the glass of milk behind, and opened my kisser to offer "g'night" when I caught just the faintest narrowing of Baskin's lids.

Damn, I'd really hoped to avoid this…

"Tell me, Mr. Oberon: Did *you* look at the photos?"

"Course I did," I told him flatly. "I had to be sure what I had, didn't I?"

"I see."

I leaned in, putting my hands on his tray. I didn't push into his thoughts *yet*, but I was gathering myself up to do it if I needed to. "Way I see it," I said, "we're just two Joes who worked together on something—not friends, maybe, but friendly-like. We can go about our business, maybe work together again in the future, and both be happy, confident that I'm hardly about to risk my professional reputation by squealing your secrets.

"*Or* you can decide to come after me 'cause of what I know. Hell, you've probably got enough on me to prefer some real charges. But right now, all you gotta worry about is Winger talking about those pictures; nobody's gonna believe him on his own. But you make me an enemy, I'm gonna have to testify to what I saw, and then he's got corroboration from a guy with no good call to want to help him. Ain't as bad as the photos themselves, but you can be damn sure it'll make the *Tribune*.

"So you tell me, Mr. Baskin. How do you want it?"

A few years passed in the next couple of heartbeats. Then he leaned back, reached for what was left of his Coke, and gave me the shallowest of nods. "Have a nice night, Mr. Oberon."

I couldn't tell you if I had a nice night, but apparently I had a long one. The sun was already poking at me through the blinds in my office window by the time I stirred the next morning. Actually, it had to be afternoon if I was getting sunlight up my nose, since my office is a basement room, and the only windows are narrow little things way up by the ceiling; but if I'm just waking up it's *morning*, goddamn it.

I admit, I was a little dizzy and disoriented for a few. I'm not actually used to sleeping all that much; just a few hours every couple of days, more so my brain can dream and take the run-out from this world of yours for a little while than because my body actually needs the rest. But after the last evening, with all the magic and me healing up from being beat like a drum, I suppose I needed it.

So it took me a minute to get my head together and peel my thoughts up off the pillow enough to dope out what woke me. It wasn't the sunlight. It wasn't the faint ringing from out in the corridor. (I don't keep a phone in my office—it drives me up the wall just being near the damn things—but Mr. Soucek was kind enough to let me use the payphone in the hall for incoming calls. It was the first thing he told all his tenants: "If pay-telephone in basement rings, is for Mr. Oberon. You tell him, okay?") It wasn't the scent of the fresh bottles of milk that appeared outside my door every morning, though now that I was awake they were awful enticing.

No, it hadn't been any of that, so what…?

Oh. Yeah, the ham-fisted pounding on my door just mighta done the trick. As I said, I was a little slow for a spell, there.

"Hold your shirt and keep your horses on, buster! I'm comin'!"

Probably not the most gracious way to introduce myself to someone who mighta been a client, but there it was.

I stood up, made sure I was more or less decent— shirt and slacks were wrinkled as an elephant's grandma from sleeping in, but they'd do—then shoved all the sheets up onto the mattress and folded the Murphy bed back up into its alcove. (A few scraps of fabric were sticking out around the edges where the doors shut, but again, it'd hafta do.)

Looking around, everything else was clean enough; not *neat*, since the place was cluttered with enough papers to rebuild a tree, but *clean*. It's not much of a home—or much of an office, for that matter—but it's what I had. Small desk with a matching swivel chair and a big honkin' typewriter. (That typewriter actually killed a man, once, but I don't ever tell *that* story.) Smaller chair in front of the desk; file cabinet; tiny, decrepit icebox, not kept as cold as most, where I keep my milk and a few dollops of cream for celebrations. There's a spindly rack, with a dusty hat I never wear—hats don't feel right on me; just because you Joes can't *see* the pointed ears don't mean they ain't there—and that usually holds my overcoat, 'cept that was currently draped over the back of my chair. Fireplace along one wall. The tools are brass; no iron in here, no way.

Oh, and over in the corner, an old radio the size of a doghouse. Yeah, I have a radio—it's about the only thing in here more advanced than a light bulb—though I gotta keep it unplugged most of the time or I go stark raving. I don't much care for what you people call "music" nowadays; give me a lute-and-flute jig or Bach's third Brandenburg Concerto over a jazz trumpet or a crooning canary any time, no matter how smooth. But Waters and Ellington and Armstrong are what you mugs listen to, so those of us who wanna fit in to your world, that's what *we* gotta listen to. Thanks for nothing.

Anything else I had to do last minute? Nah; the package Baskin gave me was sitting on the edge of the desk, but it was wrapped. Bathroom door was shut, so the client—or whoever—wouldn't see the blood and dirt clinging to the brass tub. The nook over in the far wall, where the refrigerator *used* to be before I moved in, was a little mildewed in the corners, but not enough for your average Joe to notice. Besides, I kept it that way on purpose.

So I was about as ready to entertain a caller as I was gonna be without a shower and a few more hours of shuteye.

With what I already knew was a futile attempt to straighten my shirt, I scooted to the door, slid the deadbolts aside, and pulled it open. The face on the other side was clean-shaven and just a little swarthy. He mighta been Italian, or Mexican, or just tan; features weren't ethnical enough one way or the other to be sure.

I noticed, in passing, that the payphone had stopped ringing.

He ran a hand over his hair, which was already slicked back with enough oil to lube a Ford, and said, "You keep everyone waiting this long, mister?"

"Just the people I like," I told him, stepping aside so he could enter.

"Just the people you like." He snorted, and managed, without actually touching me, to give the impression that he'd rather have shouldered me aside.

This one was gonna be fun, I could tell that already.

I picked up the two bottles of milk and then shut the door, taking a moment to get a good slant on him. The stripes on his jacket were wide and colorful, but the suit itself was pretty good quality; so he had money, but not a lotta taste. His shoes cost more than my wardrobe, but they were scuffed; and it didn't take either the keen observation of a PI or the vision of the Fae to see the bulge in that coat, or to know what was under it.

I waited until he'd seated himself, ignored the disparaging look he gave to my place of business, and then took the other chair across the desk.

"So, you're O'Brien?"

My tongue almost bled, I bit it so hard. I get three

or four of those a month. Yeah, this is Chicago, and yeah, I go by "Mick," and "Oberon" ain't exactly normal, but c'mon. The name's *right there on the damn door!*

"Oberon," I corrected, polite as I could muster.

"Oberon?"

"Oberon. And you are...?"

"Archie."

I waited. He waited for me to finish waiting. Apparently, that's all he was giving me.

"Okay, Archie. What can I do for you?"

"Well..." He hedged, and I could hear his feet fidgeting on the carpet. "You got anything to drink around here, Mr. Oberon?"

"I can offer you milk." I thumped the two bottles down on the desk, next to Baskin's parcel.

He looked at me, expecting a punchline. I shrugged.

"Milk. Yeah." He shook his head. I drummed my fingers on the side of the typewriter, waiting for him to get to the point.

He glanced up, chewing his cheek a little, and scowled. "You gotta problem with me? You're staring. I don't enjoy being stared at."

Oops. Guess I was still out of it; I taught myself to blink and fidget and all that a long time ago, but now and again I slip up. I made a show of blinking and leaned back in the seat.

"Just wondering when you're gonna quit bumping gums and tell me something that means anything."

He glowered, but I've gotten the Look from scarier guys than him.

"Fine," he said at last. "We need you to find someone."

"We?"

"My boss and me. We—"

I raised a hand. "You can stop there, Archie. I can't take the job."

"You can't take the job?! You ain't even *heard* the job!"

"Maybe not," I said, "but I've heard enough."

"You've heard enough?"

"You know, that's a genuinely irritating habit you got there." Then, before he could object any further, I said, "It's plain and simple, Archie. I don't work for the Outfit. Or any of their people."

He froze, and in that moment even the dizzying jacket didn't keep him from looking dangerous. "I don't know what you're talking about." His voice was flat as a bad note.

"C'mon, Archie, you might as well be wearing a sign. The heater, the way you dress, the way you walk. You're here on behalf of your boss. Even the look you tried to shake me with. You're with the Outfit. You *could* belong to one of the other gangs, maybe, but if I had to guess, I'd put you with Al's old crew."

"Be careful, Oberon…"

"And," I continued, ignoring what he probably thought passed for a pretty clear threat, "I don't work for you kinda people. Ever."

You gotta understand, it wasn't just that I don't care for mobs like the Outfit and their rivals, though I sure as hell ain't fond of them. But most of you mortals, you got *no idea* what they represent, what sort of effect they've had on the Otherworld…

"You don't work for my kinda people." Archie's

cheeks were trembling, and I could hear his teeth grinding together. His hand twitched, just a little, toward his left breast.

I rocked forward in my chair so I was standing, leaning over the desk, fists planted on either side of the typewriter. I didn't even bother throwing any magic at him, just *stared*.

Sometimes it helps not actually needing to blink.

"Go ahead," I said softly. "Skin it. You'll look real nice in pine; goes with your complexion."

For a minute, I thought he might actually go for it and that I would have to put him down. But then his face went even redder, he growled something—probably about me "regretting it," 'cause that's always what they say—and he stood and stomped from the office, leaving the door hanging open.

And that mighta been the end of the whole thing, or at least my part in it, if it hadn't been for my *next* visitor. They musta passed each other in the hall, because I'd barely had time to pop the cap off a bottle, take a quick gulp, and move around the desk toward the door when someone else appeared in it. The amount of bushy white fuzz on his head was unbelievable; on top, on his cheeks and chin, over his blinkers, even coming out of his ears. He was basically a walking dandelion—or a magician who'd gotten his trick wrong, and tried to hide the rabbit in his *head*.

"Hey, Mr. Soucek!"

"Hello, Mr. Oberon. I tell you before, you call me 'Jozka,' please."

"Soon as you call me 'Mick,' Mr. Soucek."

It was sort of a running joke between us, but

today, Jozka didn't look to be that into it. Of about a zillion Czech immigrants in the Pilsen neighborhood, my landlord was one of the few who'd made good. He'd actually bordered on being rich for a while there—until Black Tuesday. He'd seemed harried all the time, ever since, but I'd rarely seen him looking this blue. Not since our very first meeting...

"Everything okay?" I asked him.

"I can come in, maybe, Mr. Oberon?"

"Sure, sure. Take a seat." I shut the door behind him. "Get you some milk?"

"I thank you, no," he said. His hands were actually clenched together in his lap, and I felt a faint tingle run up my spine. Lead in my guts, I sat across from him.

"Um, Mr. Oberon..." His voice cracked. I said nothing more, just waited. "I try calling you before," he said, "on the pay-telephone."

Ah. "I heard. I was with a client."

"This client, he makes you good offer, I hope?"

That's never a good question. "I'm afraid we couldn't come to terms."

"Oh." His whole face fell; he looked like a sagging cloud. "This is unfortunate. Mr. Oberon, you need to start to look for new place."

I swallowed once, and felt my jaw and fists clench. "Mr. Soucek..."

Seems he heard something nasty in my voice. "Oh, no, Mr. Oberon! I owe you so much, ever since you find out what happen to my darling Kalene, God rest her soul. I say you can stay always for free in my building, and I keep my promise. But... is not up to me anymore. Not enough tenants to

HOT LEAD, COLD IRON

pay, so—I am losing building."

It wasn't as if I could doubt him on that. I knew how much of the joint was sitting empty, and how long it'd been that way. If I'd ever bothered to think about it, I shoulda been surprised this hadn't happened a long time ago.

The timing, on the other hand, was more'n a little hinky.

"They did this, didn't they?" I demanded. I think I might actually have growled a little.

"They?"

"The fellas you owe, Jozka. They're pressuring you to pressure me, right?"

He offered me a sad little smile that made the hair on his face twitch like a whole swarm of caterpillars. "No, Mr. Oberon. All money I owe, is owed to bank. And they are 'pressuring me,' as you say, for weeks already."

All right, then. Not arm-twisting by Archie and his boss; just rotten timing. That's Fae luck for you. How did ol' Willy put it? "When sorrows come, they come not single spies, but in battalions."

Damn it, I *liked* that office! It ain't easy for me to find a place in this town—in this *world*—where I can get comfortable, but I'd finally settled in here, been here long enough for my own aura to start drowning out the spiritual noise from outside. (Also it was underground, which is a bonus for me.) Plus, Mr. Soucek didn't charge me rent, *and* he was grateful enough to me to put up with some of my, ah, *eccentricities* without complaint.

Damn it. Did I say that already?

"Okay. How much?"

"I'm sorry?"

"How much do you need?"

"Oh, no, Mr. Oberon. Even if you had so much, it would just happen again unless I get more tenants. I could never—"

"How much?"

He sighed. "Already I have put them off for a long time, so there is much interest, yes? Three hundred dollars I need, by end of month."

Ouch!

"All right, Jozka. You worry about finding some new bodies to fill the rooms. I'll get you the scratch to keep the building. Trust me, you'd rather owe me than the bank; I'm a lot easier to get along with."

He left a few minutes later, after a whole heap of thanks and apologies that were so tumbled together and mixed up that I think, at one point, *I* was thanking *him* for agreeing to accept the handout I'd offered. But anyway, he was gone, and I was left with my keister in the chair and my head in my hands.

I've never actually needed much money, you know? Enough for milk, clothes, a little theater or opera now and then. Most of my jobs, unless something's come up, I don't charge cash except to cover expenses. I barter. I ask for—well, for whatever urge takes me, like Baskin's parcel. Sometimes the stuff I ask for sits in my cabinet collecting dust. A couple of times, somebody's payment has helped me solve another case, or even saved my life.

Your whims can do that, when you're *aes sidhe*.

But the point is, I never had much cash flowing in, because it never seemed necessary. Which is all well and good, until you run into an emergency that costs a whole *hell* of a lot more than the cush you've saved up.

The brown paper crinkled loudly as I tore it open, sliding the twine aside, to reveal a large metal bracket. It didn't look anything special; you'd pass it by as a hunk of trash without looking twice, unless you already knew what it was.

And what it was was an old switch, long replaced, to the electric chair at Cook County Jail. It didn't hold any power itself, but *symbolically* it was connected to every man who ever fried in that particular hotsquat. And symbols are the language of magic itself.

I'd probably never use it for anything, but you never know. Like I said, the whim took me, so I asked.

I went to the filing cabinet and stuck it in a drawer with my other "special" payments: a cracked and yellowed copy of the Roman Rite, the reel from an old fishing rod, a perfume bottle of a blind girl's tears, Herman Mudgett's shaving razor, signed copies of *Frankenstein* and *A Princess of Mars*, and a bunch of other stuff that more or less resembled the leavings of a rummage sale. Then, slamming the door shut, I whirled toward my chair, snatched up my coat, and was out the door.

I needed dough? Fine. But I'd be damned if I'd go running back to Archie and the Outfit, not when I had friends I could call on first.

CHAPTER THREE

"Whaddaya mean, *nothing*?"

Pete Staten looked up at me from the wooden file drawer he'd been rifling through, tugged his officer's blue jacket with one hand, and used the other to smooth out a thin, not-quite-black mustache about the same shade as his receding hairline.

"C'mon, Mick." Even though I was just two steps away, he came close to shouting so I could hear him over the ruckus from the rest of the station. "What'd you expect? Sure, there's a few missing persons or property thefts in our caseload we could toss you, but they only pay a couple of sawbucks at most. Nothing that'd cover the scratch you say you need. And even if there *was* a job that important, you think the department has the budget to *pay* for it these days?"

Probably best that my response to that was lost beneath the nine-dozen other voices that were screaming and vying for attention around the desk sergeant's and receptionist's counters.

But if Pete told me that's all there was, I could take that to the bank (or more accurately, in this case, I *couldn't* take it to the bank). I've got lotsa acquaintances, not so many actual pals, but Pete was up there with the best of 'em. Unfortunately, knowing that he'd genuinely tried didn't help me much.

"What do you need it for?" he asked, sounding sympathetic. *Genuine* sympathetic, not "professional copper" sympathetic.

"Worst case of bad timing you can picture, Pete. You sure?" I asked, even though I knew he was. "Nothing at all, not even in the, uh, *special* file?"

He knew what I meant immediately. There's a tiny handful of cops and- politicos throughout Chicago who believe all day in the weird stuff that most of you Joes only believe in at three in the morning (none of them as well as Pete himself, of course). And a few of *those* knew enough to toss me the occasional investigation that they couldn't handle, though I'm pretty sure none of 'em knew *why* I was so well suited.

Pete frowned, took a quick gander around us, and then steered me through the nearest door. He didn't have an office of his own, being a simple beat cop, but Keenan wouldn't mind us using his for a spell.

Especially since he was out, and wouldn't know about it.

The shade in the door's window flapped, waving us hello, and the racket from the main room settled down into—well, a slightly less obnoxious racket. It wasn't much of an office: barely the size of a large closet, musty and sour, with revolting bluish-greyish paint peeling off the walls in chunks to reveal *older* revolting bluish-greyish paint.

But the paint and the stink weren't any better anywhere else in the station, so it was the privacy that made the difference.

"I guess *maybe*," he said, perching on the corner of Keenan's desk. "Had a few stiffs pop up down in Packingtown with some neck lacerations and not a whole lotta the red stuff. The brass is just calling it a crime spree, but you think maybe we could be looking at a vampire?"

I snorted. "You better hope not. You're thinking of Bela Whosis in that movie last year, and I promise, that ain't the half of it. But honestly, I doubt it. The genuine article ain't exactly as neat and tidy as 'some neck lacerations.' Still... How's the lettuce look if I do stick my nose in?"

Pete shrugged. "Depends on who makes the decision and what they believe. Square, though, Mick, you won't be earning what you're asking for. Maybe a C-note, if you're *very* lucky—and probably a lot less."

Damn. Yeah, a century was great payday for a farm-out from the PD, but not even close to what I needed.

I got a lot of former clients who were happy with my work, but only a couple are anything approaching rich. I'd already been to see them before I called on Pete; nobody had any sort of job for me, not with halfway enough pay, and I don't like to borrow from anyone—especially on someone else's behalf.

Which left me with three lousy options: I could let Mr. Soucek down, watch as he lost the building, and have to find myself new digs.

I could step Sideways, see if any of the debts and boons I held were still good, and try to get the scratch I needed off someone in the Seelie Court. I liked that idea even less than I did borrowing from a mortal; Fae debts ain't something you cash in, or get yourself into, lightly. Or at all, if you can help it.

Or I could suck it up, break my policy of not working for the Mob, and hope that it didn't get me mixed up with anyone worse than human thugs and made men.

Yeah. It's basically the lady or the tiger, if the lady's Typhoid Mary.

"Okay, Pete," I said, "I understand. Can I bum another favor off you, then?"

"Sure, if I can. Whatcha need?"

I offered him a clear view of my pearly whites. "Help finding a wiseguy."

Way his face fell, you'da thought I'd just kicked his dog. Off a roof. "C'mon, Mick, you're not working with those guys."

I shrugged. "I need the dough, Pete. I give you my word, if it's anything dirty they need from me, I'll walk."

Well, I'd walk if it was anything *too* dirty, anyway...

I could see him wrestling with himself, actually taste his indecision in the air, but he knew how much I needed this. Shoulders slumping, he went and opened the door. "Hey, Shaunny! Drag your butt over here a minute!"

"Go climb your thumb!" The response drifted from somewhere in the midst of the chaos beyond the office. "I'm fuckin' busy!"

Pete winced as a number of eyes and mouths widened among the people waiting for their chance to see whoever they were here to see. "So come be busy in here, goddamn it!" He turned back to me.

"Our precinct's expert on trouble boys. Anyone can help you find your wiseguy, it's him."

A few minutes later, someone shoved his way through the crowd and stomped into the doorway. You coulda peeled carrots in his hair and never known the difference, and I wasn't sure there was a face behind all those freckles. He wore green suspenders, his shirtsleeves rolled up, and a scowl that was certainly perpetual. If they ever wanted to put the "Irish cop" stereotype to bed, someone would have to shoot this fella first.

"Mick," Pete said, "this is Detective Driscoll Shaugnessy."

Of course he was.

"Shaun, Mick Oberon, PI. You've probably seen him around?"

"Yeah, what of it? I'm workin', here."

I couldn't help but grin a little; I've known that attitude for *ages*. "I need your expertise, detective. To find a man."

"Yeah? Ain't that usually *your* job?" He sighed before I could answer. "Okay, fine. Mick, is it? You're a brave man, walkin' around with a name like that."

"And you, with hair like that."

He laughed as though he really didn't want to. "So who you looking for?"

"Name's Archie. Might be a made guy; certainly *works* for one."

"'Kay, what else?"

Unfortunately, I didn't actually *have* a lot of else. I hadn't planned on ever talking to the gink again, y'know?

When I was done, which took about as long as a schoolboy in a brothel, Pete and Shaugnessy were both looking shivs at me.

"*That's* what you got?" the detective asked me. "His name's Archie, and he *might* be a dago?" I winced at that a little, but nodded. "You know how many Archies there are in this town?"

I shrugged. He rolled his eyes at Pete. "I thought you said he was a private dick?"

"Well... Maybe you could have him look through some mug shots?" Pete offered.

"Right, 'cause I don't have a fucking thing better to do all day than to shuffle pictures in front of some cut-rate shamus. Don't you have *anything* else, *Mick*?"

Actually... "He did have an obnoxious habit of repeating most of what I—"

Shaugnessy was already nodding. "Oh, yeah, I know him. Archie Caristo, a.k.a. 'Archie Echoes.' I don't imagine I need to tell you why."

"I think I can puzzle it out," I said.

"He's a torpedo and bodyguard for Fino 'the Shark' Ottati, a *capo* who runs a crew for the Outfit. Word on the street is that he's got a pipeline straight to Tony Volpe, and actually has dinner with Frank Nitti now and again. Not a big fish, but he swims with them, and he's a good earner. Not the best guy to mess with, Mick."

A-hah! I *knew* "Echoes" felt like one of Capone's old organization!

"I don't plan on messing with him, detective. Just chatting some with his errand boy. Any idea where Archie hangs his hat?"

We jawed for a while—mostly Shaugnessy throwing information at me, me trying to squeeze the occasional question in edgewise, Pete adding a detail or two—and that was that. The detective left, with what might even have been a genuine warning to be careful, and I bent to collect my coat.

"Thanks for the help, Pete. I appreciate it."

"I'm not happy about this," he admitted. "I'm holding you to your promise."

I nodded, and headed for the door.

"See you Monday," he said.

I halted, tilted my head as I tried to envision the calendar. "Wow. Full moon already?"

He nodded. "Seems like the last one was just a month ago, doesn't it?"

"Cute." Actually, I couldn't help but smile, glad to see that Pete was adapting well enough that he could crack wise about it. "Yeah, swing by, bring the usual, you know the score."

I squeezed around, between, and in one case over the various desks, chairs, and people swarming the station like bees in a hive. It'd been a little chilly outside when I walked up, the last puffs of a dying winter, but in here everyone was so crammed in together, tighter'n butts in a pack, that I was covered in sweat by the time I approached the door (and remember, none of it coulda been mine). I'd almost made my sneak, actually reaching for the door, when I heard a voice call my name.

I was *not* in the mood for any more interruptions, but at least this one wasn't too unpleasant. A smiling, coffee-skinned woman in matching sea-foam blouse, skirt, and a floppy hat (tilted down toward one ear, of course), rose from a hardwood bench and practically lunged at me. I let her hug me—I'm not super comfortable with gratitude, frankly, even though I've earned my share of it—and even plant a kiss on my cheek. The tips of her bobbed hair tickled my nose a little, but I didn't think it'd be too friendly to sneeze in her ear.

"How've you been, Martha?" I frowned, suddenly wondering what she was doing here. "Somebody hasn't stolen the painting again, have they? Nothing's happened to your boys?"

"Oh, no, Mr. Oberon, nothing like that. I just witnessed poor Mr. Lawson down my block get beat something terrible, and the police asked me to come in and give a statement. I just saw you on your way out and wanted to thank you again for helping us."

"What I get paid for, Martha. They haven't kept you waiting out here too long, have they? I could say something, if you want." I know how things work; she'd probably been here longer than a lot of the whites who'd already done their business and gone.

"That's awfully kind of you, Mr. Oberon, but no, thank you. Wouldn't be worth the hassle they'd give me later on."

She was probably right, at that.

We exchanged a few more nonsense pleasantries— most of hers, like Mr. Soucek earlier, being variations on "thank you" that I really didn't need or want— and then I was, finally, on my way.

And if you're wondering why I bother to mention my little run-in with Mrs. Martha Ross, and her gratitude for the portrait I tracked down last year, it's because I wanna make it crystal clear that most of my cases are just as regular as you could ask. Plain, mundane, boring, with no shooting and no spells to be seen.

I figure I better mention that now, because considering what I've told you so far about my job for Baskin, and *especially* when I tell everything that happened next, you'd never buy it if I waited to make that claim later.

For some reason, Archie wasn't polite enough to just sit around waiting for me to find him, and knowing a man's haunts only helps you so much when he's got half a dozen of 'em. So I spent the next day-and-a-half looking for the son of a bitch, and my nerves were so frazzled from spending so much time on the L that I was about ready to bust—and probably take half a neighborhood or so with me.

It didn't used to be that hard, back when the L had an actual engine, way a train's *supposed* to. Then I could sit way in the back, get some distance from the machinery. Nowadays it's all electric, same as the city's streetcars, and there ain't anywhere in the train to go that's better'n anywhere else. I weathered it, because I *had* to weather it, and damn near ground my teeth down to the gums.

I almost dropped to my knees and offered a few Hail Somebodies—anybody woulda done, honestly—when I finally found him in a tiny deli called Kellman's, down on Newberry, with wide windows and a blinding blue-and-yellow awning. Just a few blocks from the Jewish neighborhood called the Ghetto, even though it's not, really,

Kellman's offered the best pastrami, mustard, and kraut in Chicago.

I knew this 'cause the banner in the window told me so, in English and Hebrew both. (Well, I suppose that's what the Hebrew said, anyway.)

A few of the customers inside looked Hasidic, with the black hats and coats and beards, but they were actually a minority of the clientele. I spotted Archie, along with a few galoots who were probably part of his crew, sitting around a garish yellow table in the corner, talking around mouthfuls of sandwich. Echoes saw me giving him the up-and-down and scowled at me, but waved me over.

The sandwiches *did* smell good, or as good as food ever smells to me, considering how rarely I eat anything solid. Guess maybe it *was* the best in the Chicago.

"Aren't you supposed to be sitting in some Sicilian café sucking down spaghetti?" I asked as I squeezed past an old man in a tweed suit and bowtie.

"Sucking down spaghetti." Archie shook his head. "Funny guy. What, I can't get a craving for a good corned beef on rye once in a while?"

"I wish you hadn't. Took me a dog's age to find you."

"Dog's age. Right." He looked at the guys seated around him, took a moment to wipe some mustard off his kisser. "How *did* you find me, anyway?"

"Um... What's my job, again, Archie?"

"Yeah, but..." He was obviously unhappy that I'd tracked him down, and just as obviously unwilling to press it. "You boys scram for a bit, wouldja? Me and this *gavone* gotta talk."

I flopped into one of the chairs just vacated, and watched Archie watching me ignore the angry glowers they heaped on me as they left. "You don't scare easy, do you?" he asked with what sounded like grudging respect.

"I try to terrify myself real good at the beginning of the week, so I don't have any left later on."

He didn't look amused, but at least he didn't repeat it.

"Get you anything, mister?"

I didn't even glance at the young boy behind my shoulder. "Glass of milk, please. Warm, if you can manage it."

Archie laughed. "What're you, stupid? This here's a Jewish deli, *babbo*. They don't serve milk; wouldn't be, ah, whatchacallit? Kosher."

I'd actually known that, just hadn't been thinking. I was a little surprised that *he* knew it, though.

"Right. No thanks, then." I heard the boy wander off to the next table.

"So, Mickey…" Archie began, reaching for the remains of his corned beef.

"Mick. Not Mickey."

"Mick?"

I was starting to get the strangest sense of *déjà vu*. What *is* it with my name, anyway. "Yeah. Mick."

"What's the difference?"

"One's me, the other's a mouse."

"Other's a mouse. Right." He smirked at me. "You don't look all *that* much like a mick, Mick."

"You don't look all *that* much like a wop, Caristo. Are we done slinging slurs at each other? Or should we keep wasting each other's time?"

I just wanna put on record that I fucking hate the way you people make me talk sometimes.

Archie bit off a huge chunk of sandwich and chewed at me. Yeah, *at* me. Finally, after a heavy gulp, "You're awful gutsy, to come in here and insult me after giving me the bum's rush."

"But that's why I'm here, Archie. I've decided to hear you out."

"You've decided to hear me out, huh? What changed?"

I shrugged. "What changed is my mind. You much care why?"

"Not much, no."

"So talk."

"Ain't that simple, Mick. It ain't my yarn to spin. Wait here; I gotta make a call. Don't touch my sandwich."

"Wouldn't dream of it. Archie?"

He stopped halfway out of his seat. "Yeah?"

"Tell whoever you're ringing up that this won't come cheap."

He frowned even deeper—I swear his chin was ready to just drop off his face by then—and headed outside. I saw the brim of his fedora swivel as he looked for a phone booth, and then he vanished down Newberry.

I only waited maybe five minutes before he was back, motioning me to stand up. "Meet's on," he told me. "Now." He gave me a quick pat-down—it says a lot about Chicago's current state that barely anyone gave him a second glance for it—and pulled my L&G from its holster with two fingers, like it was a snake he owed money.

I gave him the same song and dance I'd given Lieutenant Keenan, but I could see he wasn't buying a word of it. Either Archie Echoes was a damn paranoid son of a bitch—which, to be fair, was probably a job requirement in his line of work—or he knew more about me than he rightly should.

Either way, he stuck the wand in an inside pocket of his circus-tent-colored coat. "You'll get it back after," he said.

"I'd better."

"You'd better. Right." But I think he knew I was serious, since he had the good grace to flinch at my tone a little. He swiveled back toward the door, leaving me to follow him out onto the street. The hems of skirts and jackets kicked up a breeze along the bustling sidewalk. People tromped in and out of neighboring shops and tenements, and the air smelled a lot more of cooking meats and burning firewood and car exhaust than it did the coming spring.

Just another March day in what you saps think is the "real" world.

And then I was yanked right back out of my musing and *into* the world—real or otherwise— when Archie asked, "You got a flivver?"

"Uh…" That snake I mentioned a minute ago? My gut started churning as though I'd swallowed it, and a few dozen of its closest pals. "No, I don't drive. I'm more a train kinda guy."

"Train kinda guy. Huh. Well, I got mine parked around the block a ways. Let's go."

"Couldn't we…?" I clamped my trap shut before I embarrassed myself. No, of course we couldn't. We had a meeting to get to—possibly with Fino Ottati, if I figured right—and he wasn't about to delay it because the great detective Mick Oberon would rather stick his hand in a redcap's mouth than climb into an automobile.

My feet seemed to move faster than ever before, even though everything else was crawling through molasses, and we reached our destination way too soon for my tastes. To you, it woulda just been an oak leaf-green Model 37 Marquette, sitting on gleaming whitewalls. To me, it was a rolling torture chamber in a metal box. Archie showed surprising manners in opening the door for me, and gave me a *very* peculiar look when I reached past him to open the back door instead. "I look like a chauffeur to you, Oberon?"

"I'm more comfortable in back," I explained, in what I *think* was a steady voice. I sure wasn't going to tell him it was 'cause I wanted to be as far away from the engine as I could get.

"More comfortable in back. Okay…" He shut both doors and wandered around to the driver's side.

I suppose I've danced around this thing with me and human technology long enough; I probably oughta explain.

Y'see, it's the whole reason we—and by "we" I mean all sorts of Fae—ain't around much anymore. The whole reason, or one of the big ones, why you were able to drive most of us away over the years. We're creatures of the old world; primal, natural. Technology, industry, all that jazz, it *hurts*. Being around anything too advanced… You know those itches you get that keep moving around, so you can't ever scratch 'em good? That high-pitched hum in your ears from some lights or power lines? Those deep muscle aches that come from nowhere, and that no amount of aspirin can help? It's all of those combined, but in the *soul*, not the body. We feel it all the time, in the modern world, but some of us learn to tune it out. Mostly.

But actually using it? Talking on the horn, sitting in a car? That's awful enough to get to even the strongest of us. I've known Fae—mostly other *aes sidhe*, but a few *gancanagh* and *haltijas*—who had reasons as solid as mine for leaving Elphame, and who eventually went back anyway, just 'cause they couldn't tolerate this place anymore. Every device you build, every advance you make, your world gets that much more uncomfortable, that much more *alien*, to us.

I suppose there may come a day where I follow them. But for now, my reasons for leaving the Otherworld are stronger than my reasons for leaving this one.

Though sitting in the back of that flivver, twitching with every bump, pale and shaking hands clutching the edge of the seat, it was a damn near thing.

I couldn't tell you how long the drive was, since I was mostly concentrating on not either screaming or lashing out with my will at the engine; I *probably* couldn't do much to it without my wand, since I sure as hell wasn't in any condition to concentrate, but you never know for certain. I wasn't *completely* oblivious, though. I recognized Michigan Avenue, the fancy shopfronts and more formal dress on the pedestrians.

And down the street, I recognized the rounded corners, brick façade with terracotta trim, and big honking stone pillars of the Lexington Hotel.

"You're kidding me, right? For a meet like this? Ain't that a little cheeky?"

Archie shrugged. From behind, I couldn't tell if he was actually embarrassed or just humoring me. "Whaddaya want from me, Oberon? She got fond of the food, back when Al called all his sit-downs here."

She? We weren't meeting Fino the Shark then? Interesting… And well timed, since mulling over the implications in my head kept me distracted from the last couple of minutes of the drive. We pulled up in front of the column-flanked doors, Archie tossed his keys to the white-shirted and black-vested valet—I have to assume they already knew each other, since Echoes didn't bother to threaten the man about taking care of the flivver—and we headed inside.

I've been in palaces smaller and less ornate than the lobby of this place. Pathways of tiled linoleum ran around and between carpeted sitting areas of plush sofas, marble-faced counters, and a whole heap of shops and meeting rooms, all lit by hanging chandeliers. The Lexington mighta lost their biggest client when Capone got shipped off to the pen last year, but it didn't seem to be hurting them any.

I heard a live jazz band from the direction of the banquet hall, but Archie was guiding me in a different direction. We stepped through a couple of doors, past a couple of waiters in fancy shirts— one white, one black, which I gotta admit surprised me—and into the dining room.

The joint was crowded, but not *too*. Rows of tables draped in pristine cloths provided pathways for the waiters to bustle between the customers. I couldn't help but notice that all the waiters who were actually, y'know, *waiting* on people were white. I guess the fella at the front was mostly for show.

Nice, huh?

Archie went and traded a few quick words with the waiters at the door, and then led me to one particular table. Then, as I started to sit, he pointed to a different chair. "No. There."

"Why's it matter?"

"Why's it…? Just do it, Oberon, wouldja? You'll see."

He then draped his own coat over a chair at a table *next* to mine, and I thought I'd figured it out.

I *knew* I'd figured it out when the others arrived: two guys dressed a lot like Archie himself, only a little less loud, accompanying the woman I was there to meet. Her hair was black, a lot longer than the current fashion, and she was without a hat. She wore a burgundy dress and pearls as though she'd rather have been wearing a pantsuit, and if you wanna know what that looks like, tough. I can't describe it; I just know that's how she came across. I'd put her close to forty, at a quick estimate, and she mighta been beautiful if the worry and grief under her face hadn't twisted the skin into such ugly shapes.

I ordered a glass of milk while they were getting situated.

She returned Archie's wave with a simple nod, whispered something to her bodyguards, and headed this way. The other two men took seats at a table by the door, near enough for trouble but not enough to overhear her conversation. She sat across from Archie, and yep, he'd done what I thought he had. She and I had our backs to each other, but we were only a few feet apart. Anyone, even her boys back there, would think she was talking to him.

As for me, I twisted sideways just a little, so that I could hold up my menu, or my glass once it arrived, and her bodyguards wouldn't see me talking at all.

"I'm so glad you reconsidered my offer, Mr. Oberon," she said. Her voice was husky, just slightly hoarse. She'd either been sick, smoking a whole heck of a lot, or crying. Maybe all three. "I'm terribly afraid that you're the only one who can help me."

"Well, I'm willing to listen, anyway. No promises, you understand."

She nodded. "Thank you all the same. My name is Bianca Ottati."

Ah. The Shark's wife. "Your husband don't know you're here, does he, Mrs. Ottati." I didn't really ask it as a question.

I heard her stiffen, but she said nothing as the waiter returned with my glass. It was chilly; how friggin' hard of an order is "warm milk," anyway? He asked if I wanted anything else, I told him I'd study the menu for a while, he went to the next table and asked if *they* wanted anything, and I could tell that Bianca was about to bust by the time they finally shooed him away.

"How did you know?" she asked once we finally had some privacy again.

I shifted in my chair, raised the glass to my lips. "This whole setup. This ain't just about making sure nobody overhears us, you don't even want your boys back there to know we're talking."

"Very good, Mr. Oberon. You're quite right. I

couldn't leave the house without them—my husband's currently having some, ah, disagreements with his rivals—but I don't want them hearing this. So far as they know, I'm just here visiting with my friend."

"And Echoes over there? You trust *him*?" I didn't have to see him to know he was scowling at me when I said that.

"As I just said, Archie and I are friends—have been for years. Since before I met my husband, in fact. I trust him implicitly."

And Fino trusts him with you? But I didn't think that'd be the most politic thing to ask right about then.

"So, Mrs. Ottati. So what's the big, ugly secret you need me to handle?"

I heard her take a deep breath behind me, as well as a sniffle that could only be the forerunner of tears. "I need you to find my daughter, Mr. Oberon."

My turn to go a bit stiff. That was *not* what I'd been expecting; I'd imagined she'd lost some of her husband's money, or maybe she was being leaned on by an ex-lover. A missing girl? A Mafioso's *daughter*, at that?

"And," she continued, "I need you to find her before my husband learns she's missing. He's already involved in one war; I don't want him tearing this town apart looking for her. The distraction could get him killed, and it'll *certainly* get *someone* killed."

I nodded; she'd anticipated my first question, right enough. "Okay. How long's she been missing?"

"Sixteen years."

Um… What? "Mrs. Ottati, I'm not sure I follow. How could your husband not—?"

"That's why it had to be you and no one else."

She was crying now, openly but softly. "As far as my husband knows, our daughter's at home as we speak. But Mr. Oberon, the girl we've raised for sixteen years is not our daughter at all.

"She's a changeling."

CHAPTER FOUR

You ever experienced noisy silence before? I mean like when you're sitting in a big, public room—let's say, oh, a half-crowded dining room—and you can hear all the talking and laughing and clattering of spoons and squeaking of chairs and sparking of lighters, but it's all distant. It's all happening somewhere far, far away, so that even though it's *there*, it's all background. And around you, in your ears and your mind, there's nothing at all but quiet.

Yeah. The whole world had gone away, and I was having one of those.

I tried to say something, croaked a little, took a big slug of milk and tried again. "What?" I finally asked.

Brilliant question, Mick.

"A changeling," she said again, her tone surprised—and pretty blatantly suggesting that I was some kinda special idiot. "When they…" She sniffled. "When they take a human baby, and replace it with—"

"I *know* what a changeling is, Mrs. Ottati." I was starting to recover a little, starting to think again, and not liking anything I was thinking *about*. "I mean, what on Earth could possess you to think that your *daughter's* one?"

I was starting to get a little agitated; I picked up my menu again and shifted in my chair, making sure her boys across the room hadn't tumbled to our conversation. It's *obnoxious* trying to talk about anything important to someone when you can't face each other. I don't recommend you give it a whirl.

"Adalina…" Another sniff. "Adalina was always a sickly child, but she used to be a good girl. Such a good girl…" She sobbed softly, and I could hear the rustle of her dress's padded shoulders as she shook.

"Nix the waterworks, sister, and give it to me straight."

She gasped as though I'd slapped her, and I heard Archie's chair scrape across the floor as he started to stand, but it did the trick. She stiffened in her seat, and her voice was hard when she said, "Very well, Mr. Oberon. Straight it is."

You probably think I'm cold, but you gotta understand… I know how you humans are. It wasn't that I thought she was faking it—she *could* have been that good an actress, but the tears smelled genuine, her words tasted honest—it's just that I knew if she got on a jag, we'd be here forever.

Anger's a lot more efficient than grief, see?

Bianca said something to Archie, something calming, and he sat his keister back down. Then, her neck held rigid—I knew because of how her voice sounded—she started again.

"Adalina got very sick only two weeks after she was born," she said. "We managed to nurse her back to health, but she was always small for her age growing up. Donna Orsola and I took care of her as best we could, but she was always weak, always clumsy, always getting ill."

"Donna Orsola?"

"Orsola Maldera," she clarified. "Fino's mother."

"Ah. Okay, Mrs. Ottati, please go on."

"Well, it was a hardship, of course, but nothing too awful, and certainly nothing we weren't willing to put up with for our daughter. But it only got more peculiar as she grew older. She never, ah, she never began… her, ah…"

"Her cycle." I swear, you people are squeamish about the strangest things. "I understand."

It ain't possible, but I swear I *heard* Bianca blush to speak of such things in public, and she nodded brusquely. "Right. We thought she was just a late bloomer, what with her being so sickly, but she's sixteen now… And it's gotten worse. In just the past few months, she's developed a fearsome temper. She's getting into fights at school, and even though she's weaker than the other girls, she's doing terrible injury to them. Biting, clawing, yanking out whole handfuls of hair. She never had many friends, and now she's driven most of them away. Even Gary— her, uh, young man—walked away from her. A fact I've kept from her father," she added quickly, "since I don't really care to see the boy fall on a baseball bat half a dozen times.

"But it's not just her behavior, Mr. Oberon. She looks so *strange*, almost deformed." She started to sniffle again, cleared her throat loudly to cover it. "We thought at first that she might be possessed, but while she reacted poorly to Donna Orsola's and my own prayers and rosaries, it wasn't enough to suggest a demon or a spirit inside her. It was then that we understood what she must be—what she'd always been.

"I need you to find my *real* daughter. Before it gets worse, before she seriously hurts someone, and before my husband finds out. You know Fino's business and associates, so you know how important family is to him."

I frowned around another sip of milk. "Mrs. Ottati, everything you're describing actually *could* be the result of illness and dementia. I think you oughta—"

"Mr. Oberon, I found you, didn't I? Do me the courtesy of assuming I know what I'm talking about."

Which, of course, brought up an interesting point. "How *do* you know? Assuming you're right, what kinda modern dame jumps to 'changeling' as an answer for these kinda problems? And how'd you know enough to come to me?"

"I'm not prepared to divulge that; it's enough for you that I know."

I'm pretty sure I was scowling by then. A changeling meant a lot of legwork, asking around for people I didn't much want to deal with, possibly going places I really, *really* didn't want to go. And sixteen years? The trail wasn't just cold, it was frostbitten enough to be losing toes.

"Mrs. Ottati, I don't think I—"

"Please, Mr. Oberon. She's my *daughter*."

"I know, but I can't—"

"There's nobody else who can help us."

"I'm sorry, I—"

"I'll pay you seven hundred and fifty dollars."

"I'll need half up-front."

Yeah, sometimes I *can* be bought against my

better judgment. Whaddaya want from me? That's more than half the average Joe's *yearly pay*. With that, I could get Soucek outta his jam, and have enough left that I wouldn't have to charge cash again for a good long while.

Archie was making sounds very much as if he was choking on a live marmoset.

"Archie?" Bianca asked. "Be a dear and hand me my bag, please."

"Ghlk!" he offered, as he did so.

I heard a snap pop open, then rustling papers. "Will a check be all right, Mr. Oberon?"

"Yeah, that'll do me fine." I don't actually keep a bank account, but I know several shopkeeps who'll trade me cash if I sign the check over to 'em.

The scratch of a scribbling fountain pen crawled up my back and over my shoulder from behind me.

"Uh, Bianca," Archie said, apparently having found his voice (possibly under the tablecloth). "I don't mean to stick my beezer in where it ain't welcome, but... seven hundred an' fifty? I know you got your own accounts and all, but Mr. Ottati, he's gonna notice if that kinda rhino goes missing."

"I know," she said, casually brushing the check off the table so it drifted to the floor beside the feet of her chair—and mine. "But it'll take him some time, busy as he is."

I took a quick gander, made sure nobody'd spotted her little maneuver, and then dropped my napkin. I bent down to retrieve it, sliding the check under it in the process.

And I was right about to pick 'em both up when her heel came down on the edge of the napkin.

"As long as our daughter's been found before he does…" Bianca continued, and though she was looking straight at Archie, it was crystal clear she wasn't talking to *him* anymore. "…then I can safely explain what happened, and there shouldn't be any problems for anybody. If he notices *before* that, we could all be in trouble. You understand, Mr. Oberon?"

"I understand that your shoe's on my payday, Mrs. Ottati. But yeah," I told her as she scooted her foot aside, "I got it. Don't dawdle."

And that was the last word we exchanged. Her food arrived a few moments later—roast quail, I think, with a whole heap of garnishes—and she and Archie ate in silence. Once they were done, she rose and swept imperially from the room, barely pausing long enough for her two guards to fall into step behind.

My wand thumped onto the table in front of me, bouncing with a clatter off the edge of my glass. "Here's your dingus back," Archie said. I heard the sizzle of a lighter, caught a whiff of smoke. His fist closed on my shoulder, just tight enough to be uncomfortable. "That's a *lot* of scratch Mrs. Ottati's paying you. And a lot of personal, private stuff she told you. I dunno how much of it I buy, but I know *she* believes it. You try to cheat her, or embarrass her, or hurt her in any way…"

Interesting; it was "Mrs. Ottati" now, but it'd been "Bianca" when he was talking to her. "One, I don't chisel my clients, Archie. Ain't good for business. Mrs. Ottati's money, and her secrets, are safe with me. And two, get your hand off me before I make you eat it."

"Eat it. I'd love to see you try." But he did let go,

and the glowing tip of his cigarette appeared in the corner of my vision. "You need a lift back anywhere?"

I tensed a little, mostly to keep from shuddering. "Nah. I'll catch the L."

He nodded, dropped a few bills back on his table, and then he, too, was gone. I sat for a while longer, going over it all. It was probably a good thing nobody paid me much attention, 'cause I think I forgot to do all the little things—y'know, fidgeting, blinking—that you guys expect. What can I say? The whole situation had knocked me for a loop.

So, what'd I have?

Well, on the plus side, I wasn't actually working for the Outfit or anyone in it, though working for a made guy's frau was close enough that they might notice me if I wasn't careful.

But on the other hand, if I really was looking for a changeling—and I didn't know for sure that I was, though it all sounded right—it meant I might have to deal with other Fae, and probably the Unseelie, since kidnapping is more their bailiwick. So avoiding the Outfit directly might not have actually *accomplished* much of anything.

And to top it all off, any clues that might still be lying around were probably older than Prohibition.

Yeah, I had a *headache*, that's what I had.

Grumbling under my breath and pocketing both my wand and a check that didn't feel like quite as much dough as it had a few minutes ago, I dropped a few pennies on the table to cover the milk and shuffled toward the door.

***

If I had any hope at all of avoiding the Otherworld, it meant tracking down some people—and I use the term loosely—who might already know the score. It was duck soup finding a couple of them; the others proved a little tougher.

The wind had kicked up something fierce by that evening, whipping and spinning down the city's streets, twisting litter and fallen leaves into little spiral staircases to nowhere. People quickened their pace along the sidewalks and up on the L's platforms, clutching their coats around them. The weather was *probably* just gonna stay breezy, without any real rain—that's how it smelled, anyway—but I wouldn't have sworn to it under oath.

I climbed down the steps from the L, squeezing through the bustling crowd and trying to steady my breath from yet *another* ride on that damn electrical railway, passed under the tracks clacking and settling way overhead, and made my way up South Princeton. There, within spitting distance of Schorling's Park, was the place I was supposed to find the guy.

Course, this was the *third place* where I'd been "supposed to find the guy," and my patience was stretching thin as taffy.

I could sense the crowd—not just hear 'em and smell 'em, though there was plenty of sound and stink to be had, but *sense* 'em—before I even got near the building. Just a plain greystone, it mighta once been a row house, or a warehouse, or who-knew-what else. Now, though, with most of its inner walls knocked down and cleared out, it was a cheap, makeshift stadium for the poor folk (read: mostly black) of the neighborhood. Sometimes it hosted local jazz bands that weren't big enough, or quite good enough, to play the Savoy; sometimes a cheap-production play.

And sometimes—tonight, just for instance—they rigged up a ring in the middle of the place, with drooping ropes and sagging floorboards, and put on a boxing match.

The economy being what it was, prizefighters were earning a lot less these days than they used to, and there were a whole lot more burly galoots looking to earn a living with their knuckles, so it shoulda surprised absolutely nobody that a bunch of local circuits—some legit, some less so—sprung up outside the auspices of the National Boxing Association. I hadn't actually *been* to any before—once you've witnessed (and lived through) a couple dozen duels, boxing just don't hold the same excitement—but I could see two things straightaway, soon as I walked through the door.

First, neither of these fellas was a Jack Dempsey yet, but they were pretty good; the pro fighters would have some competition if they ever broke out of the local scene.

And second, the fight here mighta been regulated as though it was official—gloves, ref, timer, all that—but the *bystanders* sure as spit weren't.

Most of the audience was black, just by virtue of the neighborhood, but there were more than enough white faces to suggest that word of this particular circuit had spread. Voices and arms, the latter covered in everything from cleaned and pressed coatsleeves to yellowed rolled-up shirtsleeves—were raised high, and while most were cheering for one boxer or the other, more'n a few were clutching bills and shouting for the attention of anyone making book.

Of whom, without taking but a few heartbeats to get a good slant on the place, I spotted at least four. Guys weaving through the crowd or perched on a stepladder against one of the walls, collecting dough from a dozen hands at once that probably couldn't really afford to lose it. I wondered, for about a blink, which of the fighters was the favorite and what the odds were, before remembering that I had no reason in the world to care.

Yeah, lotsa ways to earn a quick buck, and to lose an even quicker one. This was definitely his kinda place. Shouldering and elbowing between bellowing bystanders, blinking through enough cigarette smoke to fill a zeppelin, and trying neither to go deaf from the roar of the crowd nor to slip on the various puddles of legitimate cola and bootleg beer, I went off in search of Four-Leaf Franky.

I got shoved a few times—once practically off my feet—and pounded by some glowers that were even harder than the fists flying in the ring, but I finally picked him out. Sure enough, he was loitering around toward the back of the joint, collecting money hand over fist, and scribbling down people's wagers in a raggedy notebook. I couldn't make out much detail from where I was, but yeah, it was Franky all right.

But I hadn't gotten another yard closer when someone else beat me to him.

From behind a curtain of sweaty meat in acrid clothes, I watched as some palooka roughly the height of the Old Chicago Water Tower, with fists that'd probably send both boxers running home to momma, put a not-too-friendly arm around Franky's shoulders. Four-Leaf's peepers went wider than his glasses, and he let the big guy guide him— since the other choice was probably being picked up and thrown—toward the closest back door. The bell chimed loudly, signaling the end of the round, as if to punctuate my own thoughts.

Is my timing perfect, or what?

Sardine-packed crowd between me and them; sardine-packed crowd between me and the front door, too, but a little less of it. I headed back the way I came, one hand on the butt of my L&G in the holster, glaring and grousing willpower out before me like the cowcatcher on a train. Wasn't easy messing with so many minds at once, but then, I wasn't trying to do anything too subtle, either. I just sort of tickled at the fear that lurks in everyone's mind, making them jump, or else ran a faint itch down a foot or a calf so that they'd shift one way or another. It didn't exactly clear me a path, not in a joint this crowded, but it thinned 'em out some, enough that I could squeeze or elbow my way through what was left. Again I got shoved and shouted at more'n once, and again I kept my feet through the worst of it.

In the doorway, I just about bowled over an older black couple who were, frankly, dressed far too nice for this sorta venue, offered a quick nod of apology, and was sprinting off down the street. Round the corner, between the walls of the greystone and a ramshackle grocer's next door, old newspaper flapping against my ankles and broken bottles crunching beneath my shoes…

And into the back alley, which woulda been ankle-deep in the same sorts of garbage if the winds weren't picking the stuff up and tossing it down somewhere else like an indecisive child. The place smelled of rotting food, stale liquor, and piss (both rat and human)—same as every other alley in Chicago, basically.

Except every other alley in Chicago didn't have Franky Donovan getting beat into porridge by a giant in a blue overcoat.

(I suppose, given what you already know about what I am and where I come from, that I oughta clarify: I'm speaking metaphorically here. Guy wasn't an *actual* giant; just plenty rugged and built to match, so he *seemed* big enough. Just so we're clear.)

I gotta admit, I was awfully tempted just to let Franky take his lumps. Heck, I'd have been tempted to let him take other people's lumps, too. Chances were pretty damn good that he'd done something to deserve whatever he was getting, and I knew that unless the bruiser pounding on him was wearing iron knuckles, he wasn't about to do Franky any permanent damage. So whatever was happening here, it was none of my business.

But then, I kinda needed Franky to be able to talk, and having him owe me one wouldn't *hurt* my cause any.

The thug was rifling through Four-Leaf's pockets when I deliberately cleared my throat. I stood, squinting, coat flapping in the wind, fist under my jacket and clenched on the wand. Impressive, if I say so myself, especially since I was focusing more'n a touch of willpower to *make* it feel impressive.

"Get off him," I said simply, "or I'll *make* you."

The big guy turned, and stood. And stood. And holy mackerel, *kept* standing! (I was starting to doubt my initial assessment that he wasn't a real giant.)

And you know what? Magic or no, I don't think he was all that impressed. It mighta been, in part, because I had to crane my neck back something fierce in order to stare him in anything other than the nipples.

"Huh," I said.

His greasy, unshaven face glowered down at me from on high. "You really wanna walk away," he told me.

"Yeah, I really do," I agreed.

He started to turn.

"I can't, though." I drew the L&G and squeezed off a burst of raw terror that shoulda had him squalling and pissing himself as he ran the other way.

But damn, the guy wasn't just big, he was *fast*. I'm sure he thought I was pulling a gat, not a stick of whitewood; either way, he'd dropped into a shoulder-roll, passing clear beneath my line of fire, before shooting back to his feet like a breaching whale. He hit me in the sternum with both open palms, lifting me off the ground and hurling me back to land in a sprawling heap amid the rest of the trash. A human woulda had half a dozen broken ribs, might even be dying; me, I just hurt. A lot.

Several old strips of newspaper and packing paper drifted down from the winds to settle over me. I sort of dizzily glanced aside, squinting against the dust the impact—*my* impact—had kicked up.

Much to my surprise, my wand was still sitting in the palm of my hand, in a slack grip that could be called a fist the same way local grain alcohol can be called a fine aperitif. "That," I muttered, wheezing a little around the throbbing ache in my chest, "could probably have gone better."

"I'd say so," the extra-large goon commented, setting a pool-table-sized foot down on my wand—and, rather more uncomfortably, the hand holding it. I actually heard the bones in my fingers creak in protest. "I... What the fuck kinda heater is *that*?"

"It's not a heater. It's a magic wand."

"Uh-huh." His tone, his gaze, his body language, all of it more or less screamed that he'd decided I was a lunatic. It didn't get him to take his foot off me, though. "And what's it do?"

"Well, among other things, it catches on fire." Which it then, with a mental nudge from me, proceeded to do.

Or at least, he *thought* it did, which amounted to the same thing.

He actually leaped back, swearing something ugly, beating at the sole of his shoe. I took the opportunity to stand, wincing a little, and to shrug the litter off my chest and shoulders. A flick of the wand yanked away a tiny portion of the big palooka's luck; as he hopped back, trying to examine his "burned" foot, his other heel snagged on the slats of a broken crate and he toppled backward, landing as hard as I had. He flung his hands out, trying to stop himself, and I saw his pinky finger snap between the joints where it dragged down the side of the nearest wall.

The fella was tough, I'll give him that. He didn't

do more than grunt at the sudden agony. But for most people, pain just makes their mind even easier to access. I strode over to him and tapped him on the temple with the wand.

To him, thanks to another tiny surge of magic, it felt more like being "tapped" on the temple with a sledgehammer, and he was out quicker'n a candle in a monsoon. Sleeping minds are even easier to access than pained ones, and I spent a good minute reaching through his dreams, dragging them to the forefront of his mind, burying his conscious thoughts as deep as they'd go. He'd sleep for a couple of *days*, now, assuming nothing too violent happened to him in the interim.

Maybe I'd call a meat wagon to take him to the hospital before I left. We'd have to see how charitable I was feeling.

I took a moment to dig through his overcoat pockets, found the wad of dough I was expecting, and wandered down the alley toward the heap that called itself Four-Leaf Franky.

He was staring at me, bleary and blurry, his broken glasses hanging from one ear. His hair, the color of summer-burnt grass, was standing up in spikes, and he was already forming two impressive shiners. His suit, which looked as cheap as mine— actually, I think it *was* mine, just in green instead of blue—was badly rumpled. But then, that might not have been from the beating; all of his suits have been slept in so often, they oughta charge rent.

I leaned in, plucked the bent frames off his ear, and stuck 'em back on his face. The lenses were cracked, but I guess it was better'n nothing.

"Oh! Hey, Mick. How you been?"

I couldn't help but notice that his lips weren't swollen or bleeding, that his teeth were all present and accounted for. "Not bad, Franky. Been better. So have you, from the looks of it."

"Yeah." I saw his gaze flicker nervously past me, toward the thug crumpled a ways down the alley. He blinked twice and went pale. "Wow. You do that?"

I pulled open his coat, shoved the cash into his inside pocket. I also found a couple of thin gold chains hanging around his neck.

Not at all unusual, not with Four-Leaf Franky. He *always* had gold on him—chains, rings, watches, whatever. He was always losing it, either hocking it for cash or, more often, getting beat-up and robbed for it, and he always had more within a few days. When you have tastes like Franky's, it helps to have his relatives, too. He's mixed-race, see, and while he's mostly *aes sidhe*, I happen to know that he's also related to an old bloodline of leprechauns.

So yeah, that Franky was wearing gold wasn't surprising. That Paul Bunyan back there hadn't taken it, however, was. At which point, I tumbled to exactly why.

Ah. Right. I shoulda expected something like this. Franky'd always been nothing more'n a cheap conman, the kinda guy who'd happily chisel little old grandmothers out of their gin money. (Cards or bottles, take your pick.)

"Smart idea, Franky. What'd you owe him for? Gambling? Hooch? Skirts?"

"I don't know what you're talking about, Mick," he protested, in a tone of voice that said very clearly,

"I know exactly what you're talking about, Mick."

"Sure, sure," I said, patting his cheek. "Next time, though, you gotta make it look more legit. *Nobody* who knows you would ever believe that anyone who was hitting you didn't sock you one in the kisser. That's the first place anybody would wanna hit you."

He gave me a wounded look.

"And make sure they take the gold, too. Otherwise, nobody inside is gonna buy that you were actually robbed. You *did* want them to think that, right? So they wouldn't blame *you* for losing all the wagers you were holding?"

Franky sagged. "You won't say anything, will you, Mick? It's just, these guys *really* want their scratch…"

I shrugged at him. "None of my business either way. I gave you back your cash; up to you what you do with it." I aimed a thumb over my shoulder. "He'll be out for a good long while, so if you stick the money back in his coat, no skin off my nose." I stretched out a hand, helped him to his feet. "But you could do me a favor, Franky."

"Yeah? What'd that be?"

"I'm looking for a human. One who was Taken, sixteen years back."

Franky nodded. "Changeling?"

"Yep. Ottati family." Franky didn't react to the name, but that didn't prove much. Franky's one of us, so I can't always read him as well as I can you mugs—and I know from experience he's a solid liar. "I know you're even less popular in the Seelie Court than I am these days—"

"Hey, now!"

I ignored his complaint. "But I also know that you keep in contact with more of the folks back home than I do. Way I see it, if anyone's heard anything about this, it'd be you."

It wasn't the longshot you might think it was. Most of the time, a changeling swap is pretty public on the Fae side of things. We brag about it, show off our new pet or slave or whatever. Hell, I've actually seen formal parties thrown just for the "coming out" of a new human child added to someone's collection.

Yeah, it's ugly. But it's also out in the open. Which is why I was more'n a little shocked when Franky said, "I dunno, Mick. I mean, I can think of a couple of swaps around the time you're talking about, but that name ain't ringing any bells. You try talking to Lenai or Gaullman? Or maybe Pink Paddy?"

"Saw Paddy and Lenai before I came to you. And you and I both know how useless Gaullman is these days." I shook my head, bemused. "Really, Franky? You got nothing?"

"Sorry, Mick." At least he had the grace to pause and mull it over again. "I'll keep my ear to the ground for you, but I just never heard anything about who you're looking for."

"Damn it! You know what that means, right?"

Franky frowned. "I dunno that it means *anything*, Mick. I don't have the kind of connections I used to, and—"

I waved a hand, already dismissing him. Yeah, it *might* not mean anything. It *might* just be that Franky missed hearing about Ottati's daughter when it happened, or any mention since.

And Lenai did. And Pink Paddy. Possible, but not too probable.

Or it meant that someone was deliberately keeping it hush-hush. And if that were the case, this was something more than your average, everyday changeling swap.

I wandered from the alley and back toward the train, leaning into the wind. I never did call an ambulance for the big guy, or find out if Franky gave him back the cash. I was kinda distracted at the time, hunting for another alternative and whimpering to myself when I couldn't find one.

There was nothing else for it. I was gonna have to visit Elphame.

CHAPTER FIVE

It was witching-hour dark by the time my scuffed Oxfords reached the steps of home—partly because I'd decided to hoof it the few miles back to Pilsen, rather than spend one more minute on the goddamn Metropolitan Elevated. The L may not be nearly as bad as a flivver, but a guy can only take so much, y'know?

I'd spent most of the walk hunched, not just against the wind but the moisture in the air, a light shower that was more or less atomized by the constant gusts, transforming the world into one big puddle of wet. I decided—kinda petulantly, I'll admit—that since it wasn't strong enough to come down in drops, it wasn't *technically* rain, and so I hadn't been wrong in my earlier predictions.

I'm like that, sometimes.

Mr. Soucek's building was also a greystone, a little better kept-up than the heap hosting the prizefight. Three stories tall—plus the basement—it was, with the exception of a few potted plants and a little dirty-white trim around the ground-floor windows, pretty much indistinguishable from umpteen-and-a-half other buildings in and around Pilsen, and a zillion more throughout the rest of Chicago. I trudged up the steps, unlocked the door with a tarnished old key, and stepped in from the wind and the not-rain. The hallway stank of wet wool… No, wait. That was me. Huh.

I meandered past rows of doors, most of which had nothing but empty rooms behind 'em. Certainly no wonder that Jozka was about to lose the place, considering that I've tossed pennies at beggars who were probably pulling in more bread than this joint. Other'n mine—and Jozka's own, of course—there were only four other offices open in the building: a dentist, which woulda been convenient if I ever needed my teeth cleaned; a cheap, sleazy realtor, which woulda been convenient if I ever planned to buy a rundown, foreclosed property; and a tax accountant, which woulda been convenient if I ever paid… Huh. Y'know, given how the Feds took down Capone and his boys last year, maybe I shouldn't finish that thought.

But there was also a membership management office for the Milkman's Local, and that *was* convenient. In fact, tired and distracted as I was, I took a minute to wander upstairs and drop a few bucks in Ron Maddox's mailbox. The local rep, Ron and I had gotten to be pretty good friends—mostly because I *kept* dropping a few bucks in his box now and again—so he made sure my deliveries were as prompt as any of the uptown markets. He told me I went through milk like a grammar school, and once asked if I was trying to figure out how to grow my own cow, but he was happy to oblige.

I thought about swinging by Soucek's office, too—it'd be easy enough to sign the check over to him and get fifty bucks back—but I just didn't have it in me to suffer through twenty minutes of tears and handshakes and hugs and whatever other profuse thanks he would doubtless bury me under. I'd had more'n enough of you people's emotions for the day, thanks all the same.

I shut my door, dropped my coat on the floor vaguely near the rack, and went straight for the icebox. Filled a glass about halfway, topped it off the rest of the way with cream; I prefer to use that for celebrating, but right now I needed a pick-me-up. Didn't even feel like waiting for it to warm up a little. Tonic in one hand, I used the other to yank down the Murphy bed and then slumped down to sit on one corner of the mussed sheets.

Turns out I pretty much wasted the cream 'cause honestly? I don't even remember tasting it.

I *could* just throw the whole job. Ask around Chicago for a few more days, tell Bianca Ottati that I'd failed, and just keep the retainer. Even that half was more'n I needed to take care of my little housing problem. And I'd be lying to you if I said I didn't spend a good hour considering just that.

But I couldn't do it; didn't feel right. Professional pride, partly. And partly... Remember what I said about getting into bargains with Fae? Yeah, that sort of includes getting into bargains *as* a Fae. Bad things tend to happen to us if we don't honor our promises. That kinda trouble, I don't need.

So all right, fine. I had to go home again. I'd rather have shaved with a rusty cheese-grater, but I was going. But that didn't mean I had to go *now*. Pete was calling on Monday, and I'd be walking him

Sideways then anyway; might as well do it all in one trip, yeah?

That meant I had a few days to follow up more Earth-bound leads, and just maybe get lucky enough that I wouldn't need to go after all. I lay back for a couple hours of dreaming, already feeling a little better, and with a pretty good idea of where to start.

Next morning I changed into a suit that wasn't made *entirely* of wrinkles—even dusted off and donned my fedora, much as I loathe the thing, and stuck my L&G in a coat pocket since I didn't think holsters would be appreciated where I was going—and got started. Step one was easy enough; just had to wander down the hall, drop a few coins in the payphone, and then try to ignore the sensation of holding a smoldering ember to my ear while I waited for the operator to get me the address I'd asked for. She talked, I scribbled, and gratefully hung up the damn contraption.

Step two took a little longer, since it involved wandering through the sidewalks of Pilsen—today was just kinda breezy, enough that you wanted a coat, but not blowing so hard as last night—until I found a secondhand shop that had what I needed.

And there was step three: Traveling way the hell across town on the L and streetcars, to Calumet and 68th, lugging a vacuum cleaner the entire friggin' way. Canister that coulda been the Jolly Green Giant's thermos in one hand, an angry python's worth of tubing over the other shoulder, I could only grit my teeth and try to ignore the people staring and the incessant hum of the electrical wires. I think if the vacuum hadn't already been kaput inside, and so not bugging me too badly, I mighta gone right over the edge.

Finally, I hopped off the last streetcar of my trip and wandered up Calumet, wheeling the vacuum along behind me and smiling nice and friendly at everyone I passed. A few of them smiled back; most just kept staring. The homes here were right nobby; nice red brick, multiple bedrooms, well-kept lawns, clean windows. Not mansions or anything—you'd have to go a lot farther north for that—but rich enough compared to most folks these days.

Exactly the kinda place you'd wanna live if your goal was to enjoy your money without being ostentatious enough to attract the law's attention. I'd have been willing to bet that one or two in every ten houses in the neighborhood were bought with bootleg profits. Be interesting to see what happened here when the end to Prohibition that everyone knew was coming finally arrived.

I found the street number I was looking for and meandered up the walk, whistling a little jig that I don't think any human had heard in a couple hundred years. The house was a nice whitewashed two-story, with crucifixes in a couple of the windows and enough twitching curtains to tell me that I was being watched by at least three different guys.

Yeah, this'd be the right place, then. The door opened before I finished knocking.

"Good morning to you, sir," I said, touching the brim of my hat before sticking my hand in my pocket, and offered the broadest smile I could manage without causing actual injury. "I represent

Credne Household Device Repair, and I would very much love to offer you a free demonstration of what we can do with—" and here I nudged the vacuum with my foot "—older and obsolete equipment such as this. Is the lady of the house in, by any chance?"

Considering that the gorilla in the doorway was a good little Mob footsoldier, and that Ottati's crew was currently at war with a rival, there was absolutely no way he should even have finished listening to my spiel, let alone think about my question. But I was hitting him with a lot more'n my toothy grin. My fingers were clenched on the Luchtaine & Goodfellow in my pocket, and my thoughts were squeezing in through his eyes and ears, insinuating themselves into his own.

Tell ya square, I probably didn't need to haul the damn vacuum clear across the Windy City, but... Mrs. Ottati was wise to me and at least some of the real Chicago skinny. Wasn't *too* likely, but she mighta taken a few extra precautions with her security; figured a prop might help me push past any resistance.

And if you're all bothered wondering why I hadn't gotten the lowdown on that kinda thing *before* I took the job... Shut up. I was thrown; hadn't thought of it when she and me were bumping gums. Whaddaya want from me? It happens.

Anyway, nope. Turned out Muscles here wasn't any more of a brain, or any more warded against "suggestion," than any other goon. I didn't need to do much to him, didn't even really control his next actions. All I did was dust some of the suspicion off my request so it sounded reasonable.

"Hang on," he grunted at me. The door shut,

and I heard footsteps moving away. A few minutes later, one of the curtains rustled again—Mrs. Ottati seeing who the hell had been convincing enough to get one of her bodyguards to even ask such a stupid question, no doubt—and then, minutes after *that*, the hardwood door creaked open once more.

"C'mon in," the goon told me, a look of vague befuddlement on his face.

"Right kind of you," I said, scooping up my vacuum and stepping across the threshold...

Fire.

Not physical, but spiritual. I felt it searing across the back of my eyelids, inside my skull. My blood felt as though it were about to boil out through my pores, my skin to flake off and blow away. The air was a poison, my own thoughts a disease that my body needed to purge. My stomach roiled, and when I say I very nearly vomited across the carpet, you have to understand that vomiting is something we simply don't do. I swear, I could actually *smell* some sort of foul, acrid smoke. Dizziness washed over me as my eardrums threatened to melt away, and if the guy hadn't been in the process of patting me down for weapons (with the usual confusion after he found the wand), I'd have fallen right then. As it was, I collapsed to one knee as soon as he was done. I had *just* enough presence of mind, when the palooka looked at me funny, to fiddle with the connections on the vacuum as though I'd just spotted a problem.

Hunched over, gasping for breath, I struggled hard to regain control—and I gotta admit, I almost lost. I squeezed the wand in my pocket until it creaked, pumping my own emotions through it like it was part of my mind and soul, trying to use the magics to calm myself down, to strip away some of the pain. I briefly rested one hand on the floor, drawing strength from the earth and soil and growing things beneath the foundation. And more than anything else, I drew on who I was—on *what* I was—on the pride of the Tuatha Dé Danann, who ruled once as kings and gods among men.

And I'll tell you, I think it was probably the pride that saved me. Because *no fucking way* was I going to collapse in front of a bunch of mortals. Especially mortal criminals!

Especially over a damn vacuum cleaner!

I couldn't make the pain go away, but I could damp it down enough so that I could work around it, same way I usually do the itch of your technology. I felt sick as a leper with influenza, and I can only imagine how pale and ragged I looked, but I hauled myself to my feet and smiled at the fella watching me.

"Loose tube," I told him, as casually as I could manage. "That woulda been embarrassing to show the missus, wouldn't it?"

He grunted and waved me onward.

I didn't actually wanna *go* "onward." Every further step into that house made the nausea worse, threatened to bring back the pain. I had to literally drag my feet; I coulda sworn I was trying to trudge through deep, smog-infused, toxic snow. But I went, because the other choice—retreat—felt even worse.

It wasn't the house itself; wood, brick, piping, same as any other. I didn't see anything in the way of unholy tomes or ancient grimoires on the bookshelves, though I didn't have much time to give 'em a thorough up-and-down. The walls and shelves boasted enough crucifixes, portraits of the Virgin Mary, and lit votary candles to supply Holy Name Cathedral, with enough left over for one-and-a-half exorcisms, but I ain't a vampire or a demon, so that wasn't my problem, either.

So what was…? Oh.

I finally recognized the sensation—the pain, the nausea, all of it—right about the time I noticed a couple of chalk lines sticking out from under the door to what I think was probably a bathroom. And seeing *that* I was finally able to pick out the rest of it: the faint redolence of incense and holly, the grit of iron shavings in the chalk, the echo of inhuman names spoken hours or even days ago, lingering like whispering spirits in the air.

Wards. Someone had warded this house.

And not just any wards, not just protections against any old ghostie or ghoulie or long-leggedy beastie. Not with that precise combination of pure iron and herbs. This was a ward against Fae, specifically (or against what most of you *think* of as Fae, which is just a subset of… but never mind), scribed and incanted by an occultist who knew what they were doing. If someone hadn't actually invited me across the threshold, I'd never have been able to set one foot inside, no matter *how* stubborn and prideful I got.

That someone led me into a sitting room, chock full of couches and chairs covered in tasteful paisleys—with cushions so overstuffed that I figured an entire dynasty of geese had given their lives for this furniture—around a central hardwood table. A tea set of fine china sat in the exact center, along with a couple of small glasses for stronger and less legal drinking, but there was nothing in any of 'em at the moment.

"Wait here," he told me, still blinking like something was nagging at him. "Mrs. Ottati'll be down in a minute."

I just about collapsed into the sofa, honestly grateful to be off my feet for a few, to try to steady myself up a little.

But I didn't have a few; I only had maybe one or two before someone else swept into the sitting room. Someone who was very much *not* Bianca Ottati.

She was short, not more'n a fifth of Scotch over five feet, though her heels added another couple of fingers. Her hair was black as a *mari-morgan*'s heart, and tied back so tight you probably coulda bounced a penny off her cheeks. She was dressed in a modest, high-necked dress, all in black, and carried a rosary as if it was a whip she was just itching to use.

Which, I guess in a way, it was. I could *feel* the power, radiating off her in waves of pure anger. If I hadn't been so out of it, so sick from the wards, I'd have sensed her coming before she even walked into the room. And the wards were hers, no question; the magic tasted the same.

Witch. Friggin' fantastic. I *hate* witches and warlocks. I'll take a werewolf or a whole Unseelie chopper squad over a sorcerer any day, and twice on the solstice. I don't like anyone who can pull off magics that I can't, and I *definitely* don't trust any of you *humans* with that kinda power.

No offense.

I stood, because it seemed the thing to do, even though I couldn't manage a whole lot in my current condition if things got ugly.

"*Vai via! Vattene, diavolo!*" She came at me, one long finger pointing. The rosary was almost a living thing, shifting and sliding through her other fist. I found myself retreating all of a step before I bumped back into the sofa. "*Io so bene quello che tu sei! Non sei benvenuto qui!*"

As best I could, given how much I felt like a used boxing glove, I let her fury wash over me and just *listened*, letting the words roll around in my ears, my mind, even my mouth, tasting the foreign tang to them.

"*In nome della Beata Vergine, ti* won't profane *questo posto! Ti caccio dalla mia* children's home!"

Almost there; almost…

"*Non so come* you found us, but I'll not allow you to—"

There it was. "Oh, enough, lady!"

Didn't know if she understood a word I said, but the fact that I said it was enough to stop her yammering for a minute.

"Look, I… Do you speak English?" Just 'cause I can *understand* most of your languages, given a few moments to adapt, don't mean I can *speak 'em.*

"I speak English just fine," she said, with only a slight Sicilian accent. "But it matters nothing in what language I address you, soulless creature. It'll not change what I have to say. I know what you are."

"And I know what you are," I told her. "*Strega.*"

No, I don't speak Italian, but I've picked up a few

words in my time. "Witch" being one of 'em.

"I'd have thought," I continued, "that with your kinda power, you'd already dealt with things a lot worse'n me."

I swear, I thought she was about to *hiss* at me. "I believe in my Lord Christ, and his Blessed Mother. I deal with spirits only when I must, to *oppose* evil beings such as you!"

"Huh." I nodded. "You're *Benandanti.*"

For the first time, her expression changed; she looked moderately startled. "I—I am. Few still know of us, *fata.*"

Since few of *you* probably know, either, the *Benandanti* were a fertility sect in Italy in the sixteenth century—eventually developing various traditions of witchcraft which they *swore* they were only using as good Catholics, to battle evil spirits and other witches, and to ensure healthy harvests.

For some reason, the Inquisition didn't buy it, which is why they ain't around much anymore.

"Look, lady…" I wracked my brain for a minute. "Mrs. Maldera, right?" She nodded hesitantly. "I ain't here to cause you any problems. I'm here to help."

"We don't require your sort of—!"

"You sent Mrs. Ottati to me, didn't you? You're the one who pieced together what your granddaughter is." I twisted to face the doorway, where Bianca Ottati had been standing for a minute or two now, her fists clenched and her blinkers wide. "Didn't she?"

Bianca nodded, and briefly waved a hand down the hall—probably sending away any of her husband's goons who were coming to see what all the shouting had been about. Then, "Donna Orsola, we need him. *You* told me we needed him. Why—?"

"I did not want him *here*!" Fino Ottati's mother shrieked. "*Madonna*, I told you what he is! Consorting with his kind is damning enough, but to let him into our home—"

"Is a short-term inconvenience you'll just have to bear," I said. "Now, can we please sit down and talk like reasonable... whatever we are?"

I gleefully yanked my hat from my head, dropped it on the vacuum, and slumped back down into the sofa without waiting for an answer. Orsola followed a moment later, choosing a chair clear across the room, leaving Bianca to pour us all a splash of tea before she, too, sat.

By the time I was done doctoring mine, it was more tea-favored milk, but I didn't wanna be rude, y'know? I'm not sure whether getting it down or keeping it down took more effort.

"I don't suppose you can do something with the wards for a few, could you?" I asked over the rim of my cup. Orsola's glare woulda done the gorgons proud, and was more'n eloquent enough to tell me the answer was "No," with a hefty helping of "Fuck you" to give it flavor.

Bianca was sitting hunched in her chair, her fingers clasped together so tight they were going pale. Donna Orsola was glaring at me, rosary beads clicking against her fingernails. Me, I was trying to keep my gorge from rising into my head, which was already threatening to burst.

So, y'know, all nice and casual.

"Mrs. Maldera—Donna Orsola," I said, "I know

you don't want me here. Fine, I dig. But there's stuff here I gotta see and do. So what I need to know from you is, which do you want more: me gone, or your granddaughter back?"

Her glower hardened to steel for just a moment or two, then wilted. She nodded to me, just once, and turned her gaze down to her lap. The beads went click, click, click against her nails. I heard Bianca whispering in time to her mother-in-law's twisting of the rosary, "*Ave Maria, piena di grazia, il Signore è con te…*"

You don't really need me to translate that for you, right? Anxious as I was to get done and get out, I figured it was best to give 'em a minute to finish their prayer.

"All right," I said once they were through. "Donna Orsola, I've already heard the basics from your daughter-in-law, but I need you to tell me, please… When and how did you tumble that your granddaughter had been snatched?"

In a voice that started angry and slowly softened into sorrow, she spoke. Unfortunately, while she gave me a little more in the way of mystic insight—how the kid always "felt wrong" on dates of power (the equinoxes, Imbolc, Beltane, that kinda thing), how she felt the magic growing in the girl recently, how she finally recognized the signs for what they were— the story was otherwise more or less exactly what Bianca had told me yesterday. And about as helpful.

"Okay…" I leaned back in the couch, squeezed the bridge of my nose hard enough to crack walnuts. "And I assume you tried to find the girl through, uh, nontraditional means as well?"

"You mean my craft. Of course I did! To find my granddaughter, I would do anything, even work with—"

"Even work with things like me. Yeah, I got that. And?"

"And I found nothing. Perhaps she is in your world, rather than ours. Perhaps it has simply been too long."

I thought for another few seconds. "Can you think of any reason you might have been targeted specifically, Donna Orsola? Any spirits or other entities holding a grudge?"

"I told you, I deal with such creatures only when I must, and when I do so, the terms of my bindings are very specific. No, I have no reason to think that any of them wish me or my family harm, beyond the harm they wish, by their very nature, on all devout Catholics."

"So what about mortal enemies? I know your son has more'n his fair share. He's at war with someone right now, ain't he?"

The women traded glances. "I'm not supposed to know much of Fino's activities," Bianca admitted. "Good Family men try to keep us—the wives and children—away from the business. But still, I hear a great deal."

"Be careful what you say, Bianca," Orsola warned.

"I'm telling him nothing he couldn't learn elsewhere, *donna*. My husband is currently, ah, *disagreeing* with the Uptown Boys."

I'd heard of them, just a little: a small splinter of Bugs Moran's Northside Gang. Vicious, brutal thugs—but then, who in any of the mobs wasn't?

"But," she continued, "the conflict with them didn't start until a few years ago. They had no, ah, 'beef' with my husband back in 1916. *Madonna*, most of this city's gangs didn't *exist* in 1916, not as they do now!"

I nodded; she was probably right, but they might be worth looking into if everything else came up snake eyes.

"There's gotta be others, though," I prodded.

Again they traded looks. "There are—other rivalries," Bianca said carefully. "Families within the Outfit, within, ah, *our thing*. You understand?"

I understood. Actual blooded Mafia families, with roots in the Old Country. Yeah, those rivalries could sure predate Prohibition. "Any in particular?"

Even distracted as I was, I could see the hesitation, the fear of betraying her husband's confidence. But Orsola, apparently, had other concerns.

"Giovaniello!" she hissed, actually spitting once on the carpet. "Scola, Reina. *Stronzi cattivi*, the lot of them! They torment our family even back in Sicily, they drive us out, they…" She just about deflated, fast as a kid's balloon. "They hate us," she whispered. "And we hate them. We always will."

Bianca leaned forward. "Donna Orsola and Fino were horrified when they discovered those families had spread here as well. And…" Her entire faced tensed. "Fino missed Adalina's birth, because someone tried to hit him on the way. He didn't have his own crew at the time, he was just a button man, but they were at war—and one of the rival *capo*'s lieutenants was Vince Scola!"

Again Orsola spit. Yeah, that family was definitely worth looking into. The name "Vince Scola" was ringing some faint bells—I'd have to talk to Pete, or maybe Shaugnessy—but it was certainly possible he was involved. I doubted seriously that Orsola was the only Old Country *strega* to have come to the Land of Opportunity.

I *really* had to move this along. It was getting harder'n harder to keep up the "cool as a cucumber" routine; I was about to start weeping bile, vomiting tears, or both.

"All right, I'll definitely get a slant on them. First, I gotta take a quick look around your place. I know you ain't thrilled with that—" directed at Orsola "—and that the chances of there being any clues or traces left after sixteen years are pretty rotten, but we better be sure, right?" I stood, and they both followed suit. "Donna Orsola, I'm not gonna find *anything* if I can't focus my magics. Are you sure you can't...?"

"No," she said again, though this time she sounded a *little* apologetic about it. "I understand what you wish to do, *fata*. And I want you to find my granddaughter. But I cannot just switch our protections on and off at whim; they would take hours to restore, perhaps days, were I to break them. I'll not leave my family defenseless for so long."

And it was then, just then, that something struck me, something I shoulda thought about from the minute I walked into that damn house. I musta been even more goofy with pain than I'd thought.

"My God..."

I hadn't even realized I'd whispered aloud until

Orsola went rigid as a railroad tie. "Don't you *ever* speak the Lord's name, creature! I'll not have it! I—"

"I'll do a lot more than offend you, *donna*. She's *here*, isn't she? You've got those wards up, and *Adalina's here*! Even if she's not your 'real' girl, the agony you're causing her—"

But the old woman was shaking her head. "No. Once I understood what she was, I sealed our home against your kind, to avoid any further danger to us. But I inscribed the glyphs around her presence. So long as she doesn't attempt to depart this place, they cause her no discomfort at all.

"I have no intention of harming her. *We* are not the monsters, Mr. Oberon."

Well, she used my name, anyway; that's better'n "creature," right?

Unfortunately, if there *was* anything to find, I wasn't in any shape to find it. I made a quick circuit of the ground floor, focusing on the doors and windows. I left my senses wide open—or as open as I could without being overwhelmed by the wards—and I got nothing. I ran the wand over the entryways, tapped on the walls, felt the resonating of magics in the brick, the glass, the wood, but everything I sensed could be accounted for by Orsola's glyphs and spells. I also got a whole heap of weird looks from Fino's boys guarding the place; I just smiled, gave 'em as much of a mental nudge as I could muster, and said, "Looking for a good place to demonstrate the repaired vacuum." I don't think they were all that convinced, and one or two even went to check in with Mrs. Ottati, but they left me alone.

I found no signs of unusual Fae interest: no

hidden patterns in the paint or the brick, nothing rusted or rotten—or, alternatively, better preserved than it shoulda been—no tricky or malicious alterations to their various holy icons, and no items or books of abnormal power. (Of course, I also saw none of Orsola's grimoires, but somehow I didn't think she'd care to show me those even if I asked.)

I'd need to check outside, too, for any toadstool rings, arches of ivy, or an excess of oak, ash, or hawthorn in the house's construction (or in the surrounding neighborhood). But I couldn't do it now; I was afraid that if I stepped outside the house—outside the wards—I wouldn't be able to bring myself to come back in.

But it was all going through the motions, anyway. If someone had been gunning for the Ottatis specifically, if this was something more'n a random changeling swap, the presence or absence of the usual signs wouldn't mean much.

I stumbled back into the sitting room where the ladies of the house waited for me. I found it interesting that, this time, Bianca was praying over rosary beads—a lot less imposing than her mother-in-law's—while Orsola was pacing the far wall. Guess she wasn't happy about me wandering around her home.

"Just one last thing," I told them, and the words were practically a prayer. *Almost done.* "I gotta speak to Adalina."

Orsola mumbled something that I was too achy to translate, and Bianca shrank in her chair.

"I have to," I said. "She was just a baby when all this began, but not all Fae grow up the same way you do. It ain't likely, but she may know something useful. If nothing else, maybe I can tell from looking at her who mighta left her."

And I could make sure that she even *was* a changeling, since I still hadn't seen any solid proof—though Orsola appeared knowledgeable enough that I couldn't much doubt her anymore.

Orsola nodded shallowly and then slumped into the nearest seat. It happened to be the sofa I'd been perched on earlier; she musta been really upset, if she was willing to touch it.

"Follow me," Bianca whispered. I did, and we made our way upstairs. The pain and sickness faded a little, since more of the wards were focused on the ground floor; not a *lot*, but at that point anything was a relief.

Above was just a couple of hallways with a lot of doors—and another goon standing in front of one of them. He frowned when Bianca told him to let me through, but he unlocked the door—a deadbolt, screwed to the frame—and stepped aside.

"You're behind the eight-ball if he asks Fino about this," I whispered to her. "No way he's gonna buy that you let a vacuum salesman up here."

"I know." She ushered me in, pulled the door so it didn't *quite* shut behind me.

It was clearly an adolescent girl's room. The walls were a subtle pink, the furniture and the closet door white-with-gold, the blankets a deep rose—with a frill, of course. A simple crucifix hung over the bed, and the shelves held an assorted mix of jewelry boxes, stuffed animals, and hats. At its lowest volume, the radio in the corner was whispering a promotional spiel for tonight's "jolly new episode" of *Easy Aces*.

It was *also* clearly the room of a girl with problems, since drawers were yanked open, jewelry boxes were dented or smashed, teddy bear parts and stuffing covered the furniture in an off-color snow, and all sorts of laundry—including a selection of camisoles and step-ins that I don't think most teenage girls woulda wanted some stranger to see— were strewn all over. Someone had gouged jagged lines in the radio's casing with what looked like a nail file, and the place stank of cheap perfume, cheaper cigarettes, and unwashed clothes.

And half under those rumpled sheets, head down and hands clutching her greasy hair, was Adalina. "Get out," she whispered at me.

I stepped to the foot of the bed. "Adalina, my name's Mick. Your mother asked me to talk to—"

"Get out, *get out*!" She glared up at me, leaning forward, and snatched a mangled music box off her nightstand, ready to throw.

"*Calm down!*" I hit her with every bit of will I could gather under the circumstances. I couldn't fully get to her emotions—they were too powerful, too deep, and I was too all in from the pain—but I could push around the edges. If nothing else, she locked up for an instant, the box falling from her hand to clunk across the mattress, and then the carpet. It started playing "Blue Danube" woefully out of tune.

If she'd known who and what she was, it woulda been harder than that. But since she didn't, her Fae nature actually made it easier on me.

And she *was* Fae, no doubt about it now. I could feel it in the air, smell it on her breath and her skin. And I could see it, see it clear enough that I couldn't be surprised anymore that Orsola had recognized it for what it was.

She was pale—sickly pale, near maggot-white—and so skinny I thought the blouse and skirt she was wearing might weigh more'n she did. Looking at her face was like looking at a photograph through the bottom of a glass: just a little *off*. Her sunken, sallow eyes were a hair too far apart, her ears a touch too high, her lips a little too thin, and a dozen other things, even more subtle. Not any one feature would stand out on its own, but all put together, it made her… Not ugly, exactly, though she was that, too, but *different*.

I took a step around the corner of the mattress, just a little closer, and held out my hands. "I won't hurt you, Adalina. I just need to talk."

"If my parents sent you, I've got nothing to say," she insisted. "Bastards! They're holding me prisoner here, you know." She pointed at the windowsill, and I saw shiny new nails hammered into the frame. I also saw that her own nails were jagged, and had what mighta been old bloodstains on it from one of her fights. "Can you get me out?"

"Not yet. Maybe eventually."

She growled and twisted her face away.

"It started within the last couple of months, right? You get angry at the littlest thing, *real* angry, and you dunno why. People look at you, and laugh or point or flinch away. You look in the mirror, and you don't recognize yourself anymore. Am I right?"

She twisted back, jaw hanging. "How'd you…?"

"I've seen it before, Adalina. It happens, sometimes, with people like you."

"People like… I'm a *normal person*!"

"I think we both know different, Adalina. But it's okay; it's a *good* thing. Once you understand what you're becoming, you can—"

"Shut up! *Get out!*" She was off the bed, coming at me with fingers curled into claws, and I didn't have it in me to stop her again—not without maybe hurting her, anyway. I made tracks, and honestly, I breathed a sigh of relief when Bianca's goon slammed and bolted the door behind me.

CHAPTER SIX

The Cook County Hall of Records was a typical government grey—more drab than the greystone flats, somehow—with images and inscriptions intended to make the place feel important. I was flopped in an old, grimy chair in an office on the top floor, with several ledgers and heaps of paper piled on a worn desk, and going blind by the light of a cheap lamp.

I also *still* hadn't managed to shake the effects of Orsola's wards, even though it'd been hours now since I dusted out of that damn house. It wasn't nearly as bad as it'd been inside, but my guts were roiling storm clouds, and my head felt like a baseball after an inning with Jimmie Foxx. But it wasn't *physical* pain, exactly; it was more... kinda the hangover you might get if your soul took off without you and got lit on bathtub hooch.

Once I'd gotten done talking with Adalina, for all the good it did, there wasn't much left for me to do there. I'd explained to Bianca and Orsola that the girl didn't seem to know anything, and that—until she was basically through changing—I couldn't accurately tell 'em what she was changing *into*. (It didn't look to be anything *too* obviously inhuman, such as a goblin or a troll, but there are *plenty* other vile bastards from my world who aren't so blatant.) I promised I'd give them a ring when I learned anything, snatched up my hat and vacuum, and made for the door like the house was on really angry fire.

I coulda cried when I got back into the open breeze; as I said, I still hurt, still felt terrible, but compared to how it'd been inside, it was heaven. Yeah, I did remember to look around, and it felt good to kneel down in the early spring grass, close to the soil and the roots—but as I'd expected, there weren't any more signs of old Fae presence outside than in. Or if there were, they were too subtle for me in my current state.

My current state was also why it had taken me three blocks of shuffling down the sidewalk, dragging my vacuum along behind like it was a stubborn dog, before I finally noticed that someone was shadowing me.

A handful of someones, actually, in a black Model 18 "Deuce" that looked more or less the same as every other flivver on the road. If I'd been hitting on all eight myself, I'd probably have felt their interest in me a lot earlier. As it was, I only noticed because I stopped briefly to lean on a lamppost in hopes that my head would stop pounding, and saw 'em brake a little too quick, to avoid passing me by.

Fino's boys, more suspicious of me than I'd thought? One of the Shark's enemies, wondering who I was? Something totally unrelated to my current job? Didn't know and, while I probably shoulda made some effort to find out, felt too ugly to care. I knelt by the vacuum—again, pretending I was trying to fix something—and slid my wand from my coat. Around the canister, I carefully aimed the L&G and let fly. I couldn't muster my full will, not around the pounding and the nausea, but it ain't hard to strip enough luck from a dingus as complex as an internal combustion engine to make *something* go wrong. I heard a loud *pop*, followed by a hissing burst of steam and a whole heap of profanity. With a shallow smile, I stood up and wandered on my way.

If I'd been in better shape, I mighta noticed that the Deuce wasn't the only flivver on my tail. But I'll get to that.

Point is, I didn't want to waste any time, and I kept thinking the effects of the wards should fade any minute—honestly, they shoulda let up right after I left the house—so as much as I wanted to climb into a hole and pull it in after me, or at least into bed, I didn't head home. Instead, after a quick ride on the L that didn't do me any good at all, I made my way here—the hall of records I just mentioned.

A combination of polite requests, mental nudges, and cheap bribes got me quick access to records that shoulda taken a lot longer, and a few that I probably shouldn't have had at all. (The expressions on everyone's faces as I lugged the vacuum through the hallways woulda had me in stitches any other day.) And so, in that little office with the little lamp, I spent the rest of the afternoon and part of the evening digging through paperwork that shoulda taken me only a few hours.

On the one hand, it didn't tell me a whole lot of

use. Fino Ottati and his mother came to the US of A from Sicily about twenty-four years ago—which, other'n the exact timing, I'd already picked up from my talk with Orsola. They came with a few cousins, which I hadn't known, and I scribbled down their names for a later follow-up. Orsola had no other kids, and Fino hadn't had any except Adalina (or whoever Adalina was supposed to be).

Bianca Ottati, born Bianca Walton, daughter of industrialist Henry Roger Walton and Pavia Angotti, daughter of immigrants. I bet Walton's family were *thrilled* with that. No sisters, two older brothers, one killed in the War, the other from complications after a bout of scarlet fever.

Yeah. *Real* efficient use of the day. Good job, Mick.

But the relatively stress-free afternoon had gotten me some rest, and I was a tiny bit more myself by the time I left. A few folks were working late, and I waved or tipped my hat at each one as they looked up, their attention drawn by the squeaky wheels on the canister.

I made a mental note, next time, to pick a cover that required less awkward props, and—bracing myself—headed for the closest elevated station. The platform was pretty busy this time of the evening, so I just stood still as a frightened sculpture and let the people ebb and flow around me. Wasn't long before the drab green cars screeched to a stop, and I slipped inside. People hurled more irritated glowers at my vacuum, shuffled around trying not to trip over it, and with a shudder, we were moving.

Much as I wanted one, I hadn't found an empty

seat, and I didn't feel up to car-hopping. So I stood for a good long while, stop after stop: swaying, one hand in the hanging loop, the other on the vacuum's hose, and listlessly watched the people around me.

Which is when, and why, I saw 'em.

Well, just one, at first. He was standing in the next car back, face pressed to the glass, staring right at me. He was wearing a long overcoat, not too much different than mine, over shirt and trousers; no suit. Coulda just been your average Joe, nothing remarkable about him, except for the *way* he was staring. I've seen it before, a lot.

No doubt at all, he was here for me. And there was something else about him, something I was too disoriented to put my finger on, that reminded me of the guys in the car from earlier.

Told you I was getting back to that.

He saw that I'd seen him, and shouted something over his shoulder—doubtless to whoever else was with him in the next car. Well, I didn't think they'd do *too* much with so many people around, and I had no intention of loitering around waiting for them. I started sidling toward the front of my car, so I could be at the exit and ready to scoot as soon as it opened.

And saw the door to the car in *front* of mine open, and a few more galoots step through. These didn't just remind me of the guys from the car, they *were* the guys from the car. Even from just my quick gander earlier, I was sure.

They were also between me and the exit. They musta been watching me on the platform, saw which car I'd gotten on, to box me in on both sides this way. And I hadn't noticed 'em at all.

I was *really* off my game.

The brakes began to squeal as we neared the 51st Street station, and damn if *everyone in the car* didn't get up to move! I don't know how many were actually planning to get off here, and how many were just wise to what was happening—Chicagoans know to clear the way when two groups of guys start converging—but either way, of all the rotten luck, I was about to lose my witnesses. Most of 'em filed out the doors as soon as they opened, a few actually ducked *past* one goon squad or the other into neighboring cars. The thugs let 'em go, a few even tipping their hats. I pondered on making a break and decided against it. No sense in just *handing* myself over.

There were seven of 'em, total; three behind, four in front. This close, I got a much better slant on 'em, and nope, they weren't the Shark's button men. Every last one was way too pale, most had lighter hair, and I damn well knew Irish features when I saw 'em.

Which, given that they picked me up right after I left Fino's, probably meant Uptown Boys.

"Okay, pal." They all looked about the same—overcoats or trench coats over casual—so the only reason I assumed the fella speaking was the leader was because, well, he was the guy speaking. "No reason this has to get unpleasant. We just wanna talk."

"So talk." I took a step to one side so I could keep my lamps on him while *also* glancing at the far windows—which were reflecting the guys behind me.

He saw what I'd done and smirked a little. "We

wanna know who you are, and what your business with the Ottatis is."

I desperately wanted my wand, actually felt my palm itching, but I didn't think these guys would take it too well if I suddenly went for my pockets. "You treat everyone who speaks with the Ottatis this way?"

His smirk started to become a lot less smirky and a lot more scowly. "If we don't know 'em and we have the chance for, uh, conversation, yeah. Now, you gonna spill?"

"Yeah, yeah, don't blow your wig." I nudged the vacuum with my foot, and then put everything I had into my words and my stare, hitting him right in the face with my will. "I'm just a salesman, mister. I represent Credne Household... Device..."

He wasn't buying a word of it, not one. I could tell because he pulled a set of brass knuckles from a pocket and slid 'em onto his right hand. On both sides of me, jackets opened, revealing baseball bats, axe handles, even a copper's nightstick. Well, at least it seemed they didn't wanna bump me off, just tune me up good. Probably because they wanted to be sure who I was before deciding if I was important enough to whack.

I didn't get it. It *should* have worked! Even without my L&G, even without more'n a minute to concentrate on him, and yeah, even with me feeling like a dirty dishrag, it shoulda had *some* effect. Get him to stop and think, if nothing else; give it *some* credence, if not make him swallow it outright.

Nothing. I might as well not have even tried.

"One more chance, pal." He ran the fingers of his

left hand over the brass knuckles. "And don't even think of lying to me."

"All right, okay." I shrugged, looked down and shuffled my feet, stuck my hands in my pockets… All nervous tics, right? They didn't even notice that last one. "They hired me to see if I could identify your mother, so we knew whether it was more accurate to call you a bastard or a son of a bitch."

I know, I know. But I was tired, I was hot under the collar, I hurt a lot, and it just sorta blurted out.

He came at me, fast, his boys just a few heartbeats slower, but I was ready—and more important, so was my wand. I kicked the vacuum at him at the same time I yanked the L&G from my pocket and hit him with a quick blast to sweep away a fragment of luck. The combination was enough to trip him up bad; he tried to leap the canister, caught his toes on the handle, and smacked down face-first. A second burst swept the palookas behind him, ensuring that two of 'em tripped over their boss and joined him on the filthy floor in a pile of arms and legs and long coats and blunt objects.

That gave me a few breaths to deal with the ones behind me. But even as I did, I felt my skin crawl— more than crawl, *writhe*, as though it was trying to make a run for it and didn't much care if the rest of me went with or not.

And then I saw why, through peepers that'd just started to sting and water. Three guys behind me; one was carrying a bat, one that billy club I just mentioned. But the third…

The third man was carrying a length of pipe.

Iron pipe.

My vision telescoped in on the weapon, like I was looking through a keyhole. Suddenly, this wasn't just a scrap, wasn't some scuffle where I might pick up a few bruises or even cracked bones that'd heal in a day or two. I could be hurt, bad.

I could die.

He had to go. He had to go fast, and he had to take the pipe with him.

There was just enough room, if they got friendly, for two to come at me at once. I shifted to one side, so that I was closest to the goon with the nightstick, and he obliged me by charging ahead of his two buddies. I let him swing and deliberately took the blow on my arm. I felt the bone quiver, and winced, but it wasn't about to slow me up. I twisted, reached across and, using the wand, pinned his billy club against my arm where it'd hit. And grabbed his wrist with the other hand, which I'm sure he expected not to work anymore.

Quick step forward, shoving into him, knocking him off balance, then a quick twist, yanking him forward and around by his arm. My spin carried him into the bench seats beside me, so his leg slammed with a loud thump into the wood.

And then, with him pressed against that wood, I kicked him hard just above the ankle, cracking his shin across the edge of the bench.

He screamed and doubled over, and I let him fall, his arm sliding through my grip until I held only the nightstick in my fist. I instantly raised that hand in a parry, catching the iron pipe that would otherwise have struck me a nasty blow across the head. My other, still clutching the wand, swung backward and I unleashed another burst of magic at the guys scrambling to their feet behind me. It was a sudden, sharp blast of pure emotion, terrible anger and shriveling fear. Again, not enough to take them out of the fight, but sufficient to buy me another few moments.

The pipe was coming at me again, but the fella on the end of it was clearly no duelist. He swung like he was chopping wood, and it was no hassle at all to knock the weapon aside, give him a good solid rap on the wrist to send the pipe clattering across the floor, and another one across the top of his skull that shoulda sent him clattering right along with.

And *would* have, except that his pal with the baseball bat stepped in and hit himself at least a double across my back.

I staggered, probably woulda fallen if I hadn't propped myself straight with the nightstick on the bench's armrest. The pain was a bolt of lightning shooting along my spine. Our senses are more acute than yours inside, not just out, so I could actually trace the hairline crack running across three separate ribs.

Those were gonna take more'n a day and a half to heal, damn it!

I spun, doing my best to ignore the agony as those cracks yawned wider with the motion, and bent sideways under his next swing at an angle most humans couldn't manage. I straightened, reached, and snagged the bat under my left arm. I poked him in the stomach with the wand in that hand, filled him with just enough magic to let him taste a little of my own pain, and then kicked his feet out from under him.

Except the bastard was *supposed* to let go of the

bat when the pain hit him, and instead he clamped up. So he was just sorta hanging there, half-lying on the floor, and I had to either let go of the bat—and leave him armed—or else take an extra second or two to deal with him further.

Which is when I confirmed that, yeah, pipe-guy hadn't gone down as hard as *he* was supposed to, either. My shot to his noggin musta gone a little off-track when bat-guy slugged me. He was back on his feet, and worse, the pipe was back in his hand.

Another parry, but this time I was weighted down by gink number two dangling off my left arm. Instead of deflecting, the pipe slid down the nightstick to rest with a thump against my right fist.

It didn't burn, exactly. But if you've ever touched something you *knew* was diseased, swore you could feel the toxins and sickness seeping into your flesh… This was similar, but absolutely *not* all in my head. Right now, it was just horribly unpleasant, but in a few heartbeats, I'd start losing skin—at *least*.

Plus, there were the fellas behind me, who were finally getting themselves sorted again. I heard the vacuum cleaner rattle and roll toward me as one of 'em kicked it out from under his feet.

I dropped the bat, jammed the L&G into pipe-guy's gut, and channeled every bit of focus I could muster through the wand. I could feel—hell, I could *see*—his aura go mottled dark with misfortune. A spiritual bruising, kinda.

And then I shoved him back, nightstick on pipe, far enough to kick him hard in the gut.

See, sometimes it's not about the magic, and it's not about the fisticuffs, but about a mix of both.

'Cause it was the kick that carried him back into the car's door—and the unnatural bad luck that caused the impact to trigger the pressure switches meant to keep the door from closing on anyone.

A "safety feature," that was.

The door trundled open with a muted hiss, and the gink—along with his pipe—vanished from the car in a lion's roar of sudden winds. Be nice to think he lived, but bouncing across the tracks at that speed, and with that much misfortune clinging to him, I expect that his bad breaks were pretty literal. And honestly, considering why he was here, I wasn't about to lose too much sleep over it. With the promise of a cold iron rubdown gone, I was already feeling a little bit better.

The rest of the Uptown Boys on the train, though, didn't look to be nearly as happy with this latest turn. Bats and axe handles hit the floor, and hands started darting inside overcoats.

Guess they weren't too interested in just knocking me around anymore. Who knew they'd take me booting one of their pals out of a moving train so personally?

Okay, I was in a bit of a jam, then. In a couple more seconds, I'd be sucking down a *lot* of lead—certainly enough to put me down for days or weeks, maybe even enough to finish me outright, iron or no iron. And my only way out was the exit my buddy with the pipe had just taken. Somehow, I didn't think I wanted to go that route, not without slowing us up a little first.

I know what you're thinking, but no, I *couldn't* just stop the train the way I'd done earlier with the flivver. It ain't that the mechanism itself is any harder to gum up; it's the *people*. In a car, you only got a couple of guys, so the weight of their belief don't add up to much. But on a train, there's dozens, sometimes hundreds. The sheer momentum of their expectations, their faith in how the train works— and more important, *that* it works—makes it just about impossible to mess with.

Magic, though, ain't the only way to stop a train.

This had to go *real* smooth, or it wasn't gonna go at all. I dropped the billy club so I'd have a hand free, crouched to snag the mug who'd been tenderizing me with the bat as he was struggling to his feet, and hauled him upright. Quick thump on the head with the wand, followed by a headbutt to the sniffer, and he wasn't thinking all that clear. I walked him back toward his buddies, step by step, blocking their line of fire. And they let me, since they figured there wasn't a damn thing I could do once we reached 'em.

Which mighta been true, but I wasn't *trying* to reach 'em.

I stopped next to the vacuum cleaner, tossed the guy into the others as hard as I could and snatched up the hose, yanking it loose from the canister. I spun it, an awkward lariat, once, twice, and threw, drawing on the luck I'd glommed from the not-so-dearly departed.

And damn if that extra dab of fortune didn't make all the difference. I not only hit the pull-chain I'd been aiming for, but struck it from the side hard enough for the chain to wrap itself around the cleaning head. It wouldn't hold for more'n a second or two, but that was long enough.

I yanked, hard, on the vacuum hose—and it yanked, hard, on the passenger emergency brake.

Everybody stumbled; everyone but me, of course, since A: I'd known it was coming, and B: most of you mooks are damn clumsy. A few shots rang out, punching holes in the ceiling or shattering the windows, but I couldn't hear 'em over the screaming brakes. Anyway, none of 'em came anywhere near clipping me. I staggered along the car, slapped the L&G against my own arm for an extra jot of luck, and threw myself from the train.

I hit hard, mashing my shoulder between the railroad ties, bruising arms and ribs—including the cracked ones, damn it, damn it, ow!—on the tracks. My skin started to burn again, and I could *feel* the bruises running deep, thanks to the iron rails, but the contact was short enough that my clothes protected me from the worst of it. Sparks flashed in front of my face, and it took me a moment to realize that they were coming from the wheels, not a bonk on the noggin or the pain of the iron. I deliberately kept rolling away from the tracks until I fetched up against the side of the elevated railway, and scrambled to my feet. A quick tick to shove the wand deep into a pocket, then I deliberately tumbled over the railing.

The train hadn't yet come to a full stop. I could feel little indentations and depressions in the wood and steel of the bridge, fingerholds that few humans coulda used but which let me climb to the ground headfirst. I almost fell a couple of times, thanks to the various aches and lacerations, but finally I flipped around and my feet touched concrete. Walking as fast as my brand-spanking-new limp would let me, I wandered away into the Chicago evening.

Oh, that extra dash of luck? No, that wasn't to protect me from injury; I knew I'd recover quick enough, long as I didn't dash my brains out on the iron rails.

I just didn't want all my tumbling and thumping around to rip my favorite coat.

By the time I got back to Soucek's building, I'd worked it all out.

See, even with Fae luck running to extremes the way it does, this had all been too much. The Uptown Boys happened to be watching Ottati's digs when I left; they happened to be in more'n one car, which I missed; they happened to keep out of my sight well enough to flank me on the platform and come at me from two sides on the L; their leader happened to shrug off my attempt at suggestion; one of 'em happened to be armed with a *fucking iron pipe*.

Any one or two of those, fine, but *all* of 'em? No. No way. And now that I knew to look for it, now that I knew it *wasn't* just a "hangover" from the wards at the house, I could sense it easily enough. I'd have tumbled to it a lot sooner, if not for those wards, if not for—well, yeah. Bad luck.

First stop, my office, where I draped my coat over the chair, yanked open a drawer, and hauled out a big bag of salt. Wand in my left hand, I dribbled handful after handful of the stuff from my right, over my left shoulder. Every seven handfuls, I'd stop and walk widdershins—that's counterclockwise, to most of you—three times around the growing salt pile. Each cascade of sifting crystals, augmented by my own magics flowing through the L&G, peeled away bits of the misfortune wrapping me in an invisible shroud. And finally, *finally* I felt the last of it fade.

I don't think I can even begin to put you wise to how exhausted I was. The wards, the fight, the iron, and of course *this*... My hands were actually shaking, my vision just a bit blurred. I just wanted to yank down the Murphy bed, if I even had the strength for *that*, and collapse long enough to give Rip Van Winkle a run for his money.

But no, not yet. There was something else I had to deal with first.

I stepped back into the hall, briefly aiming my wand at the lock to the door at the bottom of the basement stairs. I heard a faint thunk as several tumblers fell out of alignment. The chances of anyone coming down here while I was talking were tiny, but I didn't want "tiny," I wanted "none." I'd funnel the luck back into the lock when I was done, and a quick jiggle of the key should knock everything back into place.

Okay, privacy. I lifted the payphone's receiver, grimaced at the increased tickling in my head as I held it close, and slipped a nickel into the slot. I grumbled at the operator for a minute, and waited.

Despite the hour, someone answered before the end of the third ring. "Hello?"

"Donna Orsola Maldera, please."

"Who's calling?" the gruff voice asked. It coulda been one of the guys I'd met earlier today; I wasn't sure.

"Tell her... Tell her it's about her vacuum."

"Hey, buster, you got any idea what time it is? I—"

"Just tell her." Times like this, I really wished I could mess with someone's head over the blower. "Look, if she doesn't think it's worth her time, *she* can always hang up on me, right?"

I heard him grousing to himself even as the phone clicked a few times—probably the receiver settling on a table. I stood waiting, long enough that I was starting to worry about having to drop in another nickel, and then...

"It's late, Mr. Oberon."

"Donna Orsola." I smiled broadly, knowing it would carry in my voice. "And how are you this lovely evening?"

"I'm fine. I—"

"Everyone doing well? Mrs. Ottati? How's she?"

"Well. I—"

"No problems with her husband, I hope? About letting me in to see Adalina, I mean."

The old woman sighed loudly. "No, Mr. Oberon, no problems. I, ah, *convinced* Ricky not to mention it to him."

"Oh, good. I'm so glad."

Silence, for a moment. I was gonna make her ask, goddamn it.

"Mr. Oberon, what is it you—?"

I didn't say I'd let her ask *all* of it.

"I just had one quick question for you, Donna Orsola. I'm afraid it couldn't wait for a more polite hour."

"I see. And your question would be?"

"*Are you out of your goddamn fucking mind?!*"

Her gasp echoed in the receiver, and I swear I could *hear* her entire body go rigid on the other end of the line. "You will *never* use that language around me! You—"

"Language? *Language?* You put a *hex* on me, you dumb broad! What the hell's the matter with you? You damn near got me killed!"

"I've told you before, *fata*, I use my powers only against the evil and impure. The *malocchio* was a message."

"A message?" The receiver was actually creaking in my hand. "A man is dead tonight, Maldera. Your 'evil eye' set him gunning for me, and I had to croak him. That's on you, sister. Not me."

Silence again. Angry as I was, and with nobody to see, I wasn't bothering with my act anymore; anyone woulda thought I was a corpse, motionless as I was standing. I heard her pacing as far as her cord would allow.

Then, "He must have been an evil man, else he would not, as you say, have come 'gunning for you.' But still, that was not my intent. For that, I am sorry."

"So what *was* your intent? Do you even *want* me to find your granddaughter?"

"How *dare* you?" I'd rather she'd screamed, but no. It was a whisper, hoarse, scratchy, as if it was the static and distortion on the line speaking to me now. "After everyone who's been stolen from me, everyone I've lost back in Sicily, or here… Cousins, friends, my husband Piero, my *carino mio*… No." A few deep, heaving breaths rasped wetly in my ear. "No, *figlio di male*, you are not worthy even to know their names! Know only that I will stop at nothing to find my granddaughter!"

"Uh-huh. Then maybe you wanna stop gumming things up for me? I'm trying to *help* you!"

"I deal with you only because I've no other choice," she said. "I knew the *malocchio* would not cause you lasting injury. But I'll not let you endanger my family's souls! You are not welcome in our home, and you are not to return; do your job, but do it *away from us*! You refused to heed, when we first met. Now you have been punished for that transgression. I trust the message is now clear?"

"Oh, quite clear, Donna Orsola. Now let me be just as clear, you loony witch. You want me to find your granddaughter? Then I'm going where I need to, when I need to, and you're doing exactly squat to stop me. Not only are you *not* gonna gimme the evil eye again, but if I *do* have to come back by your place, you're gonna break the wards for me, and I don't care *how* long it takes for you to put 'em back up. You got all that?"

"If you think for one instant—"

"I'm *not done*! You sent Mrs. Ottati to me. You convinced her she needed me, and you've as much as told me that you're as hot to find your granddaughter as she is. So fine. Consider this your formal announcement, Donna Maldera. I now consider you to be as much a party to my hiring as your daughter-in-law. Anything you do to interfere with my investigation from now on will be considered a violation of any pact or agreement she and I have. That means, if I choose, that I can walk away from this whole mess—not just as a PI, but as *aes sidhe* and a former lord of the Seelie Court—without repercussion.

"And if *that* happens, you may just have bigger concerns than trying to find a missing girl. You get me, Donna Orsola?"

Her breath came in an angry gurgle now, but her skin scraped against the earpiece as she nodded. "*Sì, capisco.*"

"I know that you believe I'm your enemy," I said. "I get that there's nothing I can do to change your mind on that.

"So trust me, instead, when I tell you that you really, *really* don't want *me* to start believing it, too."

And with that, there was nothing left but to hang up on her with a satisfying *click*, take half a second to fix the lock, and then go collapse face-first on the mattress.

CHAPTER SEVEN

"Jesus, Mick. You look like something the cat dragged in."

"Huh. Do I?" I took a step back, leaving room for Pete to slip into my office. "'Cause I *feel* like something the cat coughed up."

This despite the fact that I was actually doing a lot better'n I had been. After flopping into bed that night, I lost a whole day to just recuperating, and then the weekend to leads that didn't go anywhere. Four-Leaf Franky, Lenai, and the others still hadn't heard a peep, the Ottati cousins I tracked down didn't know from nothing, and Pete—who'd been so busy he'd only had a minute to spare for me on the horn—could only promise to look into my follow-up questions.

He'd better have some answers for me now, or I was gonna—gonna—I dunno, complain at him.

Point is, I'd had a day of rest, and two more days that were frustrating but easy as beans, yet I hadn't *completely* recovered. Yeah, the hex was gone, and most of the marks had healed up, but I was sporting a few bruises and abrasions from the iron—or that I'd gotten when I was sick from the iron's touch—and my body was still kinda stressed from trying to shake loose Orsola's curse like it was a damn infection. So considering how Pete was used to seeing me, yeah, I probably did look a little washed up and wrung out.

Pete—who was wearing rugged denims and a sheepskin coat, rather'n his uniform, and carrying a large backpack—scooted around the desk and planted his keister in *my* chair. When I squinted at him, he just shrugged and said, "I don't *have* an office. Lemme indulge a minute."

My turn to shrug. I wandered to the icebox, poured myself a glass (I think you know of what by now), and dropped into the seat across from him. He pulled a small flask from his pack, took a slug, and offered it my way. "Flavor?"

This time, my eyebrows went *up*.

"When Congress has to deal with what I have to deal with," he said, "then they can tell me to stop drinking."

You gotta love Chicago cops. I let him pour a tiny dollop into the milk, just to be polite. "To Congressman Volstead," I said. Pete snorted, and raised his flask in response.

"Seriously, Mick," he said a minute later, after wiping his trap on his cuff. "What happened to you?"

"Just a brief tussle. They got it worse'n me."

"With?" He started to scowl. "Not Ottati's boys. I warned you about throwing in with them…"

"No, not Ottati." I sighed. "Uptowners."

"Damn it, Mick—"

"Don't start." I threw back another few swallows. "I thought the Outfit had a truce with the Northside Gang. What's the skinny?" It was one of the questions I'd asked him to look into over the blower.

"Yeah, they do, but it's pretty shaky. The beef between Ottati and the Uptown Boys is small potatoes. I think both sides are waiting to see if the two crews can handle it between themselves, without having to bring in the big guns on either side."

"Seems that the Uptown Boys are afraid the Shark's doing just that. They were pretty hot to know who I was and what I was doing with him."

Pete leaned back in his—*my*—chair. He tensed as though to put his feet up on the desk, interpreted my look (correctly) as a warning not to. "Well, the good news is, if the history Shaugnessy gave me's any guide, the Uptowners won't be a problem for too much longer."

"Yeah?"

"Yeah. Fino Ottati's enemies have a bad habit of getting into accidents."

That brought me up short. "Such as?"

"All kindsa things. He went to war with Lou Smitty about four years ago..."

"Never heard of him."

"That's because his house burned down, with him and his crew inside. And back before the Outfit and the Northside made all nicey-nice, Fino was engaged in a turf war with a crew answering to Benny Fleischer." At my expression, he clarified, "Brother of Saul Fleischer, one of Bugs Moran's lieutenants. Well, Capo Fleischer and his best torpedoes were all piled in a car and on their way to a sit-down when they were hit by a freight train. One that wasn't even supposed to be there; it'd been sent down the wrong track. How's *that* for bad luck, huh?"

Not surprising at all, if you know the fella's

mother. But what I *said* was, "Go on…"

"There's about half a dozen more of the same. Mostly other wiseguys and soldiers, but we lost a man—Detective Espenson—who was investigating some of Capone's boys, Fino included. Just stumbled and fell over a bridge railing into the Calumet River. He *coulda* just been lit enough to be that clumsy—everyone knew he was a drinker—but it fits the pattern."

"Yeah…" Oh, it fit a pattern, all right. Guess I knew what kinda "evil" Donna Orsola was battling with her magics. Not that I could entirely blame her. I wondered if Fino even knew what dear old Mum was up to. "Anything about a fella named Scola in that history?" I asked him.

Pete frowned, thinking. "Actually, yeah. 'Bumpy' Vince Scola. He—"

"Bumpy?"

"Bumpy," he confirmed with a nod. "Way Shaugnessy tells it, back in his early days, Scola was running hooch down from Canada for John Torrio. So one day, on the backroads a few dozen miles outside town, the truck's slowing up for a sharp bend when five or six hijackers with Tommies and shotguns pour onto the road and start squirting lead. Well, Scola just hits the gas like the bullets aren't even there, and runs down three of them on his way. And as they're making tracks, he turns to his partner, calm as you please, and says, 'The roads around here are kinda bumpy, ain't they?'"

I couldn't help but snicker. "Okay, 'Bumpy' it is."

"Right. So during the transition between Torrio and Capone, Bumpy got into it with Fino something fierce. Old grudges, I think." He leaned forward over the desk, resting one hand on the typewriter. "Lotta bloodshed, but at that time, who'd notice? They…" He stopped, glanced down suddenly. "They make these in plastic now, y'know."

It took me a few quick blinks (so to speak) to follow the jump. "Oh, the typewriter? I like that one."

"Doesn't it bother you having it here?"

"Nah. Steel's fine. Typewriter, filing cabinet, the joins on the bedframe, they're all steel. It's just *pure* iron that gives me problems."

"Huh. I never knew that." He stared, kinda at me, kinda off into space.

"Uh, Pete?"

"Yeah?"

"Fino? Scola?"

"Right! Sorry. So yeah, bunch of Scola's thugs are gathered outside in front of one of his speakeasies when a carload of boys working for Sam Battaglia drove past and filled the whole lot of them with daylight. They swore it was a mistake, that they mistook 'em for Northsiders. Doesn't sound too probable, but Al musta believed 'em, because he cracked down, shut down the war between Fino and Scola, and of course Battaglia never suffered any major repercussions. Sure Scola wasn't too thrilled with *that*."

"But Scola survived?" I asked him.

"Yeah. Thing is, he was *supposed* to be there, but he'd been hauled in not six hours earlier on an extortion charge. We couldn't make it stick, but he was in the cooler for a day and change. Guess we saved his life."

We both leaned back, each mirroring the other, and sat for a few minutes—me pondering on bad luck and the magics of one particular Benandanti *strega*, Pete thinking about whatever he was thinking about.

Probably nerving himself up for what was coming.

Couldn't blame him, either. I spent more'n a few minutes trying to convince myself he'd just handed me enough new leads, I didn't need to go home after all. I *really* didn't wanna go; you might've tumbled to that already.

End of the day, though? If Frankie and everyone had come up snake eyes, it meant any Mob fingers in this pie were *real* well hidden. Since finding the kid was priority one, figuring who snatched her distant second… Well, I was just angling for an excuse, and I knew it.

I left Pete to his ruminating and stood, puttering around the office a little, collecting what I'd need. From the cabinet's bottom drawer, I pulled a leather jerkin, which I slid on over my shirt in place of a suit jacket. A belt followed, complete with a narrow holster for the L&G on the right hip, an empty scabbard on the left. Then I moved to the Murphy bed—which was still down and unmade—and reached into the left side of the niche, where the mattress didn't quite reach. There, standing in the corner, was a wire-basket rapier, genuine fifteenth-century Toledo steel. Slid the blade home, threw my overcoat on over the jerkin, and I was as ready as I ever would be.

Pete was staring at me over his flask, which he was in the process of emptying in fast gulps. "Getting decked out, Mick?"

"Yeah, I'm coming along this time, not just opening the way for you. Gotta call on some of the folks back home."

"Must be nice."

"Not so you'd notice. Y'know, I been meaning to ask... how'd you talk your chief into letting you up and vanish for a three-day stretch every month?"

"Heh. Told him I have a sick aunt, lives out of town. She needs me to help her clean and stock up the house every few weeks. He's not thrilled about it, but I always make sure my shifts're covered, so he goes along." Pete smiled, a nervous, anemic little expression. "And I don't think it's occurred to anyone that it's always on the full moon. Hmm. Maybe you could, uh, *talk* to him, Mick? Make him a little less surly about the whole thing?"

I shook my head. "Not how it works, Pete. What I do ain't exactly thought-control. I can usually nudge a guy into doing or feeling what I want—especially if it's something quick and thoughtless, like dropping what he's holding or sneezing or whatever—and I can sometimes make people see stuff that ain't there. But it don't last more'n a couple of seconds after I walk away. *Maybe* a few minutes, if I laid into 'em heavy, then *poof*.

"So yeah, I could talk to the chief. I could make him cooperative as you please, right up until I step out that door. And then you're right back where you started, with a suspicious boss to boot."

"Yeah, that I don't need." Pete polished off the last dregs of whiskey and stood up. "All right. Let's get on with this."

I headed for the alcove where the fridge used

to be, the one with the splotches of mildew in the corners. Dragging my fingers along the wall, I stepped inside. "You got everything?" I asked Pete. "Remember, you can't eat anything, drink anything, accept any*thing* from any*body* while you're there. If you do—"

"Yeah, Mick, I know the drill." He hefted his backpack. "Three canteens of water, dried fruit, canned meats, and a few raw steaks for, uh, nighttime."

I nodded; it should do. The steaks wouldn't be in great shape after a day or two, but fresh enough to suffice. And given how much stronger, how much *heavier*, magic was where we were going than it is here, he *should* be able to maintain enough control, even under the light of the moon, not to eat anything—or anyone—he shouldn't.

That was, after all, why he went every month.

For a couple minutes I stood in that ugly, discolored little alcove, just *feeling* the growing things around me (even if they were just mold and mildew). I thought about them, reached out with mind and fingers both to touch them, carefully savoring and studying every sensation, every scent. I pushed my mind *through* them, linking them to me, until I could feel the whole world rotating around us, until we were its axis.

It took right about no effort at all. I let myself take a few breaths to be grateful for our timing—in addition to the first night of the full moon, we were also coming up on the vernal equinox, which made this kinda thing scary simple—and then I *pushed*.

The rear wall of the niche shrank away into the distance like it was falling down a deep (albeit horizontal) hole. From around and behind it belched an overwhelming puff of loamy air, the gasp of an awakening garden. The receding wall left behind a tunnel of moist, sifting soil that couldn't possibly exist in the soggy earth beneath Chicago's streets—which was fine, because it *didn't*, not really. Twisted roots, wriggling worms, and things that coulda been either or both looped in and out of the passage walls, floor, and ceiling. Little critters skittered and clattered and *giggled* at the edges of earshot, way beyond the light. Molds in every color of the rainbow hung in spatters across the walls. Some gleamed with a phosphorescence that had nothing whatsoever to do with chemistry or biology; a few even twinkled as if they were distant stars, or maybe winking eyes.

"Down the rabbit hole, Alice," I said. Pete threw me a vorpal glare, and we were off.

Our footsteps made a series of "fwumps" in the soft dirt, our breathing filled the air around us, and neither of 'em echoed in the least. Long minutes passed, and we strolled by dozens after dozens of roots and splotches, yet the sunlight filtering into my office from the tiny windows still seemed only a few paces behind us. The flickering fungi slowed and dimmed as we neared, picked back up once we'd moved on. Thick-stemmed mushrooms, with spotted caps in bruise-purple and drunk-nose fleshy red, started popping up from the ground, and occasionally the walls. And when I say "started popping up," I don't just mean that we happened across 'em on our way, though that was *mostly* the case; I mean that, a couple of times, they *literally* popped up in front of us, unfolding like beach umbrellas. Once or twice, I heard one yawn as it stretched.

After a dozen steps or a few hundred yards, two minutes or twenty, the light behind us abruptly disappeared from sight—and the tunnel in front began to swim into focus, brightened by a steady, golden radiance from above.

The floor sloped up, steep and sudden, and we were there.

The Chicago Otherworld. Or more properly— since there's so many more of you than of us, and your version of the city's grown a lot faster'n ours— the Otherworld a few miles outside of Chicago. Which actually works for me, since I wouldn't want someone stumbling on this particular Path and popping up unannounced in my office.

We emerged from the earth in a veritable field of toadstools, from thick white maggoty-things that barely peeked from the soil to bright-capped stalks that reached above my knees. All around us, the grasses knelt and whispered in the springtime breeze; above, the sky was an impossible blue, without any sign of the sun. There *was* no sun, not in this part of Elphame; just a brightening of the sky in the day, then darkening to flaunt the glittering stars and gleaming silver of the moon.

Yeah, there's moonlight without a sun; look, I don't sit around nitpicking the way *your* world works, do I? (Well, I guess maybe I do. Knock it off anyway.)

In all directions except straight ahead, nature stretched unimpeded. A few dozen yards behind us, an impossibly thick forest loomed out of nowhere, casting its tiny portion of the world in perpetual midnight. Pinecones the size of babies rolled around in the dirt where they'd fallen, and you would *not* wanna be under one when that happened. Branches scraped as wind and other things moved through and around 'em, and we could hear the grunts, the thumps, the growls, and in some cases the songs and poems of the animals living inside. Off to the left, a fallen oak provided room and board for another population of mushrooms; the tree itself still lived without roots, growing new branches on its upper side, its leaves waving hello to its standing brothers of the wood. Other trees stood in all directions, alone or in small copses away from the forest, and these weren't the oak, ash, and hawthorn of the woodlands behind us, but apple and pear and orange trees, their fruits ripe and enormous and ready to burst.

Short tufts of that grass I mentioned stuck up like thinning hair between the bunches of mushrooms, growing thicker and taller as it spread, until it was a couple feet high just beyond the overlapping rings of toadstools. In a couple sporadic spots, tiny puddles of honey sat where the morning dew hadn't yet seeped into the soil or the stems. The plains wore wildflowers in blinding reds and purples and blues, buzzing with bees and butterflies and wild pixies—all gangly and naked and not at all attractive (especially once you get to know 'em). They chattered and cooed at us, and snickered at Pete. Birds circled high, high above, cawing, crying, preying and praying; from here, it was impossible to be sure how large they might be—or to make out, exactly, the words that it seemed they were screeching.

And on the far horizon, jutting over the rolling hills of grasses and trees, the tippy-tops of the towers and skyscrapers of our Chicago. The kinda-civilization, at the edge of this kinda-wilderness.

I ain't doing it justice, not by half. See, it ain't just about the *what*, these expanses of Elphame, but the *how*. The aromas of sickly-sweet flowers and rich soil, wild grasses and hoary, moss-covered trees—they weren't just on the wind, or winding up our noses the way "normal" smells are supposed to. They get inside your head as if they don't even come from outside, but from your own mouth, tongue, skin. They're everywhere, a part of you, not the world around you, until your breath turns floral and your words taste of leaves.

The colors... They're *intense*, impossible, almost painful; entities unto themselves, rather'n mere traits of other objects. They're stark, standing out against each other, the richest greens, the sharpest reds, the deepest browns, the brightest yellows. You could try to capture 'em in a painting, but nobody'd buy it: too fake-looking. There's no gradation, nothing muted; the dark and light emeralds of a leaf don't blend into each other, but sit side-by-side with clear demarcation—as if no one color here would ever lower itself to *blend* with another.

No wonder Pete was squinting.

He was also fidgeting, feet shuffling, hands running up and down the straps of his pack. I gave him a few to get it out of his system; yeah, he's been here before, about half a dozen times now, but it ain't his world.

Me, though? I could feel my back relaxing, my

shoulders straightening. Much as I hated the idea of coming back, of dealing with the sorts of bastards I'd walked away from, this was my home. It felt right, felt—not friendly, exactly, 'cause there's plenty here that's not, but less universally hostile, less alien.

Partly it's the whole technology thing. We've talked about that already. Partly it's the iron. It's *all over* your world: tools, nails, pieces of trains and buildings, railings, handles, furniture… You can't get away from the damn stuff. Yeah, it ain't actively painful unless I touch it, and casual contact—brushing against it, that kinda thing—usually doesn't cause any lasting hurt. But it's there, always itching at my skin and my mind. It'd be, for you, like living in a world where random objects were brushed with lye. Not here, not for me.

And partly it's just, this was my world. My own nature, my own magic, *belonged* here, in ways they never did and never would on the other side.

Wasn't enough to make me stay, though. What's *that* tell you?

I glanced Pete's way, and couldn't help but smile. Uncomfortable as he was, he was standing taller. A few of the lines on his face had smoothed, the shallow scar on his neck—inflicted by a drunk with a bottle some years ago—was gone. Hell, even his hair was thicker.

Whoever you are, you're always more you, in Elphame.

Or in the better parts of Elphame, anyway. Trust me, you don't want to visit the places where you're *less* you, or more someone else; the things already living there are *nasty*.

"Okay, Mick," he said finally, turning back my way. "I'm ready to—*Holy hell!*"

No fooling, he jumped up and back like a startled kitten. I just about bust a gut laughing, and it took me some minutes before I could breathe well enough to answer his unasked question. (Remember what I just said about "Whoever you are, in Elphame"?)

"Some of us," I told him, "don't look entirely like our 'true selves' in your world. Far as we can tell, it's random; some Fae don't change a whit. Some just have a couple different features depending on which world they're in: eye-color, shape of the chin, that kinda stuff. And me…"

"You lose half a foot and change," Pete said, looking at me—*down* at me—suspiciously. "And your face is a little off. Your cheeks are narrower, and your nose is more hooked."

I nodded. "They tell me I got 'royal features,' whatever the hell that means. Say it makes me resemble my cousin."

"You coulda warned me, Mick."

Honestly, I'd forgotten all about it, but what I said was, "How much fun would *that* be? C'mon, let's get walking."

The hole in the soil that we'd come from just vanished soon as we took our first steps. It didn't even fill in, exactly, so much as simply stop being a hole. Just another patch of earth, until someone came along who knew enough to try and open it.

You never wanna run roughshod over toadstools and growths of that sort in the Otherworld; you never know who might own 'em, or be linked to 'em, or occasionally even live in 'em. It was easy

143

enough for me to march through the grass, since I could feel where it was okay to step and where it wasn't, but poor Pete had to keep a watch on his feet. It got even harder when we reached the thicker grasses, and I took his hand to help guide him around some of the less obvious hazards such as burrows, tree roots, and holly bushes, and—as we passed the copses and mini-orchards—*ghillie dhu* or *huldra* dens. I saw him glance up once, eying the lush, red apples, but he set his jaw and looked away before I had to remind him.

It was when he directed his attention back downward that he spotted one of Elphame's other little peculiarities.

"Uh, Mick? You don't have a shadow…"

I smiled. "Neither do you."

He actually spun, tripping over his feet, as though to catch it before it escaped. "What? Where…?"

"Living things—well, animals and people—don't cast shadows here, Pete. You never noticed before?"

"I guess not," he admitted. "I usually do my best to avoid anyone else while I'm here, and I'm usually trying to pick my way through all this *without* your help. Suppose I just never looked at my own shadow. Or, uh, my lack of my own."

"Huh. Not real observant, Pete. Good thing you haven't made detective yet." I snickered again at his glare.

"So is it like this everywhere?" he asked me.

"Nah. Different regions of the Otherworld have different traits, same as your world. Geography and weather, sure, but also little details like this. So locally, yeah, no shadows. Elsewhere…" I shrugged.

Then, "I should say, locally depending on whose lands you're in." I pointed.

He followed my gesture, over and up. Far ahead, beyond and to the right of the city that was my destination, the sky went grim. Shiner-dark clouds bubbled and swirled, filthy bathwater draining from a tub, casting that corner of the sky in a sickly yellow-grey. The terrain grew flat, as the land slid into and drowned beneath an ugly marsh—a swampy "echo" of the lands around Lake Michigan.

"It's different there, I take it?"

"Very," I said. "And trust me, you don't wanna find out firsthand."

"So whose lands are those?"

"Unseelie."

We kept walking. Right about the time we reached an actual road—well, a broad trail, mostly well-trampled dirt—Pete stopped. "This'll do." He tilted his head toward a distant wood of ash trees, a lot less dense (and less dark) than the one where we'd appeared. Big enough to run around in, easy enough to spot from a distance, and not likely to have too many of the wilder Fae living in it. It was a good pick; I wondered if he'd used it before.

"Okay," I said. "I'll be back in three days." We shook hands. "Be careful, Pete."

"Always am." He shrugged his pack into a more comfortable position and headed away. I stood and fretted for a few minutes; if the place sounds like just an exaggeration of the natural world to you, take a minute to picture the exaggerated predators, then add a bunch of unfriendly, uncivilized Fae to the mix, and stir. But Pete could take care of himself, and he'd done this a buncha times before, so eventually I tore myself away and started down the road.

It wasn't all that far to go—as I said, a few miles or so—but nevertheless, I was glad when I came across the tracks, rails of battered brass stretching off into the distance behind me, and on into the city in front. I decided to wait, see if I could bum a lift off a passing train; and if not, well, I was still close enough to walk to civilization before dark.

I came up lucky. It wasn't even a full hour, and I'd only been forced into one annoying conversation with a passing rube on his way to the big city—a *coblynau*, or what you might know better as a knocker or a *kobold*—before I heard the roar of the oncoming wheels.

It rumbled around the bend, slowing and shrieking its whistle as it came up on the road, and any of you woulda known it instantly for what it was. It had no smokestack, since we obviously need to use methods other'n steam engines, but otherwise the shape was familiar. The engine was a huge monstrosity of brass, the wheels and couplings of bronze, the cowcatcher a golden filigree clearly meant for ostentation, not any actual use. (And this wasn't even a real expensive engine. I've seen 'em constructed *entirely* of gold and silver, hauling cars of ivory.) The cars on this one were just plain wood, with brass trimming and fittings, trundling along after the engine. Clack-clack, clack-clack, it passed me, blasting winds strong enough, even as it slowed, to whip my coat around and almost knock me staggering. I tensed in concentration, collecting shreds of ambient luck—here, in Elphame, I could do it quick without pulling my wand—and then reached out and snagged the railing as the last car lumbered by. Smooth as you please, I swung up and around, cleared the brass safety chain, and settled down cross-legged on the wooden platform. It was just large enough to get comfortable, and if I didn't actually open the door and slip inside the car, the conductors might not even notice me.

I leaned back against the frame, watching the scenery whip by, snickering at the enraged squeals as some of the smaller denizens of the wild leapt clear of the oncoming juggernaut. And gradually, I also began to hear—and very, *very* faintly, to smell—the labors of the workers below, even through the careful seals meant to separate them from the passengers. And even though I hadn't seen 'em in years, I could easily imagine the cramped, dim, sour lower decks, of the engine and of every car; the scores and scores of hired *brounies* and indentured goblins hunched over their benches, hauling on their "oars": thick wooden shafts attached to the rolling wheels. And all to the steady, pounding beat, piped to them from the drummer stationed behind the engineer.

As I said, methods other'n steam engines. A few of the fancier engines actually ran on magic, but those were a *lot* more expensive, and in a culture where major fees are paid in favors and boons, everyone's a miser.

I closed my eyes, pondering on that culture, listening to the roar and the whistle of the train. And the Otherworld Chicago drew closer.

***

Which is, I figure, as convenient a segue as any to something you probably oughta know about us—the Fae in general, I mean—before I get any further.

Some of you are already wondering, why a train? If we don't use steam power, why model the engine after a locomotive? It ain't exactly the most efficiently designed vehicle for manual power, y'know?

And the answer is, we built it that way because *you* did. The thing about us is, we're mimics. It's instinctive, part of who—what—we are. Even though a few of the Fae races actually *predate* you mugs, we reflect you. We can't help ourselves.

Individually, it don't mean much; it's why I'm pretty keen at blending in with you, but that's about it. Culturally, though? Heh.

You've read the faerie tales; you're expecting a city of castles with towering minarets and flapping banners, knights on horseback, arching halls with drinking and dancing before the throne, and all that, ain't you?

Horsefeathers. Yeah, some of our cities kinda looked like that, back in the Dark Ages, and maybe—*maybe*—a couple of the oldest ones in Europe still do. (I ain't been back to the Old World since before the American Revolution, so I can't say for sure.) But everywhere else? Nah. Mimics. All tribal and covered in woad in pre-Roman Ireland, gathered in city-states and temples atop mountains in Ancient Greece, and today...

Today every city of ours is as different from each other as every city of yours. Today, we're "modern." Hip to the new age, or at least to the age of a couple years ago. Today, there's a reason I friggin' hate shuffling Sideways, *especially* here in goddamn Chicago.

I hopped off the train at another slow curve, once we were inside the city proper; no reason to wait for the station and risk being spotted. The street under my Oxfords was paved in bricks—bricks of a thousand different sizes, shapes, and colors, carefully fitted together in peculiar patterns to form a (more or less) smooth surface for wheels and feet. Most were cracked, or singed, or blackened, because here, every brick that cobbled every road came from a home or building that had been destroyed, torn down, or abandoned throughout your Chicago's history. Streets paved by fragments of the past, people's most painful moments scuffed and dirtied beneath our feet.

Tells you something about us, don't it?

I stood on a corner and took a good, hard look around, reacquainting myself with our shadow of your city. Trees grew everywhere, even in the center of town—again, mostly oak, ash, and hawthorn, with sporadic fruit trees to liven the place up. A few of the trees stood wild, but most actually formed *parts* of the various structures. In one neighborhood, a thick tree might form the central support of a house otherwise built normally of lumber and brick. Over there, an abnormally large ash—*impossibly* large, for your world, just kinda unusual here—actually *was* a small apartment building, with doors built into the trunk at various heights, and a few extra rooms tacked on to the larger branches. But those were the cheap homes, often surrounded by slumping tenements that woulda been right at home in your world.

No *Fae* lived there, of course. We didn't need to, and wouldn't lower ourselves. But others...

All these were just the outliers, though, the fringes, the "bad" parts of town. Closer to the heart, where the rich and the powerful lived—and this being the seat of the Seelie Court in the region, that meant just about everyone—*that* was where the town showed its true shape.

Mounds of grassy earth, hillocks and knolls, sat in neat rows along the sides of the brick-paved streets, filling the air with the scent of growing things—and, on occasion, dying ones. Because that's who the *aes sidhe* are, remember, what makes us comfortable: "the People of the Mounds." In each stood doors, some wood, a few stone, mostly glass in this "modern" era, leading into the tunnels beneath. A few of the fancier ones had revolving doors, or extra doors, or doors surrounded by great marble pillars—holding up overhangs of stone or more earth—and manned by doormen in formal, Victorian-age coats.

But those mounds were just the lower floors. From their crowns rose the *rest* of our great structures. Again, the shorter ones, including most of the government buildings, were granite or marble, combining the worst of classical ostentation with the most banal facades of your contemporary municipal institutions. But some were true skyscrapers, rising scores of stories toward the sunless sky; and these were made mostly of glass, magically reinforced to bear the weight, or supported by impossibly tall and narrow trees that formed the corner pillars of the monoliths. They gleamed against the sky, glowing and reflecting in the diffuse daylight, columns of static, artificial fire.

All the look of today, with all the efficiency of yesterday. We could teach you a thing or two about wasted effort, yeah?

Fae of all sorts strode the sidewalks, beneath the shadows of the great edifices: my people, the *aes sidhe*; impossibly handsome and repulsively sleazy *gancanagh*, dreaming of their next prize dame, or the beautiful and equally nasty *leanan sidhe*, making equally nasty plans for unsuspecting men; squat and knotted *coblynau*, miners and construction workers on their way home from work; equally squat but not quite so ugly *dvergr* craftsmen, beards singed with magic and fire; and a dozen more besides. Men and women, young and old (or at least young-looking and old-looking), all dressed in suits and coats or skirts and blouses same as you'd see in your Chicago, but accessorized with the sporadic leather jerkin, bronze vambraces—even, on occasion, a full-on cuirass or breastplate.

Pretty much everyone was packing, too, for ceremony and style if not actual use. Rapiers, broadswords, and daggers were common, for tradition's sake; semi-autos and revolvers and Tommy guns for more practical use. Of course, their guts were magic, rather'n gunpowder and slides and springs. Most were forged of mystically reinforced bronze, brass, or, on occasion, silver. (Steel don't hurt us, but we can't exactly *make* the stuff easily, can we?) A lot of folks carried wands, too. In a few cases, the gats *were* also wands. Rumor has it the *dvergr* who first created *that* combination is so rich now, he occasionally hires down-and-out kings to chauffeur him around, just to say he can.

Traffic clattered and clumped down the roads between those sidewalks: horse-drawn carriages, usually black, with silver trim, and white-wall rubber tires. We don't have flivvers here yet; the *dvergar* are still trying to figure out how to hammer the magic into the right shapes and sizes to make 'em work, without 'em costing more'n their worth. So for now, coaches. Some of the "horses" pulling 'em might even have just been normal animals, too.

Of course, there's only a few thousand of us throughout the entirety of "our" Chicago, so you'd expect traffic to be pretty sparse, even in a city smaller'n yours. And you'd be wrong. Because there are others here, others who walk the streets and sidewalks, others who live in those cheap tenements and the flimsiest of treehouses.

Humans. There's more humans here than Fae. Men, women, children, who got lost and stumbled into the wrong cave, or arch of ivy, or toadstool ring, and wound up here. Who made ill-thought bargains, or tried to imprison one of us, without thinking through the consequences. Who caught the fancy of a Lord or Lady of the Courts, one who don't take "No" for an answer. Who were swapped for changelings and grew up here, never knowing anything else.

Doesn't matter how they got here, really. What matters is they never got the warning I gave Pete. If you're human, once you eat the food of Elphame, or drink of our waters or our wine, or accept a gift from the Fae of the Courts, you're sunk. It's drug and dream all mashed together. Time goes by, and you don't notice, 'cause you don't *age*. (Least most of you mugs don't. Kids sometimes grow up before they go all stagnant.) Long as you keep eating and drinking, it's all euphoria and bliss—and ignorance and obedience. At night you dance and sing, and sometimes make all kindsa whoopee, for your Lords' and Ladies' amusement; during the day, you fetch and carry and tote and labor at their whim. And *you never know*, because you're too busy being happy.

The happiest slaves in two worlds.

And yeah, I had my own share, before I left the Court. I don't now—I *wouldn't* now, even if I came back; I've gotten to know you people too well—but I don't hate myself for doing it back then, even though you probably think I should.

It's just who we are.

Welcome to the Chicago Otherworld, the closest I've come to "home" in over a hundred years.

I couldn't fucking wait to leave.

CHAPTER EIGHT

"Whaddaya mean, two months?!"

I was shouting, more because it seemed the kinda situation where I was *expected* to shout than because I was actually all that shocked, but you'd never have known it. I was standing at one of the receptionists' desks, a big oak monstrosity in the main chamber of City Hall, and the volume around me made Pete's precinct look—or *sound*, more accurately—like a church in silent prayer. Fae of every kind I'd seen on the street, and a dozen more I hadn't, rushed past me in every sort of hurry, yelling and calling and grousing at people who weren't doing whatever the yeller/caller/grouser thought they should be. Dull-eyed humans meandered by, carrying boxes of files; pixies more civilized than the ones I'd seen out in the fields (you could tell 'cause these wore clothes) zipped along their way, delivering various urgent messages; *aes sidhe* in trench coats and spriggans in police uniforms dragged goblins, boggarts, and clurichauns to or from interrogation rooms. Some were to be imprisoned or indentured to pay for whatever damages they'd done, others questioned in hopes of learning whatever their Unseelie masters were scheming. Police station, courtroom (and Court), and political offices, all rolled together into a marble- and granite-walled building right in the heart of the city.

It sounded as though someone put together a friggin' war, then forgot to do anything with it.

The short woman behind the desk, a smartly dressed leprechaun with gold-rimmed glasses and holly-berry hair, wasn't at all impressed by my raised voice, either. "Indeed, Judge Sien Bheara's schedule has no openings until late May. And I fear Chief Laurelline is even busier. If you'd care to make an appointment…?"

"Not really, no."

Honestly, I hadn't expected much better, not when trying to see the King or Queen of… Huh.

Okay, quick rundown for those of you who don't know your Fae mythology. The ancient Europeans divvied us up into "trooping Fae" who gathered and traveled in groups, and "solitary Fae" who, uh, didn't. It's the trooping Fae who formed the cities and societies that you find in the Otherworld today.

And most of those civilized (hah!) Fae are split into two factions. The Seelie Court are the ones that most mortals tend to think of these days. We're the ones with the intricate laws of honor and behavior, the ones bound by pact and tradition and our word, should we choose to give it. Not all of us are nice—some are downright evil—but as a group, we don't wish humans any *particular* harm, and a number of Seelie Fae can be helpful and friendly if approached right. (Read: bribed with the traditional offerings.)

Then you got the Unseelie: the goblin under the bed, the troll under the bridge, the *mari-morgan* waiting to drag you under the water. The less said about the Unseelie, the better.

Unfortunately, I got a *lot* to say about the Unseelie. Just not yet.

The point to this little lecture is that the Seelie Court here in Chicago's modeled themselves after your own municipal government—and they've managed to twist tradition and title up with their efforts to take after you Joes. So King Sien Bheara and Queen Laurelline prefer Judge and Police Chief. We got our dukes and earls and princes and barons—titles they still hold, and still use on written edicts and certain formal shindigs—but for the most part, they're judges and aldermen and captains and lawyers. And just to make things even more of a hoot, there's no correlation. A baron and an earl might both be committeemen. A knight might be a captain. And like I just said, King Sien Bheara ain't remotely the only judge.

So how do you know who outranks who? If you're from here, you just do; and if you ain't, you keep your trap shut and pay real close attention until you work it out.

Anyway, I hadn't expected to get an audience with Chief Laurelline or Judge Sien Bheara, though two months sounded a little extreme. I'd mostly asked for two reasons: one, it's an old trick; you ask for something ridiculous, so when your next request is a little less ridiculous, it sounds reasonable.

And two, I wanted to see if I still had any pull around here. The answer to that last was looking to be a pretty resounding *no*.

"I told you who I am, doll. I was a *prince* of this damn Court!"

"Yes, Mr. Oberon." She dropped her mask of indifference long enough to look disgusted at gracing me with that name. "You did. And I should wish to mention that, in point of fact, you were never a prince in *Chicago*. Which means, at best, you were only ever a visiting dignitary here.

"And also, that pesky past tense. You *were* a prince, before you went and got yourself banished."

My fists clenched, and I'm pretty sure my ears started to steam. "Now just a minute, you—"

"If you are not planning to make an appointment, I would request that you leave. There are other folks waiting in line."

I took a couple of deep breaths. "May I please see one of the *other* courtiers, miss?" I tried to make myself sound nicely chastened, when in fact I really wanted to play some chin music on the nearest handy mug.

"I'm sure you may." She aimed a thumb at the door further down the wall, past all the receptionists' desks and windows. "Personal secretaries throughout the hall. I'm sure one of them can assist you. You are not to approach any of the offices without permission."

"Thanks. I hope I'll find them as helpful as you've been."

"I'm certain you will. Next!"

More barely controlled chaos through that door, in that same combination of precinct and courtroom. At dozens of desks scattered throughout the wide hall, detectives and file clerks, seneschals and more receptionists, all scribbled, typed, or chatted as their duties dictated. A spriggan cop frogmarched a goblin past me and cuffed him to a chair, while a pixie shot past my head carrying a subpoena bigger'n she was. The place reeked of smoke that was equal parts tobacco and crushed flower petals.

And for the next two hours, I subjected myself to every imaginable variation of the phrase, "Sorry, no," from a bunch of aristocrats' brats—relatively young *aes sidhe* and *gancanagh* and whatnot, learning the ropes of the Court before they came into their own titles. Some of 'em didn't even bother to check their calendars or ask their bosses; most were polite enough to go through the motions. I got told that some of the nobles here could pencil me in in a couple weeks, whereas others might deign to sit down with me precisely three days after Hell froze over—assuming the reports of said abnormal winter could be independently verified by three separate unbiased sources.

Have I mentioned that I wasn't the most popular fella around?

I actually thought about waiting the two weeks, to be honest. I'd just kill some time until Pete was done, come back later, have whatever meetings I could have, and figure out what to do from there. It mighta been a little annoying, just sitting around, but it'd certainly be simpler. And the girl'd been missing for sixteen years, so a few more days probably wouldn't make a difference, right?

But that was an awful important point to hang on a "probably," and I couldn't shake Bianca's warning that Fino could go to war over this if he learned what was happening. Plus, I was just feeling damn ornery over being given the brush-off. So, time for a new plan.

I picked a random bench and just watched for a few hours, observing as the high mucky-mucks, the big (and medium) cheeses, emerged from their offices to converse with their various and sundry minions. It took a while, but eventually I had a pretty good sense of who treated their secretaries and chamberlains like dirt, and who was a little more friendly to the little people who worked for them.

And once I had *that* little nugget of information, it was just a matter of time before...

Yep. A guy wandered in from outside—probably one of the *ghillie dhu*, or what some of you call a "green man," considering he was dressed in a suit actually woven from moss—and made a beeline for one of the file clerks. The young *aes sidhe* closed his ledgers, spoke to the *ghillie dhu* for a minute, and then pointed him toward one of the judge's chambers. The outsider tipped a hat with a brim of leaves, and started that way...

"Hey!" I stood, elbowed my way over, and planted myself (no pun intended) in the green man's way, right beside the clerk's desk. "What the hell you think you're doing, pal?"

The *ghillie dhu* recoiled—they're kinda shy, most of 'em, unless they're protecting their woodlands. "I beg your pardon, sir?" he asked, his voice not quite steady.

"You think I don't see what's happening here? I was just told I'd hafta wait *weeks* to see somebody, and now you think you can just waltz in, throw your weight around, and jump the line? I don't think so, bo."

"I assure you, sir, I did nothing of the kind!" His

peepers were zipping back and forth like pixies on caffeine, and I think he really wanted to cut and run. I gotta say, I almost felt bad for what I was doing. "I merely asked… That is, I…"

The clerk came to his rescue, just as I'd wanted. "Back off, mister! He didn't do anything wrong!"

"Ah!" I spun, jutting my chin as far over the desk as I could without toppling forward, and it was the younger guy's turn to recoil. "So it's *your* fault then! You're the one who decided, hey, Mr. Oberon's just a nobody, it's okay if I treat him like garbage! Is that it, kid?"

"What? No, I—"

I glanced back at the *ghillie dhu*. "Sorry about that, buddy. Didn't realize it wasn't your fault. You're free to go."

There was no *reason* for him to go, of course— indeed, he *hadn't* done anything wrong—but he was so glad to be off the hook, he was pretty much sprinting as he blew the joint.

Everybody else around us was starting to stare, as they got the picture that something was up.

"And you," I said, going back to the kid, "you wanna be insulting and disrespectful, fine. I'm more'n happy to give you satisfaction."

You humans have an expression "White as a ghost." I've *seen* ghosts, so you know I'm on the square when I tell you that the clerk went a lot whiter'n they are. "Wh-what?"

"I'll pick…" I paused dramatically, considering. "Rapiers. Dawn give you enough time to get your affairs in order?"

"You—you can't…" I think he was about to cry,

and everyone around had gone quiet as a mouse's whisper. The kid had no idea what to do about me, which was my whole point. See, a Fae of the Seelie Court ain't required to accept or even acknowledge a challenge from anyone of *lower* status, and anyone of "quality" would know better'n to challenge a servant (and the scion of a more powerful Fae, too) over something of this sort. One of those things that Just Wasn't Done—but there wasn't any law that it *couldn't* be.

"What're your terms?" I pressed. "Death? Yeah, I bet a hothead young punk like you prefers to the death, don't you? All right, fine, I can do that."

He was whimpering openly now, and if the glares I was getting got any heavier, they'd crush me down into the toes of my shoes. If this didn't work—and so far, I wasn't seeing any trace of the response I was looking for—I was gonna have a problem. I didn't actually wanna hurt the kid, and I was just scrambling for an excuse to back out (or at least let myself get talked out of a duel to the *death*), when the gamble paid off.

"Really, Mr. Oberon." The voice was resonant, cutting through the sounds from elsewhere in the hall, and deeper than a gnome's basement. "Have you nothing better to do with your time than to terrorize our faithful civil servants?"

I straightened. "Afternoon, Judge Ylleuwyn. Good to see you."

The judge—an earl of the Court, just so you know—was a gaunt shape looming in an office doorway, draped in robes of formal black, the cuffs and collar stitched with traditional litanies in Old

Gaelic. His hair and beard were storm-cloud grey, and his unblinking eyes looked quite capable of staring down his own reflection. I kept his gaze only by reminding myself, over and over, how humiliating it'd be to back down now after everything I'd done to get his attention.

"I'll not lie to you," he said, "by claiming the same. Do you truly intend to challenge my clerk to a duel? Or was this merely an uncouth pretense to attract attention?"

"Why, Your Honor, what a dreadful thing to suggest. But since you *are* here, and since your previous appointment seems to have canceled..." I smiled broadly.

He didn't. I could actually see the refusal forming behind his lips, until he glanced one more time at his clerk's corpse-pallid mug, and the amount of work that *wasn't* getting done as everyone watched to see what happened next. He sighed, loudly.

"Step into my office, Mr. Oberon." He managed, without being overtly rude in the slightest, to make my name sound even more an insult than the leprechaun at the front desk had done.

I reached out to pat the young *aes sidhe*'s cheek— he yelped and actually fell over his chair as he backpedaled—and followed.

Ylleuwyn's office was nice and roomy; probably more so, actually, than could naturally fit into the space allotted to it. (Fae architecture at its finest.) His desk was carved in patterns of oak leaves but looked more like mahogany. The entire far wall was a single large, overflowing bookcase, and a plaque directly behind him held a saber and a Tommy gun.

I had to take a second glance at the gat: this was a *genuine* Chicago typewriter—imported from your world, made of wood and steel—not one of our magic-driven copies.

"Have you any idea," Ylleuwyn asked me as he rounded his desk, "whose son you just challenged, in violation of hundreds of years of tradition?" He sat down in his great, high-backed chair. I sprawled in one of the others, opposite his desk, without waiting for an invitation that I knew wasn't coming.

"No doubt someone damn important, who'll never forgive me, and will swear himself my enemy until the end of days. He'll do everything he can to destroy me, and blah, blah, blah. Tell him to get in line."

"I'll do that. I thought we were well rid of you, Mick. Have you returned for any purpose other than making a deliberate mockery of our customs?"

"It's 'Mick' now, is it? When did we get to be such close pals, Yll?"

Fire flashed in Ylleuwyn's pupils—and if you're wondering if I'm being metaphorical or not, well, I wasn't so sure myself. "I'll not stoop to forgetting my manners with you *in public*, you wretch. But neither will I address you privately by a name to which you've no right! As though it weren't enough that a prince of the Court should be unseated and banished, you deliberately spat in the eye of every Seelie when you chose to take your cousin's name to go amongst the mortals! You are a living, breathing affront, *Mick*. A smirch on the honor of the entire Seelie Court! And some day, I will learn *precisely* what offense you committed to earn your current status, and should it be something that is even *remotely* criminal by the statutes of the Chicago Court, believe you me, I shall ensure that you suffer the full penalties permitted me by law!"

He was breathing heavy by the time he was done, not remotely as composed as he'd have been in public—and I was right there with him. My fists were clenched tight enough to draw blood, and I was seeing red flashes in the corner of my vision. I honestly dunno which it was that stopped me from lunging over the desk and slugging him one across the button: that it simply wasn't appropriate, that it'd cost me whatever leads he might have to offer, or that I wasn't entirely sure I could take him.

What you gotta understand is, I *wasn't* banished, *wasn't* stripped of my title. I walked away from it. *My* choice, nobody else's. But when the rumors started, traveling from Court to Court on wings and wheels of whispers, I didn't say a thing. In fact, I even helped spread a few of 'em. I thought it'd be a good way to make sure that nobody came to me asking for favors, or trying to rope me into whatever garbage political scheme they had going, or just begging me to come back.

I'm a lot less angry now than I was then, and I've long since abandoned my determination never to have *anything* to do with the Courts—but now that those rumors are doing me more harm than good, it's way too damn late to do anything about 'em.

So what I said instead, after pausing to let my heartbeat slow down to something a little less than a cavalry charge, was, "I didn't really violate any rules out there. There's no law against the challenge I made. You call yourself a judge, you should probably bone up on this stuff."

"No law, no," he conceded, his voice gruff enough to polish glass. "But *tradition*! You know very well they're nearly the same thing to us!"

"Yeah. Y'know what's funny about something that's *nearly* some other thing, Ylleuwyn? It ain't *actually* that other thing." Then, before he could launch back into his tirade—or find himself a new one—I continued, "But as it happens, you ain't wrong. I *am* here for a reason.

"I'm trying to find a human child. The other half of a changeling swap."

"Then why pester us about it? Go ask the Unfit, if you dare. They're responsible for far more changelings than any of the Seelie."

"More, yeah. But not even remotely *all*." I leaned back, put a foot up on the opposite knee. "But more to the point, judge, ain't that the kinda thing you guys keep track of? I know you watch everything *else* the Unfit do—and each other, too, at that. I could ask around for months, and not get the sorta info you can offer."

"I see." He, too, leaned back in his chair. "And I suppose you also have a reason why I might lift so much as a finger to assist you? Because I confess, Mick, that I cannot come up with a single one."

"I *could* tell you it's because you'd be helping out a family that's worried sick about their daughter," I began, even though I knew how well *that* argument would fly. And yep, he was already shrugging his black-robed, "honorable" shoulders before I'd finished the sentence. "Okay," I went on. "How about because the last thing you want is me hanging around for days, or even weeks, investigating this, and your help gets me outta here that much quicker?

"And because, much as you hate me, you're sharp enough to know that it'd be useful to have me owe you a small favor." I practically had to use a crowbar to pry my jaw open around that sentence. *Last* thing I wanted was to be indebted to Ylleuwyn for anything, ever. But this was a fairly minor boon, all things considered, and if it got me what I needed, it'd be worth paying.

Probably.

For about a minute, the judge said nothing. If I'd seen fire in his blinkers before, I swore that I could see copper and brass gears clicking and winding in 'em now. And then, "All right, you make an interesting point. I'll hear you out. Tell me of this human you're looking for."

"Well, she was taken about sixteen years ago." Then, since not all Fae are up on human physiology, "Assuming she's aged normally while she's been here, that makes her an older adolescent. *Almost* an adult, but not quite."

"That's still an awfully wide range. Continue."

"She's Italian, which means that she's probably a *little* darker skinned than you are, but not necessarily. She was taken from a family called Ottati…"

He was good; very, very good. Even watching as carefully as I was, I almost missed it: a single twitch in the wrinkles beside his left blinker, a quick pressure at the corner of his mouth. I kept gabbing, throwing out a few more meaningless details, but it didn't matter. He knew *exactly* who I meant.

And he didn't want me to know he knew. *That* couldn't bode well.

"No," he said after I'd finished—and after he made a pretty convincing show of giving it some real thought. "I fear I know of nothing matching your precise description of events. I shall, of course, peruse our files when I have the time to do so—I must admit, I'm rather taken with the idea of you owing me—but I can make you no promises. Where might I reach you?"

"I'll be staying at the Lambton," I told him, rising from the chair. He did the same. (And no, I didn't even consider lying about where I'd be. Even if I'd thought he'd try something unpleasant, a fella with his pull could find me in two minutes flat as long as I was in the city.) He stuck out his hand, somehow making it very clear that he did so only because courtesy demanded it; I can only hope I was able to convey the same when I took it.

I'm sure I got some murderous looks on my way outta the hall, but honestly, I didn't notice. I was too busy going over it all in my head, and getting more'n more unhappy with it each time. The weather outside coulda been responding to my mood. Darkness had fallen, and the air was filled with a heavy, steady downpour—the kind that comes with no thunder, no lightning, just a wall of wet that never seems to end. In your world, it woulda soaked me and everyone out on the street, leaving us sopping for hours, but here… Well, I'll get to that. Right now, anyway, I was drenched, but didn't much care.

Yeah, I'd learned something—something important, but not real hopeful. Ylleuwyn's reaction to the family name… At the very least, it meant that whoever'd taken the kid was someone significant, someone his

Honor didn't want to make any trouble for. And that certainly meant Seelie, since I could imagine pretty easily that the judge'd be quite happy for me and one of the Unseelie to make each other miserable.

And that was a *best*-case scenario. *Worst* case was that this was something a lot bigger'n nastier than a normal changeling swap—something that Fae of prominence wouldn't want to be associated with—and *that* was why he was keeping his yap shut. I couldn't be sure what that "something else" might be, but none of the possibilities were pleasant to consider.

Either way, I wasn't about to get any help from Chicago's Seelie Court. And that left only one other choice.

I acted before I could take the time to talk myself out of it. There was always a sporadic stream of 'em, coming from the hall: low-ranking Unseelie commoners, taken in for sabotage or theft or spying on the Seelie. Some were getting out after months or years in the cooler, or indentured servitude; others after being grilled for a while and let go.

Petty crooks, the whole lot. But their bosses…

Well, I told you, the Seelie Court of Chicago took after your Chicago's city government, the cops, and the courts. Whodaya think the *Unseelie* took after, then?

I darted through the curtain of water at the first Unseelie I saw leaving—a short, big-eared, hairy, wrinkled little goblin wearing nothing but trousers and suspenders. Before he could do more'n grunt, I had him pressed up against the side of the hall's marble stairs.

"I get it," he squawked at me. "You bastards lemme go *officially* so's you can catch me on the street without the red tape, yeah? Do your worst, copper! I ain't spilling a word, see?"

"Ah, close your head, you twit." I stepped back so I wasn't crowding him. "I ain't a cop."

"No?" He squinted and gave me a pretty solid up-and-down. "You look just like 'em."

"My name's Mick Oberon. You hearda me?"

"Mighta," he said. The wrinkles on his face were getting deeper in what I assumed was a thoughtful scowl. "Whatcha want with me?"

"I want you to get her a message."

His squint got even narrower, even more suspicious, but he didn't waste both our time by trying to pretend he didn't know who I meant.

"Yeah? And that'd be…?"

"Just tell her I want a sit-down. At her convenience, just as long as 'convenient' is damn soon." I started to relax my grip, then leaned in, nose-to-really-really-long-nose. This close, even in the rain, I could smell the reek of blood and garbage on him. "And one other thing…"

"Yeah?"

"If you decide *not* to deliver my message, and she finds out later it was something important… Well, decide ahead of time how much being lazy's worth to you. Get me?"

He nodded. "Yeah."

"Good. Beat it." I let go, and just that quick, he was gone.

I coulda hailed a cab without much difficulty— more'n half the horse-buggies on the road around the hall had the checkered stripes around the windows, or other blatant signage—but it was only a few blocks, and even in the rain, I decided it wasn't worth it. So I trudged those several hundred yards, head down, hands in my pockets. Above me, a few of the clouds glowed, lit from behind by the moon, and a couple times I heard howling in the distance, beyond the city limits.

I wondered if one of those voices might be Pete's.

In this weather, I couldn't see much of the building even once I'd arrived and was standing right smack in front of it, but then, I didn't need to. I'd seen it plenty times before.

The Lambton Worm is the nicest hotel in Chicago's Otherworld, and one of the few luxuries I permit myself when I'm here. A couple dozen stories—plus the floors inside the earthen mound at its foundation—the Lambton caters to just about every kinda Fae you can imagine. The side of the building facing the main streets is all shiny modern, glass façade with marble columns, and the rooms are straight outta the Morrison, the Drake, or the Lexington in your world. But at the back-right, the support column's an enormous hawthorn, and the rooms are framed in or carved from its branches; the back-left is a castle tower, with sleeping chambers and ballrooms accordingly. And of course, the lower levels, within the mound, have caves and warrens for those who prefer the underground.

It's ridiculously huge, since you could fit over half the entire Fae population of our Chicago here, but this is how big snazzy hotels are supposed to be, so this is how big it is.

The whole building's wrapped in the coils of a great stone serpent. The hotel's official story is that the thing actually *was* a dragon, a relative of the legendary Lambton worm for which the place is named, that was petrified by the gaze of a basilisk. But everyone local knows it's really just a fancy sculpture.

Me, I just wanted a bed, and didn't care much what kinda room it was in, long as it was quiet. I stepped under the overhang, and just that quick, I was dry. See, that's what I meant earlier, about Elphame rain. (Or again, rain in *parts* of Elphame, anyway.) It don't *stick*, don't get absorbed—not into clothes or hair, anyway. Soon as I was sheltered from the constant drenching, the water that was on me pretty much just ran off fast enough to make a duck jealous. It beaded in a few spots, but those were easy to brush away with a flick of the wrist.

That little chore done, I slipped into the glass revolving door and revolved my way inside.

A winding pathway of lush carpeting, framed in white marble, ran through a sparse forest—first of embossed pillars that woulda been the envy of the Parthenon, then actual trees, depending on what part of the cavernous lobby you were standing in. Bobbing balls of glass, sorta phantom light bulbs, floated up by the ceiling, shedding cheerful yellows and pinks. Sitting areas, some of carpet, some of soil, offered tables for a quick nip, or a game of billiards. The entryways to the various "themed" sections of the Lambton were clearly marked, as was the concierge's counter—marble, again—way the hell on the far end.

Pixies and whatnot flitted around the lights,

while nearly every type of Seelie wandered through the magnificent hall—as did smiling, blank-faced humans, toting luggage or delivering drinks.

A leprechaun wearing a red greatcoat and stilts—and no, I'm not making that up—offered to take my coat, or to call someone to lug my bags. Since I was keeping my coat, and didn't *have* any bags, he didn't get a tip. I made my way to the counter, asked for a room overlooking the city—ignoring the brief temptation to get one so deep underground it'd give Hades claustrophobia—and dumped a handful of crumpled sawbucks on the concierge. My *last* handful until I cashed Bianca's payday, in fact. (Yeah, we use cash for exchanges and services that don't warrant political favors and pacts. It's completely valueless here, of course, 'cept that everyone agrees to honor it 'cause that's what *you* people use. I swear, sometimes...)

I got my key from the nice fellow at the desk, wandered past a couple of *bean nighe* from the Lambton's cleaning service, and made for the elevators. (Which were raised and lowered by huge cranks in the basement that were hauled by humans completely tight on the delights of Elphame.) I waved once or twice at a few guys who both knew me and didn't figure I was *too* scummy, my mind already envisioning a thick mattress and clean sheets.

And if you think it all went that easy for me, you ain't been paying attention.

I was just passing one of the hotel's umpteen bars—which, according to a glass-framed poster, served twenty-seven different varieties of mead; Prohibition was one thing we knew better'n to take from you dopes—when I heard a gravelly voice call my name.

A gink wearing a thick red beard, a tan overcoat, and an orange snap-brim (and yeah, it was about as blinding as it sounds) hopped down from one of the bar stools. He was about three feet tall when he pushed off his seat, and about six foot six when he landed.

Lousy spriggans. Guess I should be glad he stopped there, instead of going full-on giant. Maybe he figured this'd be intimidating enough without drawing too much attention.

"C'mon and join me, Mr. Oberon," he grumbled. I was getting more'n a little tired of hearing my name spat like a curse. "Let's jaw fer a spell."

I didn't even try to hide my deep sigh as I wandered over. "How you been, Slachaun?"

"Oh, can't complain, can't complain. Place's been nice'n quiet fer ages, now. Y'know how much I *love* nice'n quiet, don'tcha, Mr. Oberon?"

I leaned on the bar, put one foot up on the brass railing that ran along the oak paneling near the floor. (It wasn't just meant to provide a footrest for folks on the stools; some of the bar's patrons couldn't *reach* the stools without a leg-up.) "Yeah, I remember something about that," I said. "And since I got no intention of starting anything, it's a lucky day for both of us."

"Sure it is, at that," he said, sucking the last bits of mead from the pint sitting in front of him. "'Course, with yer history, y'can understand if I'm a wee bit skeptical."

Ah, here it is. "I've never caused any trouble here

wasn't started by someone else, Slachaun."

"So y'say. But y'don't need to *start* trouble, Mr. Oberon. Y'*are* trouble. An' it's my job to keep *all* trouble out o' the hotel, not just trouble Mr. Oberon don't start."

"You've no right to ask me to leave. I've already paid—"

"Wouldn't dream've it, boyo. But I'll be takin' that wand until it's checkout time."

I froze for a flash, then made a point of slowly glancing around. Looking one way, I could pick out a dozen wands—not to mention several times that many heaters—on the bar patrons alone. The other way, a young couple of *aes sidhe* strolled past along the carpeted walkway carrying matching Tommy guns, actually inscribed with each other's names.

Slachaun was grinning openly by the time I got back to him, the thicket of red fur that was his beard split wide by a row of crooked yellow teeth.

"You're right," I told him. "You're gonna have to *take* it."

Ooh, this was going to hurt...

If you ever have the opportunity to *not* get punched by a spriggan, I strongly advise you to take it. Those bastards are *strong*. And this being Elphame—my natural environment, as it were—I couldn't just shrug off pain or minor injury the way I can in your world.

I doubled up around his fist like he was folding a towel and hit the floor on my hands and knees— well, mostly the floor; one hand landed on his shoe— coughing and wheezing. Over the sound of my own gasps, I could hear the drinking and conversation around us petering out, and the squeaking of chairs and stools turning my way.

Always happy to be the center of attention, me.

I took a moment to catch my breath and wait for the ache in my stomach to settle into a dull conflagration, and Slachaun was more'n happy to give me all the time in the world. He was enjoying this; in fact, he ordered another round while I was down.

Carefully, doing my damnedest not to shake or wince in any way, I straightened to my full (currently unimpressive) height. His grin got even wider—he was starting to look more redcap than spriggan, with that smile—as he waited for me to take a poke at him.

I stepped back and shook my head. "You still ain't getting my wand, Slachaun. You got no right." And I started walking away.

"What? Get back here, y'bastard! I—"

Thud!

I know it woulda been more impressive just to keep going, but I couldn't help myself. At that sound, and the subsequent guffaws from everyone in the bar, I had to look back.

The spriggan was flat on his face, one foot up in the air—where I'd tied his shoelace to the rail along the bar while I was slumped over his toes.

Slachaun glowered up at me, cheeks blushing apple-red, and tugged perfunctorily on the knots. And then he *grew*.

In the space of about a heartbeat, he was close to twelve feet tall, and bulky to match. The shoelace snapped with the tiniest tug and he was on his feet, coming for me with big, ponderous, echoing steps.

Nobody was laughing anymore.

But for a change, I'd attracted the kinda attention I wanted. Just as he got within a couple paces, and I was starting to think it was time either to draw the L&G or run as if the Wild Hunt was after me…

"What exactly is going on here, gentlemen? Slachaun! You stop that this instant!"

We both turned, the spriggan shrinking back to about six foot in the process, as a prim *aes sidhe*—blond hair tied back tight behind her pointed ears, and wearing a grey suit with a long skirt—stalked from a nearby office. And I do mean *stalked*; her feet hit the floor like she was trying to make sure it stayed dead.

"Hello, Ielveith," I said. "Been a while."

"Close your head, Mr. Oberon. Slachaun? Explanation. Now."

"The guy's a troublemaker, Mrs. Ielveith. I was just tryin' to deal with him before it got ugly."

"I see. And what, precisely, had Mr. Oberon done?"

"He…" The spriggan's jaw clamped shut as he glared around him, particularly at the score or so of witnesses—*some* of whom he probably couldn't intimidate.

"Your house dick might do better," I said, "if he just *looked* for problems to solve, instead of trying to make his own."

Both of them stared daggers at me, but Ielveith nodded. "Apologies on behalf of the Lambton Worm, Mr. Oberon. I assure you, this won't happen again." Then, more quietly, "Do you have to cause trouble for me *every time* you're here, Mick?"

"I'm sorry, Iel. I didn't—"

She shook her head at me. "We'll catch up later." Then, face going flinty once more, she jabbed a finger at Slachaun. "You! My office."

It wasn't until they were both gone, the office door shut firmly behind, that the entire bar broke into applause and the occasional wild cheer.

Slachaun's actually good at what he does, don't get me wrong. But "what he does" don't include making friends.

I grinned back at everyone and *finally* made my way to the elevators.

The room was nice but simple: writing desk with fountain pen, paper, and a vase of roses by the door; comfy chair to go with the desk; chest of drawers with a big honking mirror; huge window overlooking the city; and of course, the bed, which I swear had heavenly light beaming down on it and a chorus of angels singing behind the headboard. There was an attached bathroom, too, but I ignored it for now.

Despite the ache in my gut, I realized I was starving. I slumped into the bed, reached for the phone on the nightstand, and...

Oh, right. Yeah, I said "starving." It's like I told you before, Elphame's my natural world. In yours, it takes a whole lot to hurt me, and I don't eat or drink much but milk, 'cause my own nature's magical enough to sustain me. Here? Nope. We're still tougher'n you lot, even in the Otherworld, but not by nearly as much. We eat, we sleep, we hurt—and we die a lot easier.

Which, a few hours after I chowed down on

my venison steak from room service and fell off to dreamland, I just about found out firsthand when some bastard kicked in my door and started shooting.

CHAPTER NINE

I shoulda had some warning.

See, I wasn't exactly *expecting* trouble—not at a place nice as the Lambton, and not from the Seelie, at least not so *blatant*—but when you deal with the Courts, their politics and their rivalries and their secrets, you get paranoid.

So I'd prepared, just in case. I'd leaned the writing chair precariously against the door, balanced on two legs, and hung the ice bucket from the window latch. If anybody'd tried to jimmy either of 'em, the clatter-thump of falling things woulda woken me.

It just never occurred to me that some palooka would be so direct and so friggin' *loud* as to kick the damn door in. Sure, it woke me as well as the falling chair woulda, but it didn't gimme much in the way of time, y'know?

The first "shot" fired through the broken, dangling wood wasn't a bullet at all, but a wave of utter confusion, a charm of disorientation similar to the fear or pain I often shoved through my own wand. It caught me right in the midst of bolting upright and grabbing for the L&G on the nightstand. The entire room tilted sideways and I found I couldn't quite blink away the sleep and the dreams. You know that moment of faint panic when you first wake up sometimes, when your thoughts are chasing each other like barking dogs and you can't get 'em in any kinda order? Yeah, I was there. I distinctly remember fretting over how badly the noise would upset the neighbors.

It wasn't until the second or third shot—*real* shots, now, with very real bullets—that I could make myself stop woolgathering long enough to actually move.

Two or three shots that, honestly, shoulda been more'n enough to kill me dead as a eunuch's libido— except for one last bit of preparation I'd taken before dropping into bed. A moment of concentration, a quick tap with the wand, and I'd wrapped myself in a few tiny scraps of extra luck to go along with the hotel's blankets. Just in case.

It wasn't a lot, and I'd already completely burned through it, but it kept me alive, kept me outta the path of what shoulda been easy shots until I shook off the worst of my disorientation.

At which point, I gotta admit I may've squeaked a bit as I dove aside and rolled off the side of the bed. The roscoe kept right on spitting and the bullets chased me across the mattress, stitching .45-caliber holes into the fabric; each of 'em coughed a single breath of stuffing, as if the bed itself was dying.

I was too bewildered, too mixed-up, to count slugs—but even in my current state, I recognized the metallic *click* for what it meant. (And if I hadn't, I probably coulda figured it out from the gruff cursing that followed.) I took a few precious instants to pop back up over the edge of the mattress, snag my wand from atop the nightstand—I'd have loved to grab my rapier as well, but it was standing in the corner on the opposite side of the bed—and get a quick slant on the galoot trying to rub me out.

First thing I saw was the bronze-and-wood-frame heater, more or less an Otherworld copy of a S&W model 22, and I allowed myself a quick second to be grateful that he'd brought a revolver. The triggerman himself—who was wearing a beige suit, and coulda been either *aes sidhe*, *gancanagh*, or half a dozen other kinda-human-looking Fae—was crouched half outside of the door, desperately plugging shells into the back end of the cylinder. Even from this rotten angle, I could see from the way his noggin twitched that he was trying to keep one eye on the gat, the other on the hallway. Obviously, I'd ruined his evening by not having the courtesy to let myself get clipped from the get-go.

So he was rushed, frantic, worried, and frustrated. Exactly how I like 'em.

I leveled the Luchtaine & Goodfellow, took careful aim... And even a little befuddled as I was, it was no hassle at all to pluck the strings of his emotions, running through brain and muscle and soul, so he twitched at just the right moment. The roscoe dropped, half-loaded, to bounce across the carpet, accompanied by the tinkle of falling shells.

I think his howled "*Fuck!*" was louder'n the shots had been.

This, I remember thinking, *is* not *a professional hitter.* Accustomed to violence, yeah—probably someone's bodyguard or leg-breaker—but not so much a real torpedo. And *that* told me someone was in a serious hurry to get this—to get *me*—done.

Either way, I had a moment while he went scrambling for the revolver. I gathered my feet up under me and practically dove across the bed, right hand stretching out for the rapier in the far corner.

And I missed. Obviously, I remained more disoriented from the gink's initial salvo of confusion than I'd realized. I slid completely over the bed and back off onto the floor on the other side, and my fingers closed on a nice, thick handful of diddly.

I scrambled, spastic as a drunk spider, trying to get my legs under me—and rose just in time to see the thug practically leap from the doorway, coming at me with open hands. Guess he decided it was more important to keep me from getting hold of a weapon than to recover his own.

He landed hard beside me, loud enough to shake the floor even through the carpet, at right about the same instant I finally managed to grab the hilt of the sword. I spun, lashed out, and gave him a solid slash across the noggin...

With the blade still in the scabbard.

I honestly couldn't tell you if it was because of that lingering befuddlement, or just 'cause I didn't have time for anything else. Either way, it didn't do much more'n stagger him a little. *Very* little, not remotely enough. I flicked the blade off to the side, sending the scabbard flying, but he'd already lunged in again, wrapping a thick, meaty paw around my wrist.

And now the fact that he was more a brawler than a triggerman was a *bad* thing. A lance of pain speared my entire arm as he twisted, and the rapier dropped right back to the damn floor. (I suppose I oughta be grateful it didn't stick my foot on the way.) I took a poke at him with my left fist, still wrapped around the wand, but he just juked his head aside quick as any prizefighter and twisted sideways, dragging me around by the wrist. He had my back to him now, arm folded up behind me, and drove a solid jab into my kidney at the same time he shoved me face-first into the wall.

I *think* the whole room shuddered and the lights in the hallway flickered, but it mighta just been me. At my best, I could *maybe* have taken this lug. Now—bleeding on the wall from my nose, wrist about a half-inch from breaking, and someone else's confusion squatting in my head like a drunken hobo—there was no damn way...

Which meant I had to change my circumstances a little.

Struggling to focus through the pain, I stretched the L&G back and tapped the guy, just lightly, on the leg.

And fed a heaping helping of his damn disorientation right back to him.

Not all of it—I was too disoriented to channel all my disorientation, and how do you like that?—but enough. My head cleared a little, very much like just starting to sober up, and I felt the palooka's grip loosen, his body sway. Gave me just enough slack to lean forward and then slam my skull back into his face. He cried out, staggered away, and now there wasn't a schnozzle in the room that wasn't spattering nifty patterns of crimson into the carpet.

I finally had a good look at his face as he stumbled,

trying to shake it off. Definitely *aes sidhe*, now that I was up close and personal—and though I couldn't *absolutely* swear to it on the Book of Leinster, I was pretty well sure that I'd seen his mug before, in the crowd of petitioners and staff at the hall.

Apparently he didn't care much for me studying him, 'cause he came at me again—a little wobbly, yeah, but determined. And since I still wasn't all there myself, I hadn't taken the time to stoop down and retrieve the rapier.

I tried to shuffle out of his path, but he just reached out and slammed me back into the writing desk, bruising my back (and my poor kidney again, damn it!) against the wooden edge. He clamped one meat hook on my throat, the other on my left fist so I couldn't move the wand at all, and started bending me backwards over the desk.

So I reached back behind me with my right hand, shuffled around the papers while my vision started to go all sparkly and spotty, until I found the fountain pen the hotel had provided "for my convenience."

And it did, indeed, prove convenient enough for stabbing the gink in his left peeper.

It was kinda fascinating, in a grotesque sorta way. I actually saw a cloud of leaking blue ink start to spread slowly through the white before his eye just gave up the ghost completely and collapsed inward.

He threw himself back, shrieking like a goosed *bean sidhe*, yanking me forward for a few steps before his grip finally loosened. I stumbled to one knee, and by the time I could so much as regain my balance and look up, he was gone. I heard footsteps and continued shrieking receding up the hall, and the door to the stairway slam.

I probably shoulda gone after him, but I was panting and gasping myself, I'd just taken a pounding like I was Santa's runway, and I didn't much feel up to moving at all.

Well, okay, I moved enough to toss the blood-and-vitreous-covered pen across the room and wipe my hand thoroughly on the bedspread. I mean, I ain't squeamish by nature, but *yuck*.

And then I waited, taking what few minutes I had to catch my breath and decide just what, exactly, I was gonna tell the cops.

The answer wound up "almost everything," for all the good it did.

"And you're sure he looked like one of us?" The *aes sidhe* detective was wearing an overcoat over a boiled leather cuirass, and letting a uniformed copper—a *coblynau*, this one, not a spriggan like most of the others—take his notes for him. "You *real* sure?"

"Yes, damn it!" I was pacing back and forth between the hallways' white-and-green papered walls—not that there was much room there for pacing—while a swarm of coppers scurried through my room, under the watchful gaze of Ielveith and Slachaun. She was as proper and composed as ever; he, on the other hand, had slept on his beard, which was smooshed completely flat on one side.

"You understand, Mr. Oberon, that lots of Fae have the power to change their form…"

"Oh, for… I'm not a chump, detective. I know what I saw, and what I saw was *aes sidhe*!"

It was, of course, entirely possible that what I'd seen was indeed a glamour, or a shape-shifter. But one, I didn't think it probable; not a lotta guys coulda maintained a disguise like that after I hit 'em with the wand (or the pen).

And two, I was sick and tired of this mug telling me what I did and didn't know.

"So you say, Mr. Oberon. And I'm sure you *think* that's what you saw. But this is really more an Unfit shenanigan. The Seelie don't do this sort of thing."

Right. And I'm actually a pixie with a glandular condition.

"I'm giving you a few minutes to think it over, Mr. Oberon. And then we're going to go through it *again*."

"You gimme as many minutes as you want, detective. It ain't changing what happened. And I want my wand back before I leave."

He nodded politely and slipped into the room, carefully stepping over the revolver, and the various forensic runes and sigils they'd sketched around it. I paced a few more steps and then slumped against the wall, hands in my pockets.

Where, joy of joys, I was able to overhear Slachaun muttering to his boss.

"...told y'he was trouble, Mrs. Ielveith. We oughta give'm the bum's rush and ban'm from ever showin' his face around here again."

"Oh, of course," I said, straightening and taking a step closer. "Because it's my fault someone busted up the place, right? I just attract bullets. Gotta work on that."

"Look, boyo—"

"What's *really* bugging you, Slachaun? That your hotel ain't so peaceful and quiet, or that your pal didn't finish the job?"

His beard actually *bristled*, a thick, red, angry hedgehog. "What're you accusin' me of?"

"Not sure yet," I said. "I'm trying to figure if you helped the guy, or just missed him, so it's up in the air whether you're corrupt or just incompetent. Either way, this never woulda happened when *I* was working here."

Slachaun howled something incomprehensible and lunged for me, growing as he came—and a handful of coppers jumped to stop him. Several of 'em, also spriggans, grew to match. Last I saw of Slachaun that day, he was being dragged backward down the stairs by a cluster of blue uniforms, ranting and screaming curses, a few of which I *can't* translate into English, and the rest of which I *won't*.

Several of the cops remaining behind slapped me with dirty looks, and went back to work, hunched over the grass-green carpet or the bullet-riddled furniture. I heard Ielveith step up behind me.

"Was that truly necessary, Mick?"

I took a moment. "Yeah, actually, I kinda think it was."

She sighed; I felt her breath waft across the back of my neck. "You don't really think he had anything to do with this, do you?"

I finally faced her. "Honestly? Nah, probably not. He's loyal to you, whatever else he is." Then, deliberately formal, "I do apologize, Your Grace, for any trouble I've brought to your establishment. It absolutely wasn't my intention."

"Ah, forget it, Mick." Ielveith—Duchess Ielveith, to be proper—waved a dismissive hand. "As you said, it's hardly your fault someone took a shot at you. Though I *do* hope the Court locates said miscreant, since I'd love a few words with him.

"And besides, I know you're good for the cost of a replacement bed."

I winced, but nodded. Bianca's seven hundred and fifty bucks was starting to feel like a lot less dough than it had, but it was the least I could do.

"You'll hafta wait until I'm done with my current job, doll," I said. "My retainer's already spoken for. Soon as I have the rest, though, I'll square us."

"It's a deal." Her gaze flickered to one side, I nodded, and we took a few long paces down the hall, moving us out of earshot. One of the bulls tossed a lascivious leer our way, which we both studiously ignored.

Ielveith and I never did have the relationship that those rumors claimed we did. All she'd ever been to me was a boss, maybe *almost* a friend; we got along well enough, but that'd been the end of it. I worked for her a couple years as the Lambton house detective, until the rumors of my "exile" caught up with me here in Chicago. Even then, she'd waited as long as politics and position allowed before she fired me. It was a more even break than I'd gotten from anyone else in this Otherworld town.

"So what's going on here, Mick?" she asked, her voice low. "Why is someone shooting up my place to get at you?"

"It's the case I'm working on, I think." In quick snippets, I gave her the basic lowdown on what'd been happening. I even told her that I thought I recognized the fella who attacked me from the hall, which was the one tidbit I'd left outta my report to the detective. (He wouldn't have believed it anyway.) Her face was twisted up real thoughtful by the time I got through.

"Ylleuwyn's a toad," she said. "I wouldn't put this sort of thing past him, but it's a little sloppy."

"He didn't have a lotta time to put it together. If it was him at all. Seems likely, but I got no proof." I shrugged, and then frowned. "You're as well connected as him, Iel. *You* ever hear anything about this Ottati changeling?"

"Can't say I have, Mick. But I've little to do with changelings, myself. I prefer adult servants."

I'd like to think she was telling me the truth, but I know that in the Court, politics usually trumps friendship. Still, I didn't *see* any signs of deceit—which coulda just meant she was a better liar than Ylleuwyn, but I decided to take it at face value.

She didn't offer to poke around about it, and I didn't ask. I wasn't about to put her in the position of having to say no to me.

"So what's next for you?" she asked.

I shrugged again. "This is either big, or real personal, for someone—Ylleuwyn or otherwise—to take such a blatant shot at me, and in someone else's joint. You guys are usually a lot more subtle, and a *little* more honorable, than that."

"'You guys'?" she repeated with a raised eyebrow. I waved off the implication; I was *out*, damn it!

"Someone wants me dead, or at least walking away, and I intend to disappoint 'em all the way around. I'm seeing this through."

"Aren't you afraid? If they're willing to murder you over this…"

I gave her the steadiest grin I could muster. "I don't do fear." I hoped she didn't hear the quaver in my voice. "And I *definitely* don't let myself get muscled off a job, or get shot at without hitting back."

"But if nobody in the Court will tell you what you need…"

"Then I talk to someone else." I could feel my grin crumbling like a bad sandcastle, no matter how much I tried to keep it alive.

Her jaw dropped when she tumbled to what I was suggesting. "Mick, that's insane!"

"This whole thing's insane, Iel. I'm just trying to get out ahead of it."

And that was when Detective Not-Listening-To-You called me over for another useless chat. I left Ielveith a few rooms down, shaking her head and cursing, quietly but about as foully as Slachaun had been.

After another two hours of utterly useless gabbing with the detective—or more accurately, about five different separate conversations of twenty-some-odd minutes each—they finally decided that I wasn't changing my story anytime soon, and let me go. I even got my wand back, with a minimum of grumbling. Ielveith, once she got done spitting profanity like the devil with a stubbed toe, was kind enough to offer me a replacement room. I got myself a few more hours of shuteye, and woke up ready to face the new day.

Actually, I woke up ready to go hide in the corner with a blanket pulled up to my chin, but I headed out to face the new day anyway.

So I ran my shirt and trousers through the wash basin beside the tub—they were clean and dry in a matter of minutes—got myself dressed, slipped my rapier and blade into my belt, grabbed a quick breakfast of bacon and eggs in the Lambton's dining room, and… went for a walk.

Yeah, I know. Swell plan, right? But what else was I gonna do? I didn't have anybody I could grill for info—nobody I could trust or easily get to, at any rate. I didn't have any leads. And for the most part, I didn't have any friends or resources I hadn't already exhausted. All I could do was take the time to think about it, and maybe spur someone else into making a move I could follow up.

I didn't *think* I was making myself too much of a target. Yeah, I was strolling around in public as though I hadn't a care in two worlds, but I didn't think anyone would try much of anything way out in the open, in front of dozens of witnesses.

Then again, I hadn't thought they'd bust down the door and start shooting up the Lambton, either. So you can bet I was keeping a good slant on everyone around me as I ankled my way down the sidewalks.

The earlier rains had cleared some of the industrial (well, magic) smoke, and a lotta the pollen, from the air, so the city's bouquet wasn't quite so overwhelming as normal. A gentle spring breeze flipped the hems of coats and skirts, and brushed leaves (and a drunken pixie or two) across the uneven bricks cobbling the street. Carriages and buggies bounced by me, pulled by horses, ponies, bulls, goats, passels of dazed and happy humans, and—in one case—a griffon with a bum wing.

The sidewalks were just as crowded, filled with *aes sidhe* and *brounies* and all the others I've already listed for you, all dressed as dapper as you please. Most were just going about their business, headed for work or court, but I caught myself a glimpse of the same coat, the same hat, the same quickly averted stare, a couple times too many. Cops, seeing if I knew more than I'd told 'em last night? Ylleuwyn's people? Ielveith's? Friends of Slachaun? Or something related to a dozen *other* friends and enemies (more the latter than the former, unfortunately) I'd made in my years?

Just another day in Chicago—long as you're in the *right* Chicago.

I was just starting to wonder if I oughta do something about my shadows when someone took the decision outta my hands. See, there was nothing that shoulda bugged me about the sound of a coach coming up behind; there was enough of 'em on the street to make it all part of the background. But it felt *wrong*, and most Fae learn as kids not to ignore those sorts of feelings.

The ones who don't tend not to ever get to be Fae adults.

The carriage itself was a dark, thick black. The windows were sealed shut with old bronze nails, and the handles and trimmings were tarnished silver. The only sign of actual color on the thing were the whitewalls on the tires. The contraption was hauled by two black horses—or I *think* they were horses, anyway. Rivulets of water trickled from their hooves and left tiny puddles in their wake; they *coulda* been hired kelpies, then, but I chose to believe they'd just recently walked through puddles left from the rain, and decided not to get close enough to find out different. Disgusting creatures.

And there was the driver. Short and hunched even shorter, he had skin the color of worn leather, beady red lamps, and a kisser big enough to fit my whole head, full of teeth like a shark's mother-in-law. His suit was a brown pinstripe that clashed nauseatingly with his skin—except his hat, an old-fashioned bowler, that was a deep, rich crimson. And not from any dye, either.

Fucking redcaps.

People were going outta their way to avoid us, now, even crossing the street to stay well away from the coach. See, for all the political and territorial wrangling, all the rivalries and competition, all the duels and ambushes and skirmishes, the two Courts ain't *openly* at war. There's some trade, some commerce, even some business partnerships, between Fae on the two sides. So seeing one of the Unseelie in Seelie territory—or vice-versa—ain't unheard of.

But that don't mean the average Joes on either side much care for it. And they care for it even less with some kinds of Fae than others. Redcaps are popular hitmen with the Unfit, since they tend to eat the evidence when they're done, which makes 'em *unpopular* with, well, everyone else.

This one dropped from the seat and opened the door—not so much to show off his manners, I think, but to make sure I couldn't miss the brass .38 and the bronze meat cleaver hanging on his belt. He reeked of rotting beef and cheap aftershave.

"Boss wants to see ya," he growled at me, slurring a little around the not-so-pearly whites. "Get in the flivver."

I *shoulda* been surprised that she got my message and reacted so quickly, or nervous about getting into any vehicle driven by a redcap, or afraid of this maybe being a trap. Instead, I threw a tantrum. Not sure why I picked that moment for it—maybe it was frustration over my situation, or leftover adrenaline—but something about the whole shebang just rubbed me wrong.

"For Pete's sake, it's not a goddamn 'flivver'! Do you see an engine? Do you see a gas tank, or a steering wheel? 'Cause I don't. I see reins, and wood, and friggin' *horses*! You slack-jawed meatheads don't even *care* what it is you're parroting, do you? Just as long as you think you sound like the humans do!"

The redcap blinked twice at me. Then, "Get in the flivver."

I sighed, and got in the *carriage*. Damn it.

It managed to feel cramped, even though it wasn't that small a coach—possibly because of all the black and the lack of windows. The air was stale, and smelled of soap, making me think they'd just freshly cleaned it out. The seats, also dyed black, were surprisingly comfortable: a type of leather that I wasn't familiar with, *real* soft and supple as a baby's…

Oh, *fuck me.*

I shuddered, violently, and had to repress an urge

to leap screaming from the coach, or at least huddle on the floor as far from the benches as I could get.

All things considered, I don't think you can blame me for taking a minute to realize that the carriage wasn't, in fact, *completely* enclosed. A single window—a horizontal slit, barred in bronze filigree—sat high in the front wall. Through it, I could look out and see the sky ahead of us, but not the actual road or anything we might be passing.

I *also* couldn't see the redcap, who was seated next to the window; it was perfectly placed so that, even if a passenger could knock out the filigree, it'd be all but impossible to aim a blade or a heater at the driver.

So I stared at the sky, mostly to avoid thinking about what I was sitting on. I watched the passing clouds, and listened to the rattle-and-thump of tires on brick, and felt the carriage sway as it turned. And even without being able to see where we were going, I could tell that it *wasn't* the way I'd expected, not if our destination was Unfit territory. I felt my hand twitch toward my wand as I leaned forward toward the window. "Don't we wanna be taking Cobbler's Way?"

The redcap's grumble came drifting in between the shapes of bronze. "Duel."

I'm pretty sure I groaned loud enough to be heard in your world.

Here's the skinny. As I said, there's not a lotta open war in Elphame—it ain't *civilized*, see?—and the Chicago Courts're no exception. Yeah, now and again a couple of Unseelie factions might go to the mattresses for a while, but that's about it for what you'd call genuine warfare.

Which don't mean there ain't violence aplenty. It's just a lot more focused, and a *little* more organized.

How do you suppose the Fae code of honor and satisfaction looks here and now? Between the aristocrats of the Seelie Court, it's still nicely old-fashioned: two fellas with a blade or, more often these days, a gat. But when it involves lower Seelie, the Unseelie, or a beef between Fae of different Courts? No such luck.

They call it a Chicago duel. (Yeah, I know. You guys come up with "Chicago typewriter" and "Chicago lightning," so we gotta follow. Again, mimics, the whole ditzy lot of us. We can't even come up with original metaphors.) Basically, it plays out this way: we got our hits and our busts, our shootouts and our police raids, same as you. But since we don't want anything in the way of open war, we *schedule* most of the damn things. One fella demands satisfaction from another, they pick a time and place. Then they and their seconds, as many as they can gather, meet up and start plugging and stabbing away at each other until one side gives, or the right guy dies. And then they walk away. As I said, usually it's a group of coppers and crooks, just like in *your* Chicago, but sometimes it's two Unseelie, and occasionally even two Seelie (so you wind up with two "police departments" duking it out). Makes no nevermind to them; they play it the same way.

Stupid, big-time stupid. And nothing *I'd* call a duel. But it's preferable to *real* war, right?

That's what they tell me, anyway.

Anyway, we took the long way around, accompanied by the sound of *very* distant gunfire. I sat, rocking with the trundling coach, and staring at the blank blue sky through the tiny window.

Until the sky wasn't so blank or blue anymore.

It coulda just been any oncoming storm, at first, except that the clouds were *swirling* instead of going anywhere. The sky itself came over purple, but everything else took on a jaundiced cast, like the whole world was suddenly sick. The winds were barely strong enough to shake the carriage, yet they roared louder'n God's own locomotive.

Not quite so loud, though, that I couldn't hear the hoofbeats of *something* coming up beside us on either side. Something that I assumed had to be there to accompany us, since I *didn't* hear the redcap squirting metal at whoever'd shown up.

Again from that tiny window, I saw just the very tops of the tallest buildings as we drew near. They weren't *that* different from the skyscrapers of the Seelie Court: mostly glass, with the occasional stone tower. But the trees that formed the supports for some of those buildings were black and twisted, dead and rotting; and one was supported, not by wood or stone at all, but by thousands of bones, mortared together into jagged pillars. I wondered where they'd gotten that much bone, and then, with another glance at the seat, decided I *really* didn't wanna know.

I also began to wonder how this place'd smell without the constant winds, and decided I'd never been more grateful for the weather.

The carriage wobbled to a halt. I heard the driver

thump to the ground and grumble "Get out," as he hauled open the door. And the first thing I saw, other'n the redcap himself, were the two outriders who'd shown up to escort us in. My "bodyguards," in case any rival factions had decided to take a shot.

There were two of 'em, and honestly, I'd have preferred more redcaps.

Dullahan. Headless riders in black suits, on headless black horses. The riders normally carried their heads with 'em, under an arm or in a basket; I don't think any god of any time or place ever knew where the horses' heads were kept, if they existed at all. These particular *dullahan* each carried a Chicago typewriter, also black; I had to look close to tell that they were painted brass, not the steel of a human-built chopper. And each had a brass-wire basket welded to its top, where the rider's head sat on a thin layer of cushioning. It looked more'n a little funny, I'll admit, but it kept their hands free for the Tommy guns—and with peepers actually *on* the gats, you can bet the bastards never missed.

Trying not to stare at either the empty space where their heads *shoulda* been, or the unblinking peepers where the heads *were*, I climbed from the coach and slipped past 'em. The winds weren't too fierce, as I said, but they were *cold*. In the Seelie territory, and in your world, spring had moved right in, but here, winter wasn't too willing to take a powder. The mounds from which the buildings rose were gritty, covered in thorns and dead scrub, and even the glass was dark and gloomy. Distant screams rode the air like dead leaves. And way off on the horizon, the sky grew even darker—not with clouds, but with the whirling black hosts of the *sluagh*, neither ghost nor Fae but something horribly, awfully between.

Before me I saw a broad glass door, leading into a large mound. Light, yellow but a little cleaner than the sky, poured from within, and I figured that was where I was supposed to go. It didn't take me but a few steps to spot that, while I hadn't cast a shadow in Seelie territory, here I had *two*: one stretching out behind, nice and regular, and one in front of me, reaching *toward* the light.

The redcap moved ahead of me and pushed the door open, leaving the *dullahan* to stand post outside. I glanced back, and saw one of 'em put his head up on the horse's saddle to keep watch while the body set about brushing road dust off his Tommy gun. Then I turned my attention back to where I was, and saw a wall of muscle blocking my path.

A huge, pus-colored troll in a three-piece suit loomed over me, staring through black, piggy eyes. He leaned in, smiling, displaying shreds of skin and cotton between serrated teeth.

"Frisk him, Geddo," the redcap ordered.

The next few seconds were kinda how I imagine being trapped in a cement mixer would feel, but I dealt with it. The troll took my rapier and my wand, and somehow, I didn't much feel up to protesting.

You gotta understand, I could appreciate their paranoia. The Outfit in your world is run a lot more like a corporation these days (even if they want people to believe that Netti's in charge), but the Unseelie still function the way it was under Capone. Yeah, there's someone ostensibly in charge of the whole shebang, but you got lots of rival factions, groups of outsiders who don't follow the rules, and a dozen guys who'd be more'n happy to knock off the boss if it meant moving up the ladder. So the Unseelie here are at *least* as careful as Capone ever was, and with even better reason.

(Did you know that a few Unseelie actually treat the day Al was sentenced as a day of mourning? Seriously. They practically *worship* him and his ilk. Heck, that's where our little nickname for them— the Unfit—came from: *Un*seelie, Out*fit*. See? Yeah, yeah. Listen, we take our humor where we can find it. And besides, it gets 'em nice and steamed when we call 'em that, so there's a plus.)

Anyway, after getting manhandled and bruised by the troll's car-door-sized meat hooks, and after Geddo was convinced I wasn't packing any hidden heat or otherwise planning to whack his boss, he went back to his post by the door. The redcap, flanked by a couple goblins who'd appeared outta nowhere, waved at me to follow.

The wide chamber looked like another hotel lobby, though not as nice as the Lambton. Chairs ranged from rickety bundles of twigs to sofas covered in leather that looked uncomfortably similar to what I'd seen in the carriage; arches of stone or dead branches created all sorts of murky nooks, from which gleamed a heaping mess of glowing peepers (a few of which didn't even have the common courtesy to come in pairs). There weren't as many humans wandering around here as there'd been in Seelie territory, and those there were looked just as drugged, but not nearly as happy about it. Crunches, snaps, groans, and screams emerged from the darkest corners.

The center walkway, at least, was well lit by chandeliers hanging above. And I was happier in the light, if only a little—until I glanced down, and in the corners of my vision, I swear I saw my "extra" shadow moving *before* I did.

At that point, I decided on a new plan: keeping my head held rigid and my gaze locked firmly straight ahead. And it was a plan I managed to stick to, through several doorways, between multiple pairs of trolls and *dullahan*, down a carpeted staircase with mahogany banisters...

And finally into the presence of my host.

Eudeagh, queen of Chicago's Unseelie Court, herself.

CHAPTER TEN

The underground room was a study, and a big one, lit by glass-enclosed lamps of what I can only describe as "illusory fire." More of a private library, really, it was clearly designed to guide the eye precisely from end to end.

Bookcases ran along both side walls, with fancy portraits of past Unseelie nobles, in all their bloody inhuman glory, between them. The books themselves ran the gamut; in just one quick glance, I saw antique diaries and mystic grimoires, dictionaries and encyclopedias, dime novels and pulp magazines. I stopped briefly on what I swear looked like an unexpurgated version of Shakespeare's *A Midsummer Night's Dream* (I thought we'd destroyed the last of those back in the early seventeenth century), and a Bible written in Ancient Greek.

On the right wall, two of the cases stood farther apart than usual, leaving room for a broad fireplace of red brick. It wasn't burning at the moment, leaving me a clear view of the bronze manacles bolted to the inside of the chimney.

Guh…!

At the study's far end, beneath an enormous

painting of Friar Rush—the portrait's cloven feet and hooked nails were embossed with actual fingernails, the edges ragged from where they'd been yanked out—a gaggle of upholstered chairs were clustered around a tea table. Another pair of *dullahan* stood behind those chairs, coats bulging with heavy roscoes; I had no clue where their heads mighta been, 'cause I sure as hell didn't see 'em anywhere. A couple kindly-looking gentlemen in silk suits (yeah, silk) sat on the arms of two of those chairs; probably boggarts in human form, if I had to guess. At the feet of one curled a hairy black dog the size of a small pony, panting excitedly, its eyes gleaming green and its snout bared back in a very human grin. Even from here, I could smell the fear on its breath—not its own, either, but belonging to whatever poor sap last slipped through those jaws.

And between them—curled up in her chair, right in the center of everything, the way she loved it— Queen Eudeagh, Boss of Bosses, *il Capo di Tutti Capi,* of the local Unseelie. Possibly the single most powerful individual in the Chicago Otherworld, with as many enemies among the Unfit as among the Seelie, and proud of it to boot.

She preferred the title of "boss." Most of us referred to her as "Queen Mob." Look, just remember what I just said about Fae humor…

Eudeagh woulda been *maybe* three feet tall, in heels, if she'd been standing. Her hair, cut in a stylish bob, was black as unmined coal; the rest of her sat right on the knife's edge between "curvaceous" and "chubby," and made it look damn good. She wore red satin that clung like a second skin, slinky as a tipsy snake. Oh, she was one sweet tomato, no doubt—right up until she smiled at you between her ruby lips.

All six of 'em. The regular ones, where they were supposed to be, and the two smaller mouths where most of us—human, Fae, whatever—kept our peepers.

Even though I'd known to expect it, I still had to swallow hard to keep from making an unwanted gift of the bacon and eggs I'd had for breakfast.

She waved us over, and I followed my redcap "guide" to the chairs. He wandered around to stand at the queen's side, while I dropped myself into a seat without giving myself a chance to think about it. She waved again, this time at the table, which held a few different carafes of mead and wine, and two bowls, one of golden apples, the other of deep red ones.

There was also, sitting right in front of her on a napkin of purple fabric, a pair of glass peepers and a selection of false lashes. Somehow, I didn't figure she was offering *those* to me.

"You'll never have better, Mr. Oberon," she said when I hesitated. Her voice was sultry; she coulda been a lounge singer, if it hadn't been so damn disturbing watching her swap mouths in mid-sentence. "They're imported, fresh from the Hesperides and Tír na nÓg."

I gotta confess, I started something fierce at that. "Are you kidding?! Do you know how illegal it is to take apples from either…" I stopped, trailing off idiotically at the amused chuckles from everyone around me (the damn dog included). Musta forgot who I was talking to. "Right," I finished lamely. Then, because hey, why not? I reached out for the bowls.

And froze again. "And the price of this fine snack?" I asked carefully.

She laughed in three slightly different tones at once. "None at all. I offer it freely and without condition, as part of my obligation as your host."

I nodded, and took a red apple. They don't call Tír na nÓg the "Land of Youth" for nothing, I'll tell you what. Just a couple bites, and I felt a hundred times better. No more exhaustion, no more lingering pain from getting battered into, well, batter.

She went for a golden apple herself, and watching her eat it almost cost me my own appetite. She fell on it like a starving wolf, taking huge, careless bites. She chewed noisily, desperately, with open mouths. Juice and bits of pulped fruit splattered across her face, and each time that happened, her nearest tongue would come peeking out of its mouth, a fat, fleshy worm, and lap the mess clean. She wasn't done until everything, down to the seeds and the core, was gone. All she left were the bits of fruit that had fallen to the table, rather than on her, and those the black dog snuffled up in seconds.

Another wave. The redcap stood and poured her some wine, then looked at me. "Free and clear," she assured me, "same as the fruit." And then, "You're staring, Mr. Oberon. It's not polite."

"I'm sorry. I just… You're being surprisingly generous."

"For an Unseelie?" she asked, her tone gone just a touch dangerous.

"No, I mean…" I was floundering a little, knew it, and couldn't help it. "I mean for, uh, what you… That is, what you *are*."

"Ah. That." She chuckled softly.

Eudeagh, you need to understand, was what you folk used to call a "buttery spirit." (That's "buttery" as in "an old-fashioned term for the cellar," not as in "covered in butter.") In your world, they set up shop in the basements and cellars of hotels, restaurants, that kinda joint. Specifically those that shortchange their customers, or serve small portions, or stint on costs—basically anywhere they're *supposed* to be about hospitality but wind up chintzy or cheats instead. Buttery spirits *feed* on that sort of miserly behavior. People around 'em get too generous, and the little bastards can actually starve. (And they're welcome to it, frankly.)

"Do I look to you as though I'm going wanting?" she purred at me, running a hand across one hip. "I've plenty to eat here, and if I ever need to hop out for a quick bite, there's always more to be had among the mortals." She stretched out a hand and clacked her glass orbs together like marbles. "I can afford to be a gracious host. Surely you wouldn't offend me by refusing?"

"Course not. Mead, then."

I watched the redcap serving me, made sure he didn't put anything in the drink, and raised my glass to hers. She guzzled her wine with the same show of grace and manners she'd eaten with, and then stopped, cocking her head to the side.

"Can you hear them?" she asked, her voice reverent.

"All I hear's the panting of that mutt by your feet." The dog growled at me.

"The sluagh," she said; I'd have described her expression as "staring off at nothing" if she'd had anything to stare with. "They're riled tonight. Have been for weeks, in fact. Something has them stirring, something in the mortal world, I expect."

"Oh. Swell."

Queen Mob laughed again. "Nothing to do with you, I'm sure." Yet another wave—how the heck did her people tell 'em apart, anyway?—and the redcap and the black dog both strolled from the room. Guess they weren't important enough to be here for this.

"All right, Mr. Oberon," she said, twisting cat-like in her chair until she found a more comfortable spot. "It's not every day that someone with as *colorful* a reputation as yours requests a sit-down. What is it you want, exactly?"

Now that it was time, I was having second thoughts. Hell, I was probably up to fifth or sixth thoughts. Did I actually want the Unfit caught up in this? Did I want to tell Boss Eudeagh what I was doing? What if they were involved, and decided I was a liability? What if other Fae learned I was blabbing about them to the Unseelie Court? This whole thing was starting to feel like a *real* bad idea.

You know what felt like an even *worse* idea, though? Getting this far, sitting in front of Queen Mob, and refusing to tell her why. Plus, I was still pretty well strapped for leads if this didn't accomplish anything.

So, however reluctantly, I told her. More or less all of it.

To which Eudeagh thoughtfully replied, "Hmm." And then we just sat.

Eventually, for lack of anything better to say, I asked, "So why'd you agree to meet?"

"Curiosity, mostly. I thought it peculiar you sent me the request at all, even more so that someone tried to bump you off in the middle of the Lambton Worm." Then, at my furrowed brow, "I have people everywhere, Mr. Oberon. Even in the Seelie Court. Or, well, not *people*, necessarily, but you know what I mean. I knew of the attempt on your life before the detective arrived to question you about it."

So was she showing off, or was this her way of telling me that *she* hadn't ordered the hit? I wasn't entirely sure. What I *was* sure of is that I wasn't *about* to flat-out ask.

A few moments more of silence, and then the queen waved the two elderly gentlemen over. They leaned over in perfect unison, mirrors of each other, to whisper in her ears. I couldn't make out a word, but I caught the perfectly synchronized head shakes.

"Very well," she said as they straightened back up. "Neither I nor my aides have any memory of this 'Ottati' family, but we'll look into it." She rose from the chair—as far as she could "rise," at her height—and scooped up the glass eyes. Taking the napkin in her other hand, she dipped a corner in the wine and scrubbed at her, uh, "mouth sockets," transforming the lipstick into a gory smear on the fabric. Then, after a quick lick and a quick polish on the dry end of the napkin, she popped first one false eye, and then the other, into place. I cringed at the squeal of glass on teeth, and then she clamped her mini-mouths tight around them. With the false lashes and maybe a dab of makeup, yeah, they'd look real—from a distance, anyway.

"I trust you can keep yourself entertained while you wait?" she asked from her remaining mouth. "You're welcome to serve yourself, and to read anything you want. Just keep in mind that some of these books are irreplaceable. You break it, you buy it." And then she was moving toward the door.

"Wait!"

She stopped, spun, hands on hips. "Yes?"

I knew I should just close my head, not risk gumming up the deal, but some things I just ain't prepared to chock up to good luck. "You're gonna help me out? That easy?"

"Oh, Mr. Oberon, you're so cute." She shook her head and actually clucked at me. "I have to know precisely what information I have to offer you before I can decide what it's going to cost you to acquire, don't I?"

And she marched on out, leaving me there to ponder that little ominous tidbit. I looked up to meet the boggarts' twin gazes.

"You guys going with her? And if not, either of you got a deck of cards, or maybe some dominoes?"

They grinned, both of 'em in unison. And they *kept* grinning, until the corners of their mouths met on the backs of their skulls and their heads literally flopped open like they were hinged, leaving nothing but a tooth-rimmed hole at the top of their necks. Those holes then fell straight to the floor, the rest of their bodies vanishing through 'em on the way, and the boggarts were both gone.

I really hate the Unseelie.

Bound and determined not to be cowed (or not

to show it, at any rate), I sidled up to one of the *dullahan*, who clearly were *not* planning to go anywhere. "How about you, bo? Got any cards? I bet you've got a *mean* poker face."

Somewhere in the Otherworld, a disembodied head scowled at me. I'm sure of it.

So since my only companions weren't too friendly, and lacked either interest in, or a few basic requirements for, meaningful conversation, I passed the next couple hours examining Eudeagh's library and munching on more forbidden fruit. After thumbing through the musty and vaguely mildew-smelling *A Midsummer Night's Dream*— yeah, it was the uncensored original; I cringed at the descriptions of King Oberon and Queen Titania, and stuck it back on the shelf before I got too tempted to rip it up—I settled into one of the chairs with a few pulp magazines.

Yes, magazines. Whaddaya want? I've read all the ancient Celtic and other European epics already, and when it comes to modern literature, I prefer *Weird Tales* to the Brontës.

I was just about through with Smith's "The Tale of Satampra Zeiros" when Queen Mob strolled back in, one of the creepy boggart twins dogging her heels. She waved at me to stay seated—or I think that's what the wave meant; it's what I did, anyway—and glided into the chair directly across from me.

"Well, Mr. Oberon, you've certainly produced a tough nut. None of my people have any knowledge of the particular child in question. It's certainly *possible* that someone in my organization performed the swap and then traded, killed, ate, or otherwise lost track of the girl—" it was less what she said, and more the casual way she enumerated the possibilities that chilled me "—but I think *someone* would recall. It's *also* possible that the swap was performed by one of my rival gangs in the Court. We'd *probably* know of it—we keep very close watch over each other—but there's no guarantee. I have people looking into this prospect.

"But let's be honest with ourselves, Mick. May I call you Mick?"

"Uh, sure…"

"Neither you nor I believe that this changeling is an Unseelie child, do we? Not after Judge Ylleuwyn's reaction and the attempt on your life."

"No." I sighed. "We don't."

"And you," she said, abruptly angling forward, "didn't come here for information."

"Um, I didn't?"

"No. You came for our help in prying the info you need from Ylleuwyn's clutches!"

"Uh…"

"We can do this for you, Mick. We can get you what you need. What you won't get anywhere else."

I wished right about then that I could climb inside my own mouth and vanish, same as the boggarts had done, or at least slink under the chair and hide. "And in return?" Considering who I was dealing with, I'm real proud of the fact that my voice was steady.

"Well… You've a *much* greater understanding of, and more contacts in, the mortal world than we have. And even in your current state of disfavor, some useful connections among the Seelie as well.

Let's call it... a favor. A boon that we can call in down the road a ways."

Oh, *shit*. That was exactly the *last* thing I wanted—a hanging debt to the fucking Unseelie Court! And I've told you about Fae pacts; this wasn't something I could just renege on, and not only 'cause they'd hunt me down and butcher me if I tried.

It was a nightmare, pure and simple. And she was asking me to step right into it, put the noose around my own neck.

"I'm only bound to this if whatever we try works," I insisted.

"Of course."

"And I won't help you hurt anyone. We gotta understand that going in."

Eudeagh literally spit her glass peepers back out into her open palm and "gazed" at me with open mouths and twitching tongues. "I'm not entirely comfortable putting such limitations on our arrangement, Mick. I fear we may not have a bargain, after all."

Her tone hadn't changed, but I saw the *dullahan* behind her stiffen, like they were paying attention for the first time. Even without mouths, without throats, I thought I heard a pair of distant, expectant sighs.

Well, *that* wasn't a good sign, was it?

I cast about for something, *anything* to salvage this without backing me into a nasty corner. "All right, how about this? I won't do anything for you that gets me and my friends in hot water with the law, and I won't help you hurt anyone who I don't think deserves it."

For what seemed to be a few thousand heartbeats—which, at that point, woulda just been a couple minutes, honestly—she pursed all six lips at me. "You understand," she said finally, "that your honest judgment of who 'deserves it will be a formal part of the pact you swear?"

"Yeah." Meant I wouldn't be able to lie about whether I felt someone *did* deserve to be hurt or not. I *also* wouldn't be able to limit my participation to how *much* I thought they deserved it, either. I might wind up having to help the Unfit whack someone who hadn't earned more'n a mild beating or a short spell in the cooler. But I was behind the eight ball and out of options. "I dig."

"Good. Swear it."

I'm astounded she could understand a word of it, through my gritted, grinding teeth—but I swore.

And if you're thinking that I'd come to regret that someday, congratulations. You've been paying attention.

But for today, it was done. "So what's the plan?" I asked her.

"Well, Mick." She smiled and settled back in her chair. The first boggart leaned in with a gleaming grin; the other appeared from the shadows at the back of the room, behind the *dullahan*, where no entrance stood. "Let's put our heads together and figure that out, shall we?"

Dawn spread itself across the sky—sorta like margarine, really—to shine down on the brick roads and glass buildings of Chicago's Seelie Court. Other than a few white puffs casually sauntering across the brightening expanse of blue, no sign remained of the earlier rains; and *that* meant that the nostril-filling, tongue-coating, brain-smothering perfume of a hundred trees and a thousand flowers was back in full. Men, women, and otherwise strolled the sidewalks or rode the streets, making ready for the day's business.

An average, everyday morning in Elphame. For most.

Clad in shirt and trousers creased sharp enough to trim the hedges—guess he didn't bother with the formal robes until he got to the hall—Judge Ylleuwyn strode the sidewalks like he owned 'em. One hand behind his back, the other on the hilt of the Dark Ages broadsword at his waist, and his head held high as an unfurled banner, this was clearly a fellow whose hoity-toity education had somehow failed to include the definition of the word "humility." He was conversing, as he strolled, with a dog so shaggy it coulda been a walking mop.

Well, assuming your mops are leaf-green in color and the size of a calf. The thing wasn't all *that* much smaller than the black dog I'd, uh, *met* yesterday.

And when I say Ylleuwyn was "conversing," I don't mean he was jabbering aimlessly to a pet, the way some of you do. I mean they were having a conversation. The *cu sidhe* may *resemble* dogs (kinda), and they may have the personalities of hunting hounds, but they're Fae, same as the *aes sidhe* or the *glaistig*. They ain't all *that* sharp, but then, neither are a lot of the humans I know. Smart enough to hold a chat, anyway.

This particular *cu sidhe* was also about to ruin the whole damn thing; no way the judge would do what we needed him to with a witness around. We got lucky, though; just as they came into view of City Hall, the *cu sidhe* made some final comment and trotted off ahead. Maybe he was late for work, or maybe he just wanted to chase a squirrel; I dunno.

It was now or never; the streets and the stairs of the hall weren't *too* crowded this early, so it could still work. Ylleuwyn was just crossing the last street before he got there when someone appeared from behind a nearby corner.

"Hsst! Hey, judge!"

A goblin—the same goblin, in fact, that I'd accosted not far from here the night before last—glanced around furtively and then scooted over. Ylleuwyn's shoulders tensed, and he instantly peered around him, looking for an ambush, while the fingers on his hilt visibly tightened.

"I've nothing to say to you, you vile creature," he announced. Pompous jackass.

"Fine by me, judge. I'll do the talking." He was right up on Ylleuwyn, now. Several inches of the earl's blade were showing outside the scabbard—and he almost drew completely when the goblin held out a hand.

Except that what it held was no weapon, but a sheaf of papers.

Ylleuwyn couldn't have been any more immobile if the blind date knocking on his door wound up being Medusa. He didn't much seem inclined either to take the papers or to resheathe his blade. A few folk were starting to stare in his direction, but so far nobody'd taken *too* much of an interest. If that sword came free, though, or this took too much longer…

The goblin smirked. "We know you're having some, ah, *disagreements* with Alderman Rycine." (Which was no surprise, since Ylleuwyn and Rycine had been rivals since before either of 'em came to Chicago—or, for that matter, there'd been a Chicago to come to.) "Consider this your secret weapon."

The judge made no move to accept, though he did, finally, slide the sword back home. "I'm not so easily bought, you little fool. Whatever you want of me, I'll have none of it! Be on your way."

But the goblin didn't look apt to breeze any time soon—and for all his posturing, Ylleuwyn wasn't exactly walking away, either.

"Not asking nothing of you, judge. Just take it."

If Ylleuwyn's hackles had risen any further, they'd have torn his shirt. "Nothing comes free from the Unfit."

Now the Unseelie bristled, but he knew his job. "Look, buster, it's a *delivery*, see? Gift from a fella calls himself 'Oberon,' if you can believe that." The goblin shrugged. "Said he hoped this'd make you reconsider helping him out with something or other. You want more? Ask him."

"I see. Yes, he *would* stoop to dealing with your sort." Ylleuwyn started to turn away, stopped, and tried unsuccessfully to hide a grin inside his beard. "That's all you were to do? Deliver this? Not to collect any promises or oaths?"

Another shrug. "Just delivery, with Mr. Oberon's compliments."

"Very well." Ylleuwyn took a last gander around

and then snatched the documents so quick the messenger actually jumped. "Now get gone, before I find something to charge you with."

The goblin wandered away, muttering, and Judge Ylleuwyn resumed his trek to the hall, shaking his head and grinning—presumably at my "foolishness."

Where was I during all this? Oh, y'know, not too far away... A few dozen yards, in fact. Hidden by leaves and branches, and by an extra layer of ambient luck—I didn't think the judge'd spot me, but I sure as hell didn't need some curious pixie fluttering overhead and squawking at me I was crouched, nice and awkward and uncomfortable.

With a camera.

Or, well, the Elphame equivalent. It *looked* like a camera, anyway. And it did the same job.

Soon as Ylleuwyn had vanished up the stairs and through the glass doors, I was up and running. Ignoring the stares, and the occasional curse when I shoved past people meandering too slowly for my tastes, I pounded down the sidewalk, through the doors of the Lambton, and over to the elevators. (I didn't know, and didn't care, whether Slachaun just wasn't around to notice me, or whether I flew by too quick for him to do anything.) I stood rock-still— not sure I even breathed—for the elevator ride, which took about ten thousand years, and finally I was in my room.

Uh, the second one, that Ielveith had given me, not the first which was full of holes, and possibly still full of police studying those holes.

I shoved the papers off the writing desk and pulled a sheaf of parchment from my coat. I'd picked this up from a local shop, same time I bought the camera. Basically our version of "photo stock," the parchment was specially treated with herbs and reagents that… Well, here.

I spread the parchment out, positioned the camera right next to it, and whispered to it for a minute. And the camera went to work.

Atop our cameras, where yours hold those big honking flashbulbs, sits a circular frame. At my whispering, the cobweb that filled that frame began to tremble and sway, and a few dozen itsy-bitsy spiders poured out as though it was a faucet. They passed over the outer casing, where their tiny minds were temporarily imprinted with the images stored in the crystal ball that was the camera's heart. Then, their smaller-than-a-pinprick legs tracing detail finer than anything *your* film can develop, they scurried across the waiting parchment.

Those herbs and reagents? Blended specifically to react with the natural substances of the spiders. The little creatures scuttled, back and forth, round and round, and an impossibly meticulous picture began to form. From the smallest shape to the most minute differences in texture or contrast, the blacks and whites and greys revealed *everything*.

The first picture done, the spiders cleared the parchment just long enough for me to lift it up, exposing the next sheet, and they were at it again. And again.

And again.

In just a couple hours, they were done. And I was as ready as I ever would be.

***

"Oh, it's quite all right. By all means, I'll be delighted to make time for Mr. Oberon." The voice from the office door, again cutting through the hubbub and clamor of the crowded chamber, was not merely resonant, but heavy with gloating. It was damn near enough to knock a guy from his feet.

It was also very obviously an *enormous* relief to the poor clerk, who for some reason had gone pale and begun to whimper as I sauntered through the door and headed, grinning, for his desk. Now, having been saved the trouble of further tormenting the poor sap, I made for the judge's private office, ignoring the puzzled stares from everyone who knew how packed his schedule was, and the angry glowers from those who had legitimate appointments with him.

"I gotta say, judge, this is a nice change from last time. This mean we can be friends after all?"

Ylleuwyn planted himself in his chair and magnanimously gestured for me to sit. I magnanimously sat.

"We," he said, and I could see him relishing every word like a fine steak, "are nothing of the sort, *Mick*. I just wanted to tell you, to your face, that you're an idiot."

"Ah. Couldn't trust something that sensitive to a messenger, I imagine?"

"Did you honestly believe that offering me political leverage on a rival would change anything? Even if I had the information you wanted, the thought that I could be so easily bought—"

"Yeah, yeah, you're mortally offended, and would never lower yourself to so much as hold a door for me, and blah, blah, blah. You want me to get you a phonograph? You could make a record and hear yourself talking *all* the time."

It's probably petty of me to say that I was tickled pink when his expression fell, when he realized I wasn't gonna make his gloating any fun. Petty, but true.

"I think it's time that you departed, Mick. I—"

"You'd better take a look at this before I go, Ylleuwyn."

He peered suspiciously at the envelope I'd pulled from my coat and tossed onto his desk. "It won't bite you," I said.

He grudgingly tore it open at one end—and then his face went tight as a drum as he started to flip through the sheaf of parchment. "What the hell is this?!"

"It looks, *Your Honor*, like you accepting a gift. A list of names and all manner of personal secrets and skeletons—that is, leverage—of a dozen members of Alderman Rycine's staff. From a goblin." I *tsk-tsk*ed at him. "Conspiring with the Unseelie against one of your own? This is *not* gonna do your position in the Court any good at all when it gets out, judge."

You wouldn't think that a guy could flush and go pale at the same time, would you? The contrast painted targets on his cheeks.

"You can't begin to make out what I'm being handed in these pictures!"

"Not these, no. But you know as well as I do that the spiders capture that kinda detail. You just gotta have 'em sketch the picture big enough to see it. And I promise you, the crystal ball with those images is nice and safe."

"These can be faked!"

I'm pretty sure my eyebrow shot up into my

hairline. "Yeah, but it ain't easy. And there's a lot *more* magics that can *verify* 'em. Your desperation's starting to show, Your Honor."

Yeah, it really was. I saw his eyes flicker down to something behind his desk and then over to the right—trying hard *not* to move toward the plaque on the wall behind him.

"You could pull a gat or a sword," I said. "I dunno that I'd call it a good idea, though."

"Nobody in this building would doubt my word if I told them you attacked me, and I was merely defending myself."

"Oh, *everyone* would doubt it; they just wouldn't say anything. More to the point, it wouldn't make your problem go away. Anything happens to me, the pictures go out."

"You—You...!"

"I hope you're more eloquent than this in Court, Ylleuwyn."

"You dirty, scum-sucking bastard! You've whored yourself out to the Unfit! You're worse than they are! You..."

I let him sputter and rant for a minute or two, and then reached over and tapped the nearest picture on the desk. He jumped, then quieted down, glaring promises of painful murder into my soul.

I wondered if he'd feel better knowing just how much I hated being where I was. Owing the Unseelie isn't too different from owing the devil, except it's even less predictable. And the fact that Queen Mob had been willing to throw away leverage—even against a player as relatively minor as Alderman Rycine—was scary enough to make a crocodile sweat. She *said* they had no use for it, that they had better things to hold over Rycine if necessary, but I didn't quite buy it.

If it *was* a load of bunk, it meant that having me in her debt was more important to Boss Eudeagh than what she had on a noble, however minor, of the Chicago Seelie. And that just made her plans for me, whatever they were, look even more like the headlamp of an oncoming locomotive, and me tied to the tracks.

But again, it was done, and no amount of fretting over it would change anything. (Which wouldn't stop me from fretting, of course.)

"So… The Ottati changeling?" I pressed.

Ylleuwyn's glare sharpened. "I told you, I have no idea who—"

I tapped the picture again. "Do not." *Tap.* "Waste." *Tap.* "My time." *Tap-tap.* "I'm going to ask once more. And you're going to give me some useful information."

"I—"

"And if you tell me you don't know what I'm talking about, or otherwise lie to me, or make any attempt to deflect the question, I'm leaving, and I'm taking at least the next hundred years of your political career and ambitions with me.

"Now… What do you know about the Ottati changeling?"

Ylleuwyn was about to swallow his beard. "You son of a bitch, you can't do this!" Then, as I started to rise from the chair, "All right! All right, damn you."

He sighed, staring at his hands, as I sat back down. Then, "I do recall the Ottati girl, yes. I didn't take her myself, or arrange for it, but I was aware of it.

"You see," he continued, now looking up once more, "the child wasn't taken by whim or by chance. It was a pact."

A-hah! "So someone *was* targeting the Ottati family!"

He nodded. "I have no idea why, but yes. Someone—a mortal—very specifically wanted *that* child to be taken. Not slain, not kidnapped by a human, but claimed by the Fae and replaced with a changeling."

"Someone with connections here?" I asked.

"I doubt it. We were contacted through a fairly poorly enacted rite. I imagine the individual had little if any experience with magic of any sort."

I pressed a knuckle to my trap in thought. "So some Joe or Jane comes outta nowhere and decides, 'I want this kid gone. Hey, I know! I'll just ring up the Seelie Court, and have them handle it!' That about right?"

"As awkward as you make it sound, that is, indeed, what happened."

"Huh."

"Several of us sensed the ritual's calling, and discussed the mortal's petition at some length. Eventually, we decided that there was no reason *not* to grant the request—as you pointed out, the Unfit may produce more changelings than we, but we must keep up our population of servants—and the deed was done."

Holy hell, but I wanted to pound the son of a bitch in the mug until he was inhaling teeth! *The deed was done.* That casually, he and his cohorts had torn a child away from her family—and for no better reason than because someone had asked, and because hey, *why not?*

"All right," I growled through jaws clenched tight enough to bend bronze. "So who was it? Who orchestrated the pact?"

"I can't tell you that."

"Ylleuwyn…"

"I *can't*! Secrecy was part of the pact; I'm bound by oath. I literally *cannot* give you the names of *anyone* involved!"

Okay, that last part was horsefeathers. That a human would swear the Fae to secrecy about his or her name, that I could buy. But that the pact would include anonymity for the other *Fae* involved? I doubt it. More probably, Ylleuwyn was worried about the political repercussions of dragging any other nobles into this—maybe even more'n he was worried about my photos.

But that was okay by me. Much as I might *want* to know who was involved, all I *needed* was…

"So where's the girl? Who 'owns' her?"

"Mick—"

"Don't tell me if they were involved in the original pact, or if they traded for her later on. Don't tell me *how* they were involved, if they were. Just tell me who's got her now."

"I don't—"

"*Now*, goddamn it!" I don't even remember moving, just that I was suddenly standing, leaning over the desk, ready to snap it—or maybe him—in half. "If the next fucking word out of your mouth isn't either a name or a place, those photos are going everywhere. *Where's the girl?*"

A writhing, dying worm of a vein throbbed beneath his forehead, and his fingernails gouged furrows in the wood—but I had him, and no matter how foul and bilious his pride tasted, all he could do was choke it down.

"Goswythe. You contemptible jackal, we gifted her to Goswythe."

I knew the name, though only second- or third-hand. Goswythe was a hanger-on and sycophant of the Court, a gink with aspirations but no title. He just happened to be more useful and more favored'n most.

He was also a *phouka*, which made him—well, not necessarily dangerous, but damn irritating. Most of his kind ain't part of either Court; they're what used to be called solitary Fae. They spend most of their time in the form of a horse, a dog, a rabbit, or whatnot, and think it's just a hoot to trick wanderers into getting lost, or—in horse form—into taking a wild and terrifying ride. Real comedians, these guys.

But a few, a few get ambitious. They learn to take on human shapes, as well as animal, and try to make themselves useful enough to earn a position or a simple title among the Seelie. They're driven, they're obnoxious, and they lie worse'n Pinocchio on a first date.

"All right. And where do I find Goswythe?"

For the first time in long minutes, Ylleuwyn smiled, a hateful, malignant leer of crooked teeth. "Last I heard, he'd left Elphame for the mortal world.

"Where," he continued spitefully as my heart

tried to squeeze itself into my left big toe and the room seemed to close in around me, "he could look like absolutely anyone. Best of luck to you in your search, you self-righteous bastard."

CHAPTER ELEVEN

It was just as windy, but not as wet as Seelie territory or as cold as Unseelie, when I stormed across the streets and sidewalks of Chicago—your Chicago—a couple days later. My dogs were slapping the concrete hard enough to hurt through my shoes, and people were hustling to clear my way. I'm pretty sure, at one point, I actually stared down a traffic signal.

I was heading down Halstead, away from the more upmarket blocks, gunning for someone who really, *really* didn't want me to find him. I'd already called on his regular hangouts (for the second time in a little more'n a week) and with each joint he *wasn't* in, I just got more steamed. If he wasn't here, either, if I had to get back on the goddamn L one more time to find him, there were gonna be bruises.

Well, more bruises. From the lowdown I'd picked up at his last haunt, he'd already gotten the tar beat outta him once today.

Good.

It got a little cooler as I moved farther from downtown, farther away from the windows of the steel towers bouncing sunlight down onto the little people scurrying below, and the breeze was brisk enough that I wasn't getting too many snootfuls of car exhaust off the streets. Woulda been a nice walk, under other circumstances.

I knew I was getting close long before I spotted the "Soup, Coffee, and Doughnuts FREE for the Unemployed" sign. I knew 'cause I'd started passing up the people waiting some streets back. The line stretched for block after block, a shifting serpent of despair; hundreds and hundreds of people, wearing faded clothes and faded dreams, waiting dully for the Depression to end—or at least for the first hot meal they'd had in days. Not even those breezes could do a blessed thing about the sour reek that hovered overhead.

I shoved through them as I approached the door, ignoring every curse and every glower, wrinkling my nose against the smell, and made myself not care. Maybe you think that makes me hard—hell, maybe it *does*—but there were just too many of them. I couldn't carry enough sympathy to go around, not *and* leave room inside me for anything else. Fae or mortal, nobody could.

It was easier today; hot under the collar as I was, I'm not sure I'd have given much of a hoot about *anything*. After everything I'd been through and discovered in Elphame, not to mention what it meant about some of the people I'd talked with back here, I was mad enough to spit iron. (Plus, Pete'd been over an hour late meeting me, yesterday morning. Wound up being nothing big—he'd just scampered farther under last night's moon than he'd realized, and took longer getting back—but it'd just been one more thing for me to fret over.)

I finally pushed through the lines, around one

unshaven, particularly smelly bird in a ragged coat and a floppy newsboy cap, and found myself inside.

It was pretty nice, far as soup kitchens go; not as upscale as the ones Al had built during his year of so-called philanthropy before he was convicted, but following suit all the same. The chefs and servers behind the counter were dressed in cleaner whites than I'd seen at Thompson's Diner, and the soups and coffees smelled pretty appetizing. (Well, not disgusting, which for me and food means about the same thing.)

My blinkers adjusted to the shade a lot quicker'n yours would, and I was already casting around from row to row of long tables, hunting my mark, when a fella came toward me from around the corner. I saw him nodding and talking to a few folks on his way, volunteers and customers both, and saw that some of *them* were pointing my way. Guess they didn't take too well to me shoving through 'em the way I had.

Tough.

"Hold on, there, mister." He was a tall guy, a little swarthy, with his sleeves rolled up and his shirt flattened like he'd been wearing an apron. "I sympathize, but we got people been waiting here for hours. You can't just barge in this—"

"And you are?" I interrupted.

"Me? Timmy Pinetti. I run this joint."

"Well, Mr. Pinetti, I ain't here for your soup." I flashed him my PI ticket. Not as good a door opener as a copper's tin, but usually pretty effective. "I'm looking for someone."

"Huh. I'm sorry, detective…" He paused, then

went on when I didn't bother filling in the blank. "But these people come to me 'cause they've got nowhere else to go. I'm not gonna let you hassle anyone here. You'll just have to find your man some other time."

For the first time, I stopped scoping the place long enough to face him. "Look, bo, I can appreciate that. But the gink I'm looking for, he ain't one of your customers—not legitimately, anyway. Franky Donovan. You might know him as Four-Leaf Franky. He's a cheap grifter, taking whoever he can for whatever they got. If he's here—and I'm told he's here often—it's 'cause he got beat up and robbed, probably by someone he owed. He's just taking advantage of you rather'n spend an honest buck."

At this point, I was getting some curious (and some nasty) glowers from the surrounding patrons, and Pinetti didn't look too happy at what he was hearing. I'll give him this, he took a minute to think on it before he shook his head. "I'm sorry, detective," he said again, "but I only got your word on that. If I start—"

"Blond hair, glasses, suit you wouldn't use to wash a nice car."

I could see the guy starting to lose his temper—tight jaw, clenching fists, all of it—and I can't say as I could blame him. "If I start making exceptions—"

"Take me to him. *Now.*"

I hit him with everything I had, every bit of will I'd started gathering since I first recognized he was gonna be a problem, backed by the fury and impatience that'd been pooling in my mind for days. I punched into his thoughts, smacking aside his reluctance, dragging to the fore his anger at being used and his worry about further trouble in his joint. It was, without resorting to my wand, about the hardest I could hit in your world.

Pinetti never stood a chance. He *did* manage to hold off for another few breaths—he *really* didn't want to hand over one of his customers—and then he sagged. "Okay. This way."

I could see the hurt in the expressions of the folks eating nearby, the sorrow and, yeah, fear that he'd caved. What I'd done would probably cause Pinetti problems in the future, and I could tell by his resistance that he genuinely cared about these people. It made me feel rotten at forcing his hand in public, at how I'd managed to talk myself *out* of sympathizing.

Not enough to get me to back down, though.

Franky was hunched over a table toward the back, wearing either the same cut-rate green suit I'd seen him in last, or one just like it. His glasses had been broke and fixed with tape, and I could see even from here that his collar was open, and his neck suspiciously bare of gold. His jaw sagged when he saw me coming, soup actually pouring over his lip and onto the table by his bowl. He stood, tensed to skedaddle, and then about deflated when I shook my head.

Guess he saw something in my expression to suggest it wouldn't go well for him if he tried.

(Yeah, he was *eating*, though I know some fellas wouldn't call soup "food." Franky ain't full-blood *aes sidhe*, remember; not all Fae can get by in your world with milk the way we can.)

"Hey, Mick. How you been?"

"Let's take a walk, Franky."

"Uh…" He looked as though he wanted to dive into his soup bowl and swim away. "I'd, um, kinda prefer to talk here."

"No." I put a "friendly" arm around his shoulder. "You wouldn't."

"Oh. Okay…"

I guided him toward the closest door—an emergency exit—leaving Mr. Pinetti behind, horror and anger slowly painting his face as my influence started to fade.

Franky actually jumped when the door slammed behind us, leaving us in a dirty, paper-and-broken-glass-strewn alley not all that different from the one where we'd last jawed.

"Um, Mick…"

"Tell me, Franky." I moved my arm, reached over—smiling as he flinched—to straighten his collar and dust off his lapel. "You got *any* shame at all? Coming to this kinda place to grab a bite, when you and I both know you got dough—or some gold you could hock—at home."

He shrugged, smiling weakly. "C'mon, Mick. I just got beat up and robbed. Yeah, I got more jewelry, but *selling* it? Right after getting mugged? That's asking too much, don't you—"

At which point, his words turned into half-digested soup. Probably because I slugged him in the gut hard enough to lift him off his feet. He fell to all fours, his lunch spattering across the tips of my Oxfords, which I proceeded to clean off on Franky's ribs. Hard. He left his feet (and hands) again and rolled a couple yards down the alley, finally coming to rest on a heap of newspaper and used napkins that'd fallen from a nearby garbage can.

(I know I told you before that most Fae don't normally vomit. Obviously, that ain't *entirely* the case; if we've just eaten and something hits us hard enough in the stomach, the food's gotta go *somewhere*, don't it?)

His glasses had come off halfway. I picked 'em up and stuck 'em in a pocket as I stepped toward him.

"Jesus, Mick... Jesus..." He spit out a tiny length of noodle and struggled upright enough to sit back against the wall. The entire front of his jacket and vest were soaked, and already letting off a tear-jerking stink.

"You lied to me." I squatted down so I could look him square. "You got any idea how much that bothers me? How grateful I'd been to have gotten away from the Court, so I wouldn't have other Fae lying to my face?"

"What... What you talking about? When did I...?"

I picked up one of the cleaner napkins—by which I mean it didn't have any *obvious* dried soup, dirt, rat piss, or other filth on it—and wiped a few smears of puke off Franky's jacket. "Changeling. Girl. Sixteen years ago. Ottati family. Any of this ringing any bells?"

"Well, yeah, you asked me last week, but—"

"But nothing, Franky. I know how you keep your ear to the ground. I know you got connections, here and Sideways. And I don't for *one damn minute* believe that if someone like Goswythe showed up back here in Chicago, with a teenage girl in tow, that you wouldn't have heard about it!"

Okay, to be fair, I couldn't be a *hundred* percent sure they were here in the Windy City—but the odds were damn good. Ninety-five, maybe better. Not only was it the city Goswythe knew best (in both worlds), but I hadn't just sat around on my thumbs my last evening in Elphame. Once I had the name "Goswythe," I'd asked a couple more questions of the few Fae there who didn't want to see me humbled or dead. Ielveith, for instance. And based on what all of *them* had heard, yeah, Goswythe had left Elphame not too long ago, but he hadn't left Chicago.

On the *way* off chance they were wrong, I was gonna owe Franky more'n an apology.

But they weren't wrong.

"Hey, c'mon, Mick! How was I supposed to know the girl Goswythe was with was the one you were asking about? It ain't like he was shouting her real name with the newsies on streetcorners. Hell, *she* probably don't even know her real name!"

"But you did know, Franky, that the *phouka* had just shown up in this Chicago a few months before I started asking around, with a girl who was the right age, didn't you? And you *had* to know that she *coulda* been the one I was looking for. Which means, hey, you know what? You lied to me."

"Well, now…" Franky was pressing himself tight to the wall, either trying to stand up against it or to vanish through it. His hair was a drunk spider's web, sticking up and out and all directions across the bricks. "It wouldn't have been fair to send you after a guy when I wasn't *sure* he was—Mick!" I think it was probably me cocking back my fist that got to him. "Okay, *all right*! Yes, I fucking lied to you! Goswythe's a lot more well connected than you are! What'd you expect me to do?"

"I expect, Franky, for you to tell me the truth when I ask you something. Even if it means you tell me, 'Sorry, I'm not willing to get into that.'" I reached into my coat and he recoiled, smacking his head hard against the wall, but I just pulled his glasses outta my pocket. "You dig?"

"I get you. I'm sorry, buddy."

"I'm sure you are." I stuck the glasses, crooked, onto his face. "Now, where do I find Goswythe and the girl... What's her name now, anyway?"

"Celia. I've heard he calls her Celia. I don't know exactly where they are, Mick."

"Franky..."

"I don't, I swear! But I can tell you that they work mostly inside the Loop. Fleecing tourists, mostly."

Huh; okay, then. The Loop was a lotta area to cover, and just 'cause they worked there didn't mean they necessarily hung their hats anywhere nearby. But it was a start, a lot better one than I'd had—and I believed Franky when he said that was all he knew.

I think I'd been convincing enough to be sure of that.

I dropped him a few bucks to pay for the dry cleaning, and went on my merry way. Given what they were up to, the tricky twosome probably worked after hours, and I had a couple more stops to make before the sun set.

But this time I was picking up a smaller prop, damn it!

It was, as fate or fortune would have it, the same fella who cracked open the door this time as it'd been on my list visit.

"Good day to you again, sir!" I replied to his wary scowl. "I'm calling on behalf of Credne Household—"

"Household Device Repair," he interrupted, showing a better memory than I'd have given him credit for. "The heck you doing back, pal?"

"Ah, well…" I lifted the narrow plastic contraption, letting the tube dangle from my hand, a thick and lifeless plastic snake. "The lady of the house, ah, Mrs. Ottati? She wanted a demonstration of Credne's External Corner and Under-Ledge modifications. You've heard our slogan on the radio, right? 'Inside or Outside, That Dirt Can't Hide!'"

I think I hated myself a little bit right about then.

"But I didn't have it with me at the time," I continued, not waiting to see if the tensing in his neck meant he was about to shout at me or laugh at me. "So here I am."

His head tilted as he followed the tube down to the far end, coiled limply on the porch. "Where's your vacuum?"

I shrugged and tried to twist my grin into something a little more ingratiating. "Well, the lady just wanted to see how the *attachment* worked, and I know she owns a vacuum, so I thought, hey, why lug the thing all across town, right? Right?"

And then, since I'd been concentrating on him long enough while we'd been booshwashing, "Could you announce me to Mrs. Ottati, please?"

Again, it wasn't hard to make the request sound a little more reasonable than it was, and again, he was back after just a couple minutes. "C'mon in," he grunted.

Well, that was a bit of a pickle, wasn't it? I'd hoped Bianca woulda taken the hint. "Sir," I tried again gamely, "It's a head for *external* cleaning. It's best if I'm outside to demonstrate—"

"Nuh-uh, pally."

And yeah, I froze. I wasn't actually gonna walk out on my deal with Bianca, not after all I'd been through to get this far (and especially not after I'd already put myself in a couple different jams and made myself some fresh and exciting new enemies whether or not I took it any further). But I also was *not* stepping across that threshold again; never mind the pain of it all, if I backed down on my threat to Orsola now, she'd walk all over me.

I honestly dunno what I'd have done, then, except it wound up not being an issue.

"Mrs. Ottati and Donna Orsola say they wanna see you inside, so you're coming right on inside."

Orsola chimed in? Either she was taunting me, pushing to see how far I'd bend, or...

I leaned in as if I was taking a step, just enough to put my shoulders through the doorway, and I felt it. Or more accurately, I *didn't* feel it.

The wards were down!

Not *completely* they weren't. I felt a faint pressure as I stepped across the threshold, an irritating "phantom poison ivy" itch all over my skin, but it was only a smidge worse than anything I mighta felt after a few minutes in a flivver or a long chat on the phone. And as I walked inside and let the gorilla manhandle me again in his fruitless search for a heater, I could see why. The runes and glyphs were still poking out from under a door here, the corner of a kinda garish rug there. So the sigils remained; she just hadn't maintained 'em, hadn't laid any magic on the wards in a few days. Let the power slowly fade, basically.

She musta *really* wanted my help after all.

Mr. Personality led me back into that same sitting room, where I greeted Mrs. Ottati and offered Donna Orsola a deep and respectful nod. Her head twitched in what looked *almost* like she might be returning it. I started making up whatever bunk sounded good about the virtues of the External Corner and Under-Ledge cleaning head until the goon wandered from the room, and then I plopped down onto the sofa.

It felt a lot more comfortable, this time around.

"I was starting to get concerned, Mr. Oberon," Bianca said. "I've been trying to reach you since Tuesday."

"Yeah, sorry. I was, uh, out of town, following up a few leads."

She and the old woman both leaned in, their faces excited. The clicking of the rosaries they both clutched sounded synchronized. "You know where she is?" Bianca demanded.

"No." Then, as their expressions began to sag, "I'm a lot closer'n I was when we last talked, though. I ain't making any promises, but I *might* be able to find her in a couple days."

"Oh, Blessed Madonna! *Meraviglioso!*" Orsola

was actually *smiling* at me! It was, in its own way, about as disturbing as Eudeagh'd been. "But how can you do this?"

"Well, that's the trick." I turned back to Bianca. "I need a lock of your hair, Mrs. Ottati."

"What?" She looked puzzled, perhaps a little disturbed. Orsola had paled.

"I need—"

The *strega* rose from her chair. "We heard what you need, *fata*! But if you think I do not know better than to grant you such a powerful tool to use against—"

"It's not *for* you, you paranoid dingbat! I need it to find *her*. Hair or clothes or something of *hers* would work a lot better, but since that ain't gonna happen, something tied to her mother's the next best thing. And yeah, you better suck it up and live with it, or else *this* ain't gonna happen!"

"It won't work," she said, though she sounded a little calmer. "Do you believe I haven't tried, over and over through the years? Every divination I could think of, every far-ranging spirit of whom I might demand answers, and none led me to her."

"My magics don't work the same as yours, *donna*. And I ain't casting around blind, either; I know where to start, now." Which'd be why I didn't ask for the damn thing earlier, savvy? You think I didn't *know* the old bat'd throw an ing-bing over the whole notion?

The pair of 'em muttered and argued and groused in Italian for a few minutes—I could translate it all for you, but really, why bother?—and then Bianca nodded at me. "I'll fetch a pair of scissors."

Which left Orsola and me alone again, trying not

to be *too* obvious about recoiling from each other.

"Surprised you're jake with this." Yeah, I was pushing. I do that when I'm hurting and tired and angry.

"I am not 'jake' with this, *fata*. I'm well aware that I'm handing you potential influence over one of my family with which you cannot be trusted. Rest assured that while you are searching for my granddaughter, I will be taking steps to minimize your ability to use that influence. I help you with this because I must, creature, but I *can* stop you from abusing what trust we've offered. And if you attempt to do so, I swear to you, I shall stop at nothing to destroy you utterly."

I believed she would, too. But as I said before, she musta been desperate for me to find the girl to even *think* about cooperating as much as she had.

A fact she pretty much confirmed when she finished up with, "But my granddaughter is worth the risk." Her whole trap wrinkled, like the words had been marinated in lemon juice. "I will be in the next room until Bianca finds the scissors. I feel the need to pray before I do this."

Yeah, sister. You and me, both.

It all proved about as difficult as you'd imagine. Bianca brought in a pair of kitchen shears, I snipped off a small tuft of her hair, and that was pretty much that.

It was right about then, as I was shoving the lock into my coat pocket, that we all heard the front door slam and a tide of voices start flowing down the hall toward the sitting room. Bianca's blinkers went wide as the boggarts' mouths, and I wouldn't have been all that surprised if she'd fallen into 'em.

"I imagine that'd be the hubby," I said.

The door opened to reveal a small gaggle of Joes. (Do wiseguys come in "gaggles"?) Most of 'em I knew already, by face if not name. The one in the lead— kinda block-jawed, clean-shaven, wearing a rich brown three-piece with a gold watch fob—I hadn't met yet, and didn't look too happy to be meeting me now. He'd never have looked handsome, not even if he wasn't glowering like a constipated thundercloud, but his eyes were steady, half-lidded, his jaw quirked just a little. Not handsome, but definitely striking, definitely noticeable. This was a fella who, wherever he was and whatever was happening around him, was definitely *there*, if you dig what I mean.

Right now, he was *here*, and he didn't much like that *I* was here.

"Who the fuck are you?"

"Ah, hello, sir! I represent Credne Household Device Repair. I was just showing your gracious wife our new External Corner and—"

"What the fuck is this, Tony?" He'd pivoted toward one of the big lugs next to him, who was, far as I could tell, pretty much indistinguishable from the other big lugs around him. "You let this *scemo* just waltz into my house? What the fuck's the matter with you? When did you mugs turn so stupid, Tony?"

"Fino, please," Bianca began, "he—"

While I, at the same time, had started with, "Mr. Ottati, I can assure you—"

"You! Close your fucking head! Bianca, what'sa matter with you?"

"I—"

"You know better'n this! You *all* know better'n this!"

At some point during the diatribe, incidentally they'd all switched to Italian. Made no nevermind to me after a few words, of course.

"What the fuck?" Fino was going on, with a rather disturbing lack of original profanity. "A fucking salesmen you let walk in here? And leave him alone with my wife and my mother? What the fuck?"

"He's been here before, boss," one of the palookas protested. "He's harmless. Just a vacuum repair—"

"Before? He's been here *before*? You been this stupid *twice*?"

I honestly wondered for a minute if someone wasn't about to start throwing lead.

"It's not a big deal, Fino," Orsola said calmly. "We were simply discussing—"

"Please, Momma," he interrupted—though with a lot more deference than before, I should point out—"lemme deal with this." Then, to the others again, "Everything going down with Shea's fucking Uptown Boys, and now Scola's trying to convince the Outfit that I can't handle my fucking territory, and you go and let some stranger near the ladies?"

Interesting... And somehow, I figure, a lot more open than he'd have been if he'd known I understood every word. Orsola, who *did* know, cast a nervous peek my way—right after spitting at the mention of "Scola"—but said nothing.

"—searched him, boss," the guy who'd let me in was protesting. "He ain't packing."

"Yeah? You bother to search the vacuum hose, wise-ass?"

It was actually kinda funny watching a whole cluster of Mob soldiers go pale at once. Three of 'em actually stumbled over themselves getting to me and snatching the hose from the floor next to me. It was clean, of course.

"He's just a salesman, honey," Bianca assured him—in English again.

"You," he said, pointing two fingers at me. "Get the fuck out. I don't ever wanna see you back around here, you get me?"

"I understand completely, sir. My apologies if I—"

"*Get!*"

I got. I had what I needed, anyway.

And more, actually. Interesting the name "Scola" should come up *again*. Still might be nothing, but it gave me something to think about—and distract myself with—during the Elevated ride to downtown, and the long, *long* walks that followed.

You wanna hear about the next two nights? Endless hours strolling the sidewalks and shops and elevated platforms of downtown Chicago, bathed in the glow of flickering streetlamps or the light spilling from nightclubs and late-night vendors? Serenaded by an orchestra of flivvers and trains, jazz and lounge music and gasping, chattering tourists? Pushing through crowds of the Loop's nightlife as they poured from theaters and restaurants and speakeasies in a cloud of cigarette smoke and booze-breath? All the while with one hand in my coat, poking the L&G around like a friggin' divining rod?

No? Good, 'cause I damn well ain't interested in going into it. Suffice to say, those nights couldn't have been anymore wasted time if I'd sat around playing Solitaire in the dark.

But finally, early on the third night—or, well, late on the third evening—I got lucky.

Some of you are wondering what I needed Ottati hair for; some have already doped it out. It's back to magic, with all its symbolism and interconnections. If you got something connected to your mark—hair, clothes, whatever—you got a lot more power over that mark. It ain't so easy with "once-removed sympathy," like using Bianca's hair to find her daughter, but it helps.

I wasn't at all shocked that Orsola hadn't managed to find Celia. No *way* she'd had any chance while the kid was in Elphame, but even once she was back, one of the things Fae magic's best at is hiding—and making sure they kept hidden woulda been Goswythe's first priority.

But me, I wasn't using magic to try to locate the girl, not exactly. Heck, I'd barely even know how; I'm not a warlock. What I *can* do, as you've already seen a time or two, is fiddle with luck. I knew the area Celia was working, and while the chances of me just randomly bumping into her were tiny, it was *possible*. A touch of my magic—especially focused through her relative's hair—made it a lot *more* possible. What coulda taken months, if it happened at all, happened instead on the third evening. As I said, I got lucky. I *made* myself lucky.

Didn't make the previous two nights any more fun, though.

I found her across the street and just down the block from the palatial façade of the Oriental Theatre, precisely close enough for the patrons to notice her as they stepped from the whirl of Arabian filigree and plush carpets and gilded statuary. Nothing about her stood out except for how average she was, and if that doesn't make any sense to you, well, you'll just have to trust me. Her hair was a mousy brown, pretty much black in the poor lighting of the streetlamps, and standing out sharply beneath a faded burgundy cloche hat. Her blouse and skirt were nice but just a little worn, the hem a couple inches low, the colors ever so barely drab. Clean but out of style, exactly the kinda glad rags you'd expect to see on someone too poor to afford to look like she thought she oughta look. A family fallen on hard times, or maybe a small-town girl come to the big city in search of work.

Perfect choice for plucking at the heartstrings of anyone flush enough to visit the theater, without looking shabby enough to make 'em uncomfortable. I felt the urge to applaud.

She was chiseling some older couple in dark overcoats, hands gesturing expansively—no doubt describing her poor humble hometown, or the younger siblings she had to feed—and, not incidentally, swiping the geezer's watch while she was at it. Her movements were smooth, graceful; *too* graceful, if you knew what to look for. I dunno precisely what sob story she told 'em, but it wasn't just compassion made him dig into his wallet, or the old dame into her purse. Even from too far away to hear what they were saying, I *felt* an excess of emotion, pity and sympathy mostly, splashing out all around her. Best I can do is liken it to a clumsy waiter carrying a tray of soup: yeah, the bowl got to where it was going, but a lotta customers got wet and greasy on the way.

She'd been taught, and by someone good—but she was only human.

The saps moved on, a few bucks and a pocket watch poorer, and she started gunning for her next mark. I moved in just a few steps, to make sure I didn't lose her in the throng.

And she made me.

I dunno what it was, exactly. I know I didn't get careless, didn't do anything that shoulda tipped her. Maybe, having grown up in Elphame and learned a little of our magic, she just sensed me coming, same way I can often tell if someone else is Fae no matter how they look.

Whatever it was, she spun into a crouch, staring straight at me like a panicked fawn. And she did what any panicked fawn would do.

I broke into a mad run after her, cursing with every exhalation. She was smaller'n me, with plenty of crowd to vanish into; knew this part of town as well as I did; and frankly, soon as the bystanders started to notice a frightened teenage girl running from a tall guy in a cheap suit and overcoat, there wasn't much doubt whose side they'd take.

Time to cheat.

I pulled my wand and sorta whipped it forward and back, lasso-like, and literally yanked a shred of luck away from her—out from under her, really, as though it were a carpet.

One of her shoes snagged on a length of knotted twine, discarded from a local newspaper stand, and she took a header to the sidewalk with a high-pitched squeal. I winced in sympathy as she scraped her palms and knees across the concrete; that'd sting for a few.

I was pounding up beside her before she could gather her wits enough to even think of getting up or calling out. "Sweetie, are you okay? What happened!" I dropped into a crouch beside her and whispered, "I ain't gonna hurt you—well, other than a couple skinned knees, apparently—but if you make a fuss, there *will* be cops involved. I don't think you *or* Goswythe want that just now, see?"

She glared at me; it was kinda cute, especially since she was trying not to tremble. "Go away! Leave me alone!"

Yep, she'd definitely learned some of our tricks. I felt her words nudging at the corners of my mind, chiggers trying to bore into my emotions and make me feel sorry for her, or scared, or otherwise inclined to obey.

It was kinda like being punched by a toddler. Even ignoring that none of you could ever be as proficient at our magics as we are, she'd been doing this for, what, maybe ten years at most? Me, I'd been practicing for...

Well, you'd call me a liar.

"*Stop that*," I said, using a lot more'n just words, and she recoiled as though I'd hit her. I repeated my police threat and ordered her to come with me, both with enough willpower behind 'em to out-stubborn a lazy mule. She nodded, dazed, and let me help her climb to her feet. "It's okay, everyone," I told the few onlookers who'd started to loiter. "She's all right. Just a little too much, uh, excitement." I briefly lifted a nonexistent bottle to my lips, earning me a couple chuckles, some nods, and a disapproving cluck or two. But they all bought it.

This time of the evening on a weeknight, even in the center of Chicago's nightlife, it wasn't *too* hard finding us seats on the L that were, if not isolated, at least private enough if we kept our voices down. She started shaking off her stupor right about the time the doors closed and the train lurched forward. Her face tried to twist into a half-dozen expressions at once, apparently unable to quite decide on the proper outfit.

"You're safe," I said. "Nobody's gonna hurt you."

That indecision resolved itself into a look of sheer, contemptuous disbelief. "Right. You kidnapped me to tell me I won a prize. How stupid do I look to you, buster?"

"First, keep your voice down, unless you've decided you wanna involve the cops after all."

"Maybe I—"

"Second, this ain't a kidnapping. I'm *solving* a kidnapping. This is an *un*-kidnapping."

That got me a couple of blinks.

"I'm a private detective," I said. "I was hired to find you. My name's Mick Oberon."

She snorted. "Next you'll tell me you're related to the *real* King Oberon."

"Yep. Third cousin on my mother's side."

I could tell pretty clearly that she couldn't even begin to decide if I was joking or not.

"I'm working for your mother, doll," I continued. "She's been worried sick since she discovered you were—"

"Fuck you!" Yeah, she kept her voice down, but she made up in venom what she lacked in volume. My skin almost shriveled at the touch of her words. "My parents don't give a damn about me! They never did."

Oh, boy. "I dunno what Goswythe's been telling you, Celia, but your family—"

"Goswythe *is* my family!" Her shoulders were actually shaking, though I wouldn't have laid odds on whether she wanted to bolt or slug me one.

"Yeah, I know how most Fae treat the humans they steal. Yelling at you, punishing you for the smallest failure or infraction, pummeling your mind and emotions with his own... That's family to you? It don't sound like it."

"You don't know what you're talking about." She swiveled her face away, gazing down the length of the car, and then snapped back. "And what about you? Oh, I know *your* kind. Poor little *aes sidhe*. Princes of Mud pretending they're Kings of the Earth. Running around the Courts, playing your games and trying desperately to convince everyone you're still the Tuatha Dé Danann, instead of pathetic little shadows of what you used to be!"

And for just a moment, I gotta admit I lost it. Maybe it's 'cause she *had* gotten into my head and touched my emotions a bit, I dunno. But everything I'd learned to wear in the past decades, everything that was "Mick," rather'n who I'd been before, slipped away. I leaned in, and I have no idea what she saw, but she shrank back into the seat hard enough to bruise.

"Oh, blind, foolish, little girl… You have *no idea* what we used to be…"

The lights in the car flickered and went dead, only slowly recovering to maybe half their prior strength. In the dim glow, I saw the people seated further down begin to shiver, clutching their arms and their coats against an inner chill that didn't come from the air at all. A few started to glance around, seeking the source of a sudden threat, a terrible fear in their souls of which their waking minds remained blissfully unaware. A purse fell open, spilling its rattling contents across the floor, and a button popped off a brand-new shirt, as chance and misfortune swirled and mixed unguided throughout the train.

It was the squeal of the brakes as we rounded a bend that snapped me out of it. Even if I probably couldn't affect the train directly, the amount of harm I could do with my emotions running unchecked and unrestrained… I took a deep breath, straightened in my seat, pulled every memory and every thought of Mick Oberon around me in a snug blanket. The lights returned to normal, the folks around stopped shivering, and I was me again.

Or maybe it's more honest to say I *stopped* being me again. Sometimes I wonder.

For a good while, Celia kept quiet, barely even blinking as she watched me for any sudden moves, and I can't say I blamed her. Finally, maybe 'cause the silence was worse, or maybe just to prove to me she *wasn't* scared, she asked, in a soft voice, "Why 'Oberon?'"

I blinked at her. Eloquently. "Huh?"

"'Mick Oberon' isn't exactly a proper faerie name, is it? So why 'Oberon?'"

I forced a vaguely sallow grin. "I had some, uh, *disagreements* with the folks back home. When I left, I walked away from *everything*. Using my cousin's name is a reminder of who I was."

It also gets most of 'em nice and steamed every time I use it, and I was angry enough back when I picked it to consider that a plus, but I didn't feel inclined to share that tidbit just now. Heck, it's a good thing she didn't ask me where "Mick" came from; that story's even less high-minded.

"Well, but… You're not serious about being related to him, right? I mean, the *aes sidhe* are Irish and King Oberon is from, what, English mythology, or French, or something."

I think my smile became a little more genuine. "Goswythe didn't stint on your learning, anyway." Then, before she could launch into another tirade about her "family," I said, "Henry II inherited both the English throne and several territories in France. You were born American, but your paternal grandparents were Sicilian."

"Huh?" She parroted back at me. "Buddy, you wanna spend much time in this world, you better learn how people answer questions."

I snickered a little, but she was right; I was still a little preoccupied. "What I mean is, it's all just borders. Yeah, an *aes sidhe* ain't a leprechaun ain't a *glaistig*… But we're all of us all over the place. The *aes sidhe*? We were the *tylwyth teg* in Wales, the Norse *ljósálfar*, the elves of England—hell, even some of the Olympians. *Glaistigs* are also fauns, and satyrs. The differences meant a lot more to you folk, and your legends, than they did to the Fae. To most of us, other'n allegiance to a given king or queen or Court, it didn't matter any more than it matters to humans whether some mug lives in Chicago or New York."

"Oh," she said.

"How's it you know so much about human culture and so little about ours when you grew up in Elphame?"

She gave me that shrug that, throughout all the history of two worlds, only adolescents have mastered. "Goswythe taught me what I needed to know."

"Uh-huh."

She repeated the shrug, maybe in case I'd somehow missed it the first time. Then, in an even smaller voice, "So what are you gonna do with me?"

"That's—actually a good question," which was probably not the answer she'd wanted. But I was still hashing it out myself.

See, I'd *planned* just to shadow her for a while, find out where she and Goswythe were holed up, and figure it out from there. It was a good plan, right until it got nicely gummed up when she'd tumbled to me. So now?

I couldn't just dump her at the Ottati house. Leaving aside the question of how Bianca and Orsola would explain it to Fino, I doubted Celia'd just stay put long enough for them to work it all out. And whoever'd arranged for her to vanish sixteen years ago might not take too kindly to her popping back up, either.

No, that wasn't safe for anyone. So first, I needed to get her back to my office, and then…

Then I had no friggin' idea.

So we both sat on bouncing and clacking seats, staring either at each other or out the windows into the black Chicago night, and wondered.

CHAPTER TWELVE

"Whoa! You work in this dump?"

I slowly moved my hand off the light switch and did my level best to murder Celia with the weight of my derisive stare. She wasn't looking, apparently too lost in scornful teenaged horror, so at best I managed a grazing flesh wound.

"Welcome to my office," I said flatly. "Bathroom's through there. I'll see if I can find you clean sheets for the bed."

"Bed?" She swiveled toward the slatted doors that closed off the Murphy's niche. Don't ask me how, but even looking at the back of her head— hair and hat, mostly—I *still* saw her blinkers widen. "You *live* in this dump?"

"I see Goswythe hasn't gotten to the lessons on manners yet."

"Hey! I can be plenty polite, buster. You just don't have anything I want!"

The prosecution rests, Your Honor. "Why don't you go clean up?" I suggested. "You'll wanna get the dirt off those scrapes. 'Fraid I don't have any iodine or anything, but a good scrub should—"

"I *have* cut myself before, you know," she huffed. She continued to hover in the middle of the room, just long enough to show me that she *wasn't* going just 'cause I'd suggested it, and then she dropped her hat on my chair, wandered into the bathroom and slammed the door behind her.

I took the opportunity to putter around the room, straightening up a little, digging up clean linens, prepping us a couple of drinks. It was a good fifteen, maybe twenty minutes before she came back out.

"Find everything okay?"

She glared.

"Except the window, of course. I'm sure you noticed there ain't one in there."

She still glared.

"Wouldn't have mattered." I pointed vaguely toward the ceiling. "Not even you could squeeze through those, anyway."

She glared harder. Then she sighed loudly and flopped into my chair.

"Have a drink," I offered, motioning toward the glass on the desk.

"Really? You got anything stronger'n milk?"

"Sure. I got cream." Then, "You keep making that face, it's gonna stick."

So she made one that was even worse, and drank. I raised my glass in a half-toast, and followed suit.

"What, exactly," I asked carefully, "did Goswythe tell you about your folks?"

She slammed the glass down almost hard enough to break it; I winced as a few drops of milk splattered over the rim and across the typewriter. "More than enough!"

"Yeah? Lemme guess. That they were awful,

selfish people who abandoned their innocent baby somewhere to die? Or that they gave you up for adoption to a couple who were even worse, who starved and beat you, made you live in filth? And that one of the kind and bighearted faeries heard your cries, and whisked you away to a better place?"

"Stop it!" Her irises were starting to shimmer wetly in the dull electric light.

"That's it, isn't it? See, those are the usual stories, doll. And that's exactly what they are: stories."

"They're not! It's what happened!" She stared down at the table, took another few gulps. "It's what happened," she repeated, more softly.

"It's not, Celia. You were taken from your crib a few days after you were born. They left a changeling in your place, a Fae child. Your momma didn't even know the girl she raised wasn't you until a few months ago."

She shook her head stubbornly. "You're lying. You're a liar!" But it sounded, to me, more a plea than an accusation.

"Why would I?"

"Politics. You're trying to get to Goswythe, aren't you?"

I grinned at that. "I'm *aes sidhe*, sister. What've I got to fear, politically, from a *phouka*?"

To that, she had no answer. Except, eventually, despite a jaw clenched in dogged anger and denial, to yawn. And yawn again. About two minutes later, she was so far out even Prince Charming woulda had a job of waking her.

Yeah, I slipped a teenage girl a Mickey. I ain't exactly proud of it, but what else could I do, tie her up? I couldn't have her running off until I'd worked out my next step.

Of course, the drops would only work for an hour or two. I spent a few minutes concentrating on her, L&G at hand, delving deep into her sleeping mind. I shuffled her thoughts like trick cards, pulling her dreams and her exhaustion to the top, her conscious thoughts and her fear below. You folks don't have the same kinda mental defenses when you're out; it was easy enough to do, and oughta keep her snoozing until midday tomorrow. More'n enough time to do...

Whatever the hell I hadn't figured out yet.

I carefully carried her to the bed and pulled the sheets over her, took her place in the chair, and thought. Half an hour of that and I had nothing to show for it but an empty glass. My brain was chasing its own tail, round and round, and wouldn't have known what to do if it caught it.

Couldn't take her to the Ottatis, not until I could convince her to stay and I knew it was safe. Couldn't even *tell* 'em I had her, since Bianca and Orsola'd never agree to leaving her here with me. Couldn't take her to the cops or the state. Couldn't just leave her here indefinitely; even if I thought she'd stay, which she wouldn't, I wasn't in the market for a long-term houseguest. I even thought about taking her back to Elphame and asking Ielveith to put her up for a while, but again, Celia wasn't likely to just stay put. And anyway, I couldn't put Iel in the middle of this, not with Goswythe's political ties.

I had a bitter, deceitful, semi-brainwashed teenaged girl on my hands, with magic powers and a troll-sized chip on her shoulders. It was every parent's worst nightmare, and I hadn't signed up to be a damn father.

Well, fine. I got up, snatched my coat off the rack, and headed back out. If I couldn't decided what to do with Celia, I'd work on the other end of the problem while the question simmered.

It was time to learn who'd arranged for her to vanish, who I was hiding her from. And the name on the very top of that list was "Bumpy" Vince Scola.

I asked for Pete more from habit than anything. Frankly, I'd expected to have to talk to Keenan, which woulda made things a little harder. Turned out he *was* there, though; happened to be filling out some forms after his beat. Dunno if that was my unique style of luck rearing its head again or just, y'know, the regular kind.

Anyway, there were a few minutes of static and distant voices on the other end of the blower, then a thump, and then, "Hi-ya, Mick."

"Pete. How's things?"

"Got no kick."

"Good. Uh, that's good."

Silence, and a whole mess of it. Then, "Whatever you're gonna ask me that you don't wanna ask me, Mick… go ahead and ask."

"All right. What can you tell me about where I might find 'Bumpy' Scola this late?"

For a little while, all I heard was breathing. "Wow. Didn't you promise me something about not mixing with certain ugly characters on this case?"

"Wasn't my choice. And I promise, I'm being careful."

"Yeah, you promised that, too." He sighed near deep enough to inhale the blower. "All right, hang on…" Another minute, and then he was back. "You got a pencil?"

"No need. I'll remember."

"Yeah, I'll bet." Pete rattled off a few names and addresses. "Can't make you any guarantees, of course."

"Of course. Much appreciated, Pete."

"Great. You can buy me a milk." The horn clicked and went dead, and the irritating stinging in my ear faded by half. I hung up the receiver—making the other half go away—and headed upstairs to the street.

I got lucky again—and again, it was genuine, not because I was fiddling with things. There was no reason to assume Scola'd be at any of his publicly known joints or hangouts, but after *another* interminable ride on the L, I found him in only the second place I looked. In the Cicero neighborhood, there's a whole cluster of speakeasies gathered near each other. A few of 'em used to be run by Frank Pope personally; now that he's a lieutenant for the Outfit's "board of directors," he's handed over a lotta his places to his own people.

Including, in the case of a joint called Kenson's Fine Smokes, to one Vince Scola.

Even this late—or maybe I should say *especially* this late—there was a lotta folks moving in and out of the conspicuous redbrick building. Some wore working-class duds, cheap suits and driving caps or drab cotton dresses; others had donned their most formal glad rags, tuxes and gowns for an evening on the town—and most of 'em weren't bothering to even make a show of carrying pipes or stogies when they left. I swear, a rabid werewolf could teach these mugs a thing or two about subtlety. Not that being subtle was all that much a necessity in the Windy City.

I took a deep breath, hauled out the L&G, and waved it in front of my face a couple times, applying illusion like stage makeup. I said before, it ain't easy tossing magic around without any specific targets, trying to fool any eyes and any minds that happen to swing my way. But I wasn't making any *major* changes—just enough so nobody'd recognize me if they saw me again later—and since each of you humans sees me a smidgen different anyway, it wasn't too hard.

I made my way inside, past shelves full of cigars and pouches of tobacco, along with a few booths and private rooms that were empty except for a couple geezers puffing on meerschaums. Finally, at the rear of the shop, a heavy steel door marked "Private" was hanging wide open, and most of the customers were moseying on through without so much as a peep from the two bruisers standing alongside. Occasionally, one of the lugs would stop someone—not a regular, I imagined—and chat for a minute before letting 'em through.

I expected the same treatment, and wasn't disappointed. Got a few questions, asking where I'd heard about the place, whether I was a cop, all the usual bunk. Got a furrowed brow when the galoot on the left checked my holster and found the wand, and a pitying headshake when I gave 'em my "I don't carry but it's intimidating" speech.

Other customers, regulars who didn't have to endure getting pawed, were jostling past me on their way in and out, and right when the fella had finished frisking me, I let myself get shoved into his partner by some bird in a Panama hat. I traded the goon's angry glower for an apologetic grin, and made my way inside...

Carefully hiding the roscoe I'd swiped from him up my overcoat sleeve.

The backroom was basically a nightclub in full swing. Couples swirled and slid and Charlestoned across a broad dance floor under the cheerful gaze of a dark-skinned trumpeter doing a better'n-passable Louis Armstrong. Waiters gussied up in white tails circulated around the dance floor and between a couple dozen tables, delivering food that not a lotta people'd ordered, and drinks that *everybody* had. From the finest bootleg liqueurs to mid-grade whiskey to cheap bathtub hooch, you'd find it all on the menu here.

Except milk, probably.

I mingled for a few, nodding to people at random, trying to sway a little in time with the music (and again missing the jigs of past centuries). I blinked through roving banks of cigar smoke, and I gotta tell you, dressing it up in tails and cut crystal don't make the mix of sweat and booze smell any more appetizing.

And then I found him. Knew it hadda be him, with all the mugs and muffins fawning all over him, and some quick eavesdropping confirmed it. He had a private booth in the back, of course, because they always do. Boxed in on three sides, with yet another monkey-suited gatekeeper standing watch on the fourth, Vince Scola sat at a table with a blonde on each arm, and a couple more Mob-looking types gathered around. Scola himself was markedly unimpressive; his mustache looked like a gerbil's tail, and if he was more'n five-eight standing then I'm a spriggan. But his coat was spotlessly white, his shoes gleamed brighter'n the crystal chandeliers; store-bought class, all the way.

He was also human, far as I could tell from here—which, to be square, I hadn't been sure of. I'd thought maybe Fino'd made an enemy of something worse'n he understood. Had to get close to be absolutely sure, though.

I took a minute to reinforce my illusion and made for the booth.

Nobody noticed at first, since I was just a fella strolling across the joint, maybe looking for a table or a friend. Eventually, however, the goon started to straighten, uncrossing his arms, just in case... And when it became clear that I wasn't turning away, he said something over his shoulder and took a step forward to keep me from passing.

"You lose your way, bo?" he asked when I stopped in front of him. "This here's a private table."

"Nope," I said. "Wanted to give you something." And I raised my fist.

The guard's hand went under his lapel for his piece. The two wiseguys and Scola did the same, and even the two molls were hauling derringers from their bags. I had six separate pipes pointing my way before any of 'em noticed that I was holding the Colt toward 'em butt-first.

"Jumpy, ain'tcha?" I asked with a grin.

The palooka took the heater from me, then glanced back over his shoulder again and shrugged. "Boss?"

"Let him through," Scola ordered. His voice had an irritating, nasal pitch, but his elocution said "education." (Though of course, it coulda been lying; ain't as if none of these gang boys put on airs.)

"Sorry for the theatrics, Mr. Scola," I said as I arrived at the table. "The gat belongs to one of your boys out front. I just wanted to make a point."

"Dangerous way to do it, pal." As he lifted his glass, I spotted a thin chain, wrapped tight around his wrist, peeking out from under his cuff. It was simple, subtle—but quite telling if you knew what you were seeing. The links looked silver, mostly, but I could sense a few iron ones from across the table as a faint itch on my skin. No reason for that combination of metals on a cat like him—it sure as hell ain't stylish—except protection. The bracelet *had* to be a charm or fetish. "So what point would that be?" he finished.

"Security, sir. You got a problem with it."

"And you can fix that, Mister...?"

"Chulainn," I said. "Cal Chulainn. And yeah, I can."

"All right, Mr. Chulainn. Sit down, and let's talk."

I could give you the whole conversation—I claimed I was an ex-cop and a security guard for hire, spouting out enough of what I'd learned in my years as a PI and a copper's friend to make it convincing—but frankly, it'd be pointless. What mattered was I'd got close enough, for long enough, to tell what I needed to tell about Vince Scola.

He was human. I'd figured that already, but now I was sure. And he was no warlock; not even remotely enough of the smell and taste of magic on him. But there was a *little*—a slight tang to his words, his breath, his aura, faint as a sprinkle of incense in a bonfire.

Which meant that while Scola was no spell-worker, he'd spent time with someone who was. At the very least, I was right about that narrow chain, and what it was for. And *that* meant my night wasn't finished.

I eventually made my excuses, leaving Bumpy with a number where he could ring me if he decided he was interested in my services—a number I knew wasn't actually in service—and headed out. Time for yet *another* trip on the L, to the last address Pete had given me.

Scola's home.

It wasn't actually that far a trip, and if I hadn't felt the hours sifting away like flour in a sieve, I'd have just walked it rather than sucking up more of the train's lovely ambience.

See, unlike most of Chicago's Italian mobsters, a small number of 'em—including Scola—had decided to stay near their roots, rather'n move to more affluent communities. Scola's house wasn't actually in Little Italy proper, but it was damn close. Still inside the immigrant community called the Hull House Neighborhood, Bumpy's place was a small two-story affair just off Roosevelt Road. It was nicer than most of the houses around it—cleaner, a little more modern, with more expensive trim and fancier curtains—but not a *lot* nicer, and not too much bigger, so it didn't stand out much.

The entire place was ripe with marinara, thanks to the breezes coming in over the twenty-eight zillion restaurants of Little Italy, and sang with the rattle of old cars and squeaky hinges. The Hull House Neighborhood was home to a lotta Eastern Europeans as well as Italians, so in the dark I didn't stand out *too* badly. Folks and flivvers passed me on the street fairly constantly, chattering in half a dozen different languages, but I never got more'n an occasional second glance or half-hearted nod. More or less anonymous, I strolled past the house without stopping, trying to get a slant on the place—and the people who *weren't* just the neighborhood's average Joes.

I didn't think anyone was home—or if they were, they were either asleep or sitting in the dark, 'cause there wasn't so much as a flicker of light from around the curtains—but that didn't mean the place didn't have eyes on it. I counted three separate flivvers with guys just sitting in 'em, parked here and there along the street, and I had to suppose there was at least one other team a little more carefully hidden. The boys in the cars were barely making half-hearted efforts to keep their hardware outta sight—guess they assumed everyone already knew why they were here—and I spotted a Tommy in the nearest car, in addition to whatever smaller rods they mighta carried. Sharp of Scola to keep his place under guard, but inconvenient for me.

Not *too* inconvenient, though.

I crouched behind a small, poorly trimmed hedge, a few houses down the street, watching them watch the house. I drew the L&G, but even with the wand, I let the magics flow slow and careful instead of a sudden yank. I wrapped wisps of extra luck around myself, luck drawn from the fellas standing guard, but I didn't wanna do anything too dramatic—no accidental gunshots or engines coughing up steam or anything. Too obvious. Just a little bit, then a little bit more…

A coupé roared around the corner, the next street over, motor roaring and tires squealing. And every one of Scola's lugs, *every one*, jumped and twisted in his seat like someone had set his back hair on fire, hand reaching for a gat, to see what the hell the commotion was all about.

Lucky break, huh?

I was off and sprinting, ducked low as I flashed through the intervening yards and into the narrow walkway between Scola's house and his neighbor's. A tall wooden fence blocked access to the back yard, but I'd expected something of the sort. I jumped, not at the fence but at the wall of the house, fingers and toes sliding into the tiny mortared slots between bricks. I climbed up a little and then crossed over the fence headfirst, clinging kinda lizard-ish to the side of the house. I could feel the contours of every brick, every bit of mortar, find handholds that none of you could find, put weight on my joints that none of yours could take—and still my fingers ached, tendons straining and grit rubbing at the quick under my nails.

I dropped to a crouch in the tiny "alley," landing in half-grown grass, gritty soil, and what was probably dried dog shit.

Dog? Shit.

I heard the barking even before it came barreling around the corner from the back yard proper, a big honking boxer mix, all jowls and teeth and trails of splattering spit.

Funny thing about dogs, though—they're all emotion, not a lotta thought. I lunged right back at him and *snarled*, throwing every bit of anger and frustration I had (lots) behind it.

Last I saw of him was his tail disappearing back around the corner so fast his frightened *yip*—and a pungent puddle of piss—lingered in his wake. Honestly, I'd probably just ruined him as a guard dog for the rest of his life, but he'd make Scola a *fantastic* pet: nice and friendly and just a little clingy.

Keeping one shoulder to the wall, and trying to ignore the blinding stench of the newly moistened soil I was creeping through, I slid around so I could peek into the back yard itself. The entire lot was surrounded by the same fence I'd climbed over, and the yard was empty of much besides slightly overgrown grass, a couple saplings, and a ten-by-three flower garden. That last, sprouting mostly gardenias that mighta smelled nice without the *eau de* dog, was the only part of the yard that showed much evidence of upkeep.

Though I couldn't see any signs, I was sure Scola had peepers on the yard; he wasn't stupid enough to guard the front and not the back. One of the houses backed up to his, maybe? There *were* a few lights on in the one off to the left...

Well, didn't matter exactly where. I knew I couldn't just strut across the back yard and make for the door. That left the windows here, on the house's side, either of which woulda made for a fine entry if they hadn't been on the upper floor. And climbing up to 'em would put me square in the sights of anyone watching from those houses, and from the goons in one of the cars out front.

So, more waiting, more drawing of magics around me with the wand—messing, this time, with how human sight would interpret the patterns of light and darkness around me. It took a few minutes, but the silver of the moon finally dimmed behind a passing cloud, and I was climbing, jamming my fingers hard and painfully into every nook and cranny. If any of the guards *did* happen to glance my way, they'd see nothing but a little movement in the pall of shadows cast across the side of the house, maybe the waving of branches in front of a street light. They'd have to *really* look, really think on it, to notice that nothing local could possibly be *casting* that shadow.

I planned to be well inside before any of 'em had the presence of mind to do that much pondering—which, thanks to a quick poke at the lock with the L&G and then a few wiggles under the window frame with a wire pick, I was.

And *what* I was inside turned out to be a kid's room. Small bed with colorful sheets and clown pillows, shelf with a baseball glove and some model trains, brown and blue suits with short pants hanging in the open closet, a few other knickknacks scattered here and there…

No, not a kid's room. More an adult's version of a kid's room. It was way too neat, too ordered. It was also dusty enough to make a corpse sneeze.

Huh.

I slunk outta the room and down the hall, but my first impression had been right: there wasn't anyone here. Long as I didn't start making a huge racket or flipping on lights—which I shouldn't need to do, since there was more'n enough leaking in through the windows from the moon and streetlamps—there was no reason anyone should tumble to me.

The upstairs was, other'n a linen closet and a bathroom with a claw-foot iron tub (which I avoided as if it was a friggin' bomb), just more bedrooms. Scola's was easy enough to identify, since it was the biggest, with the nicest furniture, an enormous mirror, a closet bursting with suits and tuxes, and the lingering scent of several different women's perfumes.

There were also a few tiny marks etched into the door jamb and the window panes: miniature glyphs of protection, so small even I almost missed 'em. Would have, in fact, except that I tasted the magic in the air when I passed. Well, that matched up with the charm he'd been wearing, anyway. In fact, come to think of it, the ambient flavor of mysticism couldn't be accounted for by those runes alone; there was something else not quite natural in this house.

Besides, y'know, me.

Looked like one of his most trusted bodyguards lived here, too, since another bedroom—a lot smaller'n his—held an unmade bed, much cheaper suits, and an array of rumpled "gentlemen's" magazines heaped on a counter.

And one more bedroom, about the same size but much neater. The bed was covered in a pink-

and-white comforter, the walls hung with paintings of flowers. An array of makeup and jewelry boxes were arranged neatly on the dresser, in front of a gilt-trimmed mirror.

Also dusty. And also not quite right: a man's idea of what a woman's bedroom "should" be.

Huh, again.

Guess I should clarify, since I told you the house wasn't that big, that *none* of these rooms, even Scola's, were large; most were actually pretty tiny. And none of 'em were protected the way Scola's was, so I made my way downstairs—without a single groan or creak from the steps, if I can brag a bit.

You want a play-by-play of the whole downstairs? Nah, didn't think so. Bottom line, there was a kitchen with an attached dining room, a sort of living room-slash-parlor, a combination office and small library, and a utility room. They were all nice, all more or less well kept and clean, and all pretty much as mundane as you could ask for.

Except…

Except for the glyphs and runes and protections, scattered around the entire first floor in every hiding place you could imagine. It looked as though Scola had contracted out his home decorating to the Golden Dawn. Pentacles and mystic formulae, rose crosses and thaumaturgic diagrams, zodiac signs and tiny portraits of saints; whoever Scola had gotten to protect him had drawn from just about every tradition of Western magic. No way of telling if he'd just hired someone local or if he'd brought his own *strega* along from the Old Country to match Ottati's—but if the latter, then it was someone not nearly as devoted to a single tradition as Orsola was.

It also wasn't someone nearly as talented. I could sense the power here—smell it, taste it, my body practically hummed with it—but it wasn't as strong as the good *donna*'s.

Or maybe it just felt that way to me since Orsola's wards had been oriented specifically against Fae, while these were just more general protection from curses and dark magics. I couldn't be—

Protection against curses? Hmm...

Was that why Scola happened to be in police custody when his men were "accidentally" zotzed? 'Cause he'd been warded? I had a horrible image of what could happen if a Chicago Mob war ever escalated into a battle of warlocks, and shuddered.

But so far, everything I'd found here was low-grade, something any half-competent witch could cook up. No sign of darker magics or hexes, and certainly no sign of any sort of pact with the Fae—or *anything* to do with us, for that matter. All this trouble, and I was back where I'd started. I couldn't rule Scola out, since he obviously knew a little of the eldritch world—enough to get someone to protect him from it, at any rate—but neither did I have anything other than an old family grudge to suggest he *was* involved.

I shuffled around the house some more, aimlessly hunting for anything that'd tell me—well, anything. I didn't find any more about the magics, just a few more hidden protections (including an actual tuft of dried frankincense, holly, rosemary, and belladonna) that I'd missed on the first go-round. But I *did* find an answer to something else.

On the mantle over the fireplace was a photograph in a silver frame: a photo of a young mother and her son. They *coulda* been Scola's wife and kid, but she resembled him enough that I was more inclined to peg 'em as his sister and nephew. And I also knew, with no doubt at all, that they were the ones who'd lived in those bedrooms upstairs—those dusty, long-abandoned bedrooms that Scola had practically transformed into shrines.

I skittered over to the phone and dialed. Pete had taken a powder by then, and once I got Detective Keenan to take my call instead, he wasn't real shy about telling me how damn busy he was. Still and all, he was polite enough to take three winks to look into my question. I waited, he dug, he answered, I thanked him, he hung up. I stood for a few long minutes, holding the blower in my hand and staring off at nothing.

Car accident. They'd run smack into a truck hauling tractor parts, about four months before most of Scola's crew got cut down. Yeah, it coulda just been a bad break; it ain't like accidents are *rare*, right? But the timing nagged at me, and *something* had convinced Vince Scola that he needed some serious protection against the evil eye.

Was Donna Orsola really that harsh? Was she really so bitter over her own lost kin that she'd have laid a death curse on a woman, to say nothing of a *child*, just for being Scola's blood?

Well, she'd cursed me when I was *helping* her, just to send me a message. So yeah, I had to think that maybe she would. Jeez, what the hell kinda family was I working for? A witch who'd apparently gone completely off the track and an Outfit wiseguy... If it hadn't been for Bianca, I mighta started wondering if Celia wasn't better off with the goddamn *phouka*.

It gave me a lot to think about as I trudged back upstairs, made my way to the same window, and started watching for my best chance to slip back out into a night that was getting old far, far too quickly.

The sky in the east was just starting to blush a rosy pink—maybe 'cause we'd seen her before she was dressed for the morning?—as I stumbled my way back up the steps of Soucek's greystone in Pilsen. Around me, only a few flivvers and a couple of the old-fashioned horse-drawn milk wagons were rolling and clomping their way along the neighborhood streets. It'd been a long, long night, and since I hadn't yet come up with the foggiest notion what to do with Sleeping Beauty, it was looking to be a long, long day ahead.

After making a clean sneak from Scola's place, I'd caught the L and headed north, finally getting off on Lawrence. From there, it'd just been a couple blocks' walk to a fancy and really damn huge apartment, in a really damn huge apartment building. This was the home of one Nolan Shea, lieutenant to a lieutenant of Bugs Moran—and, more importantly, boss of the Uptown Boys.

It didn't go as smooth as the Scola house did, since Shea and some of his hoods had the audacity to actually be *home* when I was trying to bust into his place, tossing back hooch and playing checkers. A couple of those mugs were actually part of the group that'd jumped me on the L, so once they'd spotted me anyway, I made like I was there for some payback.

Heh. "Furious vacuum repairman seeks vengeance." Sounds like a bad picture or radio drama.

I let 'em tune me up a little, enough so I didn't come across as much of a threat anymore, and then skedaddled while they argued about where and how to murder me. (It wasn't hard to get away while they were distracted, since they thought I was way too badly hurt to move. If I was one of you, I woulda been.)

Anyway, point is I got myself a good look at the inside of Shea's place. The joint was so completely bare of anything even *resembling* the taste or feel of magic, I'd have been surprised to learn anyone had even ever tried a card trick in there. Not that it was too shocking—I hadn't thought the Uptown Boys were likely as suspects in Celia's disappearance, since the timing had been so off—but nevertheless, disappointing to hit another dead end. Waste of half a night, and a dozen perfectly good bruises.

I slouched down the stairs to my office, twisted the key in the lock with a grating squeal, and slipped inside. The place was starting to come over faintly pink, with the rising sun peeking in the high windows, more'n enough for me to see. For a second or two, I only had eyes for my chair, where I hoped I could catch a couple hours to dream before I had to deal with the "guest" occupying my bed. I was just draping my overcoat across the rack, and...

Froze. Carefully, trying for nonchalant, I turned back and gave the room another up-and-down. It was... Off. Not much—nothing missing, nothing obviously in the wrong place—but enough.

Hadn't that glass been closer to the edge of the desk? That one drawer been standing open a few more inches? Celia's hat been hanging off the other side of the chair?

There's a reason I'm a detective, y'know.

I took a few paces toward the bed. "I know you're awake," I said in a casual tone. "You can stop pretending."

Celia didn't move, but I heard the quick hitch in her breathing I'd been listening for. Oh, she was awake, all right.

It was then, in a spectacular case of "better late than never," that realization dawned on me.

Celia had been raised in Elphame. She had a grasp, however crude, of our basic magics. So yeah, just maybe the girl would be harder to keep under, and would recover quicker, than a regular human.

Oh, there's a reason I'm a detective, all right. It don't mean that sometimes I don't also make a pretty passable dunce.

I hunkered down beside the bed, staring her in the face. She breathed, softly, in and out, a pretty respectable imitation of slumber.

After a minute or two, I drew the L&G, held it over her head, and sorta *tapped* at her mind, just enough to make sure she'd notice I was doing something.

The girl bolted upright with a shriek, sheets flying, and slugged me one across the jaw that coulda taught Shea's boys a thing or two. I staggered back, already a smidge off-balance from the crouch, and fell hard on my keister.

"I see you *are* awake," I said, ruefully rubbing my chin. "I thought you—*Whoa!*"

Now that her ruse was over, she was off the bed and coming at me, my *own rapier* clutched in a competent grip. She musta had it hid under the covers with her.

Okay, that'd be right about enough of that. I rolled aside, letting the blade score a line in the carpeting, then rolled back fast. My whole torso came down on the flat, yanking the weapon from her fist. At the same time I reached up to jab her in the ribs with my wand, shoving her back physically and magically. Thanks to the tiny scrap of luck I knocked from her, her feet tangled in the wadded sheets and she fell back onto the mattress with a faint yelp.

By the time she was sitting, I was standing over her, holding the wand and rapier both.

"Trying to skewer a man with his own blade," I said, "is just *rude*." I chucked the rapier back behind me—after a quick glance to make sure it'd land safely across the chair.

"So's keeping a girl prisoner," she snapped, running a few fingers through her mussed hair and then crossing her arms resentfully.

"We been through this, Celia. You ain't a prisoner."

"No? So I can leave, then?"

"Uh… no, but not because you're…"

Jeez, I was slow on the uptake this morning.

"What the hell are you still doing here?" I almost shouted at her. "If you've been awake more'n a couple minutes, why the hell didn't you scram?"

Her entire face wrinkled in a petulant scowl, and she pressed her lips together until they went white.

"Listen, sister, you better—"

The whole office reverberated with the sudden knocking at the door.

I took a step back, trying to watch her and the door at once. Was that it? Had she called someone? Was—?

"Mr. Oberon? Mr. Oberon, is everything okay?"

I exhaled louder'n an old bellows. "Yeah, Mr. Soucek. Everything's fine."

"I heard screams."

"Nah, it's nothing." He heard Celia's shouts? From down here? Maybe he'd already been in the basement, fixing something... "Just an argument, got a little heated. You know how it is."

Celia was fidgeting; she couldn't have told me more clearly she was about to try something if she'd sent me a dated telegram. I shook my head, and she called me something girls her age aren't supposed to know.

"Mr. Oberon, please open the door, or I'll have to call the police."

I grumbled something, moved across the room, and reached for the knob...

Remember what I said about sometimes being a dunce? And being sluggish in the brain department that morning? I can only say, in my defense, that I was tired as hell and *real* distracted by a whole lotta big worries.

So I'd already cracked the door a hand's breadth when my senses finally caught up with the rest of my mind and said, *The accent's right, but when did Jozka take the grammar lessons?*

I immediately started to slam the door, but someone or something on the outside—a goddamn charging rhino from the feel of it—slammed it open. I hurtled back, empty hand clutching the side of my head where the edge had caught me, until I fetched up against the desk and dropped to one knee.

My sight blurring, I looked up to see Jozka Soucek striding into my office.

Except my sight wasn't the only thing blurring, and Soucek wasn't Soucek anymore.

CHAPTER THIRTEEN

With every step he took, the air wafting past him grew thicker with the tang of old straw and sun-baked grasses. His body shivered and swam, flesh flowing thick, like sap. For less'n a second his skin was rough and heavy, his clothes not clothes at all but a coarse layer of fur, and then the fella who'd been "Soucek" was human again.

He looked old, maybe seventy-five or eighty. He had a narrow face that was almost more of a prow, wrinkled as a wet newspaper and sprouting a scraggly tuft of beard that woulda looked more at home on a billy goat. His body was gaunt and hunched, so that he barely came up to my shoulders (or woulda done, if I'd been standing), and wrapped in a raggedy greatcoat.

I knew better'n to assume he was anywhere close to as decrepit as he looked.

"Goswythe, I presume?" I said, climbing back to my feet when he got about halfway between me and the door.

"Mick," he said with a nod.

"And Mr. Soucek?" If the *phouka* had hurt him, I swore he wasn't getting outta here alive, and I didn't make too much effort to keep that fact off my mug.

But, "Ah, don't get excited. I didn't hurt the geezer. He may sleep through a few appointments, is all." Then, "You okay, sweetheart?"

"I'll be fine when you get me clear of this bastard!" Celia barked.

"Aw, and here I thought we were getting along swell," I said. Then, "She called you, right? And you told her to stay put, instead of blowing this place... Why, exactly?"

Goswythe smirked, showing off a handful of missing teeth. "You'd just have come looking for her again, right? I figured this'd be the best opportunity to talk to you about that."

"Ah. And what've you got to say about it?"

"Don't."

I chuckled. "To the point. I can dig that. But you know I can't do that. She needs to learn the truth for her—"

"I've told her the truth," Goswythe interrupted. He gave his spindly shoulders a shrug and sidled over to the chair in front of my desk. With narrow, shriveled fingers he began idly rocking it back and forth as he spoke. "Look, Mick, it's not as though you can just hold her here against her will."

"She's a child, and her parents want her home. Legally—" And then I spun, arm raised, and handily caught the electric fan that Celia was about to use to brain me. I'm sharp enough to know a distraction when I see one.

Usually.

I shoved her with the wand in my other hand— again—and twisted back, pitching the fan at Goswythe's face even as he started to come around the desk. Both of 'em staggered, just a little, and I lunged.

At the girl, not the *phouka*.

She yelped as I shoved her, hard, sending her careening back into the bathroom. I cringed at the loud thump and a second, pained shout; something else she'd hold against me, no doubt. I jogged forward a few paces and hauled the bathroom door shut, then jabbed the knob with the L&G.

Between her shouting at me and the sound of the fan clattering into the corner where Goswythe tossed it, I barely heard the tiny clatter from inside the lock as the mechanism slipped out of alignment. She wouldn't be opening that door anytime soon.

I also made one other little tweak to the chance and probability surrounding the bathroom door. An ace in the hole, in case the next few minutes went as bad as I thought they might.

Ignoring the rattling of the knob, and then the angry pounding on the door, I turned back to the approaching *phouka*.

"It didn't have to go down this way, Mick," he said. He wasn't smiling anymore.

"Ah, sure it did. You weren't gonna walk outta here even if I *had* promised to leave you alone, anyway."

Well, he might have, if I'd actually taken a true oath to that effect; but we'd both known that wasn't gonna happen.

He slipped what I took, at first, to be a Colt .32 Police Positive from his coat pocket (and where the hell had that been while he was changing shape?). "You'll make a lotta noise with that," I warned. "You sure you wanna attract that kinda... Aw, crap."

Because it was then that I noticed the barrel was

blackened brass, the cylinder bronze. And once I'd recognized the weapon as Elphame-make, I caught just a whiff of its power on the air. Damn thing wasn't just a roscoe, but a wand as well.

Probably not as good as the Luchtaine & Goodfellow—most hybrid models ain't—but also probably good enough.

For a few heartbeats we locked stares, wands at hand, a peculiar echo of Old West gunslingers. And simultaneously, we both leaped aside in opposite directions, throwing magic as we dove.

I heard Goswythe crash painfully into the filing cabinet with bone-bruising force, his feet having got tangled in the same sheets that'd tripped Celia up earlier. But I wasn't in any position to gloat over it, since the pocket on my coat had snagged on the bathroom doorknob, yanking me to a halt as I moved and slamming me back into the wall—to say nothing of ripping an ugly, ragged hole in my favorite coat!

Wincing at the sharp twinge shooting through my shoulder blade—I shouldn't have hit the wall hard enough to hurt, but that's misfortune for you—I dropped to the carpet and crawled for the desk, L&G clenched in my teeth. I heard Goswythe scrabbling across the floor on the opposite side; this office really ain't big enough for a showdown…

A rat, big and brown and ugly, shot past the desk like a bullet in a fur stole, making a beeline for the bathroom. I wasn't entirely sure if the critter could squeeze through the gap under the door, but I was pretty sure I didn't wanna wait and find out.

Fucking shapeshifters.

Already on the floor, I grabbed my chair by the supports, right by two of the wheels, and threw myself forward, slamming it down. My rapier, which had been lying flat across the seat, went bouncing and sliding off across the carpet.

The rat skittered aside at the last second, chattering obscenely, but I'd driven it away from the bathroom. Since the chair had swiveled as it hit the floor, pivoting so it was lying back down, I shoved it forward, driving the edge under the door. If nothing else, maybe it'd block the rat from squeezing through.

Except it wasn't a rat anymore. Once more an old man, Goswythe stood over me, wand leveled. I tried to roll aside, but there wasn't much of anywhere to go. I could literally *feel* shreds of luck unraveling from around me as I struggled to dodge the worst of the blast. I slammed my knee painfully into the leg of the desk, froze for just a heartbeat at the flash of pain...

Goswythe stepped to the side and gave the desk a vicious shove. And thanks to the ugly things he'd just done to my fortunes, the screws holding that leg in place broke loose. It teetered, creaking and groaning, and then the entire dingus came crashing down across my legs, pinning me nice and tight.

And friggin' *painful*. Did I mention painful?

My heavy steel typewriter came sliding off the surface to slam into the carpet, and I *just* yanked my head far enough aside that I didn't wind up with a letter written across my face.

I heard the hammer click back on the *phouka*'s .32, and realized, now that he had me dead to rights, he was willing to risk the noise. It'd only take a single shot, too; sure, the slug itself probably wouldn't kill me, but it'd put me down long enough for him to finish the job in a dozen different ways.

Turns out that the fear of death makes for a pretty good motivator to focus past the pain in your legs and back, no matter how severe.

I clutched my wand in what I tried hard *not* to think of as a deathgrip, and sat up quick, my empty hand reaching for the fallen furniture. Goswythe came round the desk, heater raised, and his blinkers went *comically* wide as he saw me yanking a sawed-off double-barrel from the bottom drawer. He actually went pinwheeling off to one side as the shotgun roared, sending two loads of buckshot and a thick cloud of smoke into the office.

All this in spite of the fact that I don't *keep* a shotgun in my desk.

Goswythe probably recognized the illusion for what it was, sensing the magic and the deception before he'd finished his leap—and if he hadn't, the complete lack of damage to the wall behind him would sure have given the game away. But it bought me the extra time I needed to yank myself free and lift myself into a crouch. My knee screamed under me, but I ignored it.

The place was quiet, the banging from inside the bathroom long stopped. Again we paused, one of us on either side of what was rapidly becoming an *ex*-desk, each waiting for the other to make a move. And here I had the advantage; this was my place, familiar to me as the inside of my own eyelids. I listened, *really* listened, for any squeak, any clatter, anything that wasn't part and parcel of the office's normal chorus.

The faintest muffled creak of floorboard beneath carpet, and I had him. I knew precisely where he was.

Taking the wand in my teeth again, I lifted that typewriter in both hands and chucked it over the desk.

I heard a nasty *thump*, a cry of pain, and a loud *bang!* as the .32 went off. A chunk of plaster exploded from the far wall, and I was up and running long before the bits of powdery white began settling into the carpet. I dove across the floor, sliding a little, one hand outstretched toward the rapier that'd gone flying earlier, the other once again wrapped around my L&G.

Goswythe rose from behind the desk, one hand pressed to his bleeding scalp, the other aiming his weapon right for me. His finger was curled tight on the trigger, and I was pretty sure he was about to start squirting lead, not magic.

Which was fine, since it was about what I'd expected. I raised my own wand and threw everything I had through it.

Not at him, but at the gat.

It ain't *nearly* as easy to gum up the works on an Elphame gun as one of yours. We been over it already: ours may *look* more or less the same, but they work on magic, not springs and catches and whatnot. Nevertheless, there's a balance of power and forces inside that, with the right mystical nudge and more'n a little touch of bad luck, can be *un*balanced.

He pulled the trigger, and the gun made a satisfying *click*. He'd barely gotten the first of what was undoubtedly a whole caravan of curses through his yap when I was up and lunging. My knee *almost* gave out from under me, but I made it across the room.

I felt the tip of the rapier slow as it punched through something solid. Blood—a lot more thin and watery than human, or *aes sidhe* for that matter—splattered across the office, my coat, my face. It wasn't a fatal hit, not on a *phouka*; just 'cause some of 'em learn to *look* human don't mean they keep their organs in the same place inside. But I knew it *had* to hurt.

He spun away from me, toppling, his roscoe falling at my feet. I saw him reaching out his arms to catch himself and moved in behind, ready to finish him—or at least make sure he stayed down for a good long while.

Except Goswythe had other plans. And I'll tell you square, he suckered me. I thought I'd hurt him worse'n I had, thought I'd knocked the fight from him.

When he started to fall, what he'd stretched out were hands; by the time they hit the carpet, they were hooves. I had just about an eyeblink to comprehend that I was staring right at the ass end of a sorrel-spotted Clydesdale that had to weigh over a ton…

Before the friggin' thing bent forward and kicked me square in the chest with both back legs.

Ribs cracked and I completely left the floor, sailing in a disturbingly graceful arc across the room. The whole world seemed to slow down, and I actually had the time to marvel (albeit grudgingly) at Goswythe's creativity, and to note sourly that I was gonna owe Soucek a thick roll of lettuce to pay for the repairs, before I slammed into and through the office door. Slivered wood, shattered glass, and a bent brass hinge rained down around me as I crashed down awkwardly in the hall.

I actually bounced right back to my feet and managed a few stumbling steps before the deep bruises, the cracked bones, and the thousand-and-one splinters and lacerations all punched through the adrenaline and proceeded to stomp up and down on my brain. Only about a pace or so back into the office, I dropped to my knees like I was about to lay my head on the block. I had the L&G in one hand, a random shard of wood that I didn't even remember grabbing in the other, and it actually took me a few ticks to tell which was which.

Guess it coulda been worse, though. At least Goswythe couldn't create horseshoes.

And the *phouka* wasn't doing too much better'n me. He didn't even have room to turn around with his current bulk—hell, his transformation alone had shoved the broken desk even further across the room—so he shifted yet again back to his old-man shape, twisting toward me in the process. One step, one more, and then he also collapsed, hand clutching the uneven, bleeding wound where I'd run him through.

Both of us on the floor, neither quite ready or able to tap into whatever reserves we had left, we settled briefly for trying to stare each other to a pulp.

Then his gaze shifted, and we recognized right about the same time that he was now a *lot* closer to the bathroom than I was. He grinned at me through blood-slick teeth.

"Just let her go," I wheezed—begged?—as he started to crawl. "Let her make her own choice."

"She's mine," he gasped back, barely audible. "And you know what she'd pick."

"Only 'cause she believes that bunk you shoveled. Why don'tcha see what she decides when you tell her what *really* happened?"

His steady slither hitched to the side as he shrugged. "Don't know what really happened. Don't care how they got her. They gave her to me; that's all that matters." He pulled up short, then, peering first at the bathroom door, then back at me, a growing suspicion furrowing his brow.

"Ah, c'mon," I said, starting to drag myself further into the room. "The acoustics in this place? I mean, what're the odds she actually heard every word you just said through that door?"

Pretty damn slim, in fact; almost impossible.

And you know by now how much I love playing with "almost." Such as, for instance, that little extra twist of luck I wove when I gummed up the lock. Sometimes I'm so clever I could just shake my own hand, if it wouldn't look so awkward.

His whole body shaking, now—with pain, worry, anger, who knows?—Goswythe wrapped all ten fingers around the doorknob and hauled himself upright. He kept his grip briefly, probably struggling to focus long enough to make the lock's tumblers slip back into place, and then yanked the door open. He staggered, nearly fell...

Then he *did* fall, his watery blood gushing from a brand-new scalp wound as a red-faced Celia brained him with the shower-curtain rod.

"You *fucking bastard*!" Tears enough to hold a baptism rolled down cheeks already growing puffy, and her sobs racked her whole body until I thought for sure she'd just collapse. She didn't look like a young woman anymore, but a lost little girl—except for the tin rod, already bent and mangled, she was using to bludgeon the foster father who'd duped her.

"Celia, dollface…" Goswythe shoulda known better than to even try talking, since it just bought him a rap across the mouth rather than the head. Again she hit him, and again, until the curtain rod fell from her shaking fingers—and then she just switched to pounding him with her fists.

"Enough!" The *phouka* actually *roared*, his jaw and his yap distending to produce the sound, startling her back a step. He clambered to his feet once more and slapped her hard across the face. "You don't *ever* raise a hand to me, kitten! I —"

"Hands *off*, pal!" I was standing myself, now, and that long sliver of wood I'd picked up was gone, replaced by the rapier I'd recovered from the wreckage. It, and my wand, were both pointing right at him. I'm impressed with myself, too; I managed to keep both of 'em from trembling.

"We're finishing this, are we?" he asked softly.

"Imagine we'd better," I said, hoping against hope that he'd run outta steam before I did. "We—"

At which point, Celia—who I guess didn't precisely need rescuing—produced a shard of broken mirror, one end wrapped in a hand towel, and shivved Goswythe in the side.

He screamed and lashed out with a brutal backhand, but this time she'd seen it coming and jumped aside. I think he really wanted to go after her, but that woulda meant turning his back on *me*.

I decided about that point to rethink my methods of interacting with the girl; maybe I oughta be a little more careful about getting her angry. Though I did wish she coulda come up with a way of arming herself that didn't involve dismantling my bathroom.

(She had to have been *really* furious to risk breaking the mirror to arm herself. I mean, she was human, so it wasn't the same kinda bad luck to her that it woulda been to us—but still, she'd been *raised* by Fae. It couldn't have come easy.)

The three of us stood ready, each of us nerving ourselves up for whatever was coming next—except that not a one of us was prepared for what *did* come next.

An ear-smashing *crack* sounded from the hallway outside, making everybody jump. I took the risk of looking away from Goswythe long enough to lean back, craning my head to see out. As though in solidarity with my office door, the one to the stairway had blown open with matching force, splitting at the latch and sending chunks of plaster sifting down from the wall where it hit. Footsteps and voices echoed from the stairwell, and a half-dozen guys came pouring into the hall. Every one of 'em was dressed in a snazzy three-piece, and every one of 'em was packing a goddamn Tommy gun.

And standing in the lead, veins bulging in his head and teeth gritted hard enough to grind concrete, was Fino "the Shark" Ottati. Archie Echoes followed right behind him, and if he wasn't looking as hot under the collar, well, he seemed ready enough to do whatever it was they'd come to do.

You ever stare down the pipe of *one* Chicago

typewriter, let alone *six* of 'em? It's fucking scary. I may not kick off as easy as most of you fellas, but getting chewed up by one of *those* bastards ain't something I'm eager to try. It *might* not finish me off, but I'm pretty sure I'd never be pretty again. So you better believe I made like a snowman. Across the office, Goswythe did the same, while Celia...

Actually, I didn't *see* Celia anymore. Apparently, soon as the commotion started, she'd ducked back into the bathroom.

Smart girl. Right now, I kinda wished I was in there with her.

"You *fucking bastard!*" her father shrieked at me. (I decided now wasn't the time to chuckle over the "like father, like daughter" cursing.) "You stupid, fucking *leccacazzi*! What the fuck have you done?!"

"I—" Which is about as far as I got before I figured out that Fino Ottati wasn't expecting much of an answer. His face went red; Archie's lips and left shoulder twitched in what mighta been an apologetic shrug, or just a nervous tic.

Three of the choppers opened up, and I had a lot more to repair than just the door and the desk.

I hurled myself aside, but not quite fast enough. A .45 slug punched through my left hip, spinning me completely around in the air as I was toppling and spraying blood and bits of muscle in a wake behind me. I slammed hard to the floor, crying out, and felt my tongue bleeding from where I'd bit down. Pieces of my desk pretty much just ceased to exist, and my sheets and mattress turned into cheap fishing nets. Smoke choked the room in an early indoor sunset; my ears rang with the rapid *tak-tak-tak* of the

Tommies, the thump of slugs setting up shop in the walls, and a constant gong that I realized only later had been the sound of more slugs ricocheting off my steel filing cabinet.

Huddled as small as I could get, hands over my head, I glanced across the office, *through* the disintegrating desk, and saw that Goswythe was down. I couldn't tell exactly where he'd been clipped, but I saw the blood pool seeping into and spreading out through the carpet around him. He was alive—I saw him moving—but even if he was feeling inclined to help me out against a common enemy, he wasn't in much shape to do it.

After about sixteen or seventeen years that probably weren't *actually* too much more'n that many seconds, the gats quit coughing long enough for Fino and a couple of his boys to step into the room and take stock. The Shark was ranting and spitting so much that I was floored he hadn't just keeled over for lack of air, but he'd switched over to Italian, and I wasn't much in a state of mind to focus on what he was saying. Instead, I gathered my good leg up under me so I could move, tried to steady the L&G long enough to get off a few shots at the Tommies, peeped down at my busted hip, which was still bleeding and...

Smoking? The wound was *smoking*?

No, not the wound. The pocket of my overcoat. Something inside was burning. I racked my brain, wondering what could possibly...

Oh. Yeah, that actually kinda made sense.

I heard a couple of bolts yanked back, knew the choppers were about to open up again—and then I heard, instead of shots, a pair of gasps, one from the door, the other from the bathroom.

Drawn by the sudden pause in the lead thunderstorm, Celia had poked her head out for a quick peek—and her father had seen her. Ottati's peepers shimmered like he was about to cry, and for a couple heartbeats, everyone and everything froze.

And that gave me those heartbeats to think.

Orsola. It'd been Bianca's lock of hair that'd spontaneously combusted in my pocket, and it wasn't too hard to tumble why. The witch musta used it to divine where I was, maybe even that I'd found the girl; no wonder she'd finally been willing to give it up. Probably shoulda seen it coming, if I wasn't so friggin' worn out and looking nineteen directions at once. So now she'd sent her son, and she wanted to make sure I couldn't use the hair in my own magics. But could she really have done that from—?

Ottati howled something completely unintelligible and came my way, raising the Chicago typewriter again. Hopping on one leg, wishing I could ignore what it was doing to my broken ribs, I flung myself across the office toward cover—and, not incidentally, putting myself between him and the bathroom. I know it sounds heartless, but I was sure he wasn't about to open fire with his daughter in the killing zone.

Well, I was *pretty* sure... But damn it, I wasn't gonna just sit there and let him perforate me!

And I was right, mostly. He dropped the chopper and yanked a Colt "vest pocket" model from, well, his vest pocket. Guess he figured he had more control that way. "*Muoia, stronzo! Muoia!*" He was back to ranting, trying to line up his shot even as I dove behind the demolished desk *again*. "*Tutto è incazzato! Hai rovinato tutto!*"

A couple of .25 slugs dug into the wood and cheap metal of the desk, but they didn't quite have the power to punch through. I was breathing heavy, trying to steady myself, regain a little bit of focus. And that, with another second's thought, was when everything finally fell into place.

Tutto è incazzato! Hai rovinato tutto!
It's all fucked up! You've ruined everything!
Oh, swell…

"Fino!" My answer was another bullet plowing into my pathetic barricade. "Fino, goddamn it, hold your fire! For *your daughter's sake*, stop shooting!" I took a gamble and raised my hands so they were both visible over the desk. When he didn't immediately try to blow 'em off, I poked just enough of my head up to look. "She's in danger, Fino! We've gotta—"

Too late. *She was already here.*

I saw her, a short, dark-haired shape behind Fino and his boys, moving, *gliding* through the hall, her feet *never touching the floor…*

Orsola Maldera raised her hands, some kinda grey powder spilling from one, old and clotted blood from the other. She shouted, her voice more deafening than the gunfire, a horrible word, or maybe a name; something not English, not Italian, not ever intended for human mouths.

I couldn't move, couldn't act. I was too far to reach her, too weak to try, too hurt and beaten to focus whatever magics I mighta had left. A bank of darkness, not visible but *tangible*, a shadow of the soul, rolled like a bomb blast down the hall and through the doorway. I felt a horrible vertigo, a spike of nausea worse'n anything I'd felt inside her wards.

And then I didn't feel, or see, or think anything at all.

CHAPTER FOURTEEN

Nothingness, complete and utter. Absent. Empty. No dreams. You mortals spend swathes of every night this way?! How do you stand it? I'd go absolutely—

"...think I oughta put a slug right between his fucking..."

Huh. Thinking. Thoughts. Thoughts are good. Means there's not nothing, right? The nothingness is going away, and if there's not nothing, that means there's gotta be—

"...dare! We need him! *She* needs him! We can't..."

Oh, there's something all right. Pain. Oh, holy shit do I hurt!

Hey, I *hurt! I have an "I" again!*

"...from his kind! Fuck, you know what he is? He ain't even..."

Yeah, I. Me. Mick Oberon. Mick Oberon, PI, whose office was just blasted to hell and back by a lunatic chopper squad.

And not just my office, either.

"...matter what he is, he found her once, he can do it again!"

Fingers wiggling, and toes. Okay, that's good. Everything works. Really hurts, *though... Chest's aching, hip's throbbing, but I can breathe okay. Leg strong enough to stand? Dunno; not standing...*

"...need anyone to find her! I just gotta get hold of Mama, talk to her, work this..."

Better than before I went under, at least. Pain's faded, breathing's easier. Wish I had more time to rest up and heal, but...

"...told me your mother's the one who took her! We can't trust anything she..."

...but those goddamn voices *aren't about to let me, and would they please just shut up, shut up...*

"Shut up!"

I pried my lids open and rocked upright, trying to find a position to sit that wasn't pulling at my ribs or my hip, and failing miserably to find one. The light stung for just a few, 'til I adapted, and the first thing I saw was a garishly upholstered sofa.

Yep, I was sitting in that same damn sitting room, back at the Ottati house; they musta woken up faster'n I did—which probably meant I'd been the primary target of Orsola's spell, surprise, surprise—and dragged me back here. I was on the floor, obviously. Even if I hadn't felt the floorboards under me, the fact that I was nose to nose with the furniture was a pretty solid indicator. A quick glance around showed me some table legs and more chairs, farther away than I'd expected. They'd cleared the center of the room—come to think of it, hadn't there been a rug here, last time?—obviously in preparation for...

Oh, come *on*.

Yep, there it was, spread out in an uneven circle all around me. Salt, mostly, but I could see the occasional twists and bulges of the runes chalked onto the wood under it—and, more importantly, beneath the tang of tea and booze that permeated the room, I smelled the rusty powdered iron mixed in with the salt. It was sloppy, slipshod; clearly not Orsola's work. I stretched out, first with curiosity alone, then with an extended finger. Both times, I hit the edge of the circle and felt as though I was trying to push through a heavy curtain of cobweb.

I patted halfheartedly at my pockets, and even wiggled a finger through the holes in what *used* to be a pocket. Just as I'd expected, no wand. Yeah, I could get through the ward… given time. Hours.

Y'know, I just didn't think I *had* hours.

"Fucking cut it out!" This as I prodded at the barrier a second time. I blinked, popped my neck, and scooted around to see my "captors."

Neither of the Ottatis looked too good. Fino's hair was mussed, his jacket was off, and his shirt was untucked and hanging out from under his vest. Bianca's makeup was smeared, and her jaw was clenched hard.

"What's the matter, Fino? Don'tcha stand behind your work?"

"You shut the fuck up, you *stronzo bestiale*!"

"Yeah, your mamma calls me names, too." I shrugged. "It ain't half bad work, for an amateur. You been taking lessons?"

"I said shut up, before I blow your fucking head off like I shoulda done back in your office!" And yeah, maybe it was just theatrics, but he was reaching into his vest pocket even as he spoke.

"But you didn't," I said, a little more calmly. "Because you want me to find Celia. Again."

"Her name ain't Celia!" He was actually shrieking, now, and I swore I could feel a breeze from his twitching eyelid. "It's Adalina!"

"No. No, Fino. Your *other* daughter's name is Adalina."

Bianca choked on a muffled sob; Fino flushed red and turned away.

"Can you find her again, Mr. Oberon?" Bianca asked. I thought her husband's glare alone might knock her off her feet, but she stood firm.

"That depends, Mrs. Ottati. First, have you asked your husband why he arranged for her to vanish in the first place?"

I actually hadn't been positive until the words came out, but yeah, I was sure. It actually wasn't that hard to piece together, now that I had enough to work with.

"What?" I can't even rightly call it a whisper; it was just a breath dressed up as a word. Her skin wasn't pale so much as it was practically transparent.

Fino roared something that was even less of a word and skinned his .25. The first shot went completely wide, ripping into the sofa a good few feet off to my left. His whole body shaking, he swung the piece further toward me, ready for another shot with a whole lot better aim...

Bianca stepped between us, her shoulders so rigid you coulda crucified a man on 'em.

"Get the fuck outta the way! I'm gonna kill this fucking *stronzo*!"

She didn't move, didn't flinch; I'm not sure she even *breathed*.

"Bianca, *move*!"

"Is it true, Fino?"

"What the fuck? 'Is it true'?!" The gun was shaking so bad now, I think the pin might actually have missed the shell if he'd fired. "He's a fucking *faerie*! You can't buy a fucking word he says!"

"Is it true?"

"I said *move*!" Fino reached out to shove his wife out of the way, and a sharp report echoed across the room.

Not a gunshot at all, but about the most vicious slap I'd ever seen. Fino didn't just stagger, he actually dropped to one knee. His empty hand rose to his reddened cheek and bleeding lip as he stared incredulously upward. Bianca loomed over him, her fists clenched. "You son of a bitch! *Is it true?*"

"No, Bianca! No, it's—it's not…" The gun, and Fino's gaze, both dropped toward the floor. "Yeah." His voice cracked. "Oh, *Madon'*, yes. It's true."

She fell on him with a horrified, tormented wail, flailing with both fists. Fino didn't raise an arm, didn't fall back, as she hit him again, and again, and again.

I could make out part of what she said, between punches and heaving, gut-wrenching sobs, but I ain't repeating it. You don't need to know.

"Bianca," I said softly after a moment, "that's enough." She literally fell away from him, slumping to the floor, her face buried in her palms as her entire body shook. Fino, rumpled and bleeding, reached a hand out for her and stopped, clearly afraid to touch her—and not, I think, because he might get hit again. For a time, we all just sat, maybe afraid that any movement would shatter something, or someone.

Through the doorway behind them, at the top of

the staircase where I couldn't see, I thought I heard the creak of a step and the sound of something settling.

Finally, with a pained grunt, I pulled my calves in under me, sitting crosslegged; it was more comfortable for the rest of me, no matter the murder it was committing on my hip.

"Bianca," Fino began, "I—"

"Don't you talk to me! Don't you dare say a fucking word!"

Part of me wanted to let him suffer a little. I mean, the gink shot up my office, and put a slug through my hip!

But I didn't; there wasn't time. "Go easy on him, Bianca," I said. "He did it for her. Didn't you, Fino?"

They both stared at me, her incredulous, him hesitant. And then, reluctantly, he nodded.

"I don't understand," Bianca said. "What…?" Her lips kept moving, but the question wouldn't come.

"It don't matter," he began. "I—"

"Oh, it matters, Fino," I said, refusing to flinch from a glower that woulda intimidated most of his Mob rivals. "It's time for you to decide which side of the family you're on. You can't play the middle anymore."

Again he looked away. I saw him fiddling with the pistol, but at least he wasn't making any move to raise it.

"You knew, didn't you?" I pressed. "You knew what she was planning, and you wanted to protect your little girl."

"No! No, I didn't—" Fino sighed and slowly rose, leaving the roscoe on the carpet. Gently, he reached out, offering a hand to Bianca; hesitantly, she took it, and stood beside him. With a sorrowful smile, he led her to two of the chairs along the wall, guided her into one and just about fell into the other.

I thought about asking if he'd be willing to let me the hell outta this damn glyph so I could find a more comfortable seat myself—this *really* wasn't doing my hip any good—but somehow, I didn't figure this was the right time for a change of topic.

"You shoulda known her before," Fino said, and though he was looking right at me, I'm pretty sure he wasn't *talking* to me. Not mostly, anyway. "Back in Sicily, when I was a boy. We weren't *rich*, but we were comfortable. Better off'n most. I knew even then Papa was into some ugly business, that we were part of something bigger'n just our family. But I didn't get what that meant, at that age."

"*Cosa Nostra*?" I asked.

"Yeah. I mean, we didn't call it that, but yeah."

"All right." I went motionless for a minute, thinking. "You and your mother came to America well before *il Duce* started cracking down on the Mafia, so I'm figuring things went a little downhill?"

Fino snorted. "Yeah, like a fucking avalanche. We had a lotta rival families, back then. Politics, neighborhoods, routes; everybody wanted what everyone else had, yeah?

"I think… I think Mama coulda recovered from losing Papa, if she'd had time, y'know? But it was less'n two months after that when Alessandro died. He was nineteen months—*nineteen*—into a two-year bit, when someone had him whacked. We—"

"Hang on," I said, raising a hand. I was pretty sure I knew what the answer was, but I hadda be sure. "Alessandro?"

"My brother," Fino said sadly. "Mama's only other child."

Yep; that was it. "Lemme guess, Fino. Older'n you?"

"Uh, yeah. Almost three years. Why?"

"I'll get there. Go on." Actually, what I wanted was to just blurt out everything I suspected and make up the parts I didn't; anything to get 'em to let me outta this fucking cage and find Celia before it was too late. But if I didn't know exactly what I was getting into, the witch'd squash me—and besides, even if he was starting to talk, and to listen, I didn't think Fino was ready to just up and spring me.

For his part, Fino shrugged and said, "We knew who'd done it—or which family, anyway—same as we'd known when Papa was killed. Me'n my cousins hit 'em back, hard, but Mama... She just sorta stopped. Spent all her time in mourning, or in prayer. And I swear, every time anyone in our family got whacked, no matter how distant a cousin, she just got worse.

"I hadda get her away from there, so when the opportunity came to come to America..." He shrugged again. "And it worked, for a while. She seemed to shake off the worst of it, started living again. And then..."

"Then," I finished for him, "you found out the other families were here, too."

"Yeah. The Scolas, the Giovaniellos, all of 'em. I never seen Mama so angry as the first time she ran into one of 'em, over at the market, not even the day we learned about Alessandro. I actually locked up all the heaters in the house, make sure she didn't do nothing stupid."

"Which didn't stop her from cursing everyone who threatened you," I pointed out.

"Mama taught me all about the *Benandanti*, but she hadn't practiced much in the Old Country, 'cept occasionally to keep us going in lean times or divine whether a new plan would go well. But here... Well, she was angry, and I sure wasn't gonna turn away the help."

"But she didn't stop there, did she?"

He shuddered—Fino "the Shark" Ottati, vicious gangster, *shuddered*—and Bianca put a hand over his. He reached out with the other, squeezed it hard. "She was so happy when Bianca and I got married, even though..." He hesitated, glanced her way. "Even though she never really seemed too fond of Bianca."

Bianca nodded; obviously, despite how well they'd appeared to get on when they were meeting with me, this came as no big surprise.

"And then..." He looked down at his—their—hands.

"Then," I said, "you tumbled to *why*. Lemme guess again... While Bianca was expecting?"

They glanced at each other, and this time it was Fino who nodded. "Mama hadn't taught me much, but I'd learned some of the basics of her craft." I poked once at the edge of the circle, basically saying *Yeah, I can see that*. Also basically saying *Lemme the hell out*, but either he didn't get that, or he ignored it. "She'd been working hard for a few months, pretty much ignoring everything else—*except* making sure Bianca and the baby were doing okay. One day I got into her stuff to see what she was up to, and I found an old book she'd never showed me.

Real old. Parts of it were in… I don't even know. Languages I never seen before. But her notes, those were *Italiano*, those I could read. It wasn't enough to tell me much, but I got that it was a fucking ugly curse of some sort—made the *malocchio* look like cheap superstition. And…" Fino was chewing his lip and tongue something fierce, now. "And it required the blood of a firstborn relative to focus."

Bianca gasped, and whatever color had started seeping back into her cheeks disappeared. "Jesus and Mary, Fino! How could you not tell me?"

"She's my mama! She was just angry, she—"

"*Just angry?* She was going to kill our baby!"

"No! Not kill, just spill some blood! Mama would never have—"

"You can't be sure of that, Fino!"

"Yes, I—"

"*If* you were so sure," I interrupted, making no effort at all to keep the exasperation outta my voice, "why'd you interfere, Fino?"

He was starting to make a habit of avoiding my gaze. "I didn't want my little girl involved in nothing like that," he protested. I didn't believe that was the whole of it, not for a minute, and clearly Bianca didn't either. "I didn't want her caught up in black magics and curses, and… And…"

"And maybe getting hurt," Bianca insisted. This time, Fino didn't argue.

"Look," he said finally, "I done a lot of nasty things, and I wasn't in any position to refuse help, even the kind Mama was offering. But ancient curses, the blood of children…? *Maddon'*, I didn't want nothing to do with *that*. Not for me, and no fucking way for my little girl!"

"I gotta admit," I said, "your solution was brilliant." Then, at Bianca's outraged gasp, "Think about it, Mrs. Ottati. It ain't as though he was gonna kill his mother. He didn't know enough witchcraft to protect the kid, and there sure as hell wasn't anyplace he could hide her where Orsola wouldn't find her. Or at least, nowhere *here*. But in the Otherworld…"

Fino actually managed a half-smile. "It sure wasn't my first idea, but yeah. Way I figured, Mama would think it was just bad luck—the whims of the *fate*, see?—and my baby would be safe."

"*Safe?*" I couldn't hold back an ugly snicker. "You clearly don't know as much about us as you think."

"Yeah, safe! It was part of the pact. I made sure of it!"

"And the changeling?" I asked.

"We wanted a child," he whispered. Now it was Bianca he couldn't bring himself to look at, yet he was clearly speaking to her again, not me. "And I didn't want you to ever know."

"Because you knew I wouldn't approve, you—!"

"Because I wanted you to be happy."

The clack of her jaw snapping shut pretty closely mimicked the hammer on a revolver. She began picking at the upholstery on the chair, pulling tiny threads and chipping her nails, and I don't think she ever so much as noticed.

"You'd be happy," he repeated. "Nobody in the *famiglia* would ever know anything was wrong, Mama'd never have any reason to suspect I was involved, we'd have a little girl of our own, and our *real* baby'd be safe! What else could I have done, *tesora*?"

"Yeah, um," I interrupted before Bianca could even draw breath to answer, "I ain't so much interested in what else you coulda done, as I am in what Mommy *did* do. 'Cause I sure as spit don't buy that she just forgot all about the whole shebang soon as her plan went off the rails." I don't even remember standing up, but I must have, since I was looking *down* at them in their seats. Good thing Fae aren't prone to the fidgets, or I'd probably have been pacing like a caged animal. *That* woulda made 'em stop thinking of me as a "creature," wouldn't it?

"You know," Bianca said thoughtfully, "there *was* something..." She reached out for the table, also pushed back against the wall, and poured herself a cup of cold, day-old tea. It got almost to her mouth before she stopped and stared into it, seemingly unsure what it was.

"It was right after Adalina... Celia... After the baby was born," she continued softly. "Donna Orsola grew *very* depressed, unsociable. She spent all her time either in church, or locked in her room. I don't think we saw her for an hour a day for three years. I just thought..." She shrugged at Fino. "I thought she was upset the child wasn't a boy."

"You know it never mattered to me, doll. I—"

Time to interrupt again. Geez, you people get sidetracked so damn easy! "I think we can assume," I said, "that Orsola was spending her time trying to come up with a way of divining the girl's... Look, can we just call her 'Celia' for now? I know you ain't happy using the name Goswythe gave her—

that's the *phouka* she was with," I clarified to the their furrowed brows. "—but we gotta call her *something*. Anyway, looking for a way to divine Celia's location, even in Elphame. And we can also assume she came up snake eyes."

Fino rose, started pacing a little, caught Bianca's glare and quickly sat back down. "Yeah, you're probably right. She *threw* herself into those smaller curses after that, hitting hard at anyone who looked like they was threatening me and my business."

"I heard about a few," I said blandly.

"So why didn't she say anything?" Bianca asked. "If she knew Adalina was a—a changeling this whole time, why keep quiet about it?"

It was actually the Shark who answered. "What was she gonna say, *tesoro*? Even if she thought I'd buy it, the rest of the family woulda thought she'd gone fucking nuts. And we couldn't have done nothing about it, anyway. All it woulda done was distract me from everything else. Fuck, she mighta worried that we'd have lost one of our wars on account of me being, uh, preoccupied.

"Nah, what *I* don't get," he continued, squinting at me as if it was *my* fault, "is why she didn't go to you sooner. You been around Chicago for a while now, right?"

"Yeah…"

"And Mama knew what you are."

I shrugged. "I dunno for how long, but yeah, she tumbled to it. Maybe one of her spirits told her."

"Whatever. So why didn't she hire you *years* ago?"

"Because," I explained, "the crazy witch didn't—"

"Hey!" Fino was up from his seat again, fists raised. "Don't you fucking talk about my mama that way, you... you..."

I'd like to think it was my own glare of utter disdain that shut him down, but honestly, Bianca's was worse. He actually cringed away from her, a whipped puppy, before he muttered something unintelligible and sat back down—in another chair, a little farther away from the both of us.

I rolled my peepers *hard* at Bianca, who managed a feeble grin, before I continued. "Because the *crazy witch* didn't want to endanger her soul."

Fino blinked at me. "What?"

"Brilliant question," I said. "You been practicing for that one?"

"Why do you think your mother sent me," Bianca asked him, "instead of going herself?"

"What the fuck are you talking about? I don't—"

"Orsola believes I'm an unholy, soulless creature," I said. "Half a step up from a demon. It'd endanger her immortal soul to 'have congress' with me. But what the hell, no reason *Bianca* can't make all the arrangements, and Orsola just flit around the edges, right? I mean, *her* soul ain't important at all."

"Hey, Mama would never—" This time, he shut *himself* up, instead of waiting for one of us to do it for him. I think we were starting, finally, to get it through his head that, hell yes, Mama *would*.

"Are you trying to fucking tell me," he asked after a moment, "that Mama's got no problem throwing black magic curses that get folks fucking whacked, or using her own granddaughter's blood in some fucking witchcraft ritual, but making a deal with something like you, *that's* a sin got her worried about her soul?"

"Do you need me to *explain* 'crazy witch' to you, Fino?" And then, "Look, pal, I don't pretend to fully get what goes on in your mother's head. The men she's cursing are evil, least where she's concerned, and threatening her family to boot. The spirits she calls on are under her complete control, and she only uses those magics to *thwart* evil, or what she believes is evil. It ain't *that* hard to imagine how she justifies it, but that's all we're doing: imagining. You wanna know *exactly* what she's thinking, why don'tcha try grilling her instead of me. Just decide if you wanna do it before or after she does whatever she's gonna do to your daughter!"

"What, you think, after all this time, she's still—?"

"Yeah, I think so. And so do you."

Fino frowned, but nodded. "Everything I did," he murmured. "All for nothing. Fucking useless."

"It wasn't a bad scheme," I said. "You just didn't finish your homework. You shoulda known the changeling might grow outta looking and acting human."

"And once Adalina had changed enough to convince me she was some *creature*," Bianca finished bitterly, "it was easy enough for Orsola to manipulate me into hiring—"

A piercing, bitter wail whipped through the room, bursting Bianca's words like balloons. It was followed first by a hurled hairbrush, whipping across the room from the stairs and rebounding from the wall near Bianca's head, then by the sound of feet pounding on the steps and the deafening crash of the front door slamming hard enough to shake the house.

Shit! Damn it, I'd known she was there, eavesdropping, on the staircase—I'd *heard* her!—and still I'd forgotten. She'd heard it all, every last slashing word of it.

Poor kid.

"Adalina!" Bianca sprinted outta the room, was at the front door before a thunderstruck Fino had even finished rising from his seat. She fumbled at the knob, yanking the door open. "Oh, Jesus. I don't see her! Fino, *I don't see her*!"

"She *can't* have vanished that fucking fast! She—Bianca! Goddamn it, take Archie and some of the boys! Don't go searching around out there by yourself! Bianca!"

No telling if she'd heard or not. She was already gone, the door swinging gently in her wake.

Me, I was dealing with another surprise, though a pretty minor one, all things considered. *Archie? He still trusted Archie?*

Fino was practically dancing, taking a few steps toward the door, a few back toward me. Then, cursing up a storm—mostly variations on "fucking fuck"—he stomped back in and started pacing the sitting room, instead of the hall.

"You got your boys here?" I asked. "They ain't doing too good a job, if they didn't come running when you popped off that slug earlier."

He stopped his back-and-forth long enough to glare. "They're in the fucking flivvers outside. That okay with you, wise-ass? I didn't want 'em overhearing everything we hadda fucking talk about."

All right, that made a certain amount of sense. Fino went back to pacing.

"You're worried for her!"

Again he stopped. "Of *course* I'm fucking worried for her, mick!" I'm honestly not sure if he meant that capitalized, or if he was trying to rile me up. "She's my—"

I actually smiled a little—a genuine one—at the shock on his face. "Yeah," I told him, trying to come across at least a little bit gentle. "Yeah, Fino, she is."

"Aw, fuck." He turned away, his shoulders hunched, seemingly against an oncoming storm.

"Fino, let me out of here."

"What?" He nearly stumbled on the carpet, so quickly did he spin back to me. "Fuck no! Whaddaya think I—?"

"I can help you, goddamn it! I can find Adalina, I can find Celia. Whatever your mother's got going down, it's *big*, and you know it! Let me help!"

"I don't fucking trust you! You *fate* always have a Chinese angle on everything."

"Look, you idiot, I'm just trying to—"

"No. No fucking chance."

Sigh. "Okay, fine. Then tell me about last night."

"What?"

Sigh. Again. "Fino," I said, and I swear I was *trying* to sound patient, "Orsola had some kinda spell on me, so she could locate Celia. She probably tumbled the minute I first spotted the girl. So why didn't you show up to pump my joint full of lead until this morning?"

"She didn't fucking tell me you had her until this morning!"

"Right. So what was she doing with that time?"

"Fuck, I dunno. She spent some of it in church, I remember that. Otherwise..." He offered me a flex of one shoulder that was way too unambitious to make it all the way into a shrug. "I was busy."

"Oh, for the love of... This is *important*, you twit! Can't you remember—"

I actually jumped a little when the phone rang, much—judging by his quick chuckle—to Fino's amusement. He headed for the door, and out into the main hall toward the chiming blower.

"Uh, Fino? Don'tcha think maybe they can just call back? This is—"

"Important, yeah, yeah, blah, blah. So's this." Then, *clatter*, "Yeah? Yeah. Uh-huh. Where? Yeah."

I tried, I tried *hard*. But a voice on the other end of the line, with the receiver pressed hard to another Joe's ear, in the next room over? Even *my* hearing ain't *that* good, and without my wand, stuck in an iron glyph, no way I could make myself lucky enough, not in the time I had.

"So?" I asked him as he scurried back into the room. He dropped to one knee, and I thought at first he was about to be sick, until I saw he was scooping up the roscoe he'd dropped earlier.

"One of my boys," he said. "Ricky. You mighta met him, back when you were a fucking vacuum salesman."

"Okay, yeah, and...?"

"And he's calling to tell me where to find Mama." He chuckled, again, when my jaw dropped and just kinda hung like cheap Venetian blinds. "I'm not a *complete* fucking chump, Mick. You think I didn't suspect she might try something, once we'd found

Ada—Celia? Soon as she told me we hadda go find you, I had a few of the boys start shadowing *her*."

"Okay, so where is she?" And then, at his expression, "Oh, *fuck* no! Fino, you *can't* be that stupid!"

"I don't want you finding some way to show up. And no fucking *way* do I want Bianca following, and you and me both know she would. Uh-uh."

"Fino!" I actually threw myself at the edge of the glyph, stuck fast for an instant, and slowly oozed back. It felt much as I imagined trying to swim in molasses might. I tried to reach out for him, but I couldn't even punch my hand through the barrier. "Damn it, Fino! Let me help you! You *know* I can help you! For God's sake, you can't take Orsola on by yourself! You can't save your daughter by yourself!"

"I ain't by myself. I got my boys." He rose, gat in hand, and there was something in his expression, something haunted, something…

Something crying, because he could not.

"I can do this," he said softly. "She won't hurt me."

"You don't know that, Fino! You—"

"She won't hurt me. And I can't let you hurt *her*. She's my mother."

That simply, he left me, flailing and helpless in the middle of that tiny, powdery prison. And maybe Fino Ottati wasn't alone, as he marched out into the dark to find his mother and his missing daughter, but I was.

CHAPTER FIFTEEN

"Boss?"

B I couldn't have told you—still can't, to this day—whether it'd been six minutes or sixty since Fino'd split. I was too busy pushing against the glyph with everything I had left after a couple long, tiring, painful days. My brain ached, and I don't mean my head, I mean my *brain*. I felt like I'd just spent about a week trying to do calculus-based logic puzzles with random numbers missing, and I was physically pressed against the barrier so hard it was actually taking most of my weight. I was getting somewhere, and it was starting to give, but slow, way too damn slow. At that rate, I'd be outta there by, oh, Sunday.

"Boss, you in here?"

I jerked up straight as one of the Shark's gussied-up goons—I'd seen him around the house a time or two, but never caught a name—barged through the front door and into the room. I gotta wonder what he thought he saw, since for a second or two he musta spotted me leaning almost diagonal against thin air. He gawped stupidly, and I shrugged. "Ain't here, bo."

"Uh... What?"

"Your boss. Took a powder a while ago."

"But… What, he just left you here?"

"Guess he decided he trusts me," I said flatly.

"And you just been standing there this whole time?"

"It's a fascinating room. Swell acoustics. Did you want something?"

Not that he had any good reason to answer me, but I was hoping he'd be distracted or confused enough not to think about that. And, yep, "We can't find his girl. Been scouring the whole neighborhood, and there's not a fucking sign."

"Get me Bianca. Now."

"C'mon, I'll take you to her."

"Uh…" Somehow, I didn't feel that this was the right time to try explaining to the lug exactly why that wouldn't be happening anytime soon. "No, I need you to bring her here."

"What? Look, pally, the lady's kinda busy looking for her *fucking daughter*! No way I'm—"

"I can help her," I interrupted, "*if* you bring her *here*."

"I'm not your goddamn errand boy! Why don'tcha tell me what you got up your sleeve before I plug you right between—"

"How about, before you finish threatening me, you ponder a minute on what'll happen to you if the Mister and Missus find out that I *coulda* helped 'em, but it didn't happen 'cause you were too proud to play 'errand boy.' Go on, take your time. I ain't going anywhere."

"You… I… *Fuck*!"

"See? I knew you'd get there." I offered him a big,

cheery smile, then dropped it. "So go, already!"

"If Mrs. Ottati don't like what you gotta say…"

"Yeah, yeah. I been shot once today already. Come up with some new material, wouldja?"

Another few minutes—I went ahead and tried pacing my little cell, just for the novelty; it didn't do much for me, and I went back to playing statue—and the front door slammed open yet again. "What do you mean," Bianca demanded, stopping only at the very edge of the chalk rune, "he *left*?"

"I mean he's gone. He ain't here. He's currently inhabiting an alternative locality." I shrugged. "Got a ring on the horn, said he had some of his boys shadowing Orsola, and made tracks."

Bianca's blinkers went wider than the glyph. "Where?!"

"You think he told me?" I asked softly.

I swear I heard the tendons in her fists *creaking* as they tightened. "*Porca miseria! Cazzo!*" She'd turned away, but it didn't make the shouting any harder to hear.

"You know, it's still rude in Italian," I said.

Stiff-legged and stiffer-backed, she stomped around the sitting room, grabbed up the teapot, and poured out the cold, stale stuff over a length of the binding circle. Chalk, salt, and iron powder sluiced away in a thick stew, leaving a clean break, and a pressure I hadn't even realized I was feeling was abruptly gone. Kinda like your ears popping on a steep slope or a real high elevator, except all over. I stung and itched a little from the iron in the mixture, but it wasn't too bad; not even as bad as standing on an L platform near the rails.

'Course, I still felt like I'd gone twelve rounds *with* the L-train, but there'd be at least a *little* time outside that damn circle to heal, now. Whole *minutes*, even.

"Go," she said—well, more *growled*—to me. "Find Adalina."

"Sure thing. Soon as I have my wand back."

"Mr. Oberon, this is *not* the time to—"

"You're right, it ain't. So quit arguing."

Her jaw moved a little, side to side. "I don't know if he'd…" A quick head shake, sending some of her formerly pristine hair into her face, and then, "Fino locked it in the cabinet where he keeps most of his guns. I don't have a key."

"Show me."

"*Damn it!* We don't have time!"

"Show me."

Cursing softly the whole way, Bianca led me upstairs to the master bedroom—with all the usual finery I've come to expect from the boudoirs of the rich and felonious—and to a heavy walnut cabinet. It was the size of an old-fashioned wardrobe, and someone had installed a high-quality lock.

"You got a couple bobby pins?" I asked. She grunted something, went to the dressing-table, and came back with a handful. She offered, I took 'em—and then I stood, staring hard at the lock.

"What are—?"

I raised one finger, and the question died. It was replaced by more angry grumbling, but that was easier to ignore.

This woulda gone a lot quicker with my wand, but then, that was the whole problem, wasn't it?

Still, after a couple minutes, I'd unwoven enough threads of luck from the mechanism—and wrapped 'em around myself—to make up for the shabby, makeshift tools. That done, I knelt in front of the lock, and it was no time at all before I heard the tumblers click beneath the bobby pins.

It was almost funny, seeing the L&G just lying there on the bottom of the cabinet, in front of a hanging array of revolvers, semi-autos, shotguns, and a couple rifles. I couldn't help but notice a few large gaps and empty pegs, and figured Fino was packing a lot more'n that little .25.

I also took just a minute to raid the closet, swapping out my beat-up and *shot*-up overcoat for one of Fino's; no sense in attracting any extra attention, right? "Just for the record," I told Bianca as I shrugged into the black wool, "you guys are paying my tailor's bill. *And* for the repairs to my office."

And that vital pronouncement made, I was bounding down the stairs two or three at a time, and out into the blustery Chicago evening.

I didn't have to wonder long how Adalina had managed to shake everyone so quickly. I couldn't tell you if she was moving faster'n any human, or climbing and squeezing into places she shouldn't have been able to go, or if she was just cloaking herself in some manner of illusion or invisibility—woulda helped if I'd known what she was becoming—but whatever the case, she was definitely using magic to do it. Not well, and probably instinctively, not on purpose, but it was there all the same. I could feel it all around me, taste it in the air, sort of a "spiritual honeysuckle"-scented trail. At her age, in her emotional state, she'd have been sprinkling magic like a walking aspergillum no matter *what* she was doing. I held the L&G at the ready, just in case I lost the scent—fat chance of that!—and started running.

And running. And running. Damn, Adalina'd been *moving*, hadn't she? At my best, catching her wouldn't exactly be duck soup. Now? I was glomming bits of luck from the world around me just to keep myself going.

I blew past a few folks taking a late evening stroll, or just coming home from a long day's work, or taking the dog for a much-needed walk. I got my share of glares and occasional shouted complaints, especially the time or two I shoved guys outta my way, or actually jumped over a dog and leash; and maybe 'cause my sprint and the brisk breeze were throwing my borrowed coat out behind me in a makeshift cape, which was probably slapping anyone I passed too close. But the girl's trail wouldn't last forever, and I wasn't about to slow down.

Along sidewalks, across nicely landscaped yards, and even over a fence or two, until, maybe five or six blocks from the Ottati house...

The trail wavered. It didn't fade or weaken exactly, more that it... felt different. *Tasted* different.

Adalina's uncontrolled magics were spiced, faintly as you please, with somebody else's. Strong but controlled, expertly wielded; if it hadn't been for how it interfered with the more obvious spoor, I'd never have picked it up.

So who—and *what*—the hell else was skulking around out here?

It was dark enough by then that, even with the streetlamps glowing around me, I had to concentrate to make sure I didn't miss anything important. Couple of flivvers along the street (I was on 70th by then), mostly parked. People wandering around behind mostly closed curtains, cleaning up after dinner or settling down to a pipe and *Amos 'n' Andy*. Up the block, across Wabash, a dapple-grey horse was hauling a creaking milk wagon. Off to my left, a mangy possum was loitering in someone's hedges, ogling their garbage. And—

Hang on a minute...

Horse-drawn milk wagon? Sure, not at all outta place in this sorta neighborhood, 'cept that it was a little late for deliveries. By about *ten to twelve hours*.

And I was having a sinking feeling in my gut—*really* sinking, low enough to drill for oil—as to who'd be both throwing around their own magics *and* using that kinda wagon. Again, I broke into a mad dash; they were a few hundred yards away, and moving at a steady clip, but I shoulda been able to catch 'em up without too much—

If I was a boggart rather'n *aes sidhe*, I think the sudden *whooop-whooop* that split the night behind me woulda been enough to make my *literally* leap outta my skin through my mouth. As it was, I think it shaved a century or two off my life.

I shouldn't have been surprised. Around such a nice residential neighborhood—one that everyone *knows* is home to more'n its share of gangsters and wiseguys—of course the coppers have a couple prowl cars on a regular beat. Some weird bird tearing through people's yards the way I'd been was bound to catch attention. The flashing lamp cast me and the whole world around me in a washed-out, bloody aura, as the black-and-white pulled to a stop beside me.

"Okay, buddy." The bull who slid outta the car looked like... well, like a copper's supposed to. Tall, broad-shouldered fella in a blue uniform. Coulda been Pete's brother except, y'know, he wasn't. "Let's see some ID, and then you can tell me where you're off to in such a hurry."

"Officer, look." I pointed—carefully—away down the street. "I'm a PI. I'm following—"

"Yeah, you're a PI. Following a milk wagon? I wasn't born yesterday, pal. Where's that ID?"

I tried to be reasonable, I promise I did! "It don't seem odd to you that that jalopy's out on the streets at *this* hour?"

"ID. *Now!*"

I sighed once, and then very carefully and precisely socked him one in the jaw. The copper reeled back, arms flailing, rebounding from the side of the flivver with a dull *thunk*, and then sorta wound his way to the ground, a charmed snake in reverse.

All I could do was hope, between the darkness, the gleam of the red lights, and my usual effect on human minds, that he'd never recognize me if we bumped into each other down the line.

Course, if anyone'd seen that, or if he was supposed to report in any time soon, I could expect a whole fleet more black-and-whites in a matter of minutes. Even worse, the siren had apparently spooked whoever (or whatever) was driving the wagon, 'cause he'd whipped the horse into a pretty lively trot. They weren't gonna win any derbies, but with that kinda head start, the chances of me catching up with 'em were... pretty...

Slowly, stiffly, like I was being physically forced into moving, I found my head twisting around despite my best efforts so I could stare, with loathing and a growing horror, at the officer's car.

Aw, no. Oh, damn it, no...

Well, since my other option was letting Adalina get away—or, rather, whoever'd shown up and started throwing magic around get away with Adalina... Yeah.

Taking a deep breath and holding it, tensing my shoulders and bracing as if against a physical blow, I moved around the fender and scooted behind the wheel.

And then, cursing myself in three different languages, I scooted back out, ran back to the snoozing copper, dug in his pockets until I found his keys, and went *back* to the wheel.

Just sitting there was making me feel sick. My hair was standing up, my skin itching as though I was being bitten by mosquitoes made of poison ivy. I had to hold my wand in my mouth and clamp my hands hard on the wheel to keep 'em from trembling, until I'd forced myself to calm, to work through the growing agony.

It only got worse when I stuck the key in the ignition and stomped down on the starter switch. My stomach turned over along with the engine; I felt queasy, and the entire road started twisting and writhing beyond the windshield. I was panting, every muscle in my body screaming in agony as they tensed and pulled against each other. The fumes wafting in through the vents burned my nose, my throat, my eyes, my soul.

Plus, uh, I didn't know how to drive. I mean seriously, when the hell would I have learned? And *why*? Okay, yeah, I'd seen other guys do it, but I hadn't exactly been paying close attention, being too busy at the time trying not to scream or bite through my tongue like a salami.

Well, when skill ain't enough…

It was hard, *real* hard; one of the toughest things I've ever tried to do. Everything about the car around me pressed against my mind, screaming in my skull, biting at my skin. Bury yourself in an anthill, stick firecrackers in your ears, and then try listing all forty-eight state capitals alphabetically, and you oughta have some idea what I'm talking about.

And in the end, I only partway succeeded; I'm just grateful it was a big enough part.

I stomped down on the accelerator and the clutch, yanked on the shifter, and the car lurched forward in a drunken stumble. The motor whined, high and loud (I think, in retrospect, I started out a couple gears over), and the whole flivver shook, but we were moving, and before long we were moving *fast*. The emergency lamps still flashing, lighting up the streets around me in crimson lightning, I careened across Wabash—only thinking later to be grateful that whatever late traffic there was saw me coming, so I didn't plow into anyone—and roared down the street. I about *flew* past the milk wagon, startling the timorous horse into a sideways prance, and…

Well, and the extra dollop of luck that'd brought me this far gave out. I slammed on the brakes and the clutch with piss-poor timing, the engine coughed very much like an old lunger, keeled over with a metallic rattle, and the prowl car rolled at something close to twenty-five miles an hour into a parked Studebaker.

Maybe, I remember thinking, as I peeled my cheek off the cracked windshield and dully watched the blood running along the glass in nifty patterns, *I won't tell Pete about this part when I'm recounting this whole mess.*

It's probably sad that, after the last couple days, the pain of smashing my face into the windshield barely even registered. It did, however, take me half a minute or so to shake off the daze enough to throw open the door and stumble out into the street. It wasn't time I could afford to waste; *someone* woulda called in the accident by now.

Thankfully, I didn't have to worry about the wagon taking the run-out while I was waiting for my brain to get up off its back. The horse was still rearing and pawing at the air, panicked to hell and gone by the crash only a couple dozen feet away. The driver was fighting with the reins, and losing bad.

He gave up trying as I approached, threw 'em down into the seat beside him—after locking in the brake, so the horse couldn't run off with the wagon while he was otherwise occupied—and hopped down off the seat. He was shrouded in a chintzy illusion, one that *probably* woulda fooled most of you folk into thinking he was one of you, but to me it was about as effective as trying to hide behind a soap bubble. I recognized him instantly as a redcap in a bad suit; and even though they all look the same to me, I was convinced he was the same one who'd driven me to meet with Queen Mob.

He'd picked up an attractive trio of scratches across his cheek since then, though. They looked fresh, too, and I was pretty sure they'd match Adalina's fingernails.

"Breeze off, elf!" he growled, his obscenely wide mouth twisting down in a saw-toothed grimace. "This ain't your business." He opened his coat, showing off a serrated dagger and a .38 Special—a real one, too, not one of our eldritch knock-offs. I wondered who he'd taken it from, and if they'd ended up in his stomach for their troubles.

I didn't actually aim the L&G at him, but I kinda tensed that arm to make sure he got a solid peek at it. "Be happy to. Soon as you let the girl go."

"What girl?"

"Don't play the dunce with me, bo!"

"Who's playing?"

Well, there was no arguing with *that*, was there?

We eye-wrestled for a minute or two, until he decided that, no, I wasn't gonna be intimidated into leaving and, no, I didn't buy the bunk he was shoveling. He reached out to tap on the back door to the wagon, and another redcap—who I *also* woulda sworn was my driver back in Elphame, so I guess that shows what *I* know—crawled out to stand beside the first.

"The hell you think you're doing, Oberon?" the second one rumbled at me. "We got a deal, you and us."

"A very specific deal," I said. "One that don't include any-thing about not beating the tar outta you when you ask for it."

They both grinned, their faces transforming into gaping caverns of gooey flesh, their teeth into yellow-brown stalactites and stalagmites, and advanced on me in unison. I retreated a couple steps, then a couple more, flicked my wand out to the side...

And right as the redcaps were passing, the horse's tethers just so *happened* to snap under the strain of the critter's constant thrashing. Already going bananas from the crash, the horse got a good whiff of the two unnatural *things* that'd been hunkering in the wagon—guess the illusion couldn't mask their stink this close—and decided it *really* didn't want 'em anywhere nearby.

Smaller and a *lot* more frightened, it didn't kick as hard as Goswythe had, but it was still more'n enough to make the closer of the two redcaps go away.

His buddy couldn't help but turn and stare at the bushes into which the "kickee" had flown, and then at the horse that was galloping away down the road as fast as his hooves would carry him—all of which gave me more'n enough of an opening. I stepped in, thrust one foot out behind his, and planted both hands on his chest. He toppled to his back with a loud grunt, but though he glared fire at me, he was smart enough to stay down.

Maybe it was 'cause he was staring up at the business end of both my wand and his *own gun*, which I'd swiped from inside his jacket as I shoved him.

"The boss ain't gonna be happy with you," he growled.

"She can join the club. There's a waiting list, but I'm sure I can get her bumped to the top. Why'd you take the girl?"

The redcap shrugged. "What, you have plans for her? You're trying to find the human girl, ain'tcha? Whaddaya need the changeling for?"

"What do I...?" I shook my head hard enough to dislodge something. *Okay, Mick. They're Unfit; what'd you expect from 'em? Get back on track.* "What do *you*?"

"She's Seelie," he said, as though that explained everything.

And actually, it did. "She is, ain't she? And she's young, and confused, and don't know the first thing about Elphame. You could tell her, teach her, any damn thing you wanted. Mold her into your very own homegrown spy, just 'moved to Chicago' from some other Court."

"Brilliant, yeah?"

"It is. It also ain't happening."

Again with the shrugging. "Whaddaya care, Oberon? You ain't part of the Court no more."

"No, I'm not. Now let her go."

"We have a deal. You owe us. You swore an oath."

"Yeah, I did. I gotta help you out on one, uh, 'project.' You calling that in now? Is this important enough to Eudeagh to spend that particular boon?"

It's a damn good thing for me that I don't sweat, 'cause if I did I'd have been oozing bullets right about then. I dunno *what* the hell I'd have done if he'd said yes. Maybe cried.

But he didn't. He pondered on it a minute, ugly

brow furrowing, and then he said, "You're bluffing. You won't risk what might happen if you get in our way, not with that pact hanging over you."

At which point I pivoted toward the other redcap—the one who'd been kicked into the shrubbery, the one who was trying to creep up on me while his buddy kept me talking—and put two .38 slugs into his chest. I knew it wouldn't kill him, any more'n it would me, but he'd be down for a good long while.

We both watched him drop like a sack of gumballs, and returned our attentions to each other. "The girl's in the wagon," the redcap admitted, as though that were some big secret I hadn't already figured. "You take her back, you got all hell to pay. Boss Eudeagh ain't gonna take this lightly, I promise."

My guts were a ball of mating snakes—some enemies, even *I* really don't need—but all I did was nod. "She's welcome to complain. Have her give me a ring; my number's listed."

I waved the wand at the guy I'd plugged, just to make sure his *own* piece would never fire again, and then climbed up into the back of the wagon. Adalina cowered in the far corner, her peepers looking kinda glazed over—maybe from whatever spell the redcaps had hit her with, maybe just from trying to take in everything the evening had dumped on her.

I'm not sure if she recognized me, or even cared who I was, but when I offered her my hand to help her out, she took it. I had to guide her, practically carry her, but we were gone into the surrounding streets before any more police arrived to investigate the crashed prowl car or their missing bull.

We sat, dangling and twisting on a pair of wood-seated swings in a neighborhood playground, listening to the breeze flow around us, the chains creaking overhead, and sirens whistle in the distance. Place was empty now; *hadn't* been when we showed, though. Couple of local kids who'd decided—after a quick spate of pointing and whispering—that they didn't wanna be anywhere near Adalina. Poor kid hadn't even looked up since then. She kept her attention fastened on the grass and sand beneath our feet, and I had only the occasional grunt or nod to suggest she was hearing a single word I was saying.

Yeah, I was wasting time. Yeah, I had no idea what Orsola was doing with Celia, or where, or how long I had to stop it, whatever *it* was. But I'll tell you square, I didn't think Adalina was anywhere near ready to face her mom again, not yet. And I needed her to pull herself together, not just for her own sake, but because she could help her "sister."

If she decided she had any reason whatsoever to want to.

"It sounds beautiful," she said softly, still talking to the ground, not to me. "But awful. I don't think I could stand it."

"Chicago's pretty rough," I admitted. "But there are other places, better places. You think what I've described is beautiful, you should see the old lands." I know my voice drifted, as though I was floating away, and I couldn't help it, 'cause in a way I was. "The Old Elphame I knew, over in Europe and the

Isles? Oh, it'd take your breath away, make you weep in your soul. Avalon, Tír na nÓg... Nothing in this world compares, Adalina. Nothing."

"And those... the Courts? The, uh, Unseelie? They aren't there?"

"They are," I admitted. "You go to *any* city or kingdom in Elphame, you'll find the Seelie and the Unseelie squabbling. It's bad in some places, very bad, but a lot of others ain't as rough as Chicago. Sometimes, where one Court or the other's dominant, it's almost peaceful..."

"Except for the political bullshit and them snatching children!" she snapped, the chains of the swing set clinking in her clenching fingers.

"Uh... yeah." What else could I say? "It ain't perfect, Adalina. But it's good, a lot of it. Very, very good."

"And what about me?" She finally looked up at me, tears rolling down her slightly misshapen cheeks. I couldn't help but notice that those tears were grey. "Am I going to be 'good'? What am I?"

"I'm sorry, I don't—"

"Will I be like you? An, uh, *aes sidhe*? You look pretty regular, except for the ears."

I wasn't at all surprised that she could see 'em at that point. "On the square, Adalina, I don't know. I'd tell you if I did. How you look now? That could be moving in the direction you're *gonna* look, or it could be your body trying to cope with the changes and you'll be completely different, or it could be a reaction to some magics they used to keep you looking human longer'n normal. I just can't say."

"But if you *had* to!" she pressed. Those chains

were practically vibrating now; I almost thought she was gonna lunge at me.

I probably shoulda lied to her, but after everything she'd been through already… "I never heard of an *aes sidhe* going through a change the way you are," I admitted. Then, as she started to twist away, "But that don't mean anything! I told you, it could be the breaking down of a spell, or—"

"Or I could be turning into a monster," she said, barely whispering.

"There's a lot of Fae that don't look human who ain't monsters," I said. "*Lots*."

"It doesn't matter anyway. People *already* think I'm some horrible creature. Those kids, my friends, my parents—"

I whipped out a hand to snag the chain of her swing and twisted, forcing her to face me. "Your mother has been hunting for you since you bolted. She's worried *sick* over you; she only let me out of Fino's glyph so I could find you!

"And your father? You were eavesdropping all evening, but how much did you *listen* to? Fino arranged the swap. He's known from *day one* that you weren't his blood, that you weren't human. Has he ever treated you badly? Has he ever made you feel unwanted or unwelcome? *Ever?*"

She shook her head, sobbing openly now. Her hair was sticking to her face, caught fast in the moisture of her tears.

"I ain't saying your parents did everything the way they should," I told her. "And I ain't saying your father's exactly a good man. But they tried to do right by you. And right now? This thing with Celia?

This ain't about replacing you, even if maybe for a minute they thought it was. Right now is when they need you most.

"You don't wanna grow into a monster? Let's go show 'em how human you are."

I found myself holding my breath, waiting for an answer in a face that'd suddenly gone so blank that even I couldn't begin to read it. And then, with nothing more than a nod, Adalina slid from the swing and began a steady march across the playground, heading stubbornly for home.

I didn't think Bianca would ever let go of Adalina, or ever say anything more'n "I'm sorry, *piccola mia*," over and over, but finally she unwrapped her arms and led the girl and me into the sitting room. And if Adalina spent the whole hug stiff as a railroad tie, and wouldn't look her "mother" in the eye, well, I can't say I didn't understand.

Adalina took a seat, while Bianca poured herself a cup of fresh tea. Even from across the room, I could smell that it'd been, uh, *flavored* with something a whole lot stronger. "What now, Mr. Oberon?" Adalina asked.

What now? "I been thinking about that," I said, lurking in the doorway. "We still don't know what Orsola's got cooking, not exactly. Just that it's nasty. We don't know exactly what she needs Celia for, either—" the girl flinched at that name, but didn't interrupt "—but we can bet it ain't pleasant, not given all the steps Fino took to protect her after learning just *part* of it."

"Would Nonna really hurt her, do you think? Her own granddaughter?"

"Yeah, I think she really would." Then, to Bianca, "I'm not *completely* sure she wouldn't have used Fino, if he'd been a firstborn. But then, it was partly losing her firstborn that pushed her over the edge, so who knows?

"So we don't know what she's doing, and we don't know where. We ain't doing too well here. What we need to do is find her materials. Her grimoires, her notes, and all that."

"Donna Orsola keeps a footlocker full of books in her bedroom—" Bianca began.

"Which is exactly where they won't be. No way she's keeping anything this powerful in plain sight."

"Wouldn't she have taken those things with her, then? To use in…" She swallowed around the words that were obviously caught in her throat, and reached into her pocket. I heard the click of rosaries from within. "In casting her spell?"

"Nope. She's knows every detail backward and forward, you can take that to the bank. Probably dreams about it by now. She wouldn't want to be distracted, having to juggle the tome along with everything else, or risk making a mistake 'cause of some last-minute misunderstanding."

Long as she'd been planning this, she'd had plenty of time to study it, too. I, on the other hand, had *maybe* a few more hours. Only thing I had working for me is that a rite of this power probably required a hefty amount of time. Well, that, and I had…

"Adalina."

Even though she'd been listening this whole time,

peering right at me, she jumped. "Yes?"

"I need you to find 'em."

"M-me?" I hadn't thought those big dark peepers could get any wider. Wrong.

"You." I walked over, squatted down in front of the sofa where she sat. "We don't have time to tear this place apart looking. I could try finding 'em with magic, but they're gonna be *real* well protected from that sorta thing. And this house is *lousy* with mystic emanations—from the wards she had up 'til recently, a bunch of other protections, every spell she ever cast here, and, well, you. You been leaking like a sieve for months. I might manage eventually, but too late to do any good.

"You, though? You may not realize it, but you're pretty sensitive to this stuff, too. And you already know how this house is supposed to feel."

"But..." She was actually squirming; I couldn't help but think she wanted to get up and run again. "But I don't know what I'm looking for! And—and even if I can 'feel' this stuff, if she's been protecting her books all this time, the house is just going to feel the way it always does to me! And—"

"It's gonna be hard," I said. "But if we work together on it, we can do it."

"I don't think I can..."

I wish I'd had time to coddle her, to do it different. I didn't. "Then Celia's on her own," I said simply.

Bianca gasped, and then started to cry. "Adalina, please..."

The girl stared at me, a single tear of her own tracing a grey line down her face.

"Human or monster?" I whispered, as quiet as

I could while still being sure she'd hear. And yeah, maybe pushing her that way was a little monstrous on my own part.

But me, I've never claimed to be human.

Adalina sucked in her breath, and nodded at me. "What do I do?"

"Remember everything you can about this house," I began. "Not how it looks, or smells, or any of that. How it *feels*. How *you* feel, in every room. Emotions that come over you with no obvious reason. These are old and ugly magics, so depression, fear... A sense of confusion, or age, or loss..."

"I don't... I don't remember anything like that! I'm trying, but—"

"Shh. It's okay." I stood, held out a hand. "Don't worry about whether you're managing it or not. Just keep trying."

"All right..." She took my hand.

"Walk with me," I said.

So we walked. I had Adalina's fingers in one hand, the Luchtaine & Goodfellow in the other, Bianca trailing behind, winding the rosary through her own fingers over and over again. I wanted to shout at her to stop—the constant click wasn't doing my concentration any favors—but I figure she needed it more'n I *didn't* need it.

Everywhere we went, I kept whispering, working to shape perceptions Adalina shoulda already had for years. I tried to slowly, gently, draw off some of her emotions and mystic emanations through the wand, wind 'em through my own aura, infuse 'em with some sense of how our goal should feel, and then feed 'em back to her along with an extra

336

dollop of luck to help us find 'em.

And if you think that *sounds* confusing, try *doing* it.

But it worked. It took us over an hour that we didn't have to spare, but it worked.

We'd started with Orsola's room, of course, 'cause that was the obvious place to start. Adalina had felt a few "weird spots," as she called 'em, but they turned out to be simple wards or the—well, I won't say the "public" collection of witchy tomes and texts, but the ones the family knew about.

The rest of the upstairs had proved even more a waste of time, and we'd gone through most of the ground floor when Adalina had started to shake, whimpering at a pitch I'm not sure Bianca could even hear. She yanked her hand from mine and took a trembling step back.

"I…" She answered the look I tossed her. "I felt like I was falling. Like I was stumbling at the edge of a gaping hole…"

"It's just an old linen closet," Bianca protested. "We don't use it much, since we rearranged the house to have all the bedrooms upstairs."

Hmm… "Go ahead and open it."

She took a step, then stopped. "I don't want to. What if it's cursed or something?"

"It's perfectly safe. Open it."

"I… No. The books we're looking for are unholy! I won't endanger my soul by—"

"So don't read 'em. Don't even *touch*. Just open the door."

"No!" Bianca actually raised her hands, ready to claw my blinkers out if I asked again.

"Mother?" Adalina whispered.

"It's okay," I said. "I just wanted to test a theory." I moved to open the door and yeah, even *I* felt it: a fierce compulsion to leave the closet the hell alone. It started in my senses, a persistent nudge urging me not even to notice the door was there, to forget all about it, but soon as I tried anyway, it migrated into the back of my mind, where nightmares slumber during daylight.

And for a minute, I couldn't twist the knob. But only a minute.

I have been a prince of the aes sidhe, *Donna Orsola. And I have seen nightmares in my waking hours the likes of which your most vivid dreams of Hell could not match!*

I threw myself at the door—my will, my pride, and yes, my disdain. Magic burst from my hands, my eyes, and through the L&G. A pulse traveled back through my mind and my soul, a faint echo of the dark spell Orsola had chucked at me back in my office, and the twin gasps from behind told me Adalina and Bianca had felt it, too. The door still hung sullenly in its frame, but that's all it was now: a door.

I yanked it open without hesitation. The shelves were filled with old, folded sheets, just as they shoulda been. But the padlocked chest on the floor, *that* was probably something of a later addition.

Grinning, I turned back to the others, ready to make some wisecrack or other, and stopped short. I wasn't horrified or anything—I've seen much worse, sometimes on creatures I've called friends— but it was startling, right enough. Bianca pivoted to follow my shocked stare before I could recover, and she couldn't quite repress a scream.

I think she'd probably regret that for the rest of her life.

"What? Oh, God, *what's wrong*?" Wilting beneath our gaze, the thing Bianca had named Adalina—that had once looked at least *mostly* human—stared imploringly, waiting for an explanation that neither of us could offer.

CHAPTER SIXTEEN

We were back, *again*, in that damn garishly decorated sitting room, breathing in the scent of hooch-flavored tea and enough tears to drown a Norwegian rat. I was starting to feel like the rest of that house was just a dream, slowly fading away as I was sucked again and again into this one cramped chamber. The heart of a lingering nightmare.

Yeah, I was feeling a little dramatic at the time. I think it was justified.

I'd pulled a chair up to the small table, shoved a few saucers out of my way, and dropped the old tome and stack of stiff, ratty papers in front of me. For the past few minutes I'd been flipping through, my skin crawling at the touch of the old maledictions, hunting for any sign of what Orsola was up to.

It didn't help that over half this stuff was written in languages I couldn't begin to read. I could piece together some of the Latin and the Greek, but the Hebrew, the Ancient Egyptian, and what I *think* was even some Sanskrit was way the hell beyond me. (That trick of mine, where I listen to someone jawing for a few minutes and start to understand what they're saying? Yeah, that don't work with writing. No thoughts to pick up on.) Orsola had done a whole mess of scribbling in the margins and between lines, which might prove useful. Her notes were in Italian, which I also don't read—though I was starting to think I probably oughta learn—but I was carefully copying 'em down so I could get Bianca to translate. I *coulda* just given her the book, but I didn't think she'd be comfortable with that, and I wanted to make sure there wasn't anything in here that'd hurt her if she read it.

It *also* didn't help that the dame in question was constantly making sniffling or gasping noises as she slumped in her chair, twitching every minute or two like she was about to get up, or reaching out as if to stretch across the whole room. Or that Adalina was curled into a ball on the far end of the sofa, rocking in place and whimpering, well beyond her "mother's" reach. Every few minutes she'd twist around, despite herself, stare at her reflection in the darkened window, and look to me for answers she already knew I couldn't offer.

I couldn't even tell her why it'd happened *now*, not for sure, anyway. Some kinda backlash from breaking Orsola's ward? A side-effect of my pumping magics through her to improve her senses? Hell, it coulda just happened on its own, I guess, but even I have trouble accepting that degree of coincidence. No, I was pretty sure it was 'cause of something we'd just done—and that kinda made it my fault.

But I think she coulda handled not knowing "why now" if I could at least have told her "what." I couldn't even do that for her. Her eyes'd moved even farther apart, 'til she damn near had one on each side of her head, and her lips gone so thin they were almost invisible, giving her a sorta fishy look. Her skin was pale as a waterlogged corpse, and so tight I could trace the contours in her knuckles with a casual glance. She was starting to smell of some foul concoction of salmon oils and fruit juice, but just a little, only noticeable if you were right beside her.

Whatever she was, she wouldn't be passing for human anymore. And she *still* didn't much resemble any Fae I'd ever seen or heard of, not really. Either I'd been right when I suggested they'd put a spell on her to keep her looking human longer, and her body was twisting itself into taffy as it tried to fight those magics, or…

Well, I hadn't told her "or." She was having enough trouble with option number one. See, option two is that, sometimes, the changelings we leave behind ain't Fae at all. They ain't even *alive* in any traditional sense. Just dolls or old logs, enchanted to resemble sickly little babies. Most of the time they die after a few weeks, but if one was made to last longer, could this be the result when it started to fall apart? I couldn't say; never heard of it happening.

Either way, if Adalina didn't finish turning into whatever she was turning into sooner rather'n later—and maybe even if she did, if this proved to be more'n a passing stage of metamorphosis—she'd have serious problems trying to live any kinda life.

The dried pages rustled under my fingertips as I jotted down a few more lines, and thrust the pad toward Bianca. "Start with these," I said, as I carefully flipped back to the beginning of the book.

See, I hadn't been copying the *strega*'s notes in order, but instead I'd begun with the pages that appeared most important. Either they had diagrams of glyphs and runic circles, or had a larger number of notes, or just fell open more easily like the book'd often been propped open at that point.

I'd recognized enough, in those sections alone, to know that however bad we'd thought our situation was, we'd underestimated it. These were ugly, *ugly* magics; just from the phrases I could make out, some of those symbols and diagrams, and even the feel of the words on the paper, I could tell this was hellish, soul-shriveling, bloody stuff. Even your average Unseelie witch or warlock wouldn't casually mess with this kinda —

Bianca took the pad, her movements stiff, mechanical, and began to read aloud. The first few lines she translated weren't too useful; just a collection of various ritual materials, herbs and symbols and whatnot. I waved a hand in a "keep going" sort of way. She kept going.

"'Cultural ties, not just blood. Easier to acquire. Must investigate.'" Her brow furrowed. "Cultural ties?"

I nodded, thinking. "Sympathy and symbolism." Then, when her frown only deepened, "Connections between caster and subject, like putting someone's hair in a voodoo doll. Depending on how many people or families she's planning to hex, she couldn't possibly gather pieces of *all* of 'em, but something with a strong enough symbolic link to them, or their community, could work."

"Doesn't... doesn't that imply that she's planning to hurt a *lot* of people?"

"Yeah, it does. Read."

There were a few more lists of possible ingredients—again, with nothing specific enough for me to make any useful guesses—and then, "'Mortal sin? Consult scriptures or Father Leo.'" Again she looked up at me. "Father Leo's the senior priest at Donna Orsola's church. *What* could be a mortal sin?"

I had no answer, but I was getting even more nervous. What sin could be so bad that even loony old Orsola would worry about?

Bianca kept reading, and I knew.

"'Of course! Exodus 11:5. Our Lord approves!!!' Exodus…?" Her hand flew to her mouth, and even Adalina, cowering on her sofa, gasped. "Oh, *Madonna*!"

And all the firstborn in the land of Egypt shall die, from the firstborn of Pharaoh that sitteth upon his throne, even unto the firstborn of the maidservant that is behind the mill; and all the firstborn of beasts.

It'd been a *long* time since I cursed in Gaelic. I gotta say, I hadn't lost the knack.

"Is…" Adalina rose from her sofa and approached with a peculiar, swaying gait. "Is Nonna really going to do that?" Her face hadn't changed so much that I couldn't read the horror writ large across it. "Curse the firstborn of all the families she hates?"

"I wish," I muttered. Then, at their twin expressions of shocked outrage, "You don't get it! A spell this nasty, this powerful? 'Cultural ties?' Mortal sins? She ain't aiming at a couple families! She's targeting a whole fucking ancestry!"

I could see it in their faces, they still didn't understand. Well, who could blame 'em? Of *course* they didn't understand; they weren't insane.

"Using her granddaughter as a nexus," I said more softly, "Donna Orsola is going to murder every firstborn child of Italian blood."

The pad fell from Bianca's fingers with a loud *thwap*. Adalina staggered and fell back into the sofa. "*All* of them?" she breathed in an almost inaudible whisper. "Everywhere?"

"No, not everywhere," I said, working it out in my head. "Nobody's *that* powerful." *Well, not in this day and age.* "But at the very least throughout Chicago. Maybe a little farther."

Bianca was crossing herself repeatedly. I'm not sure she even knew she was doing it. "*Why?* Dear God, why would she *do* that?"

All I could do was shrug. "Maybe she doesn't know how to aim it any more precisely. Maybe she blames the whole culture for what happened to her loved ones. Maybe she just doesn't give a damn who she hurts anymore, so long as the 'right' people are included! It don't *matter* why! It's *gonna happen*!"

"Oh, Jesus... What do we do?"

Okay, Mick, think! "She needs someplace private," I began, shoving the books away and over the far end of the table. I couldn't concentrate with 'em right in front of me, not now. "She can't afford any big interruptions."

"Fino has some properties," Bianca said. "Some warehouses and shops. They—"

"Nah. Too much chance of him tumbling to what she's doing. Plus, it's missing the connections."

"Connections? Like Celia's..." She choked something down. "Celia's blood?"

"Kinda. Symbolism, like I said. She needs

somewhere connected to the Italian community or culture. Or to death and ruin. Or preferably both. *Fuck!*" I shook my head and wished I drank stronger stuff than milk. "There's still so many possibilities! Half the local graveyards would work. Hell, she could be holed up in the offices of the damn Italo-American National Union for all I know!"

I took a few deep breaths, less to calm myself down—I can do that without the funny little physiological tricks you people need—than to make it *clear* I was calming myself down. "Tell me about last night," I said.

"What?" Bianca asked.

"Orsola was preparing for this. She knew I had Celia a while before she told Fino, or moved to come get the kid herself. It—"

"Why *did* she tell Fino?" she interrupted. "I mean, if she was going to collect Celia herself…"

"She…?" It took me a second to get my thoughts back in order. "I figure she needed her boy to soften me up. She wouldn't have caught me nearly so easy if I wasn't already worn out."

Of course, Goswythe had done the job for her long before Fino got there, but no way she coulda expected that.

"Point was," I continued, refusing to keep getting sidetracked, "her delay hadda be because she was getting ready. So what'd she do? Fino didn't remember much; you *have* to."

"She… she went to church for a few hours—"

"Yeah, I already know that. What else?"

"But I don't *know* what else!" Bianca looked about ready to scream, or throw something at me, or cry; probably all three. "I saw her come in, but she went straight to her room. She was still in there when I went to sleep!"

"*Damn it!* Did she… I dunno, did she take anything with her when she left? Bring anything back? *Anything?*"

"No, I don't think—"

"Yes," Adalina interrupted softly.

Well, she had our complete attention!

"When she went into her room," the girl said, "I saw her taking a metal flask out of her coat pocket. I thought it was weird, since she doesn't drink."

"Oh, that." Bianca waved a hand. "Donna Orsola's been bringing small amounts of holy water home from church on occasion for months. She uses it as an ingredient in the wards she puts up around the house."

I was already on my knees in the doorway, digging my hand under the carpet. Oh, but this was gonna hurt…

Orsola had allowed the magic in her protections to lapse, but the chalk and other powders she used to create them remained. I poked a few fingers into the stuff, and clamped my jaw tight around a scream of pain. Several types of chalk, charcoal, lots of salt, crushed leaves and powdered herbs, *iron filings* (hence the pain)—but…

"No holy water," I gasped as I wobbled back to my feet, staring at the reddened, inflamed skin on my left hand. "Even this long after it'd evaporated, I'd feel it." I hadn't *thought* I remembered sensing anything of that sort, back when I'd first suffered under those magics.

"Then what was she using it for?" Bianca wondered aloud.

"Oh, she's been gathering it for this," I said. "I'm just not sure why. Maybe—"

"Christenings!"

Of course. I could have kissed her. What stronger link, what better "in," to a whole population of Catholic children than the waters—symbolically, if not literally—used to baptize 'em?

Bianca obviously recognized from my expression that she'd hit on something. "Does that mean Orsola's at the church?" she asked.

"No, not her own church," I said. "Again, too much chance of being found out. And I don't think she'd want to 'sully' it with these magics…"

But that was okay. Because if she was using the christening and other religious trappings as her connection to the whole community, then a church of some sort *would* make sense: it'd just compound the symbolic linkages, make 'em even more potent.

And if that was the case, I knew the perfect place. I knew *exactly* where Orsola Maldera woulda gone.

We talked about it, bounced it back and forth, looked for any holes in my reasoning and couldn't find any. Well, other than…

"But you can't be certain," Bianca pressed, not for the first time.

"No, I can't. But it's *perfect* for her, offers everything she needs and then some. So I'm *pretty* sure."

Also, like I've told you before, *aes sidhe*—okay, and some other Fae, too—have kind of a knack for these things. It's much the same as when I ask for this weird dingus or that as my fee for a case:

I dunno *why* I feel the urge to ask for 'em, I just do. Sometimes it winds up being meaningless, but a lotta the time, they prove damn useful later on. It's just instinct, or inspired speculation, or... or something. But it means that I had a better chance of guessing this right than anyone else.

I didn't feel it was worth taking the time to explain all that, though. And I still woulda happily traded for a map with a big X scribbled on it.

"All right," Bianca agreed, rising from her seat. "Give me a moment, and we'll head out."

"Uh..." I'd expected it, yeah, but I wasn't thrilled with it. "Mrs. Ottati, maybe it'd be better if you stayed—"

"You'll have to kill me."

Okay, yeah, that'd gone over well.

"It's just that—"

"No. That's my husband out there, Mr. Oberon, and my dau—*one* of my daughters." Adalina managed a misshapen smile, though I kinda got the impression it was entirely for her mother's sake. "I am *not* staying behind.

"Besides, I have the keys. Or were you planning to steal my car?"

I shuddered, but she had a point. It's not like I could afford the time it'd take to catch the L. And I sure as hell wouldn't get there in one piece if *I* tried to drive it!

"All right. Let's get a move on. We—"

The both of us turned together as Adalina also rose from the sofa. "I—"

Bianca didn't let her get even as far as I had. "No. Absolutely not!"

"But I can help! I—"

"No! You're not going. It's too dangerous."

"But, Mother—!"

"*No!*" Not sure whether it was the volume or the raw emotion, but my ears were starting to ache. Adalina squeaked something completely unintelligible and fled upstairs. Bianca and I both knew the slamming door was coming next, and we still both jumped.

"*Ragazzi! Madre di Dio...*" Muttering the whole way, Bianca followed up the steps, with rather more dignity and rather less noise. I overheard a door creaking, some rattling around in a cabinet, and a few metallic clicks. Then the faint tapping of knuckles on wood.

"Adalina? Adalina, I'm going. I... I love you. I'll see you soon, *piccola mia*."

If she got any reply at all, it was quiet enough that even I couldn't hear it. And somehow, I didn't think it'd go over too well if I asked.

I *also* wasn't about to insult her by asking if she knew how to handle the heat she was packing when she came downstairs. What I *did* ask was, "Are you sure you're ready to use those? It don't come easy to everyone."

Without blinking, she worked the slide on the Colt, checking the action, then flicked on the safety and stuck it in her pocket. "If I need to," she said.

I believed her.

She led me outside and across the street, to a rich burgundy four-door LaSalle with whitewalls so pristine they'd have been blinding in the daylight. My nails dug into the seat as Bianca stepped on the starter. The engine rumbled to life, and the all-too-familiar queasiness turned into an angry badger, burrowing through my guts. I pressed my head against the cool window and struggled to ride it out. And y'know, maybe because I was so preoccupied with what was coming up, it didn't seem quite as awful as usual.

(Or maybe it was because, in comparison to my actually having tried to *drive* the black-and-white, it *wasn't* as bad.)

We cruised along the streets of Chicago in silence—well, without speaking, since the rumble of the motor, the chorus of squealing breaks and honking horns, and the occasional rattle as we passed under elevated tracks weren't exactly quiet—and it was only after long minutes that I picked up on something. Just as my worry about what was ahead mighta distracted me a little from the pain of the flivver around me, that pain had neatly distracted me from something else.

A very faint scent, wafting up from the back, shrouded not only in the various stenches of the car and the roads and the city itself, but in a weak, amateurish cocoon of willpower. Under any other circumstances, it never woulda snowed me even this long.

"How the *fuck*," I demanded, startling Bianca so bad the car swerved, "did you get back there?"

Adalina made a noise that sounded something like "Eeerp!" Bianca went white to the roots of her hair—if she'd actually gone grey right in front of me, I wouldn't have been a bit surprised—and slammed on the brakes hard enough to give me my second windshield shave of the day. Those cars that were still out and about this late roared and screeched around us, honking and cursing and yelling at us to get outta the road. If she'd done that on an even slightly busier street, we'd have been someone else's hood ornament.

I couldn't pick out a whole lotta words from the torrent of syllables that were bursting from Bianca's trap—hell, it took me a few just to be sure if it was English or Italian—but I got enough to tell that she was more'n a little upset with Adalina.

Gosh, chalk another one up for the great detective.

Adalina couldn't possibly get a word in edgewise, but she didn't need to. Obviously she'd shimmied out the window soon as she slammed the door to her room and hid in the back of Mommy's car; no other way it coulda gone down, 'cause she sure as hell didn't sneak past me out the front. I'd pretty much have to be dead to be *that* distracted.

After it became clear she wasn't running low on words anytime soon—hell, she didn't appear to be running outta *breath*—I said, "Uh, Bianca…"

The glass behind me threatened to shatter under her look, but I persevered. Barely. "We can't just sit here. Even leaving aside the traffic hazard, we're wasting—"

"Fine. Get out!" I was pretty sure that order wasn't directed at me. "The L's not that far—"

"I'm not going anywhere!" Adalina shrieked.

"You're going *home*!"

"No, I—"

"Uh," I said again. "Actually, she's *not* going anywhere." Then, before the heavily armed dame could seriously contemplate murdering me, "Bianca, it's late, but the streets ain't *that* empty. You think Adalina could go half a block without someone seeing her?"

Bianca scowled, biting the inside of her cheek. Adalina, at the reminder of her new face, stared at the back of the seat.

"I'll *drive* her home, then!" But I could see in her peepers that she knew it was a dumb thing to say. The round trip would cost us an extra half hour or more, whereas we were less than five minutes from our destination.

Her face twisted in angry, frightened indecision until she scarcely looked any more human than the girl in the back. I started inching my hand toward the L&G, ready to *make* her start driving again if I had to, and damn the consequences, but thankfully it didn't come to that. Sounding more'n more like her husband with every profanity, she threw the flivver into gear and stomped the accelerator.

"If you stick so much as a finger outside of this car," she warned Adalina, "I swear to Jesus and Mary that I will lock you up until I've grown too senile to worry about you. You understand me, Adalina?"

In a voice grown small—but suddenly calm, far too calm—Adalina said, "I understand, Mama."

I twisted in my seat to peer at the girl, wondering what had changed, but I didn't have time to ponder on it. I wish I had.

But Bianca accelerated through the traffic signal at Grand Avenue, took another couple of quick corners, and we were there.

Pulling up in front of an abandoned lot,

surrounded by chain-link fencing. Abandoned... but not forgotten.

Because this had been the original site of Santa Maria Addolorata.

If you ain't up on your Chicago history... Santa Maria Addolorata is one of the city's largest Italian congregations, and has been for decades. It's also one of the oldest.

It's *also* standing a couple blocks over, right now, 'cause an enormous fire pretty much gutted and blackened the original building like a Cajun catfish. It'd happened just a hair over a year ago, and the property hadn't yet been redeveloped.

Which wasn't to say it wasn't proving useful to *someone*.

The lot had absolutely everything Orsola coulda asked for. The chain-link fence, and the handful of brick walls that made up the ruin, provided all the privacy she could ask for, even this close to Grand Avenue. The church'd played host to thousands of baptisms, had been the center of belief for a whole chunk of Chicago's Italian community—and people *still* prayed and sang and had their children christened in the place's namesake. That wasn't just a spiritual and symbolic *link*, it was a whole friggin' *chain*.

And the fact that the place had burned down, that the lot was covered in the charcoal and ash of holy icons and a house of worship—well, even though nobody'd died, you couldn't find a more powerful symbol of mourning and loss if you built it yourself.

It was perfect, absolutely tailor-made, for Orsola's needs. Or so I'd figured; and whether I'd reasoned it out right, or I'd been guided by those instincts I don't quite understand myself, or whether I'd just got *real* damn lucky, I've never been able to determine.

All that matters is, I was *right*.

Bianca's LaSalle fishtailed a little in the crosswinds as we pulled to the curb near three other flivvers, all of which were way too nice to be parked here at this late hour. I shot from the car, then staggered back, and I didn't need to taste the energies in the air to know that even for the Windy City, these gusts weren't natural. My hair and my coat (well, Fino's coat) were whipping around straight behind me, and I had to squint against the blowing dust and grit. I didn't know if this was something Orsola'd cooked up deliberately, or just a side-effect of the curse she was working through Celia, but either way it was aggravating.

Good for her, though, since the howling of the winds would cover any incidental sounds that might otherwise draw attention.

I made for the gate in the fence, L&G drawn and ready to do all sorts of unfriendly things to the latch, or to anyone who got in my way. But the gate was hanging open, and so was the chain that'd locked it—someone had taken bolt cutters to it—and if there was anyone lurking in wait, I sure couldn't get a slant on 'em.

Bianca appeared beside me, Colt in her small fist, and said something I couldn't hear through the wind. I leaned in, and she repeated, "Where to?"

I paused a minute, staring at the cracked, soot-blackened walls that were all that remained of the old church, opened my mouth to answer…

And the sound of gunfire reached us from around

and to the right, though the gusts were so loud even *that* barely registered.

"Uh, I'm thinking that way," I said in her ear. Her expression told me, without needing to shout at all, that I was an idiot.

We found the first body facedown in the dirt, just round the brick corner. Or, well, I shouldn't say "facedown," since there wasn't any face left worth speaking of. Fella looked as though he'd tried to French kiss a sawed-off and wouldn't take no for an answer. Bianca went a fascinating shade of green and her shoulders heaved once, but whatever was threatening to come up, she managed to keep it down. Maybe because the chintzy suit the guy was wearing made it obvious that this was one of Fino's boys, and not Fino himself.

The second body, a little ways past the first, was just as dead but in better condition. Bianca and I both recognized him as one of the thugs who'd been guarding the house each time I'd shown up pretending to represent Credne's Whatever. He'd been plugged a good three or four times in the breadbasket.

And the third, sitting in a small blood pool with his legs sprawled out in front of him and his back against the bricks... Well, the third "body" was pointing a smoking Smith & Wesson right at us. He breathed something between a gasp and a sigh when he saw who we were, and let the roscoe fall.

"You've looked better, Archie," I said as I dropped to one knee beside him.

"Looked better. You're a riot, Oberon."

He'd been clipped twice in the leg—on the outside, thankfully, away from the artery—so he'd *probably* live, if the wound didn't go untreated for too long. I helped Bianca tear a strip off my borrowed coat. Then, while she wrapped the wound, I threw a little of my will into Archie's mind, trying to take the edge off the pain. I guess it worked, 'cause after another gasp when Bianca tightened the bandage, his breathing started to come easier.

"What happened?" Bianca asked.

"Some of our own boys fucking turned on us, that's what happened," he growled, shifting to take some of the weight off his injured leg. "Opened up on us before we even got a peep at Orsola. I dunno what that bitch paid 'em, but I *promise* you they're all fucking dead men!"

Paid? I wondered if they'd been "paid" anything. Orsola coulda been slipping 'em some kinda potion or brew for ages...

Not that it made much difference on our end—or that I was about to convince Archie it wasn't their fault, even if it wasn't.

"We just scattered," he continued, waving vaguely back in the direction of the bodies. "Boss and some of the guys broke left, we broke right, and... Well, here I am. I been taking potshots at those fucking traitors," and here he craned his head toward a small hole in the bricks, "but I ain't seen 'em much. Suppose they're hanging back with Orsola, wherever she is. And I ain't exactly in any condition to go looking."

"All right," I said. "We'll keep our heads down. You got enough extra shells for that thing?"

"Oh, don't worry about me. Anybody comes round that corner ain't you or the boss, I got more'n enough lead to go around." He reached out then, snagged my collar and yanked me close enough that, even speaking over the wind, we wouldn't be overheard. "You fucking brought Mrs. Ottati with you? Are you stupid?"

"You wanna try telling her to stay behind, Archie, you go right on ahead."

"Tell her to stay... Huh. Nah, I, uh, don't think I'll do that."

"Wise of you."

I rose, keeping my back pressed to the brick, and began sidling toward the corner, Bianca inching along behind. "Mr. Oberon," she hissed over the pseudo-storm.

"Yeah?"

"Archie..."

"Yeah?"

"My husband doesn't know how much he's helped me. He doesn't know that I told Archie about Celia, or that he was keeping it secret for me. Archie had good reasons, but if Fino ever found out..."

I nodded. "No reason to tell him that I can think of."

She smiled her thanks, I smiled "You're welcome"... And then, wand gripped tight, I stuck my mug around the corner to take a gander at whatever might be waiting.

CHAPTER SEVENTEEN

W hat was waiting for us was a war zone, or sure looked to be.

The four main walls that were still sorta standing—not counting the big honking gaps scattered throughout 'em—surrounded heaps of wood that'd been too badly scorched to be worth salvaging, piles of ash-coated dirt, and the lingering remnants of a few smaller walls, now standing only a few feet tall. It really did look as though someone'd dropped a bomb on the place.

And of course, the scattered bodies just added to the imagery.

I couldn't tell for sure, squinting as I was, but I thought most of 'em were still alive. I was fairly certain I saw a chest rising and falling here, an arm twitching there. But then again, it coulda just been the wind.

The wind which, even if I hadn't already known, was now blatantly and obviously supernatural. It whipped around in a miniature cyclone, off in the far side of the ruins—where the altar once stood, no doubt—forming a curtain of dust and dirt, old papers and various other bits of refuse. Somehow, the rest of the winds we were feeling were gusting *out* from that spinning center, thumbing their noses at physics and nature as they passed. It wasn't completely opaque, and I could see the figures moving beyond.

Or rather, one of the figures was moving, circling around—*dancing* around, if those spastic tremors and twitches weren't just optical illusions caused by the windblown detritus—the other. And that "other" was...

Fuck me! Celia was *crucified to a makeshift cross*, a couple of simple broken beams lashed together. I could *feel* her screams, even if I couldn't hear 'em over the howling, and I could only hope against hope that she'd been *tied* into place, not *nailed*.

I aimed and fired, sending magics pumping into the witch, stripping enough luck from her that even tripping on her own shoelaces coulda proved fatal— or I tried to, anyway. But whatever magics kept those winds blowing, they warded her from mystical attack just as well; I felt my efforts kinda sluice off to one side. Might as well have tried to punch through a wall with water from a garden hose.

Plan B, then. I aimed the wand down and twisted it in circles, drawing the ambient luck around me and winding it through my aura, and then I broke into a mad dash for the wall of winds. It was rough going, the ground made uneven by heaps of dirt and bits of brick and wood sticking out, but I was more'n able to avoid the worst of it and build up a pretty good head of steam.

Which is, of course, when the trio of goons that Orsola had bribed—or charmed, or whatever it was she'd done—slipped out from behind the far wall and opened fire. Three choppers spat a whole fusillade of slugs my way, and all I could do was leap, corkscrewing in the air, trying to clear their line of fire long enough to dive for more substantial cover.

It was an impressive little acrobatic display, if I say so myself; no human, and not a whole lotta Fae, coulda duplicated it. I dunno that it did me much good—the ginks coulda missed 'cause of the winds, or 'cause of that extra boost of good luck I'd given myself—but miss they did. Streams of bullets flashed overhead and off to my right, but none of 'em clipped me. I let myself hit the ground as I landed, my legs collapsing under me, and kept rolling left. The slugs kept spraying, chasing after me for a heartbeat or two...

And then stopped, if only briefly, at the sound of a quick *pop-pop-pop* from behind me. Bianca, bless her, was covering me, and if her Colt wasn't a whole lot in the face of triple Tommies, she'd at least surprised the torpedoes into backing off.

My roll came to an abrupt stop as I fetched up against a small rampart of earth topped with a handful of bricks—pathetic cover, but the best I had without getting up and running some more. There I hunkered down, trying to work out what to do next, and saw that I wasn't alone in my rudimentary shelter.

Fino Ottati lay sprawled in the dirt, the stock of his own Chicago typewriter clenched in one outstretched fist. He was alive—this close, I could tell at a glance—but he was completely out. He didn't even look *unconscious* so much as *asleep*, and I even thought I heard snoring under the wailing winds.

Probably the same incantation or hex or whatever

it was that she'd hit us with when she took Celia from my office. Made sense; she wouldn't have wanted to hurt her son unnecessarily.

I wondered what, in her mind, would make it necessary.

"Hey! Fino! Wake up!" I slapped his cheek and the back of his head a couple times, first with an open palm, and then with the L&G, working to unravel the magic that held him under—or at least make myself lucky enough to wake him up in spite of it.

He snorted, then choked and spit out a mouthful of ashy soil, and blinked at me with groggy peepers. "Oberon? How the fuck—?

"Worry about how the fuck later. Right now, I need you to remember *where* the fuck."

Another blink, and his face went stiff. "Celia..."

"Yeah."

We both lifted our heads to peek out over our tiny redoubt. He muttered yet another variant of "Fuck!" when he saw the swirling barrier, and then we both ducked down as a barrage of shells hurtled our way.

But we'd both seen enough, even through the whirlwind, to know that the end was coming up quick. Orsola had drawn a foot-long *kris*—that's a wavy-bladed dagger, if you didn't know—and there wasn't a lotta room for misinterpreting its purpose.

"Jesus... Oh fuck, oh, Jesus..."

"Fino!" He whipped his head my way, glaring, but at least he'd stopped gibbering. "Can you make the shot?" I asked softly.

"What?" I couldn't hear it—I think, even if the

wind had stopped dead, I wouldn't have heard it—but I saw his lips move.

"Can you make the shot?"

His eyes started to glisten, and I don't think it was from the grit in the air. "I can't! Oh, *Madon'*, I can't…"

"All right. Cover me."

Fino's entire face tensed up hard, and then went completely blank. "*That*," he told me, "I can do."

Fino Ottati rose with a roar to shame the winds, his own Tommy gun spraying death at anyone who might even *think* of shooting at us. With the pounding of the chopper as my drummer and herald, I charged.

Barrels swiveled and bullets arced my way, but the Shark was faster. His chopper roared, cutting down one of the galoots throwing lead at me and sending the others diving for cover of their own. Again charred wood and blackened stone tried to trip me, but other'n a couple stumbles, I leapfrogged over 'em and kept going.

And Orsola's magics rose up to stop me.

It started with those same sticks and stones, suddenly jutting from the dirt, shoved by unseen things below. They poked and tangled my shoes, a few even poking *through*, scraping bloody furrows in the skin of my feet. I toppled into the dirt and rolled, barely dodging more of those makeshift spears that woulda poked right through my ribs and into God-knows-what parts that don't need any more holes. I came back to my feet, limping even worse'n I had been 'cause of the injured hip, but I was almost there, almost to that wall of swirling winds…

Chunks of broken brick and razor-edged splinters flew from the artificial storm, ignoring the prevailing gusts, hurled by some phantom hand I couldn't see. The bulk of 'em missed outright, and I juked around and between most of the rest, but a few clipped me good. Fino's coat was starting to look even worse'n the one I'd left behind, and I was leaking red from half a dozen ugly lacerations on my arms and legs.

Another step, a second, a third, and those "phantom hands" weren't invisible anymore. The dark spirits who did her will, called from the ether by her rites and rituals, lurked in the air around us, and now they wore their surroundings as gauntlets. On impossibly long, snaky arms, fists and fingers stretched from the winds and from the ash around my feet. They were spectral, translucent things, made of dirt and gravel, shattered glass and the bones of rats, broken beams and old nails—and I knew, no matter how intangible they looked, that I'd be a fool to let 'em so much as touch me.

I had the time, just, to question how this was even possible. I hadn't seen magics that potent, that blatant, in centuries; not from a human being, anyway. No way Orsola, gifted as she was, shoulda been able to manifest 'em now. And I wondered, with a shiver that had nothing to do with the chill of the night or the blustery winds, exactly what names she'd called upon to do her works, and what price she'd offered in return.

But those spirits—however awful, and whoever they answered to—weren't the only ancient power here.

I wielded the L&G as I would a rapier, dueling with the phantoms the witch had set against me, and

HOT LEAD, COLD IRON

y'know what? They never stood a chance. I stomped and spun and sidestepped, keeping my feet always just beyond reach as impossible fingers snatched at my ankles. I parried fists no more solid than smoke, and jabbed the wand deep into the wind-wrapped rubble that was their flesh and bone. And each time, with every stab and every thrust, I pierced the mystic ties binding the spirits to the bits of the surroundings in which they'd draped themselves. Magic collapsed in a flurry of misfortune; and the will of things that had never been real in even one world couldn't contend with that of a creature whose reality extended through *two*.

For a few glorious moments, I reminded Orsola Maldera what the *fate* she so disdainfully dismissed actually were. I felt the spirits fading away as I danced, coat flaring and wand spinning, between them; I felt the *strega* flinch to her soul with each phantom I popped; and I rejoiced.

And then Orsola reminded *me* what it was to be a witch, with allies even older than me.

I reached the curtain. Beyond, now clearly visible despite the gusting dirt and garbage between us, Celia hung screaming from her jury-rigged cross, her arms and feet lashed—*not* nailed, thanks be for that!—to the broken, rotting wood. Her dress was tattered, her face filthy and tear-streaked, her chest heaving as she struggled to breathe. Around the base of the cross were scattered all sorts of mystical gewgaws—candles and decanters, silver goblets and bundled herbs, an Italian flag and what I figured to be graveyard dirt, and a dozen more. And standing before them all, draped in a white habit still shiny pristine despite it all, Orsola herself. Her voice was raised in a chant part Egyptian and part Hebrew, her hair had come untied and was whipping about her head like something from Wigs By Medusa, and that ugly *kris* protruded from her left fist.

Either we'd just happened to show right before the conclusion of the rite, or she was moving up the timetable a little *because* we'd shown up—if I had to guess, I'd say the latter—but either way, we were coming up on the ninth inning.

I braced myself, took a step into the barrier…

And screamed.

Oh, it hurt. You got no idea how bad. I was sure my skin was peeling off my flesh, layer by layer; my dreams doing the same from my mind. Magics of the foulest sort, tasting of curses and blood and despair, buffeted my soul; and only now could I feel the tiny particles of rusted iron swept up in the deluge.

I threw myself away from the curtain and tumbled a few yards across the jagged ground, arms wrapped around my chest to keep myself, or so it felt, from flying completely apart. When I finally came to a halt, gasping and biting back another chorus of screams, I made the mistake of looking down. The left sleeve of my coat and my shirt were gone, and the flesh of that arm was glistening red where it peeked through the encrusted soil and shreds of lingering skin.

Iron filings. Goddamn fucking *iron*. This would take me *weeks* to heal; maybe months.

Assuming I didn't die tonight.

No way I could take down the barrier with my own magics, not without hours to work on it. I glanced desperately around me, hunting something, anything, I could use. Fino was standing out in the open, an easy target if anyone took a shot; the chopper dangled from his left hand, and he was crossing himself with his right. Bianca was squeezing off shell after shell until the piece clicked, but at that distance, through the whirlwind, she wasn't coming anywhere near her mark. She dropped to her knees, hands clasped around her rosary, tearfully praying for a miracle she didn't honestly believe was coming. The empty Colt landed beside her near a smaller piece, a revolver, also presumably empty.

"Donna Orsola!" Yeah, trying to reason with the wacky broad probably wouldn't do me a whole lotta good, but since it was taking everything I had not to curl up into a ball and whimper, it was better'n trying *nothing*. "Orsola, don't do this!"

She didn't even so much as turn her head.

"Goddamn it!" Okay, so, maybe not the most politic phrase I coulda used. "Take a look at Bianca! At your *son*! Which do you think God approves of more, Orsola? Their prayers, or your mockery?"

I finally had her attention.

"*Mockery?* You stupid *diavolo*!" Maybe it was just the surrounding winds distorting the sound, but her words came back to me hollow, strange, even echoing. It sounded a little as if there were other voices hunkered beneath hers, speaking in unison. "My granddaughter gives her life in the battle against evil! She is a *martyr*, and so I honor her even as I honor our Lord!"

Wow. Every time I think I've seen the far horizon of her lunacy, she sails right on over it...

"And the innocents you're about to murder?

What's God gonna think of that?"

"Precious few are that, *fata*. And they too are martyrs, even as is Celia. God will welcome them to Him! Their sacrifice will save so many more, as did the firstborn of Egypt."

"*Save...?*"

"Yes! When bastards like Giovaniello and Scola learn the consequences of their actions, that there are greater things to fear than their enemies—"

"What a crock of shit!" *Keep her talking, Mick; keep her talking, think of something,* of anything... "This ain't about saving anyone! This is about giving the world a bloody nose for what it's done to you."

"I've suffered! I have the right—!"

"You're a good Catholic, Orsola. Remind me. Vengeance is *whose* again, sayeth the Lord?"

She screamed something then, something incoherent through the winds—and probably even without 'em. She raised the dagger and took a slow step forward, and still there was nothing at all I could do...

"Thank you, Mr. Oberon." The voice came from just over my shoulder, carried on a waft of fishy breath—soft, sorrowful, sincere. "Thank you for trying. But I can't live as a monster. God understands."

"Oh, no. Adalina, no!"

But she was already running. With every step, her skirts flapped around tight, papery skin—skin not nearly as human as the soul inside it. I heard a despairing wail carried on the winds, and couldn't even look away to see if it had been Bianca or Fino.

Adalina reached the barrier, the deadly wall I hadn't dared cross, and dived through it.

Skin simply disappeared, flayed from flesh; and then flesh from muscle, even, in a few spots, muscle from bone. I can't begin to tell you how horrifying it was, not only to watch but to see bits of Adalina that I could *recognize* whipping around in the whirlwind with the rest of the detritus. Still I couldn't look away—and still she *didn't fall*! In what had to be agony that even I'd never known, couldn't possibly imagine, sixteen-year-old Adalina wouldn't die. Not yet.

Stumbling, staggering, maybe blind, she reached out and fell upon the woman she'd known as Nonna, wrapping her arms tight and carrying her away from the girl whose life she'd stolen, however unknowingly. They toppled backward, slamming to the earth and rolling away from the teetering cross. I heard Orsola grunt, and then scream. The dagger rose and fell, again and again. And when she rose, Adalina finally lay silent.

I dunno if there's a Heaven, not the way you folk imagine it. And if there is, I dunno if the Fae are welcome. But I swore right then that if I ever got there, and found that Adalina hadn't, I'd challenge God Himself.

Orsola stood, statue-still, and for the first time I thought that maybe, just *maybe*, I saw doubt on her face. For a long moment she gazed down at the ravaged body by her feet, and I can only hope she was wondering what kinda soulless, evil creature would do such a thing.

But the winds didn't fail, and when she spun back toward Celia, the dagger remained in her hand.

And I was outta choices.

The pain went away, washed clean in my fury over Adalina's murder. She hadn't died for nothing; I *wouldn't let her* have died for nothing! With everything I had left, I rolled over and aimed my wand, not at Orsola, not through the curtain, but at Fino. I threw my will at him harder'n any bullet, yanked at the strings of his mind.

Did I make him act, there at the end? Or was he moving anyway, a devoted son finally choosing his daughter—his *daughters*—over everyone else? I dunno, not for sure; but I'd like to think I saw his hands coming up even before I pushed him.

But whether it was him, or me, or us, Fino Ottati raised the Tommy gun in hands as white as Adalina had been, and fired.

A couple dozen slugs flew before the drum clicked empty, and at this range, even through the winds, that kinda barrage couldn't possibly miss.

Blood spattered; the whirlwind vanished, the broken bits and garbage falling from the air, impossibly and directly down. Orsola still stood, her jaw hanging loose. Her whole face bewildered, she examined the gaping, red-stained holes in her snowy habit, even going so far as to poke a finger in one of 'em.

"Fino?" she asked softly.

The dagger clattered to the earth. Donna Orsola Maldera followed.

From her, and from the ritual ingredients scattered around her, another burst of ghostly shadow erupted. It wasn't quite so dark as the one that'd knocked me for a loop in my office, and I could only hope it wouldn't anything *too* nasty before it passed over me, *through* me, and I was out.

But not for long. I blinked the dirt outta my peepers and rolled over, not nearly as disoriented as last time. Quick gander at the moon and stars said it'd only been a few minutes, and I could hear Fino stirring close by.

And weeping not far beyond.

Bianca'd been out even less time than we were— probably 'cause she was farther away—and had already made it to the eye of what'd been the storm. Tattered rope and Orsola's own dagger lay at her feet. She and Celia were holding each other, sobbing, over Adalina. Fino staggered to his feet and tottered up beside, looking down at all three—and then, only briefly, at his mother's bullet-riddled corpse as well. Then he was also on his knees, arms wrapped around the two women—one he knew so well, one he didn't know at all—he loved most.

I limped over myself, ready to rush 'em along— that much gunfire, someone might well have heard *something* even over the winds—except…

Oh, God…

They'd never have noticed, couldn't have. Not through their cries, not through their grief, not with human senses. None of 'em would.

But *I* did.

I dropped to my knees across from the Ottatis, and held my fingers above Adalina's mouth. And slowly, oh so slowly, I saw them begin to understand.

It was Bianca who reached out first, sliding her trembling hand under mine. I thought, for a moment, she would faint, that it'd all finally prove too much—

but Mrs. Ottati was one tough skirt. With her other hand she reached out, gently pulling Fino forward so he could place his fingers alongside hers.

So they could both feel the breath, so terribly faint, that incredibly, impossibly, wafted from between Adalina's skinless lips.

"It's a miracle," Bianca whispered. Over her shoulder, Fino—*Fino*—was praying.

I was too busy struggling to pump the last of my magics into Adalina, trying to help her heal as best I could, to answer that. But I gotta admit, I wasn't so sure.

A miracle? Was it? I've been in more wars in my time than you ever heard of, and I'd never seen one of the Fae take that kinda hurt and survive. It wasn't, *couldn't* be possible! I still couldn't say what she was, not really, but I didn't think even the strongest of us could come back from what she'd just gone through. Even on the off chance she survived, she might never recover.

And who would she be, then? Adalina had *wanted* to die, there at the end. If even that was taken from her, what were the odds she'd ever learn to live with—well, with living?

"Oberon?" Celia asked softly.

"I dunno," I said, rocking back from Adalina and shaking my head. "She could die before morning, or wake up in a couple days, or *never* wake up. I just don't—"

"She won't die," Bianca told us firmly. "God wouldn't let her, not after this. He wouldn't do that to her—to us."

Was that the certainty of faith, I wondered, or the

begging of desperate hope? Either way, I nodded, 'cause what'd be the point of arguing? "C'mon," I said instead. "I'll help you move 'em." So very gently, we carried Adalina to the flivver, laid her out carefully in the back seat. Then Fino and I went back for Orsola. They'd have to come up with some kinda story, sure, but having the old broad found here wouldn't help. The dead soldiers could stay: the cops'd just chalk it up to another gang killing.

"It's too much."

I glanced over at "the Shark," who was just leaning over his mother's body. "I don't…" he continued, swallowing hard. "I don't know how… Oberon, I don't know how to take care of her. Of *either* of 'em. Not like this."

"Same way you always have, Fino. Best as you can." Yeah, it was meaningless; just a stupid platitude. I wish I'd had more to tell him.

Well, maybe I did. "I can't make you any promises," I said, wondering why I was speaking even as the words tumbled out. "I ain't too popular back home. But I'll nose around a little. If I can learn anything to help Adalina, I'll tell you."

He nodded, pathetically grateful, and then tenderly lifted the body of his murdered mother from the dirt.

"They might come for her again," I warned him as we plodded back toward the cars. I wanted to keep my mouth shut, keep from heaping anything more on this family, but he hadda know. "The Unfit— uh, Unseelie—tried to take her once already. They *probably* won't again, now that I tumbled what they were planning—" *and now that she may never wake up*, I added silently "—but you never know."

"Fuck." He didn't even have the strength to yell; it was barely more'n a complaint. Then, "I got most of Mama's books, I can try and duplicate her wards, but…"

"But you ain't at all the witch she was," I finished for him. "Yeah. Maybe I can give you a hand with 'em."

"I'd appreciate that, Oberon."

"You remember that when you get my highly inflated bill, Ottati."

It got a reluctant chuckle out of him, and that was something, anyway.

Between the two of us, we managed to manhandle Orsola into the trunk with enough dignity to satisfy Fino's sense of propriety. Bianca was in the back seat, trying to dab at the worst of Adalina's wounds with a wet cloth, and having trouble *finding* 'em amid the bloody, glistening wreck. Celia stood at the open door, watching 'em both and trembling.

I deliberately scuffed my feet so I wouldn't startle her, then put a hand on her shoulder. "It's gonna be hard. *Very* hard. We both know that. But give 'em a chance before you think about taking off again, okay? Your dad honestly thought he was doing the right thing for you."

"I don't know what to believe, Mr. Oberon. I don't know if he's ever going to *be* my 'dad.' But I need…" I heard her knuckles pop, so tightly did she clench her tiny fists. "I'm not going anywhere. She did this for *me*. I have to help, if I can."

Bianca offered her a faint smile from inside, and Celia nodded dumbly in reply.

And this time, I kept my mouth shut. Yeah, maybe it was a lie. Maybe you think I shoulda told 'em that Adalina did what she did, at least partly, 'cause she didn't wanna live with what she was becoming.

I'll tell you what. *You* look the Ottatis up and tell 'em. Because I'll be damned if I ever will.

So I watched 'em drive off into the Chicago night: Fino and Bianca and Celia, and the bodies of two loved ones—one dead, one damn near—who weren't either of 'em what anyone thought. Yeah, they owed me the other half of my fee, to say nothing of the repairs to my office and my coat, but I could wait a few days to collect. I ain't *heartless*.

Course, I was still facing a long ride on the L to get home, a ride I wasn't sure I could stand on top of the pain from my arm and my other wounds. I still had to start arranging to get my place fixed up, and my furniture replaced. I still had to figure out how much of this to tell Pete.

Yeah, I'd found the girl. I'd done everything I was hired to do. And what had it cost? Maybe Adalina's life, and almost certainly her health. I'd made me two fresh enemies in the Seelie Court—one of whom was lurking somewhere in the mortal world wearing who-knew-what face, and might make a play to take Celia back—and put myself in debt to the Unfit, who were probably seriously steamed at me for gumming up their little scheme.

I was in for some really unpleasant days ahead.

Nevertheless, I found myself sighing in relief as I slowly trudged my way toward the nearest station, envisioning some long hours of shuteye on what was left of my mattress. 'cause no matter how rough things were about to get, no matter what lay ahead, my coming jobs couldn't *possibly* be any stranger or any uglier than this one'd been.

Right?

FAE PRONUNCIATION GUIDE

aes sidhe [eys shee]
bean nighe [ban **nee**-yeh]
bean sidhe [ban shee]
boggart [**boh**-gahrt]
brounie [**brooh**-nee]
clurichaun [**kloor**-*uh*-kawn]
coblynau [**kawb**-lee-naw]
Credne [**kred**-naw]
cu sidhe [koo shee]
dullahan [**dool** *uh*-han]
dvergar [**dver**-gahr]
Elphame [**elf**-eym]
Eudeagh [ee-**yood**-*uh*]
Firbolg [**fir**-bohlg]
gancanagh [**gan**-kan-aw]
ghillie dhu [**ghil**-lee doo]
glaistig [**gley**-shtig]
Goswythe [**gawz**-weeth]
haltija [hawl-**tee**-yah]
Hesperides [he-**sper**-i-deez]
huldra [**hool**-dr*uh*]
Ielveith [ahy-**el**-veyth]
kobold [**koh**-bold]
Laurelline [**Lor**-el-leen]
leanan sidhe [le-**an**-uhn shee]
ljósálfar [**lyohs**-ahl-fahr]
Luchtaine [**lookh**[1]-teyn]

[1] This sound falls between "ch" and "k," as in the word "loch."

mari-morgan [**mar**-ee **mor**gan]
Oberon [**oh**-ber-ron]
phouka [**poo**-k*uh*]
Rycine [**rahy**-see-ne]
Seelie [**see**-lee]
Sien Bheara [shahyn **beer**-*uh*]
Slachaun [**slah**-shawn]
sluagh [**sloo**-ah]
spriggan [**sprig**-*uh*n]
Tír na nÓg [**teer** na **nog**]
Tuatha Dé Danann [too-**awt**[2]-h*uh* de[3] **dan**[3]-*uh*n]
tylwyth teg [**tel**-oh-ith teyg]
Unseelie [**uhn**-see-lee]
Ylleuwyn [eel-**yoo**-win]

[2] This "t" is *almost* silent, and is separate from the following "h," rather than forming a single sound as "th" normally does in English.
[3] Strictly speaking, these "d"s fall somewhere between the "d" and a hard "th"—such as in "though"—but a simple "d" represents the closest sound in English.

MOBSTERS OF CHICAGO

While none of the characters who *appear* in this book are historical figures, a great many of those *referenced* are. If you're at all interested in learning more about them, this ought to be enough to get you started.

BATTAGLIA, SAM: A typical (but successful) Chicago gangster, Battaglia joined Torrio and Capone in the Outfit in the mid-1920s. After Capone's era ended, Battaglia remained a member in good standing of the Outfit, and went on to hold substantial power in the organization.

CAPONE, ALPHONSE GABRIEL "AL" (also "SCARFACE"): Perhaps the most infamous gangster in American history, Capone rose from being a smalltime hood to a lieutenant of John Torrio's, and eventually succeeded Torrio. A member of the Outfit, Capone was actually never "in charge" of the entire city, as many people believe, but as the man behind what was arguably Chicago's largest—and certainly most violent—gang, he might as well have been. Capone was eventually imprisoned in 1931 for charges stemming from failure to pay taxes on his criminal profits.

MORAN, GEORGE CLARENCE "BUGS": One of the biggest Irish gangsters of Chicago, Bugs Moran ran the Northside Gang from 1927 to (roughly) 1935. Violent and hot-tempered, Moran himself was one of the main causes for the constant conflict between the Northside Gang and the Outfit.

MUDGETT, HERMAN: Also known as H. H. Holmes, Mudgett wasn't actually a gangster, but was in fact one of America's earliest serial killers. From 1888 to 1894, Mudgett murdered an estimated 200 or more victims. Many of these were killed in his "Murder Castle," a hotel with secret rooms where victims could be suffocated, asphyxiated with gas, or tortured to death, before their bodies were disposed of in the sub-basements through careful dissection or submersion in lime pits.

NITTI, FRANK "THE ENFORCER": One of Capone's lieutenants, Frank Nitti went on to serve an important role in the Outfit after Al's arrest: specifically, that of a figurehead. While he did have *some* voice in the running of the organization, he was primarily a mouthpiece for the "Board of Directors." Although often portrayed in fiction as a chopper-toting psycho, Nitti was actually a bookish, white-collar criminal who rarely, if ever, got his hands dirty with violence. His nickname came from citing and enforcing Outfit rules at various meetings and sit-downs.

NORTHSIDE GANG, THE: A largely Irish gang based in Chicago's north side (obviously), this group was often at war with the Outfit over territories, routes, and the like. Capone's infamous Valentine's Day Massacre was targeted at Northsiders.

OUTFIT, THE: The hub of organized crime in Chicago, the Outfit was the organization/syndicate to which Capone (among many others) belonged. After Capone's time, the Outfit's leadership took on a very corporate form, with a Board of Directors and no single person in charge. The Outfit frequently cooperated with the Commission (a similar organization, based out of New York) and other Mafia organizations.

POPE, FRANK: A member of Capone's organization, he eventually went on to manage many of the Outfit's gambling interests on behalf of the Board of Directors.

TORRIO, JOHN: A powerful gangster during the rise of organized crime in Chicago, Torrio pioneered many of the bootlegging tactics and routes that would be used throughout Prohibition. It was Torrio who brought Capone into the fold, and eventually turned over power to ol' "Scarface."

VOLPE, ANTHONY: Volpe was one of the Outfit's gangsters who eventually rose to a position of some prominence, handling the group's gambling interests alongside Frank Pope.

ACKNOWLEDGMENTS

It's true that *none* of my books would be as good as they are without the input, advice, and critiques of various folk, but it's especially true here. Without my wife, George, and my sister, Naomi, this novel would absolutely have turned out very different— and not nearly as worthwhile.

Heartfelt gratitude to Laura Resnick, for providing the Italian translations I needed for the Ottatis' dialogue. If you've enjoyed reading about Mick, you could do a lot worse than look into Laura's own *Esther Diamond* series (DAW).

Additional thanks, as well, to C. Robert Cargill, for letting me share some of his research on the Fae, and for numerous brainstorming sessions.

And speaking of research... A great deal of it went into this book, much of which was performed online. But I need to single out a few particular books that proved absolutely invaluable to me in getting many of the details right. These are, specifically, *A Travel Guide to Al Capone's Chicago*, by Diane Yancey (Lucent) and *The Outfit*, by Gus Russo (Bloomsbury).

ABOUT THE AUTHOR

ARI MARMELL would love to tell you all about the various esoteric jobs he held and the wacky adventures he had on the way to becoming an author, since that's what other authors seem to do in these sections. Unfortunately, he doesn't actually have any. In point of fact, Ari decided while at the University of Houston that he wanted to be a writer, graduated with a Creative Writing degree, and—after holding down a couple of very mundane jobs—broke into freelance writing for roleplaying games. His published novels include *The Conqueror's Shadow* and *The Warlord's Legacy* (Del Rey/Spectra), *The Goblin Corps* and the Widdershins Adventure series (Pyr), and *Agents of Artifice* (Wizards of the Coast), as well as numerous short stories.

Ari currently lives in an apartment that's almost as cluttered as his subconscious, which he shares (the apartment, not the subconscious, though sometimes it seems like it) with his wife, George, and a cat who really, really thinks it's dinner time. He is trying to get used to speaking about himself in the third person, but still finds it really, really weird.

You can find Ari online at www.mouseferatu. com and on Twitter @mouseferatu.